I0638959

LEGACY

By Mark Eric

Legacy
Mark Eric

This book is a work of fiction. Names, characters, places, and
incidents either are products of the author's imagination or are
used fictitiously. Any resemblance to actual events or locales or
persons, living or dead, is entirely coincidental.

Editor/Copyeditor: Katherine Kahn
Cover Design: Shawn Tucker and Mark Eric

For information about special discounts for bulk purchases or
author events, please contact Mark Eric Entertainment at
MarkEricEnt@gmail.com.

Published in the United States by Mark Eric Williams
ISBN: 978-0-9960354-1-5

www.MarkEricEntertainment.com

DEDICATION

To my mother, your legacy is firmly intact. Thank you for every minute of everyday we had together. I love you.

To Allen, Bantu, and Janet, I couldn't have done this without your input. Thank you for taking the time to read and help me across the finish line.

To Kat, this doesn't get done without you. Thank you for your support and for lending your prodigious talents to this project. It means everything to me. Your legacy is intact as well.

Finally *Legacy* is for my brothers. Everyday that we live and breathe, we are faced with difficult challenges and decisions that impact our lives in profound ways. No two journeys are the same, but your strength, courage, and dignity will forever inspire me. Always remember despite the odds we face, our legacy is eternal.

For James.

1

"Fuck you, nigga!"

"Fuck you, cracka. I told you on your left. You went right, and that's why you got killed," Charlie said throwing a stiff elbow at his best friend, Chad.

Gavin, the third friend of the trio, sat not that far away at the wet bar rolling the next blunt. "Ya'll fuckers smoked so much, more than likely you're both wrong," Gavin said. "Charlie you might have said 'up' and pasty dumb fuck over there went down."

"Yeah, down on my nuuuuts," Charlie said laughing hysterically and tossing down the controller as Chad punched him in the arm.

Charlie and Chad were sprawled across the oversized custom-fitted sectional in the finished basement of Charlie's house in Covington Falls, a small, gated group of cul-de-sacs and million dollar homes to the area's doctors, lawyers, dentists, and CEOs. Gavin, who lived three houses down, called the basement the "Superior Man Cave." The mammoth-sized area possessed a fully stocked bar and kitchen as well as a state-of-the-art media and entertainment center with a deluxe surround sound system and a 110-inch, flat screen, high-definition TV. Everything they needed was at their fingertips, and nothing in the neighborhood rivaled the Jackson family's basement.

"Charlie, you wish, nigga," replied Chad as he stood and stretched. Glancing at Gavin, he continued. "And you shut the fuck up, chink, and finish rolling that thing. You been at it for like ten minutes and counting. Come on already. My system will go into shock if I get sober."

"Fuck you, pasty boy," Gavin replied, as he meticulously replaced the cigar's tobacco with his latest batch of high-priced, high-powered, organic weed. "At least mine don't fall apart half way through."

Chad rolled his eyes and made a show of dragging himself over to the bar.

Gavin glanced up at his freckled faced friend and couldn't help but lob another insult. "Anyway, I thought you pale vampire types were into blood not weed. Don't you have some chick named Bella to chase down somewhere?" Gavin smirked as he put the final touches on the thick blunt he considered a work of art. With a sigh of appreciation at his skills, he removed his lighter. After the standard two puffs, he passed the blunt to Chad, and the two boys headed back to the sofa. When Chad finished he handed it to Charlie. They repeated the ritual as they watched *The Cartoon Network* until all that remained were ashes in an empty pop can.

The expensive air purifiers worked overtime to keep the basement from looking and smelling like a scene out of a Cheech and Chong movie. As Friday night crept along, the three friends floated in their high, told jokes, complained about their classes, and laughed uncontrollably at the cartoon antics on TV.

Charlie, Chad, and Gavin were all seventeen and had been neighbors and friends since elementary school when a local real estate developer had bought up a handful of local farms in Canfield, Ohio and created one of the most sought after addresses on the outskirts of crumbling Youngstown. The small subdivision in the sleepy town had offered an escape from the urban sprawl that had crept into their old neighborhoods, so those who could afford the minimum seven-figure homes had jumped at the chance to embed themselves in a community that understood how to behave and whose shoulders to rub. To the relief of all the parents, their kids had grown up safely ensconced with manicured lawns, well-behaved playmates, and the best schools available in the area, far away from the inner city's violent, drama-plagued, and decaying educational system.

Born into new money and privilege, the boys suckled at the teats of luxuries and benefits and never gave their easy life a second thought. After all, it wasn't their money they reasoned. It was their parents', and not one of the boys gave a fuck about their parents' money as long as the credit cards still paid for their shiny toys and expensive clothes.

Gavin's father was a prominent doctor and cancer researcher at The Cleveland Clinic. Chad's father was CEO of the largest construction company throughout the Midwest, while his mother was its CFO. Charlie's father was the county's District Attorney and on the fast track to the Supreme Court of Ohio. Most of their friends and acquaintances also came from high-powered, high profile lineages.

Charlie and his father were anomalies in the nearly all white community, yet their dark cocoa skin hardly raised eyebrows because of his father's position. Neighbors, teachers, even the handful of local police knew Charlie's slim, five-foot-nine frame, his angular face, and his car. He was considered one of their own—special. Everyone liked Charlie. He was easy to like. Always quick with a smile or a funny story, Charlie never seemed to be in a bad mood.

What he was completely ignorant of though was that his conservative community liked him only because they saw him as a non-threatening Black youth. On rare occasions Charlie had heard racist whispers, but those were few and far between. In fact he actually had more difficulty relating to those who lived in the Black community than he did with those who didn't share his skin tone.

Charlie was bald by choice because the little town of Canfield with its white picket fences and tree-lined streets had no Black-owned businesses let alone barbers that cut Black hair, and shaving his head was faster and far safer than going to Smith's on Youngstown's South Side to get a fade. The few times he had made his way to the popular barbershop, he'd felt completely out of his element. While he dressed in a trendy hip hop style, he neither moved nor spoke like the other Black teenagers waiting for their cuts.

Not only was he acutely aware of his differences, but the others were as well. The last time he'd visited Smith's a neighborhood boy had jumped into the barber's chair in front of Charlie. Shocked, Charlie had just stood there. When the barber had pointed out that Charlie was next, the young man, who seemed no older but far harder, had looked Charlie up and down and with a dark chuckle replied, "No, he ain't." Charlie had shrugged and motioned that it was all right, hoping to avoid any confrontation. "See, told you," the other boy had said with a sneer before he turned to Charlie with a hard stare and continued, "Sit yo punk ass down before you make me nervous." To the sound of laughter, Charlie had turned and left instead and returned to his world and his friends.

While the physical appearances of Charlie's two best friends differed completely from his, they shared the same background. Chad's shaggy brown hair, lily-white skin, and slightly shorter but more muscular compact frame reminded Charlie of the perfect frat boy, and he had the personality to match.

Gavin was the most fastidious of the trio. Where Charlie was a solid B student and Chad didn't give a damn, Gavin was serious about school, and his grade point average proved that, which surprised everyone considering G was the local connoisseur of pot. Regardless of his nerdy tendencies, the slim Asian with his buzz-cut bordered on beautiful. He was blessed—or cursed if you asked him—with his mother's genes.

The three friends had years of history and had seen each other through the best and the roughest patches life had thrown at them. In their last few week of high school and with only a few months before college, Charlie was intent on making sure he had a good time with his two best friends, which included video games, weed, and anything else that kept the party rocking.

Tonight was going exactly as planned, and after three hours the three boys were so high and laughing so hard that they didn't hear the doorbell. What they did finally hear was the loud knock on the door that led down to the man cave. With a groan, Charlie trudged up the stairs and snatched the door open just as his father was about to knock again.

"What, Dad?" Charlie asked in exasperation.

"There's someone at the front door for you," Browning said as he started back towards his office and case files with a small bowl of ice cream.

"Who is it?" Charlie asked.

"Someone named Frank."

Fear sank into Charlie as if he had looked up to face a firing squad.

"He seems like a nice guy," Browning said over his shoulder. "Don't be rude and leave him waiting."

On shaky legs, Charlie went to the front door and inhaled deeply before slowly turning the crystal doorknob. The charming guy

Charlie's father had met minutes earlier was gone, and in his place was the man Charlie knew with hard, uncaring eyes and a murderous reputation.

Frank was the right hand of Stony Carmichael, one of the biggest bookies on the South Side of Youngstown. Stony didn't just take bets however. For a generation, his family had firmly believed in diversification, which had him elbows deep in most of the dirty enterprises that could be found in that rough and tumble area of town. Stony had held onto his inherited fiefdom because he was smarter than the rest, but most of all because he had Frank.

Frank was a stone cold killer. He was a legend, and anyone who bought, sold, or interacted with anything illegal within a twenty-mile radius knew how vicious he was. When Charlie had first seen him months ago, he'd almost lost control of his bodily functions. Now here he was at Charlie's front door.

"Whattup, Frank?" Charlie said as he tried to stifle a nervous, weed-induced giggle.

"You know what's up. Let's go," Frank said with the calmness of a mortician.

"Okay. Uhhh…can I grab my shoes?" Charlie asked.

Frank looked pointedly at his Timex. "Nigga, you got one minute before I come in and snatch you up outta there, and we both know no one in that house wants that. You feel me?"

Charlie nodded quickly in agreement.

Frank smiled wide and chuckled as Charlie nearly tripped in his haste to close the door. Rumor had it that a couple of years ago Stony had sent Frank to pick up a squirrely guy trying to get out of town before paying the ten grand note he owed for picking against Miami, but things hadn't gone all that smoothly. Word had spread that Frank had kicked in the door, killed everyone in the house, and even flushed the goldfish down the garbage disposal just because. Now when Frank knocked on a door, folks got up, got dressed, and willingly went with him regardless of the time of day.

Charlie ran back down to the cave, and while tugging on his sneakers, he told Chad and Gavin they had to go because Frank was waiting.

"Holy shit," Gavin said jumping up from the couch.

"How the fuck did he get past security at the gate?" Chad asked as he also scrambled to his feet.

"How the fuck should I know? You wanna go ask him? He's right outside," Charlie said.

Unwilling to meet up with Frank, they said their cautious goodbyes and quietly slid out the back of Charlie's house. Charlie laced up his Jordans, downed a Red Bull, and went out to Frank who sat on the fender of his pearl black 5 Series BMW complete with dark tint that hid passengers from probing eyes.

Glittering in the moonlight, the modified monster crouched in Charlie's driveway on twenty-inch black on black rims with high performance tires from somewhere in Italy or Japan. His whole set up was legal by a hair, and even when standing still, the car looked like it could run you down like a black bullet. Tonight, Charlie saw it as his hearse. As dread clawed at his insides and his high quickly began to fade, Charlie climbed into the cool cream and black interior and buckled his seatbelt.

Sparing only a glance at him, Frank smirked and asked, "Are you high?"

Charlie nodded.

"Good, don't say a word then."

Frank gently shifted the car into drive and slowly pulled away from Charlie's impressive house in bucolic Covington Falls.

2

No words passed between the quiet killer and his nervous passenger. Both of them understood why Frank had collected Charlie. This ride wasn't a mystery, and neither was their destination. With every passing second the sleek BMW slipped away from Charlie's safe, polite affluent town with its trimmed hedges and manicured lawns and into a part of Youngstown, Ohio that many in Charlie's social set essentially considered a war torn country thousands of miles away rather than the neighboring town.

The South Side wasn't a place where those with pedigrees like Charlie and his friends—those with a future—chose to spend their time. They turned a jaundiced eye to the decay and destitution that made up the majority of the streets of Youngstown. Those who did brave its streets either had floundering family there or needed a fix for whatever addiction demanded attention. It was a mecca for those who craved a dopamine escape or any other illicit vice.

Fifteen minutes later, Frank smoothly pulled up to the curb in front of Romare's, a busy corner club on a dark narrow street that possessed an abandoned building, condemned dwellings, and a few rundown homes with broken steps and sagging porches. Despite the blight, there was a throng of Friday night patrons out front yelling, laughing, and smoking. A scuffle broke out down the block drawing the crowd of gawkers who kept their distance in case a gun appeared, but when Frank climbed out of the car everyone went quiet. A few people offered up greetings, but Frank acknowledged none of them. He instead eyed the fight for a few seconds, and when he felt it wasn't anything serious, walked around, opened the passenger side door, and waited expectantly.

Charlie tried to unbuckle himself as he stared at the crowd milling around the windowless bar. He'd only been here twice before, and both trips were in the early afternoon when the streets and the bar were nearly empty. This was his first visit when the place was in full swing, and his fear and nervousness wouldn't let go of him long enough to free himself from the seat belt. Out of patience, Frank reached in, unbuckled the belt, and lifted him out of the car by his shirt. Charlie again glanced around at the ogling crowd and quickly lowered his eyes to his sneakers as if seeing them for the first time. The sea of people parted as if Frank was Moses and Charlie his staff.

In the front room of the building stood a dark stained bar with less than a dozen backless stools. A twenty-foot mirror ran along the wall behind the rows of well and call liquor, so whoever tended bar could keep an eye on the crowd. As they weaved through a handful of small tables, Charlie saw the old balding barkeep with quick hands acknowledged Frank with a nod while everyone else in the room kept their eyes on their drinks.

In the deeper recesses of Romare's was the low-key strip club with a small two-poled stage. Three topless ladies swayed and gyrated as seductively as they could to the bass heavy music in their attempts to pry as much money from the crowd as they could. Charlie started to blush even as Frank yanked him through the heavy industrial double doors that led to the one time kitchen area, which housed Romare's illegal sports book operation and gambling.

Walking past the two sets of crowded blackjack, craps, and poker tables as well as the slot machines, Frank finally let go of Charlie's shirt but kept a firm hand on his back until they made their way to a security door. Frank punched in a code and motioned for Charlie to go first. Hesitantly Charlie took the first step and looked back uncertain only for Frank to suck his teeth and shove him ungraciously up the stairs. At the top was another security door. Before Charlie could knock, a loud buzz sounded.

"Push," Frank said.

Charlie entered a thickly carpeted spacious L-shaped office. A sleek black leather sofa and matching chairs stood a few feet from the door and faced a two hundred gallon fish tank full of exotic saltwater fish. Before Charlie could become transfixed by their stunning colors, Frank shoved him towards the back of the room.

Behind the desk with his feet resting comfortably on its smooth dark surface was Stony Carmichael, a slim built man with a dark chocolate complexion, watchful eyes, and a grimace on his lips. The young head of the Carmichael family was only a half a dozen years older than Charlie, but his hard and unforgiving eyes had lost any twinkle of youthful optimism. However Stony wasn't your average stereotypical thug. He never carried a firearm. That was Frank's job. Stony's weapon was his mind.

Charlie sat nervously in one of the two Chippendale chairs that faced the desk, but his host didn't speak. Stony's eyes simply assessed him. Completely sober now, Charlie could feel the icy grip of terror creep up his spine.

"What's up, Stony?" Charlie said, but his attempt to smile collapsed.

"You know what's up," Stony lazily replied as he sat up and slowly pulled a ledger from his drawer.

Charlie's heart thudded like he was in the last quarter mile of the New York City marathon and was in the middle of his kick. "How's Lamont?" Charlie asked nervously, trying to turn on his usual charm.

Lamont was Stony's younger brother and a schoolmate of Charlie's. When the kids and staff at Canfield High School had realized that Lamont was from the South Side they'd either avoided him like he was about to pull a gun and rob them or flocked to him as if he was a first round NFL draft pick. Charlie and his boys had flocked, eager to hear firsthand what life was like "in the hood," and when Lamont had told them about his family's illegal gambling operation, the boys had jumped at the chance for some action, placing bets through Lamont.

Charlie had won more than both Chad and Gavin combined, and at one point during the NFL season, his roll was so impressive that Stony had wanted to meet him. Chad and Gavin had declined their invitations to tag along, intimidated by the reputation of the South Side. Charlie had jumped at the chance to spend a couple hours in the neighborhoods that his dad had warned him "were a dangerous place full of desperate people."

Once Lamont and him had crossed the city limits, Charlie had only seen a smattering of rundown or abandoned houses on nearly every block, torn up streets, and uninviting dirty storefronts that catered mostly to payday loans or pawn shops. He had been expecting to be shot at or at the very least hear some gunshots, which had made Lamont laugh until he couldn't catch his breath. "Oh that happens, but this ain't Syria, Charlie. At least not yet," he'd said.

Stony's chuckle brought Charlie back to the present. "'How's Lamont?' This is not a social call with tea and crumpets, Chuck. The first time you were here I wanted to meet the lucky kid and pay him his winnings in person, but now…now it's an altogether different story. So there is no asking about my little brother. There's no staring at the damn fish or getting a can of pop either. What this is right now, right this very instant, is you telling me just how in the fuck you are going to pay me what you owe."

"H-how much do I owe you?" Charlie asked fidgeting in his seat. "I know I haven't picked a lot of winners lately, but I…ummm…guess I lost track."

Stony smirked, opened up the ledger, and read off Charlie's list of losses. He continued minute after minute, and the more he read the harder Charlie found it was to breathe. Finally he slammed the black ledger shut. "All in all, Charlie, you're currently into me for a little over two hundred big ones," Stony announced flatly.

Charlie swayed slightly in his seat, and his eyes glazed over in shock.

Stony steepled his hands and summed up the facts. "You should have stuck to betting on football, Chuck. Basketball is clearly not your game."

Charlie had been almost perfect at picking football scores and at one point had fourteen winning Sundays in a row. However once the cheers of the Super Bowl had faded so had Charlie's luck. He had tried his hand at basketball with horrible results, but that hadn't stopped him from placing more wagers. Stony had continued to accommodate him until now. Now there was no more accommodation. Now it was time to discuss payment. Charlie wanted to run. He wanted out of that claustrophobic office, but he had no idea where exactly he was or how to get home. He hadn't even remembered to bring his cell phone or wallet.

"Relax, kid. I learned a very long time ago that dead men don't pay, so relax. No one is going to harm a hair on your head. That is if you had hair. Isn't that right, Frank?" Stony asked the silent killer who lounged on the sofa at the far end of the room and watched the lionfish stalk its prey in the colorful fish tank.

Without even glancing their way, Frank replied, "Not a hair."

Smiling broadly, Stony continued. "See, you'll be back in the warm confines of your million dollar house in little Covington Falls in no time. We just need to figure out how you're going to pay me. Any ideas?"

Charlie didn't have a clue how he was going to raise that kind of money, so he sat mute.

"I don't hear you, Charlie."

Silence.

"You know what else I learned, Charlie? I learned that the best way to get people to pay what they owe is with a little thing called incentive. It's a nudge in the right direction, so to speak, to square their tab with me. It's done in all kinds of ways, and while dead men don't pay, other things often inspire all kinds of trips to the bank and creative financial maneuvering." After a few seconds he asked, "Do you know how I plan to incentivize you?"

Charlie shook his head still unable to find words.

"It's real simple. You have forty-eight hours to either get me my money or explain to me in detail how you're going to get me my money. If you don't…know that somewhere out there in this big bad world of ours…is a chainsaw," Stony said before he paused for effect, "with your father's name on it."

Charlie sat up ramrod straight, and his face flashed with fear before he slumped back in his chair.

"Nod if you understand, kid."

Trying to keep the pizza he'd eaten earlier from spilling all over his shoes, Charlie managed a meager nod.

"Great. Have a great weekend, Chuck. Frank?" he said without a flicker of compassion. Somewhere in the inky shadows of the room punctuated only by the tank's purple neon glow emerged Frank. "Take him home, please."

"Let's go," Frank said and tugged Charlie roughly to his feet. Charlie couldn't feel his legs as they walked towards the door.

When Stony yelled out Charlie's name, he slowly turned. "Forty-eight hours, homie, and then I'm calling. And don't duck me. I hate when motherfuckas duck me," he said before he turned his attention back to the monitor on his desk.

3

Once the door closed behind Frank and Charlie, Stony lost himself again in the video security feeds from the various cameras installed at Romare's. Staring at the flickering images calmed him. Even after four years, he still hadn't fully draped himself in the burden of his uncle's inheritance. He ignored invoices, paperwork, and receipts for as long as he could.

Truth be told, while he still loved his uncle, he slightly resented him as well. Thrusting Romare's on him, making him responsible for the financial security of a good portion of the family, was a nightmare. This was not where he wanted to be. This was not supposed to be what he was doing with his life. Yet here he was, back in the clutches of a community he wanted no part of. He took money from people who couldn't afford to lose a dime, and that embarrassed him.

Stony remembered how excited he'd been at Charlie's age, knowing that his future lay ahead of him like a glimmering jewel and believing—at least for a little while—that it didn't involve the decaying landscape of broken dreams that littered Youngstown. His dreams had once been so much bigger and grander than this place. His uncle had made him believe those dreams could one day come true, but in the end he'd also been the one most responsible for destroying them.

Stony had been in his second year at Berkley studying art history when he'd gotten word that his Uncle Leonard, the moneyman and patriarch of the family, had died suddenly. He had rushed home for the funeral, crushed to have lost the only real father figure in his life, the one who had helped raise him and taught him so much about the world outside of Youngstown's city limits. Once everyone had paid their respects, Leonard's attorney had gathered the family together and read his uncle's shocking will. Leonard's wishes had ruffled feathers and hurt a number of family members, but Stony's uncle had never given a damn about anyone's ego or emotions and even from the grave had handled his business with the same callous attitude.

Leonard, who had been there for Stony after his father had become a victim of the streets, had left his favorite nephew in charge of his diverse empire, which included five apartment buildings, five houses, an auto repair and detailing shop, a pawn shop, along with the jewel of his uncle's kingdom, the bar/strip club known as Romare's, named after the famed artist and writer, Romare Bearden. Leonard's will had demanded Stony take immediate ownership and control.

Legal stipulations allowed him to sell any and everything if he so chose, but Leonard was clear that the empire he'd built and bled for could not fall into the hands of any of his brothers, their children, or his sister, Stony's mother. The lawyer explained it in the simplest terms. "Stony, if you don't want any of it then you must break it up and sell. You can burn it all to the ground if you're inclined, but it's either yours or no one's." Without saying a word, Stony had left the reading and the bickering, intent on putting that last option in motion as soon as possible, so he could return to college and the life of culture he wanted clear across the country.

However later that evening his mother had spoken at length to him about what selling would mean for the family. The majority of the money their family enjoyed came from his uncle's legal and illegal enterprises. A handful of trusted family members worked at several of the properties and businesses. Some from the older generation were taken care of with their bills quietly paid each month. Selling any of the businesses or real estate holdings would mean losing streams of much needed revenue, something the family couldn't afford. "In other words," his mother had told him, "It's all on you whether we live or die."

He had listen without complaint or argument, and the next morning Stony dropped out of Cal Berkley and became the reluctant heir. Stony's sole inheritance had upset his family, but it had incensed his competition. Leonard had gained and held the lion's share of the street business through the decades thanks to the help of some Youngstown's most notorious criminals. His most recent right-hand had been Frank, a deadly and efficient hustler who had once been childhood friends with Stony. With the patriarch gone, Leonard's competition had figured Frank and his hard-hitting crew would come to one of them. However Frank had kept a low profile after Leonard's death, and as a result Stony had found himself with a bounty on his head.

Lenard's nephew hadn't known how to handle the pressure or defend himself against his newfound rivals. Street politics, mercenary mentalities, and hostile business tactics had never been his world. His uncle had purposefully insulated Stony from the darker world of Youngstown's South Side and instead surrounded his nephew in the intoxicating and gentlemanly world of fine art.

Swimming with sharks had been foreign to Stony. One day he had been an art major in California. The next he was the head of a quasi-legal empire where everyone knew he was untested and vulnerable. His life had hung in the balance on whether Frank would continue to align himself with the Carmichael's or shift his allegiances and launder his money elsewhere.

Two weeks into his new lot in life, while holed up in the bar one afternoon, Stony had been haphazardly going through delivery receipts when there was a loud knock on front door. No one had been there but him and the bartender, Turk, who had been quietly prepping the bar for the evening ahead. With a nod of his head, Stony had sent the bartender to open the door as he gripped his uncle's .50 caliber Desert Eagle with a nervous hand. When Turk had opened the door, there stood a smiling Frank.

For a moment Stony had stood stunned as Frank filled the doorway like his guardian angel. Then snapping out of his awe, he'd greeted his old friend with relief.

Frank motioned to the gun. "Whatchu gon do with that?"

"Whatever I had to," Stony replied.

Frank nodded. "I'm sorry about your uncle."

"Thanks, man. It's damn good to see you. It's been a minute," Stony said as he closed and locked the door.

"Yeah, it's been a few years since I seen you. Heard you was out in Cali doin ya art school thing. Whatchu doing here?"

Stony shrugged. "It's what unc wanted, me in charge."

"Yeah, when I heard that I ain't believe it at first. 'Whatchu still doin here?' is the better question."

"I don't have a choice really."

"You all right?" Frank asked as the old friends sat at the bar.

"No!" Stony said quickly. "No I'm not all right, man. Fuck I know about this world? Got people putting bounties on me and shit. I'm walking around with a damn gun, Frank. ME, with a gun," Stony said as he dropped the monstrous handgun on the bar.

"That's actually more like a cannon than a gun, and please don't drop it like that again," Frank said motioning to the Desert Eagle. "You ever shoot that thing?"

"I've never shot a gun of any kind, Frank. I think the last person I ever shot with a gun was you. Remember those foam dart guns we had?"

Frank nodded and smiled.

"That's the last thing I ever shot."

"Good," said Frank. "Because the kick back from that thing would probably break your arm."

"Fuck," Stony softly said eyeing the gun with a new found respect.

"You know," Frank started, "if it wasn't for your unc, I might be dead or doing life. That man saved me in more ways than I can count."

"I know. He told me about all of it. The money he sent you when you were locked up in juvie. The people he intimidated or paid off so they wouldn't testify against you. He told me all of it."

"Not all of it but that's a good amount. He was a good man."

"He was a bastard, Frank, but I loved him."

"Hard not to. So who do I have to kill to get a drink around here?" Frank asked.

"What you want? The selection is kinda weak," Stony said as he walked behind the bar.

"There's a bottle of Johnny Blue up under the bar."

"Bullshit!"

"No lie," Frank said matter-of-factly.

"He's right," Turk said as he returned from the restroom. "I'll get it."

Stony returned to his stool with a shrug. "Who knew?"

"I did," Frank said with a laugh. A few seconds later Turk placed two glasses of the most expensive whiskey within a five-mile radius on the bar. "Compliments of the house," the old bartender said with a smile.

"Before we drink," Frank started, "I came here to help. I know what the word is on the street, and it ain't good. I'm here to help you in any way I can, out of loyalty to your unc and out of friendship to you. If you don't want it, I'll drink my drink and bounce. If you do then we work together, deal?"

Stony picked up his glass, and Frank followed suit. "Deal."

Frank clinked his glass against Stony's and in one gulp downed the contents in his glass.

Since that day, the two men had been inseparable and successfully kept Leonard's legacy alive and thriving, as they gained the respect of not only those who worked for them but also from those who wanted them dead.

Stony glanced at the ledger still on his desk and read Charlie's line again.

Hold on, Chuck. A storm's headed your way, Stony thought as a smile slowly crossed his lips.

4

After a slow, leisurely ride through Youngstown's South Side, Frank had Charlie back on the familiar soil of Covington Falls. As Frank's powerful BMW slipped down the silent street and back through the gates, Charlie stumbled into the house. Suddenly the dimensions seemed off, as if he was in someone else's home. He looked at the furnishings, and nothing felt familiar. The air even smelled different. Instead of the usual fresh scent of home, the foyer was stuffy and stale.

Charlie walked deeper into the house, passed the kitchen, and ran his hands across the upholstered sofa in the living room. He stared at the crystal and porcelain vases his stepmother fawned over, and he wondered how much she'd spent on those. Seeing his home through a new lens, Charlie gazed around and saw a wealth and a pretension he'd never been aware of until now. He marveled at all the money spent on things that did nothing but collect dust and shook his head.

Leaving the opulent living room, Charlie stumbled down to the basement and tried to calculate the amount of money it must have taken to outfit the ultimate hang out spot. There was the flat screen TV and theater quality surround sound system from *Bang & Olufson* as well as the custom-built sectional that Gavin swore was more comfortable than his own bed. Every make, model, and generation of gaming console sat inside the solid oak and frosted glass multimedia center next to a matching wall unit, filled to capacity with every video game Charlie had ever wanted. On the other side of the spacious room was the wet bar, microwave, and fridge, while vintage Ms. Pac-Man, Asteroid, and Centipede arcade games stood at attention next to the custom pool table in the far corner. Charlie roughly estimated that the entire basement bill must have bled at the very least eighty grand from his dad's pocket. Charlie shrugged. Not even that amount of money would square what he owed Stony.

Queasy with that realization, Charlie plopped down on the sectional and turned to ESPN. He kicked off his sneakers and reached for his favorite distraction under the sectional, his secret stash of three tightly rolled blunts. He lit up and slumped along the length of the sofa.

Try as he might to not think about it, Stony's words came back to him. He had forty-eight hours to either pay or at least come up with a way to clear his gambling debt. *Fuck*, he thought, *I don't have 200 grand!* Charlie couldn't understand how his luck had just upped and walked out on him without so much as a goodbye.

There was no way he could tell his father, who would either disown him or worse get the authorities involved which would make things cataclysmic. His stepmother was gone for two weeks on her "Girls Only Annual Cruise" to the Bahamas, so her help wasn't possible either, not that she'd do anything other than tell his father. He knew his friends couldn't help. The kind of money he owed was well out of their realm of their assistance. Charlie took a long pull and closed his eyes. He didn't want to be the reason his father violently met a chainsaw.

Charlie had never felt more alone except after his mother had died. Doing what he usually did when he was unable to come up with any realistic solutions, he happily let his high take him away from all his problems.

5

After waking up midway through the morning stiff and sore, Charlie had grabbed some cold pizza from the fridge for breakfast, stumbled upstairs for a long shower, and spent a couple of hours browsing social media and watching reruns of sports highlights. Nothing satisfied him. The sense of dread he felt stayed with him like a deep merciless chill in his bones. Gavin texted him wanting to hang out, but Charlie wasn't ready for the third degree, so he let him know he'd catch up with him and Chad later on. Bored and restless, he meticulously picked out his latest fashion ensemble and decided to get out of the house in case his dad decided to come home early.

Charlie ambled into their three-car garage and climbed into his sixteenth birthday present, a black on black Volkswagen Jetta Turbo. He had begged and pleaded for a Porsche, but that request had sent his father into an apocalyptic fit. Before their conflict had gotten ugly, his stepmother, Bailey, had suggested a compromise that still allowed Charlie to get German engineering but kept Browning from paying Porsche prices. She recommended Volkswagen, and Charlie had begrudgingly agreed. When he'd asked for aftermarket bodywork and rims though, his father had once again adamantly opposed the idea. They had argued for hours.

His dad had explained that being the Mahoning County District Attorney, he was well aware that Black men were more often pulled over just because of the kind of car they drove. "I don't want my son's car to be an excuse for any overzealous cops, so no matter what you say, I'm nixing any and all 'Pimp My Ride' fantasies you may have." Charlie's argument that everyone in town knew who he and his father were didn't sway his father's decision in the least. "And what happens when you cross the city limits and run to Pittsburgh or Cleveland with Chad and Gavin?" Charlie didn't understand his father's paranoia and laughed off his 'nightmare scenario.'

The car issue had done nothing but push Charlie further away from his dad. In defiance, while his parents were off to Chicago for a weekend, he and his friends had torn out the factory stereo and speakers and replaced them with a far more powerful sound system, including two twelve-inch subwoofers in the trunk.

When Charlie turned the key, the Jetta's engine roared to life, and Kendrick Lamar's *Money Trees* rumbled through the interior. Charlie's head bopped along to the song's bass line as he slowly drove out of Covington Falls and headed towards Boardman's shopping area.

Twenty minutes later Charlie strolled into the Southern Park Mall still searching for a satisfying distraction, so he indulged in one of his favorite rituals, a soft pretzel. The first time his mother had given him one he'd been twelve, and he'd immediately fallen in love with the warm, soft, chewy treat that carried a hint of butter. From then on, whenever they had gone shopping, they shared the salty bread, and every time he devoured one now he could almost hear her playful voice admonishing him not to eat so fast. Biting into one brought his mother vividly back to him. Those memories were always bittersweet.

With pretzel in hand he lazily sauntered through the mall, occasionally running into other classmates as he made his way to his favorite store, a mom-and-pop operation that sold sneakers and other cool casual gear for teens called Pistachio's. The entire staff knew Charlie, and when he walked in, Big Red, the store manager, greeted him with a broad smile and a fist pound.

Brian Reddington was a couple years older and a student at YSU studying business management. He was about Charlie's weight and height, but they called him Big Red because of his blazing red hair. Despite his freckles and his emerald green eyes the size of silver dollars, Big Red wasn't like most white boys Charlie knew. Red worshipped at the alter of hip hop like Christians did at the feet of Jesus, which was why Charlie and Red enjoyed each other's company so much. Every now and then he would hand Charlie a homemade CD of old school hip hop that would rattle the Jetta. Charlie in turn would introduce Red to various new artists coming up on the scene.

"What's up, Chuck? I was about to text you."

"Whattup, Red? You got something good for me?"

Red leaned in and whispered conspiratorially, "I stashed a pair of vintage, white on white Jordans in a size twelve in the stockroom."

Charlie's eyes lit up.

"Just for you, man," Red said with a light punch to Charlie's chest. "You wanna see em?"

"Is the sky blue? Of course I wanna see em."

"Cool, be right back," Red said before he headed to the storeroom.

"Hi, Charlie," came an all too familiar melodic voice from behind him.

He swallowed hard in anticipation. Still wearing his grin, he turned towards the sweet musical voice. Standing on the other side of the counter was the amazing Clarissa Moore. She was the one girl outside of Lily Fernandez who always made Charlie's pulse race. Clarissa's father had once played football for Ohio State, and her mother had run track for Michigan State, so Clarissa had been blessed with truly gifted genes. Standing at a statuesque six foot one inch, her curvy and muscular frame was stunning. She ran track for their high school and was headed to Southern California to run for the Trojans of USC on a full scholarship. From the waist up she was shapely with broad shoulders, carrying what every guy in school thought was a perfect C cup. From the waist down, however, Clarissa's powerful form was jaw dropping.

Today she wore her hair in a tight clean French braid, a style Charlie always thought looked great because it accentuated her high cheekbones, long lashes, and a radiant smile. Her brown, almond shaped eyes gleamed and danced with light against her flawless café au lait colored skin that capped off her beauty.

Charlie walked over to the counter as cool as he could, hoping she couldn't hear his heart pound in his chest. "Hey, Clarissa," Charlie said mimicking her playful tone and looking around the store. "Busy in here today."

"You know how it is on weekends. You're here enough to know," she said at the same time a young white boy and his mom approached the counter, arguing over the kid's choice in clothes.

The kid tossed an armful of clothes on the counter while his mother made her way forward searching through her purse. The woman grumbled loudly to her son. "I don't see why you want to dress like those rap guys in those ridiculous videos. That's all I'm saying. I hope you grow out of this thuggish phase and quickly."

Considering Charlie wore many of the same styles the boy had placed on the counter, he rolled his eyes at the ignorant woman's tone. When she realized others had overheard her, her critical eyes looked Charlie up and down and wrinkled her nose before she turned her attention back to her child, who continued to plead his case.

Clarissa rang up the items, handed over the shopping bag to the annoyed mother, and said, "Thank you for shopping at Thugs."

Taking her purchase, the ugly woman sneered and asked, "I'm sorry. What did you say?"

"Have a nice day, ma'am," Clarissa replied and flashed her irresistible smile. The mother glanced at Charlie and tightened her grip on her purse before she and her son quickly left the store. When they were gone, Clarissa and Charlie looked at each other and broke out into peals of laughter. Fifteen minutes, some playful flirting, and two bags later including the Jordans Red had put aside for him, Charlie left Pistachio's with a wink at Clarissa and her invitation to "Come back to Thugs anytime."

Charlie wasn't quite ready to leave the mall. He was finally feeling good, so he wound his way through the concourse and strolled into Lady Foot Locker, hoping to grab some time with one of his favorite people. Standing at the wall of sneakers, he carefully eyed each pair.

"May I help you?" asked a distinctive dusky voice that made his toes tingle.

"Yeah, do you have these in a size twelve?" Charlie asked holding out a hideously multicolored track sneaker that glowed in the dark.

Lily smiled at Charlie's silliness and snatched the sneaker from him.

Charlie's joy was palpable. He had eyes for only one girl, and while Clarissa was stunning, time and his heart stood still for Lilibeth Fernandez. Lily's Mexican-American heritage gave her skin tone a shade of honey mixed with a dash of cinnamon. Whenever she smiled, her eyes would almost close to slits, and two deep dimples sunk sweetly into her cheeks. While Charlie daydreamed about it often for almost two years, neither he nor Lily seriously acted on their mutual attraction. Instead they had developed and maintained a fun, solid friendship since the beginning of their junior year. There was no point trying to be more than friends. After high school he was going to Michigan, and she was headed to NYU. While they talked about staying in touch once they went their separate ways, he knew they wouldn't. Charlie understood that people typically never looked back once they left their hometowns and old friends.

Lily pursed her lips. "Hmmmm...I can check our stock, but I doubt we have anything that's a size twelve in men's."

"Why's that?"

"Well," Lily started as she returned the sneaker to its shelf and he took in her short curvaceous build. Charlie loved Lily's curves, but what he loved most about her was her nimble mind. She was the smartest girl he knew, and he enjoyed being around her, even if she did often make him the butt of her jokes. "I know you sometimes have a hard time reading, Charles, but this is Lady Foot Locker, keyword is 'Lady.' There aren't many women walking around with a sasquatch-sized foot like yours."

His mouth watered at the scent of her, but he stuck to their usual playful banter. "Hmmm...that would explain all the pink," Charlie muttered with pursed lips. "Well could you check for me? I really like that ridiculous sneaker and would love to have a pair. The hot pink, red, black, and neon orange swirls somehow call to me," he said loudly.

"Shhh," she whispered slapping his arm. "You got some secret life you care to share with the entire store?"

"See...I came in for a pair of sneakers, and you attack me. Where's your manager?"

"Fine, sir," she said trying not to double over in laughter. "Please wait right here, and I'll see if we have those in a...what size was that again?" Lily asked with a hand on her hip.

"You know," Charlie said, "now that I'm looking at them from a distance, I don't think I want them. They'll clash with my yellow spandex onesie. I'm going to keep looking if that's all right."

Choking back giggles, Lily tried for a serious tone. "Absolutely, sir. If there is any way I can assist you, please let me know."

Charlie flashed a mischievous grin and whispered, "With you looking as fetching as a glass of water to a thirsty man in the desert in that uniform, I think you could definitely assist me." Her husky laughter was his reward and squeezed his heart.

Lily smiled, blushed, and shook her head at his flirting. "What are you doing here, Charlie? You trying to get me fired?"

"Hey, you approached me. I was minding my own business, seriously contemplating that pair of sneakers, being conscientious, and all that, and you came up to me but whatever." He shrugged. "What time do you get off work?"

She glanced at her watch. "In an hour."

"Fine, I'll be back in an hour to get you. I'll take you to dinner, okay?"

Lily cocked her head considering. "Sure," she said finally.

Charlie let out the breath he'd been holding. "Just one catch though. You have to wear that lovely uniform," he said tracing the clinging material across her shoulder. "Deal?"

Shaking her head, Lily crossed her arms under her ample breasts inadvertently plumping their already ample form. "Nope."

Charlie swallowed hard and with puppy dog eyes. "Come one, you look sooo good in it. Pretty please?"

She nudged his shoulder pushing him off balance. "I wore my own yellow spandex onesie to work, so if you like me in this, you'll love me in that," Lily said with a sly smile.

Charlie laughed. "Perfect, I'll go home and throw mine on too, so we can match."

"I swear you are the craziest boy ever," she said, her warm laugh again rolling over him like a fire on a chilled night.

"And don't you forget it," he softly said. He cleared his throat, and again said loud enough for the store to hear. "I'll be back in an hour for my hot pink, red, black, and orange sneakers, ma'am. Please make sure you save me a pair. Thank you."

Lily blushed and rolled her eyes as she escorted him to the front of the store.

"Size twelve, understand?" he yelled before Lily shoved him into the main concourse.

Lily turned and found herself face to face with her manager, Marsha, a flaxen-haired, freckled, middle aged woman with a warm smile and a figure that looked like she got the most out of her gym membership. She had watched them with her arms folded. "Was that him?" she asked with a nod in Charlie's direction.

"Yep."

"He's cute, loud but cute," Marsha said as the two women walked back into the store.

"He's all yours if you want him," Lily offered. Unbeknownst to Charlie, Lily had sworn off guys her senior year because her sole focus was on NYU, but she couldn't resist Charlie. He tempted her in a way no other boy ever had.

"He's too short for me," she said.

Lily looked her boss up and down and laughed. The two women were the same height at a mere five-five.

"What?" Marsha asked raising her hands at Lily's dubious stare. "I like my men tall, and besides, he's too young for me. Perfect for you though, lil mama," she teased before she walked away to help a customer.

Marsha missed Lily's sigh and glance toward the front of the store. "Yeah, I know," Lily whispered. "That's the problem."

6

Forty-five minutes later, Charlie slowly made his way back toward Lady Foot Locker carrying a few more bags. He felt slightly better, but his dark storm cloud still hung low overhead. He couldn't escape it. The thought of Stony refused to stay in the back of his mind. He still had no idea how to pay off his debt, not really. An idea had come to him at the food court, but he wondered if he could sink that low.

Not up for any additional temptation, he strode past Pistachio's. Clarissa waved, and he waved back but kept moving and grabbed a bench outside of Lily's store.

Ten minutes later, Lily walked out wearing pink spandex leggings, white track sneakers, and a fitted white t-shirt, which accentuated every curve of her shapely figure. She approached him with a smile and a little runway strut.

"Yeah…yeah…you're right. While it's not the yellow onesie you promised me, it is way better than your uniform," he said standing to meet her with an appreciative grin. Glad I didn't go home and put on mine. I'd have felt like a lonely banana. Speaking of uniforms, you got my sneakers, lady?"

Lily sucked her teeth and smacked him in his arm. "Will you let go of the sneaker thing?" she demanded as she pulled on him to walk.

"Sure, okay, but I really liked those ugly things."

"You do not. No one likes those ugly things."

"That's because only I can see the genius in those beautiful hideous sneakers. They are beautifully ugly."

Lily rolled her big brown eyes. "So where are we going?"

"Well knowing how much you love movies, I thought I would take you to a movie, get you a huge bag of popcorn, a giant pop, and afterwards, if you're hungry, a big juicy burger from Stymie's."

"Sounds like the perfect end to my day," she beamed. "What movie?"

"That new sci-fi thriller, *The Ambassador.*"

"Yes! I was hoping you would say that. I love the director." All she could do was smile at him and slipped her arm around his. "Okay, okay so you know me, so what? Don't go feeling yourself, buster."

"But I feel so good. Really, Lils, you should feel me sometime. I'm so amazing to the touch that you'd be all 'OMG' and stuff."

"Whatever, Charles," she said with laugh and a roll of her eyes. "Just because you do what most don't doesn't mean you're special, you know."

"What do I do that most don't?" he asked apprehensively coming to a stop.

"You pay attention, which is why I like you. That and you never tell me I'm stupid or crazy about seeing a movie more than once or wanting to be a director someday. You know what, thank you, Charles."

Charlie looked at her in confusion. "For what?"

"For letting me be me. I like that," she said tugging on his arm to walk.

"Oooookay...well, you're welcome, loco. Now tell me why are we going this way?" he asked her. "My car is in the other direction."

"We're going to take the long way. I want to walk by Pistachio's with you."

"Why?" Charlie asked a little nervously.

"It's a girl thing," she said patting his arm. "You wouldn't understand."

Charlie sighed. "You wanna bet?" he said under his breath.

After their little parade past Pistachio's where Clarissa smiled and waved sweetly, they jumped in Charlie's car and headed to the theater on the other side of the mall complex. For two and a half hours they sat side-by-side transfixed. They laugh, they jumped, they shared the biggest bucket of popcorn the theater had with extra butter, and they sipped a supersized pop. When Lily cried, Charlie leaned over and wiped her tears before he put his arm around her. When the credits rolled, they left reciting lines and reenacting scenes. They laughed until they couldn't breathe anymore, and for the first time all day, Charlie felt happy.

"Are you hungry?" he asked after regaining his composure.

"Yep! On to Stymie's," she said with a charging bugle sound effect as they jumped in the Jetta for the drive across town.

Thirty minutes later after copious amounts of laughter, they arrived at Stymie's and grabbed a booth before Lily headed to the ladies room. As Charlie perused the menu he lost himself in thoughts of Lily and those pink spandex leggings.

"Whattup, nigga?"

Startled, Charlie dropped the menu and saw Chad's smiling face. His big blue eyes were glassy, so he instantly knew his friend was baked. "Hey, Chad."

"Where ya been all day, fucka? I thought maybe aliens snatched your ass up and was anal probing my boy. Gavin got a hold of some killer chronic. You gotta try this shit, man. I been tryin to reach you. Gavin been trying to reach you," Chad said throwing his hands in the air.

"We call, we text, and nothing. No reply. No phone call. Nothing. Wasammatta, dick? You don't love us no more?"

"I've been busy, and you need to go, man," Charlie said with one eye on the ladies restroom door.

"Why? Wait…Hold up, Chuck. Whose bag is this?" Chad said picking it up with a grin.

"It's Lily's, so get going," Charlie hissed.

"Ooooh…You lovin on that big bootie Mexican?" Chad asked with a wry smile. "Do your thing, playa," Chad said as he slid out of the booth just as Lily walked up behind him.

"Ahem," she said, announcing her presence.

Chad spun and said, "Oh! Hey, Lils. Nice outfit."

Lily slid into the booth. "Hi, Chad. Thank you," she said dryly.

"Well you two kids have fun. Lily, you are in the best possible hands around. I'm sure you know that though. Charles, be a gentleman and don't do anything I wouldn't do, and if you do, use protection," he said with a wink as he stumbled a few steps away from their booth. Turning back he shouted, "Charlie, call me tonight when you get in. Cool?"

"Leave, Chad," Charlie said.

"I'm going. I'm going. Sheesh."

When Chad finally left, Charlie started to apologize, but Lily stopped him. "There's no need, Charlie. You didn't do anything wrong. I've known Chad for years. I know how he is and who he is, but for some reason he seems to be getting worse," she said shaking her head.

Charlie sighed. Everything about Lily appealed to him. Not only was she smart and silly and had the cutest dimples when she smiled, but she was also compassionate and understanding. Most of all though, for some odd reason and more surprisingly, she was genuinely interested in him and who he was rather than how much money he had or who his dad was. She asked him questions that no one had ever cared enough or thought enough to ask. She wasn't the prettiest girl in school, but in Charlie's opinion, she was the total package.

"So," she started after they ordered, "what did you get from Pistachio's today?"

"A throwback pair of Jordans, two pairs of shorts, five t-shirts, and a new hat," he answered with a shrug. He hadn't needed any of it, but spending money made him feel good.

"Nothing else?" she asked innocently looking out the window to avoid his gaze.

"Nope, there was nothing else I wanted."

"You didn't get a phone number or anything like that?" she asked wearing a sly smile.

Charlie chuckled at her curiosity. Her little concern over Clarissa made him wish college wasn't right around the corner. "No, I did not get a phone number."

"Just checking," she said and began looking through her bag to hide her face.

"And why are you just checking?"

"No reason," she said as she applied lip-gloss to her already glossy lips.

"That's bull, and we both know it."

Lily pouted and took in the silverware.

"Why are you 'just checking' about that, Lily," Charlie asked again.

"Well, I heard she has a thing for you so...I wanted to know if that was true."

Alarm bells clanged in his head. "What did you do?" he asked bracing for her answer.

"I asked her."

"WHAT?" Charlie asked incredulously.

"I asked her if she had a thing for you," Lily answered bluntly.

"Which she doesn't."

"Oh yes she does, buster, big time. Told me so straight to my face,"

"Bull."

Lily feigned shock. "You calling me a liar?"

Charlie eyed her suspiciously for a few seconds. "Fine and what did you say?"

"I politely told the Amazon to back off," Lily said, her dimples on full blast.

"Or what?" Charlie asked with laughter in his voice.

"Or else I'd have to make her bleed," she said with an emphasis on the last word which made them both break into uncontrollable laughter.

"Well thankfully," said Charlie, catching his breath, "there's enough of me to go around." When Lily slowly picked up her butter knife, he held up his hands. "Okay, okay, easy killer! I was playing."

"Good, because I wasn't," Lily said and flashed her dimples again. "So what did you do last night other than the usual?"

"What's the usual?"

"Video games and weed, of course."

"Wow, am I that predictable?"

"No, that unoriginal," she answered glibly.

"Ouch. Okay, you got me," Charlie said. "Gavin and Chad came over. We smoked and played video games all night."

"Like I said, sadly unoriginal."

"What would have been original?" he asked.

"Are you still working on that novel you started last year?"

It was Charlie's turn to avoid eye contact. "Nah, I gave that up."

"Why?"

Charlie thought about for a second. "Because I have nothing to say. I thought I could come up with something, you know, interesting, but I haven't done anything or gone anywhere yet. So I figure get some life experiences, maybe go on an adventure or two, and then I'll have something worth writing about."

"Okay…that makes sense, but have you ever heard of this little thing called an imagination? It's a device used by all good artists. You might want to look into getting one. Besides, how exactly are you going to get any 'life experiences' when all you do is shop, play video games, and get high?" she asked. "See…working on your novel, that would have been original."

Charlie couldn't think of a reply because he knew she was right. Thankfully their food came, and they dug in hungrily. Once they cleaned their plates and in no hurry to leave, they sat in their booth and discussed the movie, school, their friends, and future plans.

"Why Michigan?" Lily asked?

"Two reasons. One, I want to be a writer, and Michigan is one of the best literary arts colleges in the country. Secondly and most importantly, however, attending Michigan will truly piss off my father, an Ohio State alum. How bout you?" Charlie asked. "I know you want to be a movie director, but why go all the way to NYU?

"Because, my good man, they have one of the most amazing and accomplished film schools in all the world, and what better school to go to if I want to make movies? Plus I got fam in New York, so it's a win-win."

"Yeah, but why not UCLA or USC?" he asked.

"First off, because UCLA and USC aren't New York, and I don't know if you've heard, but New York is the greatest city in the world. There is no way I would go west if I can go east. And I swear to God

Charlie, you mention USC one more time, and I'm gonna kick you till you're dead." She punctuated her threat with a smile.

"Ahhh, Trojans…gotcha," he said with a cringe realizing he'd mentioned Clarissa's choice in school. "What's with the 'kicking me till I'm dead' thing though?"

"It's a line from *Moonstruck*, but I will do it," she said, pointing a limp fry at Charlie. "Don't push me, buster."

"Geez, so violent. I think you need some anger management classes before heading to New York," he said laughing at her silliness getting up to pay the tab and drive her back to her car.

"Can I ask you a question before you go?" Charlie asked twenty minutes later as they sat in Charlie's Jetta neither quite ready to say goodbye.

"Sure," she said tucking a bit of hair behind her ear.

"Why do you like me? I mean…why me?"

"If I tell you why, will you tell me why you like me?"

"Sure."

"Okay," she said apprehensively but turned to face him, "Remember that writing assignment in Mr. Whitmore's class at the beginning of the school year? The one where he had us write about the memory that was most precious to us?"

Charlie nodded slowly.

Lily lowered her eyes, softly took his hand, and continued in a hushed tone. "You…you wrote about how your mother taught you how to ride a bike and cook an omelette and wash your clothes. You wrote about all the things she taught you before she died and how thankful you were for her and for those memories. I cried when I read your words, Charlie, and in that moment I realized that there was so much more to you than just a cute class clown who takes nothing seriously."

Charlie swallowed and stared out the window remembering the words he'd written. He'd almost torn it up and considered taking an incomplete for the assignment. He'd waited until the night before to write it, and the only memory he could remember had been his mother's face that day she taught him how to ride, how her eyes had sparkled, and how she'd shouted praise over and over while running behind him until she was out of breath. Then suddenly other memories, memories he had long forgotten, had rushed in from the cold. Mr. Whitmore had given him an A+ on that essay. There hadn't been any other dreaded red pen editing marks on the pages. "How…how did you read that?" he whispered.

"It fell out of your book on the way out of class, and I was right behind you. I picked it up and was going to give it back to you, but you started roughhousing with your friends the second you hit the hallway, so I kept it, planning to give it to you the next day. I never intended to read it, Charlie," she said quietly and squeezed his hand. "But when I found it that night in my backpack and after I read the first line, I couldn't help but read the rest. Then…knowing what it was about…well, the time never seemed right. I hope you don't hate me," she said, raising her eyes to meet his, but Charlie continued to stare through the windshield.

"How could I hate you, Lils? " he said when he was finally able to speak. "You didn't plaster it all over school or post it everywhere online. You didn't tell anyone about it, and that means a lot to me. Thank you for keeping that between us," he said as his finger ran along the contours of the steering wheel. Lily squeezed his other hand again and breathed a sigh of relief.

"Okay, your turn," she said attempting to lighten the mood and pull Charlie out of his reflections.

"I like you because you're…different, in a good way," he said, still staring at the steering wheel. "Like, all the other girls I know don't seem…pleasant. You're fun to be around. You make me laugh all the time. I don't know. I just really enjoy your company."

"Charles, look at me."

He turned his head and met her warm brown eyes. Lily leaned in and kissed him softly on the lips. Charlie was shocked but instantly tilted his head in invitation. Timidly they tasted each other, nipping softly. With a sigh Lily opened her mouth slightly, and Charlie tentatively slipped into her warm sweet mouth. His heart raced, but when things were about to get hot and heavy, she pulled away slowly.

"I liked that. I should have done that sooner," she said a little out of breath but with a contented sigh. She placed her hand on his cheek softly. "You should come to New York with me, Charlie. You can go to school with me. You write, I'll direct, and together we'll find some sucker to produce our projects. Whattaya say, buster?" she asked, dimples on full blast.

How could anyone resist this girl? Charlie thought. "Let me think about it," he said leaning his head back on the seat trying to calm his revved up libido.

"Nah, forget it. Bad idea," she said suddenly as she pulled back her hand. "You'd get tired of me, and god knows there are a million better looking girls than me in New York," she continued as she grabbed her bag.

She was about to get out of the car when Charlie stopped her lightly placing his hand on her arm. He could tell she was somehow distressed, but he wasn't sure why. "No, Lily," he said softly but firmly. "There aren't."

She paused to meet his eyes, then leaned in quickly, and gave him another kiss on the lips. This one was far less sensual than the first but equally as passionate. Silently, she opened the car door and left without looking back.

7

"You owe HOW much money?" Gavin asked Charlie.

"Don't make me repeat it. Saying it out loud makes my head hurt," Charlie said as he walked to the fridge in the man cave. He pulled out an energy drink and downed it. According to Gavin, Chad was home sleeping off his super high from earlier in the day, and given how he'd acted at Stymie's, Charlie wasn't surprised.

"Yeah, I heard you. I just don't believe you," Gavin said.

"Believe me," Charlie said before taking in a long deep drag of much needed weed.

Rubbing his pounding head, Charlie plopped down on the plush sectional and grabbed the remote. His impromptu date with Lily had given him a welcome albeit brief reprieve from his troubles. No matter what he was dealing with, she had the ability to take his mind off his issues, but as he'd watched her taillights fade in the distance, Stony, Frank, and the chainsaw with his father's name on it had climbed into his car and come home with him.

"Shit, dude! What the fuck were you betting on? And how much were you laying down?" Gavin asked stunned.

"Remember that hot streak I was on during football season?" Charlie asked. Gavin nodded taking the half-smoked blunt. "I thought my luck would ride, so I started betting on basketball, a little hockey, and tennis too."

Gavin coughed. "Charlie, what the fuck do you know about hockey or tennis?" he asked passing the blunt back.

"Apparently nothing." Charlie groaned and rubbed his face. "I am so fucked," he sighed.

"Maybe not, what were you told exactly?"

"I have forty-eight hours to either pay him or come up with a way to get the money to pay him. Stony's gonna call tomorrow, and he's gonna wanna know what I'm gonna do to get him his cheese,"

Charlie said which made Gavin explode into laughter. Charlie stared blankly at his friend. "What the fuck is so funny?"

"You said 'cheese,'" Gavin answered and couldn't stop laughing.

Charlie chuckled himself. "You're a dork, dude."

"I know. I know. My bad," Gavin said as he tried to stop snickering.

Charlie almost told his friend about Stony's threat to his dad, but he wasn't ready to face that part of the nightmare and saying those words out loud would make the danger all too real. He lifted the blunt to his lips and pulled another deep hit.

They sat in silence for a few minutes contemplating possible solutions as they watched ESPN baseball highlights in silence. Charlie passed Gavin the blunt as Gavin asked, "Charlie, you think your pops would miss, say...fifty thou?"

"What?"

"Do you think your dad would miss fifty thousand dollars?"

"My dad would miss ten dollars. Why?"

"Well," Gavin started slowly, "if you could get your hands on fifty grand, you could give Stony that, call it like a good faith payment kinda thing. Give him that right, and let him know that it's like the first of four payments. Each payment another fifty thousand," Gavin said with a shrug.

Charlie turned and cocked his head in annoyance. "Really, G? Are you smoking something different than I am?" Charlie asked. "Where in the hell am I gonna get four payments of fifty thousand dollars? Out of my ass?"

"Dude...yo...that's the brilliant thing. You don't have too. All you need to do is come up with one. That payment should buy you enough time, and before you have to make your next payment, you'll be off to college. Boom! Besides how's some idiots from the South Side ever gonna find you on that big ass campus? Hell, can they even read?" he asked pulling on the blunt.

Charlie knew Stony and Frank weren't some kind of dumb ignorant hoods from the South Side. He sighed. "First off, dude, they found my house, and I never told them where I lived. And even if that plan had any chance of working...they'd find my dad."

"So? Your pops can take care of himself, dude," Gavin said. Glancing up, Charlie's friend caught the look of apprehension flash across his face. "What? They threaten you or your dad?" he asked passing the smoke back to Charlie.

Charlie closed his eyes took another long drag and held the draw as long as possible. Slowly releasing the smoke from his lungs, he leaned back and absorbed the lift-off to his desired high. After a few minutes, Charlie finally answered quietly. "Yeah, man. They threatened my dad." Charlie stared at the smoldering end of the blunt before he tapped out the cherry. "Stony looked me in the eye and said somewhere out there, in this big bad world, is a chain saw with my father's name on it. I almost pissed in my fucking pants, dude."

Gavin lit up the second fat blunt and puffed. After a long exhale, he said, "Fuck, that's some brutal shit right there."

"Yeah...So I'm thinking those idiots aren't into payment plans. They want their fucking money, but your idea isn't really a bad one, G. All I'd have to do is get my hands on fifty grand and see what happens."

Gavin leaned forward slowly and squinted at Charlie through the hazy cloud between them. "Nope, forget I said that, man. It was a bad idea."

"No. No. It has some legs, G." Charlie slipped the blunt from Gavin's fingers and took another long hit, hoping if he got high enough the tightness in his chest would disappear like his headache.

"Yeah, until those legs get cut off by a chain saw. You ever seen *Scarface*?" Gavin asked.

"Nope." Charlie said as his high settled in firmly. He then leaned back, closed his eyes, and smiled.

"How are you the only person I know who's never seen that damn movie?" Gavin asked, his words coming out far slower than usual.

Charlie shrugged.

"Anyway, there's this chainsaw scene in the movie, the bathroom scene. These crazy Columbians...or Cubans...whatever, anyway they got Scarface, Tony Montana, and his right hand man handcuffed to the shower rod, and they wanna know where the money is. Tony and his man won't talk, so the bad guys start up a chainsaw and cut up Tony's man right in front of him. Dude…it was insane. Blood's splattering everywhere, all over Tony, all over the guys who were cutting the guy up, all over the bathroom, but Tony just stands there and watches his boy get chopped up into little pieces while he's covered in his boy's blood. Fucking wild, dude."

A more relaxed Charlie looked at Gavin and snickered. "You sound funny when you high."

"Whatever, just…forget my idea," Gavin slowly repeated.

"Come on. You said yourself it's only a movie. Maybe they're just trying to scare me." Charlie then turned to face his friend. "Do you really think they'd take a chainsaw to my dad? MY dad?" Charlie waved a dismissive hand. "C'mon, man, they ain't messing with my dad. He's the fucking District fucking Attorney and shit."

"Charles Robert Jackson…have you ever watched the local news?" Gavin asked, sounding like he had cotton in his mouth. "Those cats are craaaaaaazy," he said, his eyes wide like a cartoon character. "Shit, man, I bet it's the fact that your dad IS the district attorney, who's job is to lock them away, probably makes it more of an im…im…impetuous to take him down. You think they SCARED of your dad? Really?"

Charlie laughed at his friend. He knew Gavin was completely done whenever he used his full name, and he was even starting to trip up on his words. "You mean 'impetus,' douchebag?"

"That's what I said, man."

"Whatever," Charlie replied, but Gavin's points did make him pause. He stared at the ceiling thinking back on last night, seeing Frank and Stony in their element and how everyone around them respected them. *Neither one of them fools would be scared of going after my dad*, he thought. *Shit, Frank would be a legend then. Killing the D. A. would make him big time.*

"No," Charlie eventually answered. "They'd be about as scared as I'd be racing against a blind cripple."

"I heard them blind cripples are fucking fast, dude," Gavin said with his head tilted back and his eyes closed. "And they cheat, so watch ya back."

Charlie shook his head at his friend.

"Then yeah…I'd take that chainsaw threat as gospel," Gavin quipped.

"Fuck, dude. Enough. You're killing my high." Charlie replied closing his eyes.

Gavin sat up and shrugged. "Whatever, man. I got a few grand I can give you. It's not much, but it might buy you some more time."

"How much is a 'few grand'?"

"I can give you about ten right now. I need the rest to re-up."

Charlie was surprised. "Maybe I should start selling drugs."

"It's weed, man. Weed ain't a drug. It's only classified as a fuckin narcotic by the government because they–"

"All right, all right," Charlie said cutting him off before Gavin got on his soapbox. "Didn't mean to get you started. Thanks for the offer, but I can't take your money. Sides, Stony wants all or nothing. I walk up in there with ten, and they'll likely send me home in some kind of ridiculous pain."

"Shit, ten grand ain't nothing to sneeze at."

A frustrated Charlie said, "You're right, except when you owe one hundred and ninety thousand more. Then ten G's is like shooting a BB gun at a charging rhino. No effect at all."

He glanced over and saw that sleep had taken Gavin. Sensing he was close to nodding off himself he stamped out the blunt and grabbed a throw pillow. He dozed off to the sound of sports highlights.

8

Sunday morning, Stony stumbled into the bathroom and started the shower. Even after more than six years, Stony continued to think of it as Leonard's shower, just like the house itself. Leonard had left Stony not only his businesses but also his spacious two story house in the heart of Youngstown's South Side. Despite being surrounded by blight and disrepair, the house was a masterpiece inside and out, so much so that initially Stony had been willing to sell everything left to him but the house. As a child, it had been his sanctuary.

Despite Leonard's roots in Youngstown's rough South Side, he had been a Renaissance man with an unbridled love of art, and while other kids had been climbing trees or beating each other with sticks and dirt bombs, Stony had been content to stare after each piece in his uncle's modest collection of prints and reproductions. By the time he was nine, Leonard, the patriarch of the family, had taken Stony further under his wing and became like a surrogate father, taking the quiet intellectual young boy to art shows, museums, and galleries not only in Youngstown but also in Pittsburgh and Cleveland. Eventually the two of them had also traveled to famous museums in New York City, Italy, Spain, and France.

Leonard had made sure Stony wanted for nothing and even designated one of the bedrooms in his home as Stony's, so his nephew would always have a safe and nurturing place to stay. To Stony those days with his uncle had been the happiest days of his life, where he could be himself.

Once showered and dressed, Stony ate and was watching the morning news when a pounding knock came from the front door. With a slight tap of his thumb Stony changed the TV's input feed to his security cameras. Seeing Frank waiting in black slacks and pressed dark shirt, he quickly wiped his fingers with a linen napkin before he walked to the front of the house to let in his friend. The two men greeted each other warmly with their customary half handshake-half hug.

"Is everything all set?" Stony asked as he finished his glass of orange juice.

"Yeah, we got him over in one of those abandoned houses by the park."

Stony smiled. No one knew the streets better. Frank and his relentless crew were almost the equivalent of Navy Seals. They always found their man. "Where'd you find him?"

"Hiding out at his girl's place. He made the mistake of steppin on the front porch late last night. When the boys rolled up in there they found him in her closet wearing her underwear," Frank said.

"Bullshit!" Stony said with a callous laugh. He slipped on a khaki-colored short sleeve button down over his white t-shirt that complemented a pair of olive cargo shorts and sparkling white sneakers. Frank smirked but didn't elaborate, which meant he was telling the truth. "Get the fuck outta here. Wow, you never know about some people," Stony said under his breath. "Okay, let's go."

Once they were in Frank's BMW and headed to the other end of the South Side, Stony browsed his email.

"Why you smiling?" Frank asked.

"Do you know who Jean Michel Basquiat is?" Stony asked still scanning the digital display in his hand.

"Should I? You got beef?"

"No," Stony laughed, "Jean Michel died in the late eighties. He was an amazing contemporary artist. He started off with graffiti, but some of his works are currently valued in the double digit millions."

"Yeah, that's all you, man. I don't get into the artsy stuff," Frank said as he checked his mirrors and turned left. "You know that."

"Yeah, I know." Stony shook his head missing how his uncle had shared the same passion for art. Now there was no one around who understood that beautiful transcendent world.

Frank continued, "So what about him? What has you going on bout some nigga named John Michael?"

"C'mon man, not everyone is a nigger."

"My bad," Frank said.

"And his name is Jean Michel," Stony corrected. "He was Haitian."

"Fine, fine, whatever. What about Jean Michel?" Frank asked mimicking Stony's pronunciation.

"I just got an email on the new exhibits coming to town, and in a few weeks one his paintings will be on loan at the Butler," Stony explained.

"Cool, so you'll get to see one of his joints up close and personal like."

"I've already seen several. I'd actually love to own this one. It's one of my favorites."

"They gonna let you buy it? Like an auction or something?"

Stony chuckled. "While that would be cool, this particular painting sold for 13.5 million eight or nine years ago, and we don't have those kinds of funds, so no...there won't be any buying it. But...you know... maybe this could fit nicely into something I already have cooking...." Stony stared unseeing out the window lost in his thoughts.

Frank eyed his friend and partner. "That devious mind a yours is puttin something together. I can smell the smoke. What you got cooking?"

Stony barely hear Frank's question. His mind was intent on the soon to be displayed Basquiat painting and how he could possibly get his hands on it. He wasn't aware of the twisted smile painted across his face.

"Yo! You aiight?" Frank asked.

Stony shook himself from his thoughts. "Huh? Yeah, I'm fine."

"What the hell were you thinking bout, man?"

"I'll tell you later."

"So be it. We here anyway," Frank said as he pulled into a driveway alongside a black Suburban. A few of Frank's crew stood on the porch of the abandoned house smoking and laughing. Frank's eyes tightened. When the two men climbed onto the crumbling front porch, the guys immediately quieted down, but Frank still eyed each of the young men.

"What the fuck is this?" he asked without raising his voice. "A fucking party? Ya'll do know this house is abandoned, right? As in none of you motherfuckas should be in or out let alone on the porch actin like fucking fools. What if someone called the cops or five-oh rolled by? Ya'll ever heard the word discretion? Who's inside?"

"Chill, Frank." one of his boys said. The thug nodded toward the street. "Everyone round here know what time it is. Ain't no one gonna call no damn cops," he said with a sneer, holding his gun loosely in his hand like a toy.

Frank stared at the dark boy for a long tense moment before he pulled out his own nickel-plated, pearl handled Colt 45, chambered a round, and walked up to the gold-toothed teenager. In a flash Frank had the barrel pointed at the boy's forehead. "Fuck did you say to me?" he quietly asked as his eyes bore into the watery-brown ones of the brash teen, who wisely chose to keep his mouth shut.

Sweat immediately formed on the kid's forehead, and all his arrogance vanished. Everyone knew if he said another word, Frank would put his brains all over the porch.

Another member of the crew bravely stuttered a reply. "B-B-Blake's inside, Frank."

Frank glared at the other two teens. Only the creaking of the porch's aged boards dared to breath. "Fine," Frank said quietly as he slowly lowered his gun and tucked it behind his back. "I want the rest of you no clue havin niggas to get in ya truck and get the fuck outta here. Understand?"

The three boys scrambled around Stony and off the porch without hesitation.

"C'mere, Ripper," Frank said stopping the one who hadn't yet said a word. He pulled a thick roll of cash out of his pocket and peeled off two crisp one hundred dollar bills. "Go get something to eat somewhere, and I'll call ya'll later."

Ripper winked and sauntered towards the SUV. Once their truck had rumbled down the street Frank searched Stony's face. "You ready for this?"

Stony swallowed hard but responded confidently. "Yeah, I'm good."

"Remember what that cross-dressing fuck and his boys did. He earned this, Stone. Just give me the nod when you're ready. I'll take it from there."

"I got you. I'm good. Let's get this over with," Stony said darkly and walked into the house.

The abandoned two-story held a strong dank, musty odor. Sunlight streamed through the cracked living room windows to highlight the peeling wallpaper and pieces of broken dishes scattered across the mottled carpet. What had once been someone's dream was now an abandoned nightmare. While not loud enough for the neighbors to hear, they could make out Blake singing *Fake* by Alexander O'Neil in the back.

"I swear that boy can't hold a tune to save his life," Frank mumbled.

They made their way to the kitchen that no longer cradled humming appliances, the smell of food, or the chatter of family. All that remained were two forgotten mismatched kitchen chairs and a battered red milk crate, which held an older model radio tuned to the local R&B station. Sitting on a ripped vinyl chair was Blake, lost in song.

The other chair groaned under a bound overweight, dark skinned man who wore a ruby red lace bra stretched tight across his hairless barrel chest. His protruding gut buried the matching thong, and a pair of unlaced black sneakers covered his feet. Sweat rolled down the cross-dresser's face as he stared in horror at Blake's off-key performance.

Stony stifled his urge to laugh at the inane scene, but Frank's face somehow remained placid. When Frank and Stony entered the room, Frank's lieutenant stopped belting out lyrics about a phony woman mid-note and jumped up to turn off the radio. The sudden silence was deafening.

Stony moved closer while Frank leaned against the doorway to keep an ear out for any abnormal Sunday morning street traffic. Where a stove had once cooked dinners sat Appleton Harris, the leader of one of the most violent gangs in Youngstown and their main competitor. His wrists were tied behind him and his ankles to the chair legs. The left side of his face and lip were swollen.

Stony leaned casually against the dusty counter with his hands in his pockets and looked down at the beaten yet defiant Appleton and smiled. "What up, App? They treatin you okay?"

"Ain't nothin, man. It's your world," the obese cross-dressing gangster replied.

"Nice outfit," Stony remarked. "You know why you're here?"

Appleton raised his chin and tried to look confident. "I got some idea," he said with a hint of a smile that flashed a few missing teeth and bloody gums.

"I'm sure you do. What you and your pack of wild dogs did to one of my boys was fucked up on so many levels," Stony said as he turned Blake's seat around and straddled it. "When you came to us and demanded a cut of our action and we told you to fuck off, I had no idea you would take it so personally. It's fine if you get all butt hurt, App, but to then turn around and put little ass Earl in a coma? That shit was uncalled for." Stony tilted his head and in wide-eyed wonder asked. "What did you expect us to do, App? Nothing?"

A pool of sweat had collected in the space between his breasts and gut, and it rippled when he spoke. "I had nuttin to do with that. That was some overzealous niggas actin out on they own accord. That shit ain't got a thing to do with me!" Appleton shouted.

"If that were true, which we know is not, that's YOUR crew, right? You told us you run shit over there, remember? Those boys move if and when you say move, right? Those were your words, right? The money goes to you, right? The buck stops with you, RIGHT?" Stony yelled making Appleton jerk in his restraints allowing the puddle of sweat to run free down his left side.

The bound man locked eyes with Stony, and after a few tense seconds Appleton yelled back. "What you want me to say? Fuck you want from me, man?"

"Do you know why you're here, Appleton?" Stony softly asked again.

"Yeah, nigga. I know why," Appleton spat.

"Anything you want to say to me?"

"Whatchu think? I'm gonna beg for my life? Get the fuck outta here, man. I ain't never begged anyone for shit. I damn sure ain't about to beg your fuckin punk ass for my life."

Stony nodded slowly. "I can respect that, admire it in fact. Last thing I want is some fat motherfucka in a matching bra and thong begging me for his life."

"Never that, Stone," said a suddenly very calm Appleton. "You know how I know, nigga. When we choose to live this life, there ain't but two outcomes, jail or the grave. We do what we do knowin that. It is what it is, so get on with it," he said embracing his fate.

"You like movies, App?" Stony asked changing the subject. "Me, I love them. My collection is so fucking huge I could open up my own video rental store if people still did that. These days everyone's downloading and streaming and all that shit."

"Yo...your point?" asked Appleton.

"Out of all those movies I own though, one sticks out as my all time favorite. I can watch this damn movie every day and never get tired of it. You got a movie like that?" he asked Appleton.

"Why, nigga?"

Stony ignored the question and continued, "That movie for me is *The Untouchables*. You've seen that movie, right? Sean Connery, Kevin Costner, a really young Andy Garcia, and the man himself, De Niro, playing Capone. I do a great De Niro as Capone."

"No, you don't," Frank interrupted.

Stony turned and looked up at Frank bemused. "Yeah. I do," he stated.

"I'm just saying not really is all," Frank said with a shrug.

"Don't be a hater," Stony said before he brought his attention back to a puzzled Appleton. "Anyway, the reason I love that movie is because it gives you damn near a tutorial in how to handle yourself in these types of situations."

"A what?" Appleton asked irritated.

Stony sighed. "A tutorial. It's like an instruction manual, a how-to guide. You with me now, you dumb uneducated fuck?"

Appleton sucked his teeth and rolled his eyes.

Stony continued. "The part of the movie I love is when Sean Connery schools Kevin Costner's character in the church."

No one noticed the slight shift in Frank's movements as he slowly pulled out his gun and held it at his side while Stony went on with his story.

"Kevin Costner's character is like a fish out of water, floundering. He doesn't know who to trust or how to bring the fight to Capone, and do you know what Connery's character tells him?" Stony asked as he stood, turned to Frank, and gave an almost imperceptible head nod. "He tells him," Stony said turning back to Appleton. "'He brings a knife. You bring a gun. He sends one of yours to the hospital. You send one of his to the morgue. That's the Chicago way.' Now while this ain't Chicago, I agree with that philosophy a hundred percent. Later, App. Have a nice ride to the fucking morgue," Stony finished with a sneer before he walked past Frank out of the kitchen.

When Stony got to the dilapidated dining room Frank's gun boomed twice, but Stony didn't stop. He simply left the house.

Blake stood next to Frank taking in the scene. Appleton lay face up, two holes in his fleshy chest. His blood pooled underneath him in an ever-growing puddle. The body wore a sly smile on his face, and Frank found something odd and dangerous in that death mask. In all the dead men he'd seen, Frank had never seen anyone go smiling. He suddenly felt a twinge of concern that he and Stony had possibly made a major tactical error in killing this man.

Frank put his gun away and ordered Blake to pick up and dump the shell casings and wipe down the place. Frank walked out as Blake got to work.

When he sidled up next to Stony, who was leaning on his BMW, Frank looked at his partner, "Why you didn't ask him about The Wolf? We still don't know where that bitch is."

"You really think he would have told us if I asked him?" Stony asked.

"No."

"Me neither so we'll deal with that when it comes," Stony replied.

"Yeah," Frank agreed. "Oh, so what was that shit you was tellin me about this Jean Michel Basket guy?"

"Basquiat, man," Stony corrected shaking his head. "Basquiat. He's Haitian."

"Whatever, man," Frank said.

9

Seth checked his watch on the way out of his Harlem brownstone. With one minute until 11 a.m., he was on time. The ride to his restaurant would take less than ten minutes. In his typical fashion, Seth had dressed for comfort in a style that complemented his six-foot-one frame, flawless milk chocolate skin, and smooth baldhead. Wearing a black button down shirt, black pleated slacks, and black Stacy Adams gators with pale blue accents, he would have been intimidating if not for his easy gait, quick smile, and bright dancing eyes. He strolled to his new gleaming black Cadillac ATS-V tucked perfectly at the curb on 137th Street.

Seth loved Cadillacs. Ever since he was a kid he thought of them as the automobile only real men drove. He had gotten his first one almost fifty years ago at seventeen, and as soon as he'd turned the key and cruised down Lenox Avenue he'd felt his manhood settle firmly into place. Chuckling at the memory, he chirped off the alarm and climbed into the sporty black and taupe interior. The supple leather sighed as he made himself comfortable. He loved that sound.

Feeling content, Seth pushed the ignition button, revved the twin turbo V6 engine a few times, and chuckled. He loved that sound too. The sun had no company in the New York City sky, so he slid on his shades, lowered all the windows, and opened the sunroof inviting the outside world to join him. When he turned on his stereo, his favorite group of all time, The O'Jays, began to sing about backstabbers in crisp highs and rumbling lows.

He had to admit that the new ATS-V was growing on him. Paulie, his oldest and closest friend had to convince him to upgrade from his DeVille. It was only after much cajoling and a long test drive upstate had Seth relented. With only a few days behind the wheel, he realized Paulie had been right. *I owe that old bastard a hundred bucks now, dammit*, Seth thought with a smirk.

After waving hello to the handful of ladies headed to church services, Seth deftly pulled away and rolled to a stop at the light at the end of the block. He had lived his entire life in Harlem. It was not just his home. It was his kingdom. When the light turned green, Seth turned right onto St. Nicholas Avenue and headed north.

In his youth, he and his bear of a best friend and now business partner, Paulie, and their gang, The Known Men, had controlled Harlem and treated her like the tough but soulful lady she was—with respect and a firm hand. Nothing had gone through their territory without them knowing about it, taxing it, and tolling it. The Known Men had ruled with an iron fist sheathed in a velvet glove, but when it was time to fight the glove came off, and whoever dared to bring the fight to them had felt their full uncompromising brutality.

Today, thirty years later, Seth and Paulie were still a part of Harlem's success. On the northwest corner of 145th Street and St. Nicholas Avenue stood The Pearl, the neighborhood's favorite restaurant and bar, which they had owned and operated for the last nine years. It had originally been a dive that had been slowly crumbling since they were kids. Paulie was sure they had even robbed the place once or twice. Seth however couldn't recall that.

The two men had always worked well together whether running The Known Men or handling business at The Pearl. Paulie, who tended to be more abrasive, took care of the nuts and bolts while Seth used his charm to handle the staff, distributors, and their customers. They both understood each other's strengths and limitations, which allowed them to be great friends as well as successful business partners.

After ten minutes of talking with anyone except Seth, Paulie would typically begin to consider ways to kill them—literally. While his talents had been a definite benefit in their early days of violence and struggle, they tended to create occasional unnecessary drama in the business world.

Luckily, Seth possessed limitless patience for people as long as they never crossed the line. Seth was as violent as Paulie, and like Paulie, he had no stomach for stupidity or bullshit, but he did have a degree of empathy for humanity that Paulie had never truly developed.

Neither man had known how to run a restaurant. While they had been warned about the high rate of New York restaurant failures, they had seen it as a good investment opportunity and a great way to retire. The early days of The Pearl had been another fight in a long line of battles they had engaged in over the course of their lives. Battles they usually won. The learning experiences of owning a restaurant though had amounted to very little bloodshed, only some mild cajoling coupled with a few "Paulie moments" as Seth had dubbed them. Together the two friends made every financial decision and split everything down the middle even though on paper Seth owned fifty-one percent of The Pearl due to the flip of a coin. After years of hard work, luck, and intuition, The Pearl was a thriving neighborhood eatery that appealed to both the working class stiffs and the corporate professionals who made up the community.

Seth cruised into his parking spot, right behind Paulie's white 7 Series BMW. Paulie had volunteered to oversee the prep for their famous Sunday Brunch that many of the older ladies from the neighborhood attended after church services. However, Seth knew his friend was only there in case his morning meeting with Chico and Roscoe went south. Even after all these years and their transition to legitimate businessmen, they continued to watch each other's backs.

On his way inside, Seth caught sight of Ray-Ray, a neighborhood homeless Iraq War vet with the complexion of coal and eyes the color to match. The towering man ambled around the corner of The Pearl and froze in place when he saw Seth. Even his tattered coat seemed to stand still despite the light spring breeze. Ray-Ray was a shell of his former self, who had returned home after the war to find his grandmother, the woman who had raised him, had passed. With nowhere to go, he'd turned to self-medicating and soon become another one of Harlem's lost addicts. Now he walked 145th asking for spare change and looked almost as old as Seth, when in reality he was half his age.

"Mornin, Seth," Ray-Ray said in a gravelly whisper as he ambled towards Seth.

"Morning, Ray. Whatchu doin out here?" Seth asked. "You all right? You know if Paulie sees you out here that could be bad for you."

"Just doing what I gotta do to survive, man," the vet wheezed as his eyes flitted nervously to The Pearl's glass front door.

"I hear ya," Seth said as he reached into his pocket and pulled out his money clip. He snapped off a crisp twenty-dollar bill and handed it to Ray. "Take this and get yourself something to eat. And looka here, Ray, you get yourself in a program somewhere, get yourself clean, and there's a job waiting for you on the other side of that door. You hear me?"

"What about Paulie?" asked Ray-Ray as his ashen hand quickly took the twenty and stuffed it into an inside pocket for safekeeping.

"You let me handle Paulie. You go take care of yourself, and I'll be here for you, okay?"

"Thanks, Seth. I appreciate that, man. I really do. You the nicest person I know, man."

Seth shook his head with a hint of a smile. "Ray," he said with a light pat to the homeless vet's arm, "I ain't that nice. Now get on the move before Paulie comes out here."

"Thanks again, Seth. I'm a get that help, and I'm a get clean. You'll see, Seth. You'll see," Ray-Ray promised before he quickly shuffled off down the block.

"I hope so," Seth whispered as he watched the addict go. With a sigh, he walked into the cool atmosphere of The Pearl and found Paulie perched on a barstool sipping coffee and reading the paper.

In his younger days Paulie had been built like a tank, and while he still possessed shoulders that could block out the sun, he was far softer around the midsection these days. Even at this age he was blessed with a full head of hair and kept his moustache and goatee sharply groomed, claiming the gray proved his wisdom. Seth gave up an inch to Paulie, but unlike his partner Seth kept himself in shape and his face was clean-shaven.

Seth's smile was broad as he took the stool beside his friend.

"How much did you give him?" Paulie asked gruffly without looking as he turned a page of newsprint.

"Good morning to you too," Seth said motioning for the young lady behind the bar to bring him a cup of coffee. He tilted his head and watched the efficiency of the tall woman blessed with traffic stopping curves as she crossed the bar to grab the coffee pot. He raised an eyebrow at his partner. "Who is she, Paulie?"

Paulie flashed a toothy grin. "That, my friend, is Tamara."

"And how old is Tamara?"

"Twenty-five." Paulie answered taking another sip of his coffee as his usually cynical eyes softened following her every movement.

With full lips and broad nose Tamara was more handsome than she was pretty, but everything else about her—her buttery complexion, her long dark hair, and her shape—favored the pop singer, Mariah Carey. Seth shook his head in amusement. She was exactly Paulie's type. "She looks damn near seventeen. When did she start?"

"Last night," Paulie replied still smiling.

Seth lowered his voice and asked, "How is it that every time I take a day off I always come back to a new employee?"

Paulie shrugged.

"Can she bartend at least?"

Paulie shrugged again. "Don't really know yet, but she makes one hell of a cup of coffee."

As if Paulie words were a stage introduction, Tamara strolled down the length of the bar with a killer kilowatt smile and placed a steaming coffee mug in front of Seth.

"Good morning, Tamara. I'm–"

"Seth," she interrupted with a friendly tilt of her head. "Mr. Paulie told me all about you, and I am just so thankful for this opportunity. I promise you won't regret it!" she exclaimed with a little hop that made certain attributes jiggle appealingly. With that she sashayed back down to the far end of the bar to continue stocking the bar glasses.

Seth added cream and sugar before sampling his coffee. Paulie was right. The coffee was far better than usual, and the scenery wasn't so bad either. "Where did you find her, Paulie?" Seth asked already knowing what his friend of almost fifty years would say.

"Where you think?" Paulie asked returning his attention to the metro section of the paper.

Seth chuckled softly. "When are you going to leave them damn strip clubs alone, old man?"

"When I find a woman like the one you got," Paulie said as a victorious smirk broke across his face.

Seth chuckled. He was beat, and he knew it, so he stole the business section of Paulie's paper and silently finished his coffee. When he was done he rose from the stool. "I told Roscoe and Chico to be here at 11:30. When they get in send them up to me, please," he said as he walked across the polished ebony stained hardwood floors through the empty dining room and headed deeper into The Pearl toward their shared office on the second floor.

Paulie grunted but nodded his head.

10

Paulie hated Chico. The smart-mouthed, spoiled, wannabe gangster, whose mother had begged them to hire her son to keep him off the streets, had little to no respect for anyone or anything. Paulie had little use for people who talked loudly but said nothing, and Chico fit that bill perfectly. Paulie thought Seth's meeting was a waste of time and energy. Until someone went upside Chico's head, the boy would continue to push all the wrong buttons. Lately Chico had been intent on pushing Roscoe's, and Paulie actually liked Roscoe, which was rare. Paulie hardly liked anyone.

Where Chico played at the role of tough guy and street hood, Roscoe didn't need to play. Early on, Paulie had recognized a lot of himself in Roscoe, which is why he'd hired the ex-con. Still on parole from an assault conviction, Roscoe was the silent observing type who never showed his hand until he absolutely had to, and with Chico he hadn't had to…yet.

Everyone who worked at The Pearl knew that moment was coming though, and both of the older men understood that Roscoe had probably already mapped out several ways to kill Chico and had a few locations where he could dump the body. This meeting was Seth's attempt to keep that confrontation from happening. If Seth could help it he wasn't going to allow pride and foolishness to destroy the lives of two more young Black men.

Paulie had suggested a couple days ago that he could quickly solve the problem, but Seth, ever the diplomat, had balked at that idea and wanted to resolve the conflict "with an amicable solution." While Paulie had scoffed and accused Seth of taking the fun out of things, he knew his friend was a smart man and a fair one to boot, which was why Paulie loved him. However, Paulie secretly hoped Roscoe would put his fist through the diminutive muscle-bound punk's face. He smiled to himself at the thought and gazed in appreciation at Tamara's curves as she sashayed the dirty dishes to the kitchen in a way only a former stripper could.

"Whattup, pops?" Chico said with a snide smile as he bopped into the bar, interrupting Paulie's lecherous thoughts.

"Office," Paulie said not even glancing at the thick, young, cinnamon-colored boy.

Chico stopped behind Paulie's stool. "So it's like that, huh?"

"Like what, youngin?" Paulie said as he slowly turned on his stool to face the brash boy. Chico was a squat, nineteen years old, who slept in the gym. His shoulders were well developed, and the blood red wife beater he wore barely contained his chest. Even with his arms relaxed his biceps were coiled knots, and his veins crisscrossed over his arms like a road map. Chico was over confident in his build, and Paulie was well aware of the kid's physical flaws. His muscles might be intimidating, but in a fight his bulk would result in slow reflexes. Chico's lower body was also greatly underdeveloped, making him little danger to anyone who knew what they were doing in a fight, and despite Paulie's age, he hadn't forgotten what to do in a fight.

Chico tipped his chin in defiance. "Like you can't say good morning or something, old man?"

Paulie felt a familiar warmth creep down his spine. The sweet sensation was a joy he hadn't felt in awhile. "I said something, youngin. If you feel it's a good morning then I'm happy for you, but get your ass to the office," he finished with a cool tight-lipped smile and a hard gaze.

Anyone who had ever known Paulie knew that infamous smile well. It was a look his enemies saw more than his friends. However, Chico didn't heed the warning, and he mumbled under his breath as he made his way past Paulie. Before Chico could blink Paulie leapt from his barstool, grabbed the kid by his throat with his right hand, and slammed him against the dividing glass block and wood wall that stood between the bar and the dining area.

"What did you say?" Paulie asked with icy calm even as he squeezed Chico's thick neck. The kid's meaty hands pounded on Paulie's arm with no effect. He tried to grab Paulie's face, but his massive arms were too short. Finally he frantically clawed at the older man's ever tightening grip, but Paulie pressed on without pause. "What did you say?" Paulie calmly asked again.

The boy started to gag, and his face flushed. Paulie could see he was trying to say something and relented a fraction. The young man gasped for air. "I said…one day…it's gonna be me…and you," Chico sputtered in continued defiance.

"Is that so?" Paulie squeezed again. "Well you said it was a good morning. How about now?"

Chico began to turn purple and again flailed at his grip, but Paulie had no desire to let go. He simply continued to squeeze, lost in the warm haze of violence that to him was absolute bliss. He'd missed that drama of kill or be killed situations, where the outcome would be fatally different for someone when it was all said and done. Chico's effort and struggle was weakening by the second, and the kid was about to drop.

11

Paulie in the throes of his violent haze intimidated everyone, everyone but his best friend. Seth rushed up behind his larger friend, looped his right arm under Paulie's and braced his right hand behind Paulie's neck. He pulled at his friend with everything he had, but Paulie didn't budge.

Seth knew Paulie was gone, and he knew Chico was in the final moments of life. Desperate to save lives, Seth wrapped his left arm around Paulie's midsection and pulled again. This time Seth found some traction and heaved once more, throwing Paulie off balance enough to loosen his grip. The kid slumped to the floor, choking and gasping for air.

Ignoring Chico, Seth rushed Paulie out of the bar, head down, feet pumping as if his friend was a tackling sled. Once they burst onto the sun-drenched sidewalk, Seth positioned himself between Paulie and the entrance and braced himself like a linebacker waiting for Paulie's charge.

It never came.

Instead Paulie blinked, reared back, and howled with laughter. After a several long minutes, he clapped his large hands and bent over out of breath.

Seth relaxed.

When Paulie finally stood up a few seconds later, he took in his friend. "You a hell of a lot stronger than you look, you know that?"

Seth came out of his crouch but still blocked the door and looked at his friend with a mixture of concern and respect. "You too, old man. I thought you were done with the 'moments.' What the hell was that all about?" Seth asked breathing heavily.

"That boy…that boy don't know how close he came," Paulie said, trying to catch his breath.

"I think he has some idea." Seth looked up and down the block and then glanced at his watch. Services would be over soon, and he wanted no more drama today. He took a deep breath. "Tell you what," he said as he slowly approached Paulie, "get in that car of yours and go. I'll send Tamara out, and you take the rest of the day off. I'll take care of things."

Paulie eyed Seth. "Seriously?" his partner asked still bent over at the waist. "You know how busy and hectic the next six hours are likely to be?"

"Yeah, but get the hell on outta here anyway. Take Tamara to a movie or something. I can handle the place."

"Yeah? Who's gonna bartend?"

"I will." When Paulie smirked, Seth asked, "What? You don't think I can tend bar?"

"Not well."

"Well then it's a good thing it's Sunday. The church ladies only want virgin drinks or mimosas anyway. Go on, man. I got this," Seth said as he nudged Paulie towards his BMW.

Paulie relented. "Fine, but let Tamara work the day though."

"You sure?"

"Yeah, she could use the practice, and you could use the help," Paulie said as he deactivated the alarm, climbed in, and started his 750 LI.

Seth still didn't move.

Paulie was about to pull away from the curb when he put the BMW back in park, climbed out, and looked over the roof of his car at his best friend. "Seth?"

Seth nodded his head. "I'll send her out, old man," he answered and walked into The Pearl.

Ten minutes later Seth turned his focus back to Chico and Roscoe, his kitchen assistants. At the far end of the bar Chico rubbed his neck and relished each breath while Roscoe merely sat trying to piece together what he'd missed.

Seth took aim at Chico. "I'm not going to ask what the fuck you were thinking, but you almost died today," Seth stated. "For the life of me, I don't know what made you think going up against a man like Paulie was a good idea, but do you see now how stupid it was?"

Chico slowly shrugged his shoulders.

"Yeah, that's what I thought," Seth said shaking his head. "I called you both in today to get to the bottom of this problem you two have for each other, but now I don't give a damn. I'm tired, sweaty, and brunch is about to fuckin start. Roscoe, get to work. Chico, you're fired," Seth said as he reached into his pocket and again pulled out his money clip. He counted off ten one hundred dollar bills and slid them to Chico. "Get your ass out of my establishment."

Roscoe smirked on his way to the kitchen while Chico scooped up the money before making his way to the exit.

"Hey!" Seth yelled at Chico who stopped at the door. Seth slowly walked towards him. In a low menacing growl, Seth addressed the hot head. "If anything happens to this place, anything at all, like if the plate glass gets spray painted or broken or the place catches fire one night or if someone trips and falls at the corner, I'm blaming you! And if I blame you, so will Paulie. Don't make us pay you a visit. Do you understand me?"

The young man and Seth locked eyes until Chico dropped his and nodded.

"Fantastic, good luck to you."

12

Seth made his way through the dining room to the kitchen. Stocked with state-of-the-art equipment and top of the line stainless steel cookware and cutlery, the kitchen was the heart of The Pearl.

When the two friends had initially opened The Pearl there hadn't even been a kitchen or dining area, just the bar. Two years later, Seth and Paulie had decided to expand, but in order to do that they had to buy out the failing hardware store next door.

Roland "Old Man" Robertson had owned and operated Robertson's Hardware for nearly fifty years. He was a compassionate soul and often did work in the neighborhood for nothing. If you needed new locks or a busted doorframe repaired after the police removed an abusive boyfriend or someone kicked in your door and robbed you, Old Man Robertson was there the next day at no charge.

Everyone in Harlem had loved Old Man Robertson.

About eight years ago, his business had begun to struggle. He simply hadn't been able to compete with the big chain stores that had begun to move into Harlem. Knowing Old Man Robertson's difficulty to stay afloat after decades of hard work and service to the community, Seth had invited the genteel man to the bar for a drink as he was closing up shop. Sipping slowly over a round of top shelf scotch, Seth brought up the idea of buying out the old man. He had expected vigorous pushback, but Roland had sat back, downed what was left of in his glass, and asked Seth what his offer was.

Seth pulled out a slip of paper and slid it over to the old man. "The number on this paper is what Paulie and I think your place is worth...not a penny less or a penny more."

Roland's eyes had tightened, but the dark-skinned old man had simply nodded. With a scarred hand nicked by thousands of jobs throughout the years, his stubby fingers had picked up the slip.

Seth poured them both another glass with a knowing smile.

"Seth...," Roland had whispered before he visibly swallowed, "this is too much...too much money for my place," he'd croaked. "My store ain't worth all this. I can't take this from you and Paul."

"Yes you can. Do you know why?" Seth asked patiently. The old man had shaken his head. "That price isn't just for the space. It's also a portion of what we calculated was the dollar amount of free work you've given everyone in this neighborhood. You changed and saved lives. You made people feel safe in their homes. That's priceless. What's on that paper doesn't come close to what you deserve or what you've earned, but that's the best we can do. Now, if you don't take the money, Mr. Robertson, Paul and I will be offended."

The next day Seth had the keys.

Seth had wanted to honor the old man, so over the entrance of the kitchen hung the actual faded window sign that Roland personally had handed to him before he'd left to see all the places he'd dreamt of seeing. Every so often a postcard showed up letting his "boys" know how he was and where he was in the world at that moment. Those postcards always made them both happy.

Seth smiled fondly as he walked under Old Man Robertson's sign and into the kitchen toward the grill. Latin jazz hummed from the radio as the staff efficiently prepped for their Sunday brunch rush. When he saw her, like she usually did, she took his breath away.

Marta Concepcion was the head chef at The Pearl and the second most beautiful woman Seth's eyes had ever seen. His deceased wife Penny would forever be number one to him, but Marta was as close a second as he had ever found. Her solid jaw line, high cheek bones, and full lips were set in total concentration as she pulled fresh baked bread out of the oven while shouting instructions to her team. She was a slim, complicated, full-blooded Puerto Rican woman with exceptional curves and a fiery personality. Barefoot, she stood no taller than five four, but Marta was always in heels, even in the kitchen. When not cooking her thick black hair fell in a stunning silk cascade to her waist, but her most noticeable feature were her piercing dark brown eyes.

They had met several years ago when she had catered Broome & Crowe's annual client reception. Seth had been looking for a new chef, and after a surprisingly creative and delicious dinner that blended soul and Latin flavors perfectly he had gone into the kitchen to meet and hopefully steal the chef. When he'd approached her time had stood still. He hadn't expected such a lovely commanding woman. Not even her blockish chef whites could dampen her appeal.

Seth had introduced himself and praised her food. However when he'd asked if she would be interested in setting the menu for his kitchen, she had immediately thanked him but turned him down flat and explained that she had too much on her plate with her own catering business booked well into next year. He'd left, but not before he had warned her that he wasn't a man to give up easily. Her stormy brown eyes had drilled into his almost in a silent dare before she'd smiled and told him she would be disappointed if he did.

Seth had indeed persisted, and Marta, a successful, independent woman, had continued to resist, but she enjoyed his attention and tenacity enough that she'd never told him to hit the bricks. From what he'd picked up over months of their small talk and banter, he'd become intrigued not just professionally but personally. After months of turning down Seth's business opportunity she agreed to dinner.

However, Seth never mentioned The Pearl's need for a new chef. Instead it felt surprisingly like a date, so over scallops, steak, and caviar at *The House* Marta had explained that when she'd turned fifty several years ago, she'd vowed to stay single and that she was finally at a place where she could stand on her own and planned to do everything she could to keep her promise to herself.

Seth had simply nodded before he'd asked, "Okay, but that doesn't mean we can't have dinner and build a friendship, does it?"

After sitting back in momentary shock she'd finally laughed and asked, "Friends huh?"

Seth nodded again. "Two friends sharing a meal. There's no law against that, is there?"

"No, I guess there isn't. You're not easily intimidated are you?" she asked as she fed him a cracker covered with caviar.

Seth chewed and shook his head. After observing her for so long, he firmly believed she needed a strong man to match her strength, a man who could handle her attitude and her mouth and not cower in a corner after getting gut punched in his ego. He chased his first taste of caviar with water and smiled.

"Impressive," she said, "most men yak when it comes to fish eggs on crackers."

Seth smirked. "I am indeed not like most men."

Neither had taken the easy road through life, and slowly they opened up and showed the other their scars and bruises. Over the following few months, in bits and pieces she'd revealed pieces of her history and confirmed the kind of insecure men Seth had suspected they had been. When Seth never made a hard play at her, Marta had begun to look at him more seriously, and eventually she stopped running from both him and the idea of running Seth's struggling kitchen.

When Marta finally accepted his offer to run The Pearl's kitchen, she jumped in headfirst, firing half the staff. The reenergized kitchen had instantly become The Pearl's heartbeat, and Marta kept the pulse lively, infusing their comfort soul food menu with Latin and Mediterranean flare. Thanks to Marta, The Pearl had been reborn and quickly became just as popular outside the neighborhood as it was within it.

Working side-by-side had only strengthened their burgeoning friendship. The day-in-day-out stresses of running a very successful Harlem restaurant quickly showed them both their true colors, and it hadn't taken long before their friendship turned romantic.

Remembering to breathe again, Seth watched Marta running her limited Sunday crew ragged. He sighed in relief and knew with her at the helm they'd get through the hectic shift without any tension or additional drama. When she spun to grab a knife, she caught him standing by the sub-zero fridge.

"What are you doing in my kitchen?" she asked with a flirty gaze placing a hand on her lush hip. She wore an ochre-colored pencil skirt covered by a khaki colored apron, a pale blue blouse, and blue heels. Her makeup was flawless.

"Making sure you were working, woman. Someone has to keep an eye on you young kids or else you'll get on your phones to troll the Internet and text or something," he said as she approached him with her usual playful sass. She smelled seductively of men's cologne. "You smell good," Seth murmured into her ear when he took her in his arms.

"Don't I though?" she agreed with a low provocative hum.

"Yeah, you smell like me actually."

"Then you smell good too," she said flashing her one dimpled smile. Her warm brown eyes turned serious and searched his gaze. "I heard what happened with Paulie and that ass, Chico. You all right?" she asked rubbing his arms.

"I'm fine," he said. "Where were you?"

"I had to pick up some produce," she answered as the two of them left the kitchen and grabbed a seat at the nearest table. "How's Paulie? In fact…where is Paulie?" she asked looking around the bar and dining room.

"I sent Paulie home or somewhere with the bartender."

Marta smiled. "Ahhh…Tamara, I like her, but I don't know if she can tend bar."

Seth laughed. "Same here."

"Though I'm pretty confident that's not why Paulie hired her, and I do find it quite odd that damn near every time we take a day off there's a new face in this place," she said with a laugh.

Seth sighed and checked his watch. "You and me both."

"And now that you fired Chico—something I did a month ago, but who you HAD to bring back for whatever reason—there's going to be another new face in the place."

"Yeah, yeah woman. You were right. I was wrong," he said with a shrug and a chuckle.

"As usual," she said shaking her finger playfully and laughing as she stood.

Seth swatted the round curve of her bottom. "I'll let you think that."

She simply laughed again before she leaned over and kissed Seth on his forehead. "I have to get back in there and make sure the kids aren't on their phones trolling the Internet or texting."

Seth gently took her by the wrist to keep her from dashing away. "You could have at least said good morning this morning, you know."

Her eyes grew soft, and she sat on his lap. "I wore your ass out last night, baby," she said stroking his smooth jawline and planting a kiss on his full lips. "You needed your sleep."

"I woke up. You were gone. No word. No nothing. I half expected to see some money on the night stand," he said with a pointed look.

"You charging now?" she asked trying to keep things light.

"You know what I mean, Marta," he sighed.

"I'm not going to apologize for getting in here on time, but I'll make it up to you. Okay? Ya big baby," she teased with a casual swat.

"I got your big baby right here."

Marta smiled, wiggling seductively in his lap. "Mmmhmm...I can feel it, but hold that thought," she said with another quick kiss before she sashayed back to the kitchen.

Seth smiled at the view and after adjusting himself headed to the bar just as the first wave of church ladies walked through The Pearl's doors.

13

Charlie sighed and threw his hands up in frustration as he and Chad finished another round of *Call of Duty*. "Hey, I'm hungry. You hungry?" It was almost 4:00 p.m. on Sunday, and the last thing Charlie had eaten was a late breakfast.

"When am I not hungry?"

"I'm gonna order a pizza."

"Order two….and get some wings…and some cheesy bread…and–"

"Are you paying?" Charlie interrupted.

"Left the wallet at home, homie."

"Then two pizzas it is."

"Where's the chink?" Chad asked. "I was hoping to score more of that Purple Nirvana shit he's working with. I so need something a tad stronger than my stash. Ya feel me?"

"Dunno. Ain't seen him since last night," Charlie answered with a careless shrug. "I guess he's busy, but you know his number. Call him. I ain't your damn secretary, cracka."

"Last night? I thought you were on your date with that big booty Mexican mamacita? PLEASE tell me you hit that by the way!"

"Why, so you can blab that shit online and then jerk one out? I look like a dumbass to you?" Charlie asked laughing. "Anyway, Gavin saw me pull in afterwards and came over. He said you were asleep."

"Yeah, I probably was. And since when have I ever gone online and…" Chad stopped short and cringed as at least one of a dozen memories came to mind.

"I'm sorry. What were you about to say?" Charlie asked holding a hand to his ear. "It sounded like you were about to say 'When have I ever done anything like that?' When we both know you did some shit like that last week."

"I was high," Chad shrugged leaving the sofa to ransack the mini-kitchen.

"And drunk and mad. You lost your mind for everyone to see. The world did not need to read your rant on how Jenny did porn star level shit to you cause you weren't invited to her party everyone else was at. Yeah, I don't see me spilling my guts to you about anything Lily and I do."

"You get that call yet?" Chad asked after a long chug of his energy drink.

"Not yet." Charlie ran his hand over his smooth head and tried to soothe the anxiety the subject of his debt and Stony always sparked.

"Nervous?"

"Wouldn't you be?"

"Fuck yeah," Chad admitted walking back and throwing himself on the sectional. "Want me to roll one with what's left?"

"You roll like shit, and you know it."

"Fuck you, nigga. I'm getting better."

"If you say so, homo. Man, I have no fucking idea how I'm gonna come up with two hundred grand. It's like this black cloud of death hanging over me, dude. It's mental torture."

"Chill. You know he's not going to kill you so don't go stressing yourself out. He'll call you soon enough, and you'll know what's what. Try to relax before you make me nervous," Chad said, reaching into his pants pockets to pull out a plastic baggie of local weed, a lighter, three Phillies, and a razor blade wrapped in newspaper.

"If you have all that why you crying for G?" Charlie asked as Chad spread out his stash on the coffee table.

"Cause he has the better weed, nigga."

Charlie almost leapt out of his skin when his phone buzzed. He looked at the screen, and breathed a heavy sigh of relief when he saw it was Lily. He answered as he walked across the room towards the pool table and away from Chad's nosy ears.

"Hey buster, you busy later? Want to get together after I get off work?" Lily asked.

Charlie kept his back to Chad and grinned broadly. "Absolutely, I'd love to."

"Great, meet me at 8:00 by my car. Same place it was last night, and don't be late, or I'll bust your lip. Gotta run. Someone wants your sneakers. See you later."

He could picture her smile as he slipped his phone back in his pocket. Her call had been the first ray of sunshine in his otherwise gloomy day.

"Yo, you should call Gav," Chad yelled from across the room interrupting Charlie's thoughts.

Charlie groaned and walked back to see his friend put the finishing touches on a badly rolled blunt. "I already told you. I am not your damn secretary. You call him."

"Fine, fucker," Chad said picking up the phone only to see Gavin come up to the sliding glass door. "Well, look what the cat dragged in. I hope you brought your stash, chink."

"When don't I bring some of my stash, pale face? Get off my dick."

Just then Charlie's phone rang again, and his stomach knotted up seeing a blocked caller. He knew it was Stony. He threw his wallet at Chad for the food, walked into the backyard on numb legs, and answered the call.

Minutes later Charlie bent over with his hands on his knees and dry heaved.

Chad and Gavin dropped their food that had just arrived and rushed out to Charlie, but he couldn't respond. They eventually brought him back inside to the sofa. After five minutes of silence, Charlie began to mumble to himself as he stared straight ahead unfocused.

"Charlie...what the fuck is up, dude?" Chad asked waving his hand in front of his friend's face.

"He's like in a fugue state," Gavin explained matter-of-factly before taking another bite of his slice of pizza.

"How do we break him out of it?"

"We don't. He has to come out of it on his own."

"Fuck that," Chad said and picked up his lighter. He flicked it and slowly lowered the long yellow flame to the top of Charlie's hand. After a few seconds Charlie jumped and smacked at Chad's hand.

"What the fuck, bitch?" Charlie yelled as he stumbled to his feet and clutched his hand. "Are you crazy?"

"Dude, you were out of it, so I thought that would bring you back."

"Burn me again, and I'm kicking your ass," Charlie stated rubbing the burn.

"You all right?" Gavin asked.

"Hell no, I ain't all right. I got this motherfucker here trying to set me on fire, and I got Stony who now wants me to steal some goddamn painting like I'm in *Oceans 11* or some shit, like I do that shit every other day," Charlie said and sat back down clutching his head.

Chad choked on a mouthful of half-chewed pizza. "He wanth thou tho dooo whaaat?" he shouted.

"Steal some stupid painting."

"What painting? From where? Why?" Gavin asked.

Unable to be still, Charlie began to pace back and forth in front of the TV. "It's by someone named Basket Yacht. It's going to be at The Butler in a couple of weeks, and the why is because he fucking said so since I don't have two hundred grand to fork over to him."

"You mean Basquiat?" Gavin asked.

"Yeah, that's not what I said?" Charlie replied.

"Fuck me. There's gonna be a Jean Michel Basquiat on display at The Butler? Cool," said Gavin with a small smile.

"Forgive me if I fail to see the cool-factor in this shit," Charlie said rubbing his churning stomach. He looked down and grabbed a slice of pizza.

"Sorry, but a Basquiat is a huge deal actually. Jean Michel was and is one of the most renowned American artists in the last forty years. He died young, like 27 or 28 when he OD'd. He even painted with Andy Warhol. Some if not most of his work is worth millions," Gavin explained. "Yeah, security's gonna be heavy."

Chad just stared at Gavin before grabbing his second slice. "Well, thank you for the info, G. Leave it to you to know all about that art shit."

Charlie sat down between his friends on the sectional. "Yeah, and I have to steal it, or they go after my dad," Charlie whispered before he collapsed against the back of the sofa. "Fuck it. I really need to get high."

"Great, I'll join you," said Chad.

Gavin shook his head at Chad but immediately started rolling a fat one for Charlie with the best weed he had from his collection.

Later that evening, after the boys had eaten both pizzas and smoked all the kush Gavin had brought, Charlie looked at his watch and saw he only had a half an hour before he was supposed to meet Lily. He slowly stood and brushed crumbs and ashes from his clothes.

"Yo, I gotta head out," he said as he swayed a bit and patted his pockets for his car keys.

"Where you goin?" Chad asked with both his eyes closed.

"Gonna meet Lily. She wants to hang out after work, so I need to bounce."

"You ain't in any fucking shape to drive, dude," Chad said with a squint in his friend's direction.

Charlie laughed and asked, "How you know?"

Chad opened his bloodshot eyes wider and looked at Charlie. "Cuz I'm not, nigga, and you definitely smoked more than I did. Sit your ass back down, pick up your phone, and cancel. That fat juicy ass ain't goin nowhere."

"Nah," Charlie said checking his balance. "I'm good."

"Yeah, good and high but whatever."

"Whatever, cracka. Look, clean all this shit up before ya'll leave," Charlie said as he carefully made his way to the bathroom. He washed his face and hands, brushed his teeth, and squeezed some eye drops into his eyes. When he turned around Gavin was standing in the doorway he'd left open.

"What up, G?"

"You sure you can drive?" Gavin asked.

Charlie shrugged. "Yeah man, I'm good. Make sure pale face makes it home safely," he said as he brushed past Gavin and headed up the stairs.

"You mean three houses down and across the street?"

"Yeah, or he might spend another night in the bushes. Make sure you bitches clean up before you leave!"

14

When Charlie got behind the wheel of his Jetta he knew he probably shouldn't drive, but he desperately wanted to see Lily. She was the only positive uncomplicated joy of his life at the moment. *I'll just drive slow and take the back roads, and it'll be cool.*

Twenty minutes later he pulled into the mall parking lot, a little after 8:00 p.m. and found her leaning on her car waiting for him. She sent a happy wave as he pulled in beside her. He quickly walked around the car, and she smiled that smile he loved before greeting him with a hug.

Lily immediately recoiled. "Wow! Are you high?" she asked pulling from his embrace.

Disappointed at the loss of her warmth, Charlie let her go. "Why'd you ask me that?"

"Because seriously you smell like you've been rolling around in weed all day," she said with a dramatic display of pinching her nose.

"I smoked a little bit, yeah," he said with a shrug. "No biggie."

"Wait, so you drove here high?" she asked putting her hands on her hips.

Charlie shrugged again.

Lily threw back her head as if asking a higher power for patience. "That was so unbelievably stupid, Charles."

"What are you talking about? I'm here in one piece, right?" he said with a laugh.

"Which is a fucking miracle, but what if the cops had pulled you over? You do remember where you live, right? The cops around here don't necessarily appreciate someone of your complexion? What if they pulled you over and then your father had to get involved? What then?"

"Well then he would have to do something he rarely ever does," Charlie grumbled.

"What's that?" Lily asked a little confused.

"Get involved," he softly replied leaning back on his car to stare off in the distance.

Lily was about to say something but stopped. After a minute of silence she quietly said, "Wow, so that explains it. I'm sorry. I didn't know."

Charlie didn't elaborate. He'd shocked himself by sharing even that bit of information. He did his best to keep those emotions away from everyone. He simply never spoke much about his father to anyone, but as usual though, things were different with Lily. Charlie shoved his hands in his pockets and tried to get back to their friendly banter. "So what do you want to do?"

Lily stared at him with concern that made him feel both cared about and uncomfortable. She sighed. "I just wanted to hang out, spend some more time with you, and talk, but I didn't expect you to be baked. You do realize that's not my thing, right?"

"Are you saying," Charlie said getting off his car, "that you've never smoked or gotten high?"

"No. Never," Lily proudly confirmed.

"How is that even possible?" he asked dumbfound. Almost everyone he knew did something.

It was her turn to shrug. "It's easy when you see what that stuff does to the people you love."

"Wow, that rhymed," he snickered. He was doing his best to hide his buzz, but he hadn't been able to help himself.

Lily rolled her eyes. "Whatever, I think I should go home. I'll see you tomorrow in class. Hopefully you'll be sober," she said as she started fishing for her keys. She turned to get in her car, but Charlie reached out and softly grasped her arm. She glared at his hand until he let go.

"I'm sorry, Lils. I had a really bad day. Please, don't go home," Charlie pleaded softly.

"Why not?"

Charlie swallowed the lump in his throat. "Because…I need you."

"For what?"

He could hear the doubt and suspicion in her tone. "To talk to Lils," he said as tears he could no longer fight began to well in his eyes. He turned away, but she had already glimpsed the emotion that was all too obvious on his face.

She called his name, took his arm, and gently asked him what was wrong.

"I just had a really bad day and have a lot on my mind. Look, if you want to go home that's cool. I understand. I'll catch up with you at school," he said as he headed to his car.

"Charlie, stop!" Lily demanded.

He stiffened, but he didn't turn to face her. Charlie didn't want her to see his tears.

Lily walked over to him, and she reached up with both hands and wiped his face dry. "Whatever it is, it'll be all right," she said softly. "Come on. It looks like we both need to get away from the world. Get in my car."

Charlie couldn't meet her eyes. "Where we going?"

"To my most favorite spot in the world. I go there when I'm feeling like shit. Now stop asking questions, buster," she said giving him a little push. "Get in, roll the window down, and don't forget to buckle up."

15

Charlie stared out the window as trees and houses flew past in the dark. With Rhianna playing softly on her car stereo, Lily took Route 224 through Boardman and Canfield and kept going. He had no idea where they were headed, but he trusted her.

A half hour later she took a couple of turns into Mill Creek Recreation Area and drove them to the edge of a large placid lake. He had no clue where they were except that they were all alone, and the sign at the entrance said "Berlin Lake." He hadn't known this pretty spot was so close to home. She parked the car next to the shore but a nice distance away from the haze of overhead lights that dotted the parking area.

After Lily cut the engine and the lights they sat in the dark without speaking for a few minutes. Charlie took in the glittering moonlit lake. Taking a quick breath, she opened her squeaky door, hopped out, and with a practiced grace climbed onto the hood to lean against the windshield. The other girls he knew believed in non-stop chatter or preferred to hang out where everyone could see them. Once again Lily set herself completely apart from the pack. He wasn't sure what to do next until he heard her quiet call for him to join her.

Charlie slowly got out of the car to the sound of crickets. He nearly opened his mouth to make one of his usual smartass remarks about the inky blackness, but when he glanced over and took in her curvy outline reclining across the wide hood in the moonlight, he knew this wasn't the time or place. At that moment she was both sweet and enticing, and he knew what he needed more than breathing—her. Sighing deeply, he slid onto the hood, hovered above her, and kissed her deeply. Instantly, he was lost in the kiss. It was only when Lily gently pulled away did the world return. He lay down beside her and softly asked, "What are we doing here, Lils?"

She stared out over the calm water. "This is my favorite spot in the world, Charlie," she said with a sigh of contentment before she turned and locked eyes with him. "I wanted to share it with you."

Charlie understood without her saying it that she'd never brought anyone else here. "Why this place?"

"Well for starters, it's away from everything and everybody," she said with a shrug. "Sometimes I need some alone time, ya know." She then smiled gently at him and leaned her head back against the windshield. "And secondly because tonight the skies are clear."

"Meaning?"

"Charlie," she said softly, "look up."

Charlie gave her a quizzical look and then turned his face skyward. He gasped. Millions of stars sparkled against the dark night sky. He rarely looked up to notice the usual smattering of stars. The stunning view he saw lying next to Lily on the hood of her car, however, would be sight he would never forget. "Holy shit," he whispered.

"I know, right?" Lily said with a light giggle. For long minutes they gazed at the glittering magic show. Eventually Lily softly broke the silence. "This is where my dad proposed to my mom, and every year on their anniversary, we would come out here to look at the stars and celebrate. We'd just talk and laugh and love as a family," she explained, smiling at the memories.

Charlie was happy she had those moments, but he also felt a slight pang of jealousy. That kind of family outing hadn't happened for him in years. He could barely remember his family's last camping trip together. He shook that thought quickly from his mind. "That's only the second time you've ever said something about your father. You never talk about him. What happened?"

When Lily didn't answer immediately, Charlie looked back at her to see her chew at her lip. "I'm…I'm going to tell you something very few people know about me," Lily said still looking at the stars. She inhaled deeply. "Two years ago I was raped by a neighbor. We had grown up together. I was best friends with his older sister and used to spend the night at their house all the time, at least once a week. Over the years her brother told me he liked me, but I'd never felt the same way. Even though he was only about six months younger than I was, I saw him as a little brother. One day he called my house and asked me to come over and help him with some math homework since his sister wasn't home. I knew how bad he was at math, so I went," she said with a tremor in her voice.

Taking another deep breath, she continued in almost a whisper. "He was so strong. God…I never knew he was so strong, Charles. He held me down. When I fought back and yelled at him to stop, he slapped me, punched me, tore my clothes, and…."

Charlie reached over and gently took her hand. "You don't have to tell me anymore, Lils," Charlie said quietly.

She squeezed his hand. "I'm okay, had quite a bit of therapy, buster," she said as she sniffed and wiped her tears. "When my mother got home and saw my bruises and the scratch marks, she demanded to know what happened. After I told her she called my father home from second shift."

Lily dragged her free hand nervously through her hair while Charlie tightened his grip on the other. "We came out here that night, and I explained everything to them. I could see the hurt and shame on my mother's face that she hadn't been able to protect me. On my father's I only saw rage. I begged him not to do anything. I made him promise, and he said okay, but we all knew he was lying. He couldn't leave it alone, not when they lived right across the street, not when it was a boy we'd thought of like family, so almost as soon as we got back, my father…he stormed over to their house and tried to kill him."

Charlie stared across the lake in stunned silence. Nothing like that had ever touched his life. He tried to comprehend the horror that she must have gone through that day. He couldn't understand why a guy would do such a thing to a girl, but especially Lily who was the sweetest and coolest girl he'd ever known.

"My dad beat that boy to within an inch of his life," she continued calmly and practically, "and when his father tried to help his son, my father pummeled him too. His wife, a woman I'd looked at like a second mother, rightfully called the police, probably saving both of their lives. I lost so much of what made me who I was that day. I lost my faith in people. I lost my best friend, but worst of all…I lost my dad. He's currently doing ten years for attempted murder and aggravated assault."

When Charlie looked over at Lily, her round face was tear streaked. Without thinking he moved closer, brought her to his chest, and held her tenderly in his arms. Very gently as if she might break, he ran his hand from the top of her head, over her long dark hair, and down her back. She curled into him and his heat.

"That reality and all that comes with it, the loss, the pain, the humiliation...those are memories I have to deal with every day. That's why I keep almost everyone at a distance. That's why I work so hard in school and why I have that annoying job selling hideous sneakers you like so much," she said with a small chuckle. "I don't want to give my mother something more to worry about, and I do whatever I can to help her make ends meet for us."

His high now gone, Charlie didn't know what to say, but he was sure that whatever might come out of his mouth at that moment would have sounded stupid, so he opted to stay quiet and listen.

"I wanted to bring you here because this place is sort of sacred to me. It's always made me feel better, and I could see how upset you were. I thought that maybe this place would work its magic and make you feel better too somehow," she whispered.

He thought about her words as the bugs, frogs, and crickets laid down a cacophony of sound around them. He felt incredibly protective of her, and while he already liked her for a long time, his admiration for her had shot clear past the stars in the heavens.

"I wish I was Superman and that I could have rescued you," he murmured. Her arms tighten around him, and her affection made him feel good. He squeezed his eyes shut hoping this moment would last forever, but then he heard a tiny giggle against his chest and then another. "What?" he asked quietly.

"Superman, huh?"

"Hey, don't laugh. I'd bet I'd look pretty damn hot. A bright blue leotard and that cape? You wouldn't be able to resist," he teased. "Chicks dig capes."

Lily giggled a bit more and placed her hand onto his chest. "Okay...speaking of super power, if you could pick one, what would yours be?" she asked.

"I'd want to be invincible," Charlie answered with no hesitation still stroking her back.

"Been thinking about this recently, buster?"

Charlie shrugged.

Lily looked up at him. "You wouldn't want the coolest of cool power of flight?"

"Nope, don't like heights. I don't need to be super fast either. Just give me the ability to shrug off bullets and walk through life invincible, and I'd be happy. What would yours be?"

"Flight, definitely flight," she said. "Would you want to be super strong or just invincible?" she asked.

"You said only one, remember?"

"I did say 'or' remember?"

"That's a tough one, but I still gotta go with invincible," he said.

"Well I would think you'd be incredibly powerful if you were invincible, right?"

"I guess so," Charlie said. "What would be the first place you'd travel to with your powers of flight?"

Lily paused for a moment to consider. "You know what I'd do?"

"What?"

"I would swoop you up and fly you to where my dad is, have you break him out, and then fly him away."

"And leave me behind, huh?"

"You're invincible," Lily said with a shrug and a smile. "You'd be all right. Besides I'd be back for you once I got him someplace safe."

"And how long would that take?"

"Five, ten minutes tops."

"Then yeah, I'd be fine, but you better not forget me," he said with a playful tug to her hair.

"How could I forget my hero?" she asked turning her face up to him.

He looked down, met her eyes, and swallowed. She was absolutely beautiful, and in that moment there was nothing else he wanted more than to be her hero.

Slowly she rose up and straddled his hips with her warm thick thighs. "Thank you, Charlie," she whispered before she leaned down to kiss him slow and deep. Charlie's hands clenched her narrow waist and savored her sweet taste.

For almost two hours they found comfort in each other under the moonlight far away from their everyday world. Between soft kiss and slow touches, the two of them debated topics ranging from which restaurant had the best burritos in town to if there was a God. She teased him about how fashion conscious he was, and he grilled her about her future dreams for directing remakes of *The Gumball Rally*, *Midnight Run*, and *Wonder Woman*.

As the night wore on they shared a half a dozen more passionate kisses and long minutes of cuddling before they headed back to the world. Holding hands, Lily drove Charlie to his car in the deserted parking lot, and he kissed her goodbye one last time before he followed her to her house. Once he was sure she was inside safely, he headed home. This time though, Stony, Frank, and their chainsaw didn't join him.

16

Hours later across town, after their last patron had stumbled to their car and Stony had locked up Romare's, he and Frank huddled together at the far end of the bar in deep in conversation. They discussed the weekend's business as they slowly sipped on cognacs and debated potential threats and future strategies with a seriousness of men making life and death decisions.

Turk, who had worked there almost as long as the place had been open, carefully washed and restocked the glasses not that far from where the two sat. While he respected them, he smirked at the young men's attempts at sophistication.

The short, cinnamon-colored, wiry black man with a salt and pepper five o'clock shadow and a receding hairline was from the old school. He believed in keeping it real instead of pretending to be something you weren't. It was one of the reasons Leonard had valued his perspective despite his history.

When Turk was younger he had figured he would never be President, so he'd chosen to run the streets rather than attend high school. That choice had led him to become mixed up with the kind of people everyone knew about but wanted nothing to do with, and it hadn't taken long before he'd graduated from recreational drug user to junkie.

One night forty some years ago on his way home, Leonard had found Turk crumpled in the street. Without hesitation, he'd stopped his car and thrown the bloodied and swollen kid who'd take a beating into the back, taken him home, and called in a few favors to get medical help. After several weeks when Turk was on the road to recovery from both his injuries and addictions, Leonard had offered him a job at his newly opened bar, and the grateful young man had jumped at the chance of a steady paycheck. Working together every day, Turk had become like a younger brother to Leonard and eventually become his most trusted employee and sounding board.

When Romare's had been accepted into "The Network", the underground information syndicate, the two men had celebrated the accomplishment with a quiet drink after closing.

The brainchild of an influential New York City hustler, The Network provided Black-owned bars, restaurants, and clubs that were paid members with key information and occasional financial backing as well as those in need a safe place to hide from authorities, rest, and grab a meal. Romare's inclusion into The Network had been vital to Leonard's expansion and made him one of the biggest fish in Youngstown's small pond. Eventually Romare's had become The Network's Midwest hub. That night over their third celebratory round Leonard had charged Turk to be his point man for everything related to The Network including payments and information.

Turk smiled at the memory of his old friend as he ran through his mental checklist for the night. Grabbing a washrag, he wandered close enough to overhear Stony and Frank while he wiped down the bar.

"Why'd you bring the Colt though and not the Glock?" asked Stony.

"Cause the Colt's my killing gun?"

Stony's brows rose in doubt. "Your what?"

"My killing gun," Frank repeated.

"What does that even mean?" Stony asked amused.

"I have show guns, guns I carry that are big, intimidating, but they clean. People see the Glock, and they usually straighten up. No need to use it. There ain't no bodies on the guns I show, and if I do happen to catch one on a gun I'm holdin, it usually never gets seen again. My Colt, she got crazy bodies on her, so she rarely sees the light of day, but she's a powerful bitch. Going in there's no muss. Coming, though, ain't nothin but fuss."

Stony still looked slightly confused.

"Turk," Frank called.

Turk stopped what he was doing and walked over to the young men.

"Turk, how many guns you got?" Frank asked still looking at Stony.

"I got five."

"How many of em killin guns?" Frank asked.

With no hesitation Turk answered. "One's a killin gun."

Stony shot his bartender a look, surprised to discover Turk had taken a life.

"You still carry that .22?"

"Sure do. Got it on me right now," he said as he reached behind his back and pulled the small pistol from its hiding place and placed it on the bar. "Your Uncle Leonard gave dat gun ta me."

Stony's eyes widened. "Really? Why?"

"Quick story, I'd been workin here bout a year, and one night some wannabe pimp slapped a woman clean off her stool. Sounded like a gunshot up in here he hit her so hard. Anyway, nobody moved, and this fool was stadin ova her grinning, bout to swing again. I grabs the closest thing to me, a bottle of Wild Turkey, and went upside his damn head," Turk said with a coarse laugh. "Anyway, that's when everybody started callin me Turk, and dat night after we closed Leonard hands me dis .22 and told me not to waste no more product or he'd shoot me hisself."

They all laughed knowing Leonard would have threatened exactly that.

"Any bodies on it?" Frank asked nodding to the gun in the older man's weathered hand.

"Hell, I ain't never even shot it. I just shows it. I takes it everywhere I go cause them streets…they can be mean some nights."

"See," Frank said. "Show guns and killin guns."

"Wait," Stony said holding up his hand. "What about the rule that if you show your gun you better use your gun or else?"

"Looka here, Stone. When you show your gun," Turk began slowly, "You better make sure you pull it an make sure you point it at the head a da sumbitch you showin it to. You wanna let em see it up close. Let em feel that cold steel on their forehead. That way they knows you ain't scared to make it a killin gun. See, showin involves pullin, and pullin makes em think twice bout comin back on some revenge mess."

"In fact," Turk continued as he slipped his gun back into its hiding spot, "if you do show it, pull it, and don't use it, that person may even see it as you sparin dey miserable life, might even show you some gratitude for not puttin em in dey Sunday best six feet deep."

Frank nodded his agreement. "Got it now?" Frank asked Stony before he finished his cognac.

"Yeah, I got it. Thanks, Turk," Stony said with a nod.

"Don't mention it."

"Now I see why my uncle kept you around."

Turk smiled and went back to wiping down the bar but stayed within earshot.

"So tell me the plan for this painting," Frank said as he refilled his snifter.

Stony smiled. "It's simple. I told the kid that since there's no way he can pay off his debt, he has to steal the painting that's going to be at The Butler in a few weeks. If he doesn't do it, we take out his dad, the fucker that came after my uncle. If he tries to get it, his little prince will likely get caught of course, which will ruin his life along with his father's career as D.A.," Stony said and took another sip of his drink. "And if the kid somehow does get it done, we take them both out, and I'll have a Basquiat," he said confidently. "It's a win-win-win."

Frank's expression darkened as he thought over Stony's plan. "And when you say 'We take them out.' you mean me, right?"

"You or you can get someone else to do it. Maybe get some out of town shooters. Don't matter," Stony said with a shrug.

"I ain't never balked at getting someone who deserve to get got, and this D.A. deserves his for what he did to Leonard, but he IS the D.A. This is a dangerous game you're playing, Stone."

Stony gazed into the dark auburn liquid in his glass. "It's a game I'm committed to," Stony slowly said. "This has been a long time coming. I put on the smiles. I've played the part for a long time, Frank, a long damn time. Now it's time for some payback."

Frank nodded his head. "I hear you talking, but honestly you and I both know that boy got about as good a chance of gettin that painting as a crackhead does gettin into Harvard or some shit," Frank said as he raised his glass.

Stony laughed. "True but I no longer underestimate the power of those with ample bank accounts, resources, and connections. Besides, I really want that Basquiat."

"Who IS this motherfucka? The second coming or some shit?" Frank asked.

"I'm all done here, boss," Turk called from down the bar. "I'll be back tomorrow at four."

"C'mere a second, Turk," Stony called to him.

Turk ambled back in their direction.

"You ever heard of Jean Michel Basquiat?" Stony asked.

"Sure have," he replied proudly. "Your uncle talked bout him all the time."

"What'd he say?" Stony asked taking his turn to look pointedly at Frank.

"Your uncle, he could talk for hours bout painters bout what they styles was and stuff. Shit way over ma head, but when it came to Basquiat, man, Leonard could talk for days. He'd go on and on bout how that young Black man was a brilliant, bone a fide genius," the grizzled barkeep answered.

"Thank you Turk," Stony said smugly. "Take the day off tomorrow. You never take one, and you've earned it. I can get John to cover for you."

Turk waved off the offer. "That boy don't know how ta work no bar. I'll be here at six."

"Turk, 'day off' means you don't come to work. Relax. Come back on Tuesday, capisce?"

"Ka-what? Looka here, I'll be in tomorrow at six if that's okay witchu."

Stony shook his head and relented, knowing his efforts to give the old man a day to himself were a lost cause. "Turk, why do you work so hard for this place? What is it?" he asked as the two men walked to the front door. Stony unlocked the door and held it open.

"Cause your unc and this damn place...they saved my life," Turk explained. "See yous two tamorrow," he said and headed to his car.

"At six," Stony yelled at him.

"Six," he yelled back.

When Turk got home he went through his usual routine. After a hot shower and a sandwich he walked to his nightstand, pulled out his address book, and flipped to the F's. He sighed and plopped down on his bed. *Hope I don't regret dis, but I gotta do somethin fore them negroes mess up all Leonard done built,* he thought as he placed his phone on the page he needed for his call in the morning. With a sigh, he turned off his bedside lamp and stretched out on his single bed.

17

When Turk's call came through first thing at 9:00 a.m., it went to voicemail. Florida, The Network's current overseer, was a strong believer in starting the day off right with a quick staff meeting and had his voluptuous secretary, Ivelisse, bent over his desk taking it deep. "Evil," an ex-prostitute he'd rescued years ago from her abusive pimp, happily obliged since Florida paid her handsomely and lavished her with gifts, shopping sprees, and vacations.

With the phones ringing frantically first thing in the morning, a rarity, Evil efficiently finished off her duties with her learned skills before she readjusted her thong, affixed her red horn rimmed glasses back on her face, and pulled herself together. Then the half Puerto Rican, half Cuban siren originally from Miami dashed back to her receptionist desk to answer the phone and check messages.

Five minutes later Evil leaned over Florida's desk flashing him a deep v of cleavage and placed the priority message in front of him. "Looks like there might be a whiff of trouble in the Youngstown area, Daddy," she said with a wink.

He watched her sashay out of his office on patent leather red stilettos, her red pencil skirt struggling to contain her curves. When she was out of sight and the spell was broken, he read her note.

"Damn, I do not need this shit today," Florida growled and picked out a disposable prepaid phone from the top drawer of his desk. His return call to Turk was brief. According to his South Side contact some serious unsanctioned illegalities were about to take place in Youngstown that could bring not just local but federal heat down on one of The Network's major hubs.

"Many thanks for the call, Turk, but do me a favor and keep your ears and eyes open. If Leonard's boy really plans to do something this dumb it could burn a lot of people, so get me as much info as you can cull together and call me when you know more. I'm gonna be sending someone around too. When he's on his way I'll let you know," Florida said and then paused to listen to the older man.

"No, you're damn right," Florida continued. "Leonard would not be down for this kind of shit, but he's dead, so we have to deal with the issue currently on the table. I know this is hard on you, but I promise you I won't forget you. There'll be a package coming," Florida promised before the two men hung up.

Rubbing his brow at the headache forming behind his eyes, he couldn't move on anything from a single overheard conversation, so he needed specifics. There was a reason The Network was so well respected. Before Florida put anything into action he always made sure he had at least two verifiable sources for every fact. It was time to scour his connections and deploy an operative.

"Evil!" he yelled.

She came to the door in seconds, teetering in her heels. "Whatchu need, Daddy?"

"Find out if there's anyone out in the Youngstown area that owes me."

She put a hand on a hip and said, "You want the names of ALL the people that owe you, or just a few?"

"Get me the top three."

"Comin right up, Daddy," she said with a nod and returned to her desk.

Ferociously efficient, inside of thirty minutes she had three names of men who owed Florida either a lot of money or a major favor. From the three he picked Percy Hammersmith, a nervous, fast-talking, coward of a street hustler originally from New York. The Known Men had run him out of town over a misunderstanding. Word on the street had been "kill on sight", but Florida had intervened and sent Percy to Chicago. While his actions had put a strain on his relationship with Seth, Florida had thought it was the best thing to do for all involved to avoid any possible jail time or hospital stays. Over time Seth had reluctantly agreed with his logic but still felt Florida owed him one.

From Chicago Percy had slowly made his way back east to Ohio over the years and eventually settled in Youngstown.

Florida called and chuckled when he heard Percy's nervous voice again in his voicemail greeting. Florida left his office number and a message demanding a return call. He then hung up and threw the phone back into the drawer with the others.

Florida simmered. If the game the old bartender told him was for real, the trouble it could bring would throw business in that area into a tailspin. One thing Florida refused to allow was anyone's ego or feelings to effect business.

The Network had been the creation of Florida's now retired father, Kellogg, who currently lived in Key West. In his youth, he had called Harlem home, but with family down in Tallahassee and his paralyzing fear of flying, Kellogg had driven the I-95 corridor down and back every summer. Along the way he'd made numerous stops and cultivated friendships with Black business owners of back road establishments.

Kellogg would grab in a meal, a drink, a haircut, or even a tune up and spread good amounts of money. Being a people person and a natural talker, almost anyone would open up to him. He would share information he'd learned from his travels if pertinent with other owners. They'd loved him, and those with the say so in those parts had quickly declared him off limits. It wasn't long before all involved saw how valuable Kellogg's resources, information, and connections were. Information was as important as money. Kellogg being a savvy businessman had quickly begun to treat it as such, and The Network was born.

However the actions of two young arrogant men with too much power and apparently too little sense could deal a serious blow to the other members and the organization Florida now ran. He popped a Tums and promised himself he wasn't going to stress this yet. *It could be nothing, just an old man whose mind is playing tricks on him*. He'd wait for confirmation.

Then Ivelisse popped her head into the office, and with her thong dangling off her index finger. "How bout another staff meeting and an early lunch, Daddy?"

Florida smiled in agreement, and for the next hour he did his best to forget all about Youngstown.

18

Tuesdays were quiet days at The Pearl. Only the bar opened at noon because the bulk of their deliveries for the week arrived in the morning. Today it was Paulie's turn to handle the incoming supplies, so Seth had planned an evening with Marta with the intent on sleeping in past dawn.

Unfortunately, Seth woke early in an ornery mood. Instead of their quiet night together, Marta had been attached to her cell phone most of the evening. After she'd taken it with her to the bathroom, Seth had wanted answers. When she had offered none his temper had spiked, and he'd demanded her phone. Her response had been to grab her things and leave. He hadn't moved a muscle or said a word to stop her.

Seth had fumed for the rest of the evening. When he'd tried to get some rest, he'd hardly slept. He'd been upset with himself for behaving like an ass and frustrated at Marta for pushing him away and being rude. She acted out from time to time, her M.O. almost from the moment they'd met, to see how far she could push him.

Seth didn't understand why she sometimes felt the need to poke the lion. He usually laughed it off and chalked up her behavior to a case of insecurity. However, last night he simply hadn't been able to make light of her antics. They'd been together exclusively for years, and he felt he'd more than earned her trust and that these kinds of games should be over and done with by now.

The Rippingtons' *Aspen* hummed in the background as he drank his coffee. The track was his go to smooth jazz song and usually helped him to find his "happy place" when he was in a foul mood. While the music had removed some of the knots in his shoulders, his mood hadn't brightened all that much.

Oddly enough he hadn't discovered his happy place until prison. Many of The Known Men's rivals and enemies had been locked up with him, and they'd all wanted to see one of the leaders of the most feared NYC gangs bloodied if not dead.

He'd had help on the inside from his connections, but still his enemies had cornered him into too many fights that could have ended in death had it not been for the C.O.'s interventions. After one particularly vicious altercation where Seth made sure his attacker would never talk again, the prison review board had given Seth a choice since he hadn't started the fight, the hole for six months or prison therapy. Seth had chosen therapy, and with the help of a counselor Seth had created his happy place, a mental space he could retreat to for peace of mind. Over the years, the strategy had often given him the emotional cushion he needed to quell his anger enough to where he could snuff out his instinctual desire for violence. Seth had tried to help Paulie develop a happy place, but that idea had crashed and burned amid raucous laughter.

Seth was still trying to find that place when he climbed into his Cadillac and turned on *War* by Edwin Starr. By the time he got to the light at the end of his street he'd started grooving, and fifteen minutes later when he pulled into his spot in front of The Pearl he was firmly ensconced in his happy place and ready to tackle the prep for the week.

19

When Seth walked into The Pearl singing, Paulie nearly spilled his coffee. He spun on his barstool and faced Seth who greeted him with a few lyrics of Edwin Starr's classic *Agent Double O Soul*. Paulie grabbed Seth's shoulder before he could strut past.

"What happened?" Paulie asked alarmed. "Some bad shit either went down or is about to go down. Which is it?"

Seth smiled and patted his partner on the back in reassurance. "Everything's cool, P."

"Whenever you sing, you set me on edge. You know that?" Paulie squinted at his friend in concern. "And it's never a good sign when you call me P. You sure you all right?"

"Yep."

"How did last night go?"

Seth shrugged. "It could have gone better, but I'm cool," Seth answered as he pulled his shoulder out of Paulie's grip and headed to the office.

"Where the hell's my damn gun?" Paulie said under his breath clutching frantically at his pants pockets.

Once upstairs Seth slipped out of his blazer, and for the next thirty minutes leafed through the invoices on his desk, checked the business email, and printed off the purchase orders for the day. *Work's gotta get done.* With a deep breath he readied himself to see Marta and to apologize for his part in last night's debacle. With a grin on his face and a hop in his step, Seth went down to the kitchen still humming *Agent Double O Soul.*

From his perch at the bar, Paulie looked hard at Seth as he came through the back of the dining room. With a growl he hollered, "Alarm bells are clanging in ma head!" Seth dismissed him with a wave, but Paulie left his coffee and newspaper on the bar and followed.

Seth pushed through the swinging doors into the kitchen before coming to an abrupt halt. Near the back door, the paper delivery guy had an arm to the wall cozying up and flirting with Marta. Hearing her giggle echo through the kitchen, Seth's happy place closed shop and hung up a 'Gone Fishing' sign in the window.

Seth's shoulders knotted again in anger and frustration. It wasn't because the young good-looking man was coming onto his woman. Marta was beautiful. Any man with a drop of testosterone would desire her attention. What lit the flame of violence inside him was that she flirted in return, right there, in his kitchen. Unlike Paulie's warm response to violence in the air, Seth's blood ran cold. His hands turned to ice, his senses sharpened, his breathing quickened, and his mind raced.

Neither Marta nor the younger man noticed him as they continued their suggestive banter. Without a word, Seth calmly walked to a prep area and snatched one of the butcher's knives off the wall. When he turned back, Paulie stood in front of him, blocking his path.

Paulie motioned with his chin at the knife. "Whatcha gonna do with that?"

"I'm going to fix a situation," Seth said quietly through clenched teeth.

Paulie checked left, checked right, and then with raised eyebrows asked, "Something in here needs fixin?"

Marta's husky laugh echoed again through the kitchen. Seth squinted in consideration. "Mmmm, not really fixing," he said as he approached Paulie. "More like a serious adjustment is needed. Now get the fuck out of my way."

Paulie glanced cautiously at the weapon in Seth's hand but stood his ground. "Tell you what. Why don't you go to the bar?" Paulie suggested. "Tell Tamara to make you one of her special fancy mocha things I was just sipping on. She puts brandy in it. Go and let me handle this one, partner." Paulie stuck his hand out for the knife.

They locked eyes and waited out each other.

After a few tense seconds, Paulie said a word very few had ever heard him say. "Please."

Surprised by Paulie's plea Seth ground his teeth for a long minute then reluctantly gave the blade to his friend handle first and walked out of the kitchen.

Paulie sighed and placed the knife back where it belonged before he then hustled over to Marta and the delivery guy who were still flirting with each other. He tapped Marta on her shoulder. "You're needed at the bar. We gotta talk to you. Now."

Marta flipped her hair in obvious annoyance. "About?"

"We have a situation. Seth can fill you in on the details," Paulie lied.

"I'm almost done here," she said before she turned her attention back to the delivery guy. "Hold your horses. I'll be there in a minute."

"It's an emergency, Marta," Paulie said as his facial expression darkened.

Marta heard the change in Paulie's tone and sucked her teeth. "Fine. Catch you next week, papi," she said to the delivery guy before she slowly sauntered toward the bar area.

The delivery guy stared at the rhythmic shake of Marta's curvy backside.

Out of patience, Paulie shoved him in the chest. "You done here?"

The man shook himself out of his daze. "Huh? Yeah. I'm good," he said and handed Paulie the invoice. "Here you go."

Quickly skimming the order, Paulie pulled out a wad of cash and paid the bill. "Leave. Now."

With a shrug, the delivery guy left out the back door to the alley where he'd parked his van.

Paulie exhaled in relief but turned around only to see Marta storm back into the kitchen.

"I don't know what bullshit game you're playing, but I don't appreciate being lied to, Paulie."

"What are you talking about?" he asked confused.

"Seth isn't at the bar, jackass, just your latest young thing. Now, where's Walter?" she asked trying to look over Paulie's shoulder.

"I just sent Seth to the bar," Paulie told her. "And who the fuck is Walter?"

"Well he's not there, and Walter was the cute delivery guy. Did you run him off?" she asked, planting her fists on her hips.

"You mean did I save that man's fucking life, Marta? Yes. Yes, I did, and you can thank me later," he said as he brushed past her and plowed through the kitchen's swinging doors. She was right. Seth wasn't there. Paulie dashed to the stairway door and shouted up to the office, but he got no answer. He darted to the front door and saw Seth's Cadillac still sitting curbside. "Did this motherfucka up and disappear?" Paulie growled under his breath. His nerves were on fire. His alarms were clanging louder than they had in years.

20

Walter whistled to himself as he loaded his hand truck into the back of his van. He even took a couple of salsa steps as he made his way to the driver's door. With a quick glance at The Pearl's back door he shook his head, smiled, and jumped up into the driver's seat.

Walter reached into his pockets for the keys when he froze and his heart stopped. He saw Seth silent and still as a statue in the passenger seat. Even with his arms folded across his chest, Seth radiated danger. Walter tried to play off the surge of fear he felt. "Hey, Seth. Shit man, you scared the hell outta me," Walter said with a nervous laugh. His hands shook as he adjusted the rearview mirror. "What's up? You need something? Hey…what's with the tire iron, man?"

Seth turned his head and looked at him dead in the eyes. "You want me to crack your fucking head open, Walter?" Seth asked coldly.

The hostile energy in the van intensified, and his gut clenched. "Say what?" Walter said, his voice quivering.

Seth blinked once and repeated himself slowly. "Do you…want me…to crack…your fucking head open?"

Walter rolled his eyes and hoped the older man was playing with him. "Man, go head with that bullshit," he said with a nervous laugh.

"Get out the van," Seth ordered.

"What?" Walter asked, alarmed. He wasn't sure what to do. In all the time he had known Seth he had never heard him speak like this. It was the kind of tone that made people lock their doors and call the cops.

"Get the fuck outta the van!" Seth yelled as he threw open his door and quickly stalked around the front of the van as Paulie burst out of The Pearl's back exit.

Walter instantly hit the lock on his door and began to fumble in his pockets for the van's keys. Seth's face contorted in rage, and when he pounded the squat-nosed hood with his fist, Walter jumped, squealed, and dropped the keys.

Seth tried to put his foot through the driver's side door. He took a step back and swung the tire iron. As Paulie ran up behind him, Seth bashed in the window and reached for Walter.

Paulie grabbed Seth in a reverse bear hug just before Seth could get a firm grip. Paulie locked eyes with Walter. "Get the fuck outta here!" he yelled at the same time Seth slammed Paulie's shin with the tire iron. With a growl of pain, Paulie fell to the ground reaching for his leg.

When Seth looked back at the van, Walter finally snapped out of his terror stupor, started the van, threw it in drive, and rocketed away.

Seth stumbled, regained his balance, and took one last swing at the fleeing van. The back window shattered and glass flew everywhere. Walter wisely kept his foot on the gas and sideswiped a parked car as he made the right turn onto the main street and disappeared.

"Fuck is wrong with you?" Seth screamed as he wheeled on Paulie. "Don't you ever fucking do that! Don't you ever touch me, mothafucka!" Seth warned pointing the tire iron at Paulie.

"Fuck you," Paulie shot back from the ground still holding his leg. "What were you going to do? Beat the faggot bloody and get sent back on a bullshit assault charge over some dumb shit? Use your fucking head, dumb ass. This ain't the old days. These kids are pussies, and you know it. He's probably on the phone right now with the damn police."

Seth paced the shaded alley. He took a swing at the dumpster as his rage continued to boil. He knew Paulie was right. One more case and he'd be sent up for good, and punk-ass Walter was not worth losing his freedom for. He dropped the tire iron and leaned against the building. After a few minutes Seth began to calm down and let out a deep sigh.

Paulie glared up at him. "I thought I was the one with 'moments,'" he grumbled. "And for the damn record, I will touch your Black ass whenever I feel like it."

"What did I tell you about touching my ass?" Seth asked walking to Paulie. "My ass is off limits to you." He reached down and helped his friend to his feet. "And by the way, 'faggot' isn't politically correct, you know?"

"No?"

"No."

"Well what is?"

"Gay, I think."

"But 'gay' is boring. With 'faggot' you can truly express how you feel towards someone," Paulie reasoned as he leaned on Seth.

"I know, but 'faggot' is considered a slur these days."

"A slur? What? You mean like 'nigger'?" When Seth nodded his head, Paulie laughed harshly. "Get the fuck outta here!"

"Yeah, I know," Seth said.

"Oh that's some bullshit right there. When their people go through what our people went through for centuries, THEN they can call something a slur. Oww!" Paulie yelled when he tried to put weight on his leg.

"Shit. Did I break you, Mr. Glass?"

"I'm just fucking with you. You must be getting slow. I'm fine," Paulie said with a chuckle as he stood straight under his own power.

Eyeing his friend doubtfully Seth continued to watch his stance. "You sure?"

"Yeah, you hit like a little girl. You know what you can do for me though?" Paulie said as he made his way toward The Pearl's back door with Seth in tow.

"What?"

Paulie looked back at him and with a smirk said, "You can leave. Take the rest of the day and go. In fact, you look like you need to go back to fuckin bed with those damn bags under your eyes."

"I'm exhausted actually," Seth admitted with a sigh. "You can handle things?"

"Don't insult me, grandma. Get your shit, go get your woman if you want, but get the fuck out of here. No telling if little Walter might roll up in here with the boys in blue, and you don't want to be here for that." Paulie said as he walked back into the kitchen area.

Paulie was right again. If Walter did show up with the cops, things could get ugly. Seth followed his partner back into the restaurant, cut through the kitchen, but didn't see Marta. After grabbing his things from the office he waved goodbye to Paulie and walked outside to find her leaning on his Cadillac, purse in hand.

21

Seth paused and took a deep breath but said nothing. While the fog of frustration and anger still hung thick on his mind, he was relieved to see Marta. With a flick of his wrist, he unlocked the doors, and they both climbed into the car's buttery leather interior.

After he'd pulled from the curb he said, "I have to get groceries." Marta nodded, and Seth noticed her slightly trembling hand. Ten minutes later they entered Fairway supermarket under the West Side Highway at 126th Street. Seth grabbed a cart and followed Marta. Watching her walk, he couldn't hold his fury, but he was content giving her the silent treatment.

When they walked into the bakery area, Marta grabbed a sourdough salt loaf she knew Seth loved and wordlessly added it to their cart without looking at him. Seth knew Marta loved ginger lemon cream cookies and tossed in two boxes, which put a hint of a smile on her face. He loved a particular brand of raspberry walnut vinaigrette salad dressing, so she grabbed two bottles of the tangy stuff. She loved Kalamata and Sicilian green olives. Seth bought a jar of each.

For nearly an hour they silently strolled through the aisles, tossing items they knew the other liked into the cart, which was overflowing after Marta added several pounds of ribeye steaks. At the checkout, they unloaded their haul, and before Seth could reach for his wallet, Marta had swiped her credit card, ignoring Seth's frown. Together they loaded the groceries into the trunk, but before they climbed in, Seth grabbed her arm and pulled her close.

He gently moved her hair out of her face and looked deeply into her big brown eyes. "It's time for the fucking games to stop, Marta. No more. Do you understand?"

Marta nodded, her almond eyes boring into his.

"Say I understand," Seth ordered.

"I understand, baby," she whispered. "And I'm sorry. I love you," she said sincerely.

"You better," Seth replied with a glare.

Marta smiled seeing the playful gleam in his eye. "Or what?"

"You'll see."

"Such a tease you are, Seth Jackson, such a tease."

"Takes one to know one," he said as he slid behind the wheel and softly closed his door.

22

"I need a favor."

Those four words spoken by a ghost from his past had sent chills up Percy Hammersmith's spine. Percy had ignored the first call yesterday, hoping there wouldn't be a call back, but this morning Florida had put his ever-faithful and doggedly determined Evil on his ass, and she'd blown up his phone and every social media channel he used to kill time. The woman was the queen of digital stalking. With every new message she had promised worse and more painful consequences if he didn't get in touch with them by 3:00 p.m. She'd eventually threatened to puncture his scrotum with her stiletto, and he didn't doubt that she knew how to make that happen.

Percy had never been a brave man. He was for the most part, a coward, so it was no surprise that he caved in to Evil's bullying and called Florida with minutes to spare.

"Bout time your ass got back to me. I was beginning to think you were ducking me. You wouldn't duck me, would you, Percy?" Florida asked.

"Hell nah, Florida. You know I wouldn't do you like that, man," he replied, his voice dripping with sincerity.

"I didn't think you were, but my secretary thought different. She thought your cowardly ass was holed up somewhere with the blinds drawn and the curtains closed hoping like hell you wouldn't have to man up and return the favor you owe me for saving your life. I had to tell her that that's not the Percy Hammersmith I knew. No, I told her the Percy Hammersmith I knew wouldn't duck the man that gave him the most precious of all things…more tomorrows. I said he was probably busy and didn't have the time to call me back and that when he could he would."

"Exactly. I was just in the middle of some things. That's all. I had to, you know, untangle some knots is all," Percy nervously explained.

"You all right? You need any help with them knots?" Florida asked sounding sincere himself.

"I'm solid, man. I'm solid. So you need a favor?"

"Indeed I do, and you are the first man who came to mind."

"Cool, but how can I help you from way out here? You know I'm still in Youngstown, right? Not sure what I can do, Flo."

"First off, you know better than to ever call me Flo," Florida stated darkly. "Secondly, and this is the beauty of the favor, Percy," he said in a more friendly tone, "what I need help with is a set of ears, yours exactly, listening to the noise that's going on in your own backyard."

Florida's rickety office chair creaked in the background as he explained exactly what he needed. Percy swallowed hard and listened very carefully to the third most dangerous man he'd ever known.

Percy walked into Romare's some hours later per Florida's instructions and immediately felt uncomfortable. It wasn't the South Side that made him jumpy. He knew the area well and had even earned some money there from an occasional hustle. It wasn't the raucous crowd or the flashes of skin he could see on stage in the back. What made him uncomfortable was the hard, cold gaze that hit him the moment he arrived from the guy at the end of the bar with the low fade. He was not much taller than Percy, but everything about him screamed violent and deadly.

Percy had a decision to make then and there. He could tuck tail and leave and suffer Florida's wrath or shrug off the death stare at the bar and get Florida the information he needed. Percy swallowed the bile rising in his throat and glanced around the bar. As long as there wasn't any immediate physical threat, he'd rather cope with the unwelcoming vibe of the bar than deal with Florida's very long reach and even longer memory. There was nowhere to hide from his influence.

Percy flagged Turk, the grizzled bartender and Florida's contact, for a drink. As he expected, Turk wasn't welcoming either.

"Whatchu want?"

"Hi there. My man Florida told me this was the place to be."

Turk said nothing.

"You got Heineken here?" Percy asked.

For a quick second the old man looked at Percy as if he had grown another head and then turned and grabbed his choice in beer out of the fridge under the bar. After the bartender popped the cap and slammed the bottle down in front of him, Percy felt like a dumb ass for asking the obvious. He quickly paid for his drink and settled in to watch the playoff basketball game and did his best to seem unaffected by everyone's hostility.

Mr. Dangerous continued to stare at Percy as if he were looking through him. Halfway through the first period, Percy finally realized why the man made his sphincter squeeze shut. The eyes that bore into him reminded him of eyes that had belonged to two stone cold killers he'd once come across back in Harlem. Percy did his best to control his trembling hand as he clutched his beer bottle and took an anxious swig. *Fuck you, Florida. Fuck, fuck, fuck you, man*, he thought. *Fuck you and your psycho secretary too.*

After a couple of minutes, Percy let out an audible sigh when Mr. Dangerous left the bar and headed towards the back.

Turk checked in a few seconds later as he wiped down the bar. "You gon be watched all night, so be easy. Nobody likes virgin faces round here if ya get what I'm sayin."

Percy motioned with his hand to the game as if he were into it but nodded in understanding and ordered another beer. Florida had explained that this "favor" might take a while. He cringed knowing he'd have to keep coming back to Romare's night after night armed with only small talk and a smile.

An hour later, Percy shook his head when the game ended and tossed back the last swallow in his bottle. He hadn't heard a word about anything that would matter to Florida, and he dreaded what could be a lot more trips to the bar. With a sigh he hopped off the stool, waved goodnight to Turk, and managed to leave without running for the door.

Fuck, fuck, fuck you, Florida.

23

With virtually only days left of high school Charlie and his fellow seniors were pretty much going through the motions. Once in class, they had nothing to do other than browse their social media feeds or take selfies. The majority of them had mentally checked out of high school. SAT's were taken, scores were tallied, and college acceptance letters were received. Pretty much everyone had a plan including Charlie. That is if he made it through the summer.

He'd applied to UCLA, USC, Texas, Miami, and Michigan. When he'd received acceptance letters from UCLA and Michigan, his father had announced that he would happily send Charlie to UCLA, but there was "no way on God's green earth" he would give one thin dime to the University of Michigan. His father's careless comment had made up Charlie's mind for him. *Michigan, here I come. Fuck you, Dad.*

While his classmates milled about and exchanged phone numbers, email addresses, and promises to stay in touch, Charlie sat at his desk in Mr. Whitmore's English class and paid more attention to the cloudless sky.

Unfortunately, Mr. Whitmore noticed his detachment, and after posing for his third selfie with other students, he walked over to Charlie with his brows furrowed. "Charles, you feeling okay?"

Charlie gave his favorite teacher a quick nod and a smile before returning his gaze to the blue sky.

Charlie knew he was one of Stanley Whitmore's best and favorite students. While Charlie hardly studied or took notes, he aced every test, and English was the only class where he actually turned in his papers on time. He felt Mr. Whitmore deserved that kind of effort because he was the one teacher in the whole school that gave a damn about his students. It also didn't hurt that Charlie loved his English class. Mr. Whitmore didn't just lecture. He encouraged debate, asked opinions, and settled arguments that arose from reading authors like

Orwell, Hughes, Shakespeare, Morrison, Baldwin, Hemingway, Bradbury, and even Octavia Butler. What proved just how much he enjoyed Mr. Whitmore's class was his perfect attendance, especially considering it was the last class of the day.

Stanley searched Charlie's placid face. "You need to see the school nurse or something?"

"Nah, I'm fine, doc," Charlie said. Once Charlie had found out that Mr. Whitmore had a Ph.D. in Literature, he hadn't been able to resist the nickname. None of his other students knew or cared about his distinction, but Charlie had been impressed.

Mr. Whitmore smiled at their inside joke.

Charlie didn't want to be rude, but he didn't feel like chatting and tried to zone out again, hoping Stanley would let him be.

"You don't seem fine, staring out the window when everyone is doing…whatever it is they're doing." Mr. Whitmore looked over at a crowd of students and shook his head. "What are they doing?"

Charlie turned and glanced at the impromptu dance that had broken out in the middle of the classroom. "I think it's some form of the Macarena, doc."

"The Macarena? They still do that?"

"What can I say? It's got staying power."

"At least they're not twerking," Stanley stated with a shrug.

Charlie raised his eyebrows at his balding, freckled faced, middle-aged teacher. "What do you know about twerking, doc?"

"Not much, but I know I like it," Mr. Whitmore replied with an appreciative smile.

Charlie shook his head in amusement. Thankfully the bell rang. As he began to rise from his desk Stanley touched him on the arm.

"Stay for a sec." Stanley said.

Charlie slowly sat back down, curious to see what was on his teacher's mind. Occasionally, Mr. Whitmore asked him stay behind to go into more depth on a question Charlie had asked that was beyond the normal class discussion, so his request wasn't a complete surprise. Once the last kid had left the room, Stanley squeezed himself into the desk next to Charlie's and looked him.

"What's up, doc?" Charlie asked.

Stanley smiled. "You want to tell me what's going on?"

Charlie's stomach clenched a little. He had no desire whatsoever to share with anyone else the latest drama in his life. He contorted his face as best he could in mild confusion. "What do you mean?"

"I mean what's going on with you."

"Nothing's going on with me," Charlie remarked as he flashed a perfect smile and a thumbs up sign. "Everything is great."

"After four years, you think I don't get to know you guys a bit and don't know when something's up with any one of the kids in this school, especially with you?"

The sincere concern in Mr. Whitmore's eyes took him by surprise. It had been a while since an adult had paid this much attention to any one thing he really did. Most of the time he felt invisible. He blinked, refocused, and settled his mask a little more firmly in place. "Doc, is this because I was staring out the window? Say it ain't so."

"You do know how much I hate that word, right?"

Charlie grinned. "I know, but the phrase doesn't work with 'not,' so 'ain't' gets the nod."

"Look, real talk," Stanley said using the vernacular he'd picked up from his students. "If you're in some kind of trouble or if something is going on at home or with your friends, you can talk to me. I hope you know that, Charles."

Mr. Whitmore's words hit Charlie like a heavyweight jab to the head. In an instant he ceased seeing Mr. Whitmore as a charming, intelligent, and talented teacher and saw him as a person, an average, law-abiding, middle-aged white man with a not big but certainly noticeable paunch. His pleasant enough face probably once upon a time had attracted a few ladies, but those days were gone. He more than likely lived in an okay duplex and maybe had a wife, maybe a kid, and a dog. He definitely had a dog.

Charlie also knew this man wasn't in any position to help him out with his kind of problems. First sign of a shark and this white man would no doubt go screaming to the cops. No, while Charlie appreciated Stanley Whitmore's offer, Charlie liked him too much to tell him anything that could potentially get them both killed.

"You married, Mr. Whitmore? I mean is there a Mrs. Whitmore waiting at home for you?"

"She tends to get home after me, but yes there is a Mrs. Whitmore. Why?"

"So with you getting home first, do you do mosta the cooking?"

"I do most of the cooking, yes," Stanley said, putting the emphasis on 'of.'

"Then maybe you should go home and get your Betty Crocker on, doc," Charlie said with a fond smile as he rose to his feet. He strode to the open classroom door with the confidence of a senior and stopped. He turned and met Mr. Whitmore's concern gaze.

"Thanks, Mr. Whitmore. For everything."

"See you tomorrow, Charles?"

"You just might, doc. You never know."

24

Hannibal Wolfe aka The Wolf steered his Chevy Avalanche into his driveway and cut the engine. Seated in the passenger seat, her cheeks still wet with tears, was his fiancé, Monique. The shock of identifying Appleton's body an hour earlier still hadn't worn off, and Hannibal's fury roiled like hurricane-fueled waters. Monique remained quiet, her hand on his thigh in comfort, patiently letting him work through the relentless waves of emotions.

Appleton and Hannibal were first cousins, and for most of their lives, they had been virtually inseparable. When Hannibal had blown out his knee in his senior year of high school, the college recruiters who had pestered him for years with slippery promises of glory had vanished like early morning fog. With his dreams of playing pro football destroyed, for the first time in his life Hannibal had had no goals to chase down and tackle, so Appleton, a self proclaimed 'street genius', had offered his rudderless cousin a place at the table as his number two in his hustle to supply whatever his customers demanded, typically weed, coke, and pills.

Passed from grade to grade because of what he could do on the gridiron and not in the classroom, Hannibal had had few options and willingly had become the brawn his cousin needed. The Wolf's six-four muscular frame as well as his brutal and uncompromising nature kept their East Side crew in line and their enemies on high alert. Hannibal had quickly developed a street reputation for being an uncontrollable Alpha that mirrored his on the field nickname.

The only person Hannibal didn't frighten was Monique. With her he wasn't The Wolf. She saw him for all that he was, a flesh and blood man with passions, emotions, and pain. Monique was a soft spot where he could lay his head and forget the outside world.

Appleton had taught Hannibal what he knew, and for years they had made money hand over fist by diversifying their holdings. Monique, using her university-sharpened business acumen, had invested their profits and washed the money with stock market ventures, real estate holdings, and local business investments. With each success, their assets and reach had crowded out their competition until they controlled most of the East Side.

Before Appleton's murder the team had discussed expansion into other areas of Youngstown. Hannibal had been ready to take by force, but Appleton had wanted to negotiate alliances, hoping to keep any large-scale violence at bay. Most of their competitors had succumbed to either the promise of profits or the threat of The Wolf and his gang and agreed to join them.

However, one rival on the South Side had refused to bend a knee. Surrender wasn't in Frank's DNA, and everyone knew he would never share the corners that he and his boys had worked so violently to keep. Weeks ago, Stony and Frank had made the situation clear. If Hannibal and Appleton wanted any action on their side of town then they would have to get wet.

With their already expanding enterprise Appleton had no interest in a war with Frank. They knew his vicious reputation and thought it best to focus on their burgeoning success. They were living good and lavished their crew with money, gifts, and trips whenever they could. When Stony turned down Appleton's buy in attempt, the two men had established a tenuous and uneasy arrangement to stay in their respective territories, but that informal treaty no longer mattered.

Appleton was dead. All because a few of their overzealous soldiers had roughed up a member of Frank's crew. In the business they were in, everyone knew death or prison was their only fate, but the counterstrike was completely out of proportion. It was illogical to take out a general for a soldier's ass beating, and for that Hannibal was determined to bring hell to their doorstep. *Fuck Frank and his rep*, he thought, pounding the steering wheel as a tsunami of pain-fueled rage overtook him yet again. Monique's tears continued to fall as he grappled with his anguish.

Monique's calm touch pierced his rage, and he froze. As her soft warm hand slowly rubbed the back of his head, Hannibal took a deep breath and closed his eyes. Monique could soothe his beast with just her touch. Eventually his violent emotions subsided, his muscles relaxed, and his breathing returned to normal. After a few long minutes, her man was again in control.

He wiped away the trail of hot tears that scorched Monique's smooth cheeks. She loved Appleton like a brother, and he knew she wanted someone to hurt dearly for bringing this anguish down on them. With their foreheads touching his fierce, future wife asked him quietly, "What are you going to do now, baby?"

Hannibal didn't answer immediately as he thought over for long minutes how Appleton might want things handled. Finally he sat back in his seat. "We gon have a barbecue...yeah, a big one," he whispered. "It's gonna be massive, steaks, burgers, fish, corn, beer, Henney, your special macaroni salad I love. You name it. I want everyone here this weekend."

"Everyone?" she asked with a sniffle. He knew her nimble mind had kicked into gear as she began to plan.

"From the corner boys to the captains," he said turning to look at her. "Everyone."

"Why, baby?"

"Because after we eat, drink, smoke, be merry and all that good shit...we goin to war."

Monique flinched in the darkness, but he was grateful when she swallowed her instinctive urge to argue. That was the last thing he wanted to deal with at that moment. She searched his face and knew there was no changing his mind.

"I want and need some get back. The streets demand it, baby. You know that."

Resigned, Monique kissed Hannibal's cheek and grabbed her purse.

"Where you goin?"

"Aren't you headed to the gym?" she asked.

A faint smile tugged at the edge of his lips. His woman knew him too well. "Yeah. I need to get my mind right, work through this."

"I know. You do what you have to do. I'll be up, so don't worry about waking me when you get in," she said softly.

"What you gonna do?"

"You want everybody here this weekend, so I have calls to make," she said before she leaned over to kiss him and climbed out of the truck.

Without a backward glance and Hannibal drove off to find temporary solace and clarity the only way he knew how—through physical punishment.

The Wolf's Den had been a gift from Appleton a few years ago. Staffed and operated by select members of their crew along with a handful of neighborhood kids, the sparse renovated warehouse was the one place Hannibal felt he could let go and be his most vicious self. Other than in bed with Monique, it was the only place that centered and calmed him. Lifting weights, pounding the heavy bag, working the speed bag, and sparring with anyone who dared step into the ring with him allowed The Wolf to push himself until he couldn't go anymore. He loved and hated the pain, but more than that, tonight he needed it.

The Den and the rigors he put himself through allowed him to clear his mind and think. He'd learned the benefit of strategic planning at App's side, but his best friend and only family he'd had was gone. Now any current and future business moves fell upon his broad shoulders.

Gotta get this right. Somehow. Some way, Hannibal thought. He knew his cousin would hate the idea of war. "War don't bring no money, and we in business to get money," he'd often said, following with, "Somebody is always gonna to try to fuck up your money. Don't help em."

Wise words, but this is different cuz. With his hands taped and gloved he pawed slowly at the heavy bag. Once he built up a good lather he began to pound. With practiced precision he rotated around the bag, sidestepped it, jabbed and viciously hooked it. The resounding booms echoed throughout the gym, and those few still there stopped what they were doing to watch The Wolf tear at his imagined prey.

Hannibal knew his cousin had pulled him back from the brink more often than not, but he couldn't this time. *This time, cuz, them mothafuckas are gonna pay,* he thought as his tears fell and his fists continued to jackhammer.

25

Early Thursday morning Frank stalked into Stony's office as Stony began to feed his fish. "We need to talk," Frank said with an edge in his voice that his partner rarely had heard.

Sensing Frank's unusual tension, he put down the fish food and took a seat on the leather sofa.

Frank followed suit. "I just got a call from one of my informants that The Wol–"

"Wait," Stony interrupted, "You have informants? Where?"

"I got people everywhere, and I got one in Appleton's crew. He told me The Wol–"

"How many we talking?" Stony interrupted again.

Frank visibly clenched his teeth. "Does that fucking matter right now?"

Stony ignored Frank's impatience to consider the implications. "That's ballsy. Whoever they are, they get found out they're a dead man. They know that, right?"

"Whatever, nigga. Listen."

Stony bristled. "You need to calm down and breathe, seriously. Whatever this is can't be something we can't deal with. So relax."

Frank took a deep breath and let it out slowly before speaking again. "My guy was at The Wolf's Den."

"What's that?"

Frank winced. "Seriously…are you done?"

Stony sighed and raised his hands. He sat back and gave Frank the floor.

"The Wolf's Den is Hannibal's gym on the East Side. The Wolf came through last night and put in some serious work and pretty much tore the heavy bag off its hinges. I was told he only goes that hard when he's plannin on doin something crazy. He may be goin to the guns."

Stony's eyebrows rose in surprise. "War?" While the thought of bullets flying and bodies falling in the street didn't make him nervous, he didn't want anything to get in the way of his other plans.

Frank nodded. "He and his girl got back into town yesterday, and the cops notified them first thing. They went down to the morgue last night to ID App's body."

"So he knows his cousin is dead, so what? How does that come back to us?" Stony asked with a shrug "Didn't nobody see shit."

Frank looked at him like Stony had shat a golden egg from his ass. "It doesn't as far as the cops is concerned, but that's because cops need evidence. The Wolf don't give a damn bout no evidence." Frank's impatience got the best of him, and he rose from the sofa to pace. "Look, them niggas beat down Lil Earl. It ain't hard for Wolf or anyone on the street to connect that mess to App's death and then bring it to our doorstep. You got the crew's respect for goin hard at App, but now the Wolf's gonna want revenge, and make no mistake, he won't hesitate to bring that shit to us, Stone. We need to get ready. You need to get ready."

"I was born ready," Stony said with a dismissive wave unworried about an ex-football jock's temper or reach. He knew first hand how cunning and dangerous Frank was. "And I am confident you'll make sure everyone else is too. I'm confident that you won't let anything slip and that you'll make all the right decisions when the time comes. Am I right?"

Frank stopped pacing, crossed his arms, and assessed Stony. "Of course. I'm not about to let us get caught sleeping with our dicks in our hands. I'm just starting to like you. Can't let you get killed now," Frank stated dryly.

"You got jokes, huh?"

"I'm not joking, Stone. You need to be strapped at all times," Frank said, the edge in his voice left no room for further discussion.

"Starting when?"

"Starting right fuckin now. Plus I'm having a vest brought by tonight for you. You'll wear that at all times. Understood?"

Stony nodded with a shrug.

Frank sat back down on the sofa and continued to lay out his plans and preparations as Stony watched and listened to a man who could likely have been the brightest military strategist of his day had he not been brought up without a pot to piss in.

Frank was cool, manipulative, and left nothing to chance. He'd been through plenty of street skirmishes before and had always come out on the other side. He may have been both psychologically and physically scarred, but he came out alive. If Frank said do something, Stony would follow his lead.

"We also need to put shooters on the roof," Frank said.

"What roof?"

"This roof."

"Seriously?" Stony laughed. "You think he'd target this place? In the heart of our territory? C'mon man. You trippin."

"We'd be damn fools to think he might not try us here. If I were him, I would." Frank's eyes blazed with life as he mapped out tactics in his mind. "I know his gym is on my list of targets if this shit jumps off."

Stony stood and took his turn to pace the length of his office and consider what a possible attack on Romare's would do to business. While slow money was better than no money, Stony hated slow money, and if this war popped off like Frank thought it might, it would definitely choke their cash flow. He had other streams of revenue, but he didn't like the idea of using those to keep Romare's afloat. This was his doing though, and he realized that he may have overreached a bit in his response to Earl's beat down.

Frank and crew had originally hunted the cousins. They'd wanted to take the head off that entire organization out in one fell swoop, which would have been a masterstroke, but The Wolf had been in the wind, so they'd settled on Appleton and had hoped to get a fix on Hannibal a day or two later. Unfortunately, the heir to the throne hadn't resurfaced until the day the cops had found Appleton's body. Now here they were, preparing for his blowback instead of planning on how to dice up the East Side.

Fuck that, thought Stony. *If that muscle bound motherfucker wants to go to the guns then so be it.* Stony walked to his desk and pulled out his Uncle's nickel-plated pearl-handled Desert Eagle, chambered a round, clicked the safety on, and laid it on his desk.

Frank finally cracked a satisfied smile.

26

Charlie sat outside with Lily at a picnic table, basking in the bright late spring sun over their last school lunch. While she munched on an apple Charlie chowed down his second burrito, courtesy of Ms. Brown. For some reason Ms. Brown, the cafeteria lady, had taken a liking to Charlie. She always had a smile and an extra helping of his favorite foods.

After cutting school with Gavin yesterday to play video games and get high, Charlie had decided to attend his last day of high school. Graduation was coming, but that pomp and circumstance wasn't for another two weeks. He was only on campus to see Lily and say goodbye to a couple of teachers and other faculty like Ms. Brown. More importantly, Charlie wanted to say goodbye to his English teacher, Mr. Whitmore. Out of everyone who worked at his school, he was going to miss that man the most.

"Are you seriously staying the whole day?" she asked after swallowing a bite of her fruit.

"Yeah, why not?" Charlie shrugged. "Last day and all. I'm never coming back, so why not?" he asked before shoving the last of his burrito in his mouth.

"I don't know. It seems so unlike you."

His mouth stuffed with ground beef, rice, beans, cheese, and tortilla, Charlie held up his hands in mock offense while he tried several times to speak. Finally he said, "Hey, I'm not a bad student."

"Never said you were a bad student," Lily said as she stood and flung what was left of her apple into a garbage can about fifteen feet away. "But I'm a better shot than you are a student, and that shot was pure luck."

"We both know that's bullshit, Lils," he said.

"What is? That that shot was pure luck?"

"No, that you're a better shot than I am a student."

She pursed her lips in thought and looked him over with a cynical gaze that quickly softened. "Well you did ace your SAT. I'll give you that, buster. How you did it I'll never know."

Charlie puffed out his chest and lifted his hands above him and boasted. "Cause I'm gifted, and you know it."

"Anyway," she said with a playful roll of her eyes. "What are you doing after school?"

Charlie leaned back and glanced up at the puffy clouds. "I don't know. I was gonna maybe hit the mall before heading home. Why?"

"Going to see Clarissa?" she teased.

"What would make you say that?" Charlie asked.

"I don't know. Maybe it's the way she looks at you, like she wants to tear your clothes off or something."

"I like that look," Charlie said knowing that would rile Lily. "But it's rare."

"My ass it's rare. It's every time she looks at you," Lily said as she stuck her tongue out at him. The light blue silk tank top and white cotton shorts she wore popped against her tanned skin and straddled the line between appropriate and indecent. As she turned to gather her things, he stole a glance at her ass. "Stop looking at my ass, Charles," she warned.

"You brought it up," he said.

Lily shook her head at him. "You ever wonder why Ms. Brown likes you so much?" she asked changing the subject as he walked to the trashcan to dispose of the wrappers. "I mean she doesn't hook anyone else up but you. What's up with that?"

"Don't know and don't care, but my belly loves that woman," he said with a smile as he rubbed his stomach.

"Maybe she likes you, thinks you're cute or something."

"Well that makes at least two people in this world who thinks I'm cute," he said.

"Just two?"

"According to you it's Clarissa and now Ms. Brown. It's a really exclusive club."

Lily pouted which made Charlie smile. "You want to join the club?" he asked.

"Only if I can be President."

"I would have it no other way."

"If you know what's good for you, you better not," she said shaking her fist at him. "Hey, you want to hang out tonight? Catch a movie?"

"Absolutely but I'm supposed to hang out with Gavin," he said prompting Lily to pout again.

"Didn't you hang out with him yesterday?" she asked.

Damn, I love when she pouts, he thought. "Tell you what, I'll text him and cancel."

Lily smiled. "Great, meet me at the mall around four," she said and kissed him.

"You're not gonna say goodbye to Stanley?"

"I already said my goodbyes to Mr. Whitmore yesterday. If you had been a good student and showed up you would have known that, but nooo…someone spent the day bumming around with his friends doing whatever it is that you all do." she chided. "But I'm glad you came today, Charlie. Shows commitment. Anyway, I'm ghost. See you later," she said and pecked him again.

When she turned and started across the lawn to her car, he yelled, "I love those shorts on you!"

"Stop looking at my ass, Charles!"

When Charlie finally strolled into his last high school English class, an unexpected wave of sadness tugged at him, and a lump formed in his throat. Only about eight other students milled around the front of the classroom. Mr. Whitmore caught his eye and made a point to welcome him. Charlie greeted his fellow classmates with fist bumps, hugs, and a few kisses on the cheek.

The tiny crowd soon thinned until he was the only student left with Stanley. Each kicked back in a desk and discussed sports, summer plans, and the future. They talked about cooking though Mr.

Whitmore did most of the talking on that subject. The two spoke as if they were out on a lake with poles in the water and a bucket of ice-cold beer between them. Had anyone told either of them that they would have been sitting there like this when Charlie was a freshman, both would have doubted that claim vociferously.

When the bell rung Stanley asked, "Walk out with me, Charlie?"

"School's over?"

"High school is. C'mon," Staley Whitmore said as he grabbed his satchel. After locking the classroom, the two wound their way down to the main floor and stepped into the warmth of a beautiful afternoon.

As they passed the tennis courts, Stanley searched Charlie's strained face. "Something on your mind?" Stanley asked.

"It's hard for me to explain, so I'm not even going to try, teach."

"I'm not your teacher anymore, Charles, so you can call me Stanley."

"If it's all the same…Stanley, you'll always be my teacher, so I'm a stick with that or doc."

"'I'm going to' not 'I'm a.' You can do better than 'I'm a.'"

"See, that's why you'll always be my favorite teacher," Charlie said with a wan smile.

"Hey, are you still working on your novel?" Stanley asked.

Charlie's head swiveled in shock. "How the hell did you find out about that?"

"A little bird told me."

"I may have to pluck her wings. I stopped, doc. I'm a…I'm going to pick it up again one day."

"Good, I think you'll make a fantastic writer, Charles. I really do, and I can't wait to read it."

They approached Stanley's faded yellow dented Volvo. "I have something for you," he said as he threw his satchel in the back and gathered something off the backseat.

"How'd you know I was even coming to school today?" Charlie asked.

"It's burrito day, Charles. You never miss burrito day. Here," Stanley said as he handed Charlie a gift bag. "A little something for my favorite student."

Charlie reached in and pulled out two books, *The War of Art* by Steven Pressfield and *This Year You Write Your Novel* by Walter Mosely. Charlie smiled even as his eyes welled up at Mr. Whitmore's faith in him and his talent. Unable to find words, Charlie hugged him.

"Whatever you want to do, Charles, do it," Stanley said as the two separated. "Don't let anyone stand in your way, including yourself. Understand me?"

"I think so, doc."

"I know this world can be shit at times, and the people in it can be unforgiving, heartless, even cruel, but never let those people stop you. Do whatever it takes to never become like them. You can be whatever you want to be, Charles. Don't ever forget that."

Charlie considered his mentor's words. "I'll do what I can, doc but nony promises."

"Why is that?"

"I don't know. I just can't," Charlie said unwilling to explain as the ghosts of Stony and Frank kicked in the door of his consciousness. He took a deep breath but kept his fears of not making it to eighteen to himself. He checked his watch. "Hey I have to go. Thanks for the books," he said as the two shook hands like men who were on equal footing.

"I'm gonna miss you, Charles."

"'Gonna?' Really? It's 'going to' as in…I am going to miss you too, Mr. Whitmore."

Charlie's correction brought a smile to Stanley's face. "Touché, Charles."

"Thank you for everything, doc. Now go get your Betty Crocker on, and say hi to Mrs. Whitmore for me," Charlie said backing away about to break into a run.

"Charles, come back and pay us a visit sometime."

"Again, no promises, doc, but if I do it'll be on burrito day!" With that he turned and sprinted to the student lot and his car before his old English teacher could see his tears.

27

This time it was a sober Charlie who met Lily outside of Lady Foot Locker. He was determined to leave behind the thoughts of the South Side and all its drama for the evening. He again gratefully admired Lily's tempting ensemble of white shorts and light blue tank with a low whistle and enjoyed her smiling blush even more. The evening was off to a good start.

Lily had reluctantly given her okay for Gavin and his friend, Jennifer, to tag along with them to the movies and dinner. The two couples met at the food court in the mall, and Gavin introduced Jennifer to everyone. "She just moved here, and our families know each other, so I thought I'd show her around," Gavin said.

"And you want to subject her to us so soon?" Lily asked. "That's not very nice of you."

"Speak for yourself," Charlie said. "I think he could have done way worse than hanging out with us." He looked at Jennifer and opening his arms wide said, "On behalf of the Canfield-Boardman welcoming committee, I bid thee welcome to our little corner of the realm."

"Thank you," Jennifer said with a giggle. She looked at Gavin. "You were right."

Gavin grinned. "Told you."

"Told you what? What are you talking about?" Lily asked Jennifer and Gavin suspiciously.

"I told her that Charlie was super funny and super charming, like Lando Calrissian," Gavin answered with a shrug. "Jennifer is a gigantic *Star Wars* fan."

"Live long and prosper," Charlie said as he flashed the Vulcan salute.

Lily rolled her eyes. "That's *Star Trek*, silly, and yeah, I can see the Lando thing, but he was cuter."

"I try and be nice, and everybody's got jokes," Charlie said.

As they took a leisurely stroll through the mall, Charlie carried on a mutated version of Lando meets Spock and kept the group in stitches. During a moment when the girls were grabbing frozen mochachinos, Charlie pulled Gavin aside and asked, "Dude, you heard from Chad?"

"Nope and I'm guessing you haven't either, huh?"

"I got some garbled text from him about skiing at some killer all-day party in Akron."

"What in the hell is he doing there?"

"I don't know, and I have no idea what any of that meant, but I'm worried that he seems to be pushing the edge lately."

Gavin shrugged. "Yeah, but he's always been this way. Nothing bad has really happened."

"Yet," Charlie said somberly.

After seeing a film that failed to impress, they grabbed a table at Stymie's and introduced Jennifer to the best burgers in town before the two couples called it a night.

As Charlie drove Lily home, he was caught off guard when she explained why her car wasn't in the mall lot. "So is that why you left school early today, to sell your car?"

"You are so swift sometimes. I don't care what anyone says about you," she said with a playful punch to his arm. "You are most certainly not slow, Charles Jackson."

"Got jokes I see. Seriously though, I can't believe you sold The Beast. You loved that car."

"I'm leaving for New York soon, Charlie. I needed pocket money, and besides, you don't need a car there like you do here."

"Leaving soon, huh?" Charlie asked, trying to ignore the sudden discomfort in his chest.

Lily turned in her seat to look at him. "Yes, which is why I wanted it to be just us tonight. Though Jennifer was sweet, and Gavin, wow, he's prettier than ever."

Charlie swallowed and attempted to maintain their usual light banter. "Don't be calling my friend pretty. You tryin to make me jealous?"

"Of course, I live for that," she said with a sly smile.

Charlie tried to smile back, but it didn't stay long. "Your news isn't really something I feel like smiling about, Lils. I kinda thought you'd be around until the end of summer."

"Charlie…I want to spend as much time with you as I can before I leave," she said quietly. "I don't know when I'll be back, if I'll come back." Lily closed her eyes and continued in a whisper. "I'm going to miss my family and my friends so much, but I need to get away from the memories and ghosts that chase me down every street, corner, and neighborhood. I crave a fresh start, and that begins in New York. I hope you can understand."

Charlie quietly absorbed her words. He understood her motives and was slowly coming to grips with how little time they had left. Catching a red light, he met her warm brown eyes. "My time is yours," Charlie promised threading his fingers between hers. "Just you and me, deal?"

She squeezed his hand and sniffled a little. "Deal," she replied with a hesitant smile. "Maybe I'll even let you try to convince me to come back and visit once in a while."

"Oh really? Then you better count on coming back more than a few times," he said with a chuckle before hitting the gas.

28

Seth leaned against The Pearl's bar as he enjoyed an Amaretto sour and grooved to the sounds of the live jazz they featured every other Friday night. The group was a trio he had heard in a downtown subway station. He'd liked their sound and their style so much that he'd left the threesome his contact info, and they had quickly negotiated a standing gig at The Pearl. Known as the FTS Trio, not one of the young Black men appeared to be a day over twenty-five, but their growing number of fans ranging from eighteen to eighty-five packed The Pearl every time they played.

Squeezing through the throng of people, Marta placed a bowl of cooked-to-perfection honey-mustard glazed chicken wings in front of Seth with a quick kiss on his cheek. He couldn't contain his appreciation and kissed her full on the lips before he dug in with both hands.

A few feet away, Paulie grumbled to himself behind the bar alongside Tamara, who'd shown a natural ability for bartending after all. Paulie hated jazz music. "Prissy music for prissy pseudo-intellectuals who think they're smarter than the rest of us."

Seth laughed at the comments because he knew what Paulie did love were the barrels of money those "prissy intellectuals" brought into The Pearl several times a month.

As FTS kicked off their rendition of Thelonious Monk's classic *Ruby My Dear,* Paulie opened the cash register, and a big smile broke across his dark weathered face. He glanced back at Seth, pulled most of the money, and made a quick deposit into the safe under the bar. Then he reached above him and grabbed a bottle of Johnny Walker Black before walking over to Seth and Marta. With a wide toothy grin, Paulie refilled Seth's empty glass with the top shelf whiskey and poured one for Marta and himself. They raised their glasses to one another and to the FTS Trio.

For the moment, Seth felt great. His place overflowed with customers, he and Marta were good, his friends were healthy and well, and his chicken wings tasted like sweet honey on sunshine. Right now there wasn't a thing in the world that foretold of the storm coming his way.

29

Hannibal sat in the front pew with Monique by his side. They had both dressed in red, Appleton's favorite color, while the rest of the church had embraced traditional black. Though sniffles filled the church, Hannibal's eyes were dry. He stared at the altar in silence as he finally quelled the emotions that had threatened to explode. His anger and grief had been so strong that morning that Monique had needed to help him with his buttons and tie. However, seeing his cousin resting peacefully in a casket surprisingly calmed him. Soon the ones who put Appleton in his red silk lined, gold handled box would join him. Hannibal's plans for war gave him solace. *Don't worry, cuz. I promise. You'll have company soon.*

After the ceremony only family went to the crematorium to say goodbye one last time. The group was a small one, him and Monique. Appleton had been an only child, and Appleton's parents were already deceased. Hannibal eyes flooded as he took charge of the ashes. His best friend—his only family—was gone.

Hannibal drove silently back to their house with Appleton's ashes resting in Monique's lap. He hadn't said more than two words all day, but she didn't fuss over him. She knew tomorrow the words and the emotions would flow freely. Today was a day of grieving, so she let him be. Once home she handed him the red and gold urn, and watched silently as her man took it to its final resting place, in his den where it would be prominently displayed. She closed the door behind her to let him say his own goodbye.

Moments later after Monique had unpinned her hat she was not surprised when she heard him howl in pain and sorrow. The mournful sound echoed like a wounded animal through the silent house and broke her heart.

"Let it out, baby," she whispered, "let it out."

30

The Wolf's barbeque was jumping thanks to the bass that pounded through the amped-out speakers around his backyard. Nearly every member of what used to be Appleton's crew packed Hannibal's place. Soldiers brought their significant others, and the obscene seven-foot double-door smoker and grill worked overtime, pumping out enough mouth-watering barbeque chicken, baby back ribs, and steaks to feed a small country for a few days. The drinks flowed, and fat tightly rolled blunts made the rounds as well.

On this day the boys conducted no business on the streets. Everyone came together in a day of honor and celebration. Teenagers hung out in the basement, their younger brothers and sisters ran around in the backyard, and the babies sat on their mothers' laps as the ladies talked, laughed, and gossiped.

The guys played everything from dominoes to spades to cee-lo, talked about the NBA playoffs, shared stories, and enjoyed themselves. Every now and then one of the crew would pour some Hennessy out for dead, and every last one of them made the pilgrimage to visit the urn. All the while Hannibal presided over the festivities like a benevolent king. Unlike the previous days, this afternoon he freely doled out smiles, pats on the backs, bear hugs for the kids, and kisses for the babies. Uncle Wolf even hooked up his video games systems in the basement.

The man on the grill, Big Bones, had brought his secret rub and sauce, slathering it over pounds of meat and shrimp and even a few pesky children whenever they got too close. Bones had folks lined up for thirds and fourths.

The DJ spun the latest grooves as well as a good amount of soul classics. There was dancing and reminiscing. Everyone shared stories of App, but it was the original inner circle—the ones he'd grown up with and started the organization with—that laughed the loudest and talked the longest, especially about how they'd run the streets together as kids or the first time they'd met his "big muscled neck" cousin. Their memories brought a different kind of howl from Hannibal, one of warmth and joy.

For the moment peace and calm held in the hood, and no drama touched the festive atmosphere. The music rattled windows, and cars of all kinds parked on his lawn and down the block choking the street, but none of his neighbors complained. Some out of respect, some because they were in attendance, and others out of utter fear. When the police did roll through, the crew handed them to-go plates of steaks or ribs and bottles of water. The neighborhood kids mingled with his crew's kids, and they roughhoused in the inflatable ball pit and bouncy castle. They showed off their latest dance moves in multiple dance contests and ran themselves to exhaustion. While Monique was the perfect hostess and kept everything running smoothly, Hannibal made the rounds to make sure no one wanted for anything. He refilled cups, restacked plates, and told them all to eat up or be prepared to take a mountain of food home with them.

During a momentary lull, Hannibal pulled Silas into the house and led him to the den. Silas was one of the crew's most loyal and trusted captains. The husky, light-skinned charmer was also a great earner and the only member that never had to look up to Hannibal since he was slightly taller at six-five. His corners never came up short, and on that rare occasion when they did, he put his own money in to cover the difference. Because of his leadership and experience on the streets, Hannibal had tagged the younger man to be his number two. Silas readily agreed, and Hannibal quickly laid out his immediate plans.

Once Silas was on board, the two men walked out to the deck, and Hannibal signaled for the DJ to kill the music. When silence fell, the crowd's attention focused on their new leader, The Wolf, eager to hear what he had to say.

"First off, I wanna thank ya'll for comin. Don't make no damn mess in my house," he said, which made everyone laugh. "I hope ya'll are enjoying ya selves. Second, I wanna announce that Silas has been bumped up to number two status."

The gathered throng applauded and shouted their approval.

"He'll be picking who will take his place with his crew in a minute, so you boys hold tight," Hannibal said with grin and a wink at Silas' team.

Taking the Heineken Monique offered him, he continued. "Hey, it's been a minute, my niggas, since we all been in the same place like this, and it makes me feel good to see you all, seriously. We all know App's up there grinning at us and…we miss you, brother." The Wolf raised his bottle in honor of his cousin, and everyone joined him. "Someone took our King off the board, feel me?"

Everyone nodded in agreement.

"We took a loss, no lie. It's been hard the past few days for me and mine as I'm sure it was for you, but don't worry. We gonna get some get back, feel me?"

Every member of his crew murmured their agreement or nodded their heads again.

"So eat up, drink up, smoke up, and be fuckin merry and all that shit. Smoke it down to the fucking filter peoples until you see three of me because tomorrow…tomorrow we go to fucking war." Hannibal took a swig of his beer.

No one said anything for what seemed like an eternity.

Then the howls came.

One by one each voice added to the whole in tribute to their new general, mimicking The Wolf's signature call that everyone had heard him do either on the football field or in the streets. Today his crew howled long and loud. The chilling sound echoed through the neighborhood. After he'd taken it all in, their new Alpha reared back and added his distinctive powerful howl that promised retribution.

Hannibal signaled to the DJ to crank it back up, and the music throbbed again with Big Sean's *My Last*. He smiled. His crew was ready for a war meant to get the cowards who killed their King.

Before anyone got too wasted, Hannibal pulled every one of his captains into his den and held a brief sit down. He explained what he wanted from them, what he had for them, and the course of how he wanted things to go down. They were to report to directly to Silas their statuses and needs, so Silas could bring that all back to him, and Hannibal promised to take care of them.

"This is gon prolly slow our money down, gentlemen, but this shit won't last long. Them punk asses will fold, and we'll get the nigga that pulled the trigger on App. With what we bout to do to them, they'll give his ass up in a minute, feel me? Don't worry about your corners. Keep an eye on your stash houses, but don't sweat them corners. Our money is right, so we can afford to take those losses for a few, ya'll feel me?"

Everyone nodded in agreement.

"Good. Back to the party. Enjoy yourselves."

After everyone filed out of the room, Hannibal stood and went to his best friend's urn and whispered, "Company's comin soon, cuz."

Uncle Wolf then headed down to his basement to check on the kids and see if they wanted ice cream.

31

Blake Connors did what he usually did each morning. He grabbed a bowl of cereal and parked his ass in front of his TV to watch cartoons until the spoon had scooped every last crumb from the puddle of colored milk. His mind devoured the animations like he devoured his sugar-laden breakfast. He studied the lines, the splashes of color, and the characters movements. It didn't matter which cartoon he watched. The art form fascinated him.

At just eleven, Blake had carried the household responsibilities. His mother had suffered from a myriad of medical ailments, which hadn't allowed her to work. The worst of her challenges had been her chronic asthma. When a neighbor had told Blake's mother that ginger might help ease her breathing, Blake had been determined to get his mother the spice.

"Alls you need is some ginger, right, mama?" he had asked, taking her soft hand.

His mother had looked at him with watery brown eyes that were the size of fifty-cent pieces and nodded as she took another wheezing breath.

He searched her face, and her listlessness only increased his resolve. "All right," he said. "I gotta go to the nice store across town cuz they not gonna have that over here. I'm gonna go and come back as fast as I can. Okay, momma?"

That was the last time he'd seen his mother alive. After the nasty store manager had pulled the small tin of ground ginger from his pocket, the old man had refused to listen to Blake's promise to return the next day to work it off. Instead he'd called the police. When the officers sauntered into the manager's office and pulled out his handcuffs, Blake smacked one of the cops as he fought to escape and get back to his mother. The police hadn't asked any more questions and had simply taken him into custody, which led to a standard juvenile detention sentence of ninety days for a first timer. A little less than a month later a frazzled social worker visited to tell him that his mother had passed away. When she'd begun to question him about next of kin, he'd simply walked away from her and returned to his bunk.

Blake was never the same. He'd stayed to himself, and with every day the little bit of light left in him flickered and faded further away. The larger, more hardened teens in his block had tormented him, breaking his pencils and tearing up his artwork.

One afternoon when another altercation started over his drawings, Blake had had enough. As he balled up his little fists tighter and prepared to stand his ground against the teens that surrounded him, an inmate he hadn't seen before approached the group.

The older boy lightly tapped the lead bully's shoulder with his bandaged hand and gave the ringleader a bemused look that sent the gang scattering. As he approached Blake, he raised his hands in surrender. "Hey, lil man. Be cool. I ain't gonna hurt ya. I'm Frank" Moving slowly toward the distrustful boy, Frank studied the destroyed drawings on the floor and after a few tense minutes picked them up and offered them to Blake. "Not bad. Not bad at all. You got skills. I like the horse one. How long you been drawing?"

A feral Blake snatched his drawings from Frank never taking his eyes off him.

"Look lil man, everything that happened before today stops today. Ain't no one gon touch you again, and if they do tell me, and I'll deal wit em."

"Whatchu want?" Blake asked suspiciously.

The teenager chuckled. "Can you do Batman? I like Batman. Errbody else likes Superman. Fuck Superman. Can you handle that?"

"That's it? That's all you want?"

"That's it. We gotta deal?" he asked extending his hand.

"Fuck Superman," Blake said as he shook Frank's hand.

From that day until the morning of Frank's release Blake basked in the older boy's shadow, and before Frank left juvie he gave word that the boy was still under his protection.

Thirty-two uneventful days later, Frank was the only one waiting when Blake walked out of the juvenile center. Frank secured Blake an apartment in one of Leonard's buildings and gave him a job. He taught the boy how to cut, cook, and bag product as well as how to sell, spot a cop, hide the stash, and handle himself in the streets. When Blake was older Frank taught him how to drive and shoot.

Now nineteen and standing at a lanky six-one and blessed with a baby face, Blake still sketched when he had the time, but it was only a hobby. Dropping his cereal bowl in the sink he headed out to do his afternoon rounds. As the stereo bumped with one of his favorite songs he cruised in his 2012 Honda Accord over to Romare's to pick up the day's supply and deliver it to Frank's corners.

Frank greeted Blake at the door with a fist bump.

"Whattup, boy? You good?"

"Can't complain. You straight?"

"Everything's good here. What was you singin to in the car just now?" Frank asked with a rare curve of his lips.

Blake laughed. "I went old school today, the Gap Band's *Burn Rubber*."

"Ahhhh a classic fo sho," Frank said as he reached under the bar and placed six packages in front of Blake. "But is he saying 'Burn rubber on me, Charlie' or 'Charlene'?"

"Hell if I know. I think it's 'Charlie'."

"Yeah but that don't make no sense, does it?"

"Not really but I gave up trying to figure that shit out long ago. I sings it as I hears it."

"You mean you try singin it as you hear it. Way you sing, the whole world knows you ain't hearin them songs right," Frank said with a slight chuckle.

"Why you hatin?" Blake asked with a smile.

"Am I lyin?"

"Nah, but one day I'm a sound good. Be up on one a dem singing shows and shit. Watch."

"That's the spirit. Let me know when that happens, so I know to sell my TV," Frank said.

"No love in the club."

"Whatever, nigga. Here." Frank handed Blake an envelope. "That's your usual plus a little extra for the way you handled yourself in that kitchen."

Blake nodded and tucked the envelope away before he grabbed the packages, stuffing them in a plain black gym bag. He headed for the door, but before he got passed the end of the bar, he stopped and looked back at Frank with a furrowed brow.

"Whattup?" Frank asked.

"Remember back in juvie when we met?"

"Yeah, of course."

"Why'd you look out for me?"

Frank shook his head and chuckled to himself. "I done already told you this like a thousand times, lil man."

"Yeah but sometimes the answers change."

Frank walked up to Blake and searched the younger man's face. "Like I told you, I saw a little of me in your scrawny ass. I never had a little brother, and you looked like you could use an older one. Besides, I really wanted a Batman drawing."

"I did need a older brother, Frank," Blake said as he gave Fred a grateful pound and walked out the door. "Fuck Superman."

"Fuck Superman," Frank repeated their standard goodbye.

The temperature climbed as Blake made his rounds through the mazy streets of the South Side. Hot and humid, people left their stuffy homes to sit on porches, and the kids escaped outdoors to play in the johnny pump or find a sprinkler in the park to cool off under. Blake loved the summer. As he crisscrossed through neighborhoods the weather allowed him to chitchat with the ladies, laugh with the kids, and catch up with the fellas.

After Blake's third stop, he stepped once again to his latest infatuation, a petite young lady with flawless milk chocolate skin he'd been eyeing a while. For over a month he'd unsuccessfully tried to get her attention, but every time he stopped at the curb to say hello, she would hardly even look his way let alone speak to him. However, today was his lucky day. She'd finally given in and replied with a hello. That was all the opening he needed, and after making her laugh a few times, she broke down and passed him her number. Smiling broadly, Blake promised to call her that night before he sped off to finish his last stops as his stereo blasted *If It Isn't Love* by New Edition.

Crooning the last notes with Ralph Tresvant, Blake rolled up on his next drop, a run-down little corner market that sold more Mad Dog and cigarettes than bread and milk. Blake hopped out of his car whistling as he considered what he might say tonight when he called her.

Blake had opened the store's door to the usual chorus of bells attached to the broken handle when he heard someone shout his name. The lanky teen spun with a smile and was met with gunfire that shattered the summertime sounds of the ice cream truck melody and playing kids. An onslaught of bullets rained down on the corner store with such relentlessness that no one stood a chance. Blake was cut to shreds. Bullets pierced his chest and chewed up his baby face as he was blasted back through the store's door. The young clerk behind the counter ducked and prayed to Allah while those who ran from the corner took shots in the back. Pools of blood spread quickly over the hot pavement of the sidewalk, framing bodies under the scorching summer sun.

Hannibal confidently stepped out of the lead car. A mask hid his face, and a baseball cap covered his head in case someone foolishly whipped out their cell phones with the intent to make this the next viral video sensation. With spray can in hand, he painted the nearest wall with brilliant red letters as one of his boys grabbed the gym bag out of Blake's car. Hannibal quickly surveyed the street justice he and his crew had served up and swallowed the urge to unleash his distinctive howl of triumph. Satisfied with the carnage, he scrambled back into his ride and the three cars peeled off in different directions.

Frank and Stony were in Romare's office when they got word. Frank shouted for Stony to stay put and lit out in his BMW. As he flew over the crumbling Youngstown streets, Frank tried unsuccessfully to reach Blake on his cell or his boy at the market. Ten minutes later he understood why.

Emergency vehicles surrounded the corner. Frank jumped out and sprinted passed the yellow tape. When he spotted Blake's car, his pace slowed. His jaw clenched and his nostrils flared as he scoured the scene. Bodies littered the sidewalk, and he knew everyone was dead. Just as he knew his product and money were gone as well. He searched for Blake and in the bullet riddled doorway, he found his lifeless little brother as a cop stood over him taking pictures. Frank turned away and closed his eyes. His hands fisted, craving someone or something to destroy. When he opened his eyes, he found the message left for him. On the bright yellow wall pockmarked by bullets were two words that gave Frank all the information he needed.

Following the police officer's demands to get behind the tape, Frank left the corner for the authorities to find their answers. He had his, and as he drove back to Romare's, he left the red scrawled words "FOR APP!" in his rear view mirror.

"Fuck Superman," he whispered.

That evening a shy young girl never wandered far from her phone as she waited for a call that never came.

The war had begun.

32

For the rest of the week Stony and Frank kept most of their men off the streets. Some corner and street business still went on, but Frank made sure his boys weren't caught sleeping again and that no one made a move alone. They also packed enough firepower to hold off a military platoon for a few days if needed.

Thursday brought the first of several funerals, and since Blake had no family, Frank solely handled the details and expenses. Once Frank, Stony, and their crew had paid their respects, the partners hustled back to their strategy session. Every hour counted. They had essentially turned Stony's office into a war room where they debated moves and potential countermoves. Unfortunately they'd yet to come up with a plan Stony would sign off on.

With a sigh Stony rubbed his temple as he attempted once again to reason with his partner. "No, Frank, there will be none of that."

Frank continued to analyze the local street maps layering the coffee table. "Why the fuck not?" he yelled in a rare sign of impatience. "It could work, and we could end this shit before it gets started."

"Fuck is wrong with you? I've never seen you this...crazed. I know you're upset about Blake but dynamite? Really? Youngstown may be a crumbling town, but it ain't motherfuckin Middle East."

"You sure about that, Stone? Blake's closed casket puts you on the wrong side of that fuckin argument."

"YOU knew this was coming, Frank. You warned me yourself. The Wolf didn't waste a damn day. We need to figure out what to do, but we can't start throwing fucking dynamite into the mix. Think about it for a minute and be reasonable. What kind of heat would that bring us if we start using explosives? Hell, even our own people will think we've lost our damn minds. We'd end up bombed out of here like what happened to that group MOVE in Philly. Remember them? No, we'll stick with guns and ammo to handle them jackasses."

Frank slowly paced the length of Stony's plush office like a caged predator as he ran through other strike options. "Appleton's crew jumped Earl at Chico's, right?" asked Frank.

"Yeah, why?"

"That was a truce spot. They violated." Frank hard gaze turned to meet Stony's. "So all safe spots are up for grabs then? Is that what they saying?"

"They just shot up one of our corners," Stony stated, "so I don't think they give a damn about safe spots right now."

"Then we shouldn't either, right?"

Stony considered Frank's implications. Scattered across town were a dozen "truce" spots where any beef between rival crews and gangs was momentarily squashed. These included most of the barbershops, a few grocery stores, the mall, two pizzerias, the hospitals, and Chico's sneaker store. These safe zones allowed everyone to handle basic necessities in peace, helped the "mom and pop" businesses, and kept collateral damage from rival skirmishes to a minimum. "Apparently not," Stony said.

"Cool," Frank said with a sadistic look of satisfaction, which made Stony's chest tighten with dread.

"What are you thinking?" Stony asked.

"A little get back, my man. Just a little get back."

33

Smith's, the iconic South Side neighborhood landmark, had been around since the sixties and still had the best barbers and the best conversation in a 60-mile radius. Men and boys flocked there not just from the South Side but from all over the Youngstown and outer areas as well. Some folks, typically the old timers, hung out there during the day simply for the entertainment of dispensing whatever knowledge they had on the uninitiated. For as long as anyone could remember, Smith's was a truce spot, where a soldier from one crew could drop his sword and shield and chill with a rival from another crew without a skirmish.

Occasionally tempers flared, but the seasoned barbers did their best to keep the peace and shut down drama with laughter and jokes. If that failed they didn't hesitate to kick out anyone who stepped out of line. If any soldier got the boot, truce spot rules gave him ten minutes to leave the area, or he was fair game, and no one would lift a finger to help him.

About a half hour before closing, Silas's younger brother, Vincent, strolled into Smith's wearing his brother's off-limits Wolf's Den t-shirt that he'd "borrowed" that morning. He held the door as another young man exited with a smooth scalp and face smelling of sweet jojoba oil.

With a quick head nod to Vincent, the exiting teen didn't hesitate to dial Frank's number before he took off for home.

Ten minutes later as Silas' brother sat down in the front chair, a man in a ski mask purposefully strode into the shop, calmly raised his gun, and blasted a hole in the boy's heart at point blank range. Without any fanfare he left and disappeared. The fatal assault was over in seconds.

The handful of men left unharmed stared in silent horror at the dying teen's ripped open chest as the heavy flow of blood splattered onto the scuffed white linoleum floor. There was nothing anyone could do. Once their initial shock faded, a few called 9-1-1, others called their wives or girlfriends, and someone called Silas.

Word spread like bacteria in an open wound. The safe zones were no more.

34

Later Thursday night Percy strolled into Romare's and marveled at the subdued vibe. Usually his short wiry frame had to fight the crowd to get to the bar and grab a stool, but with tonight's lack of patrons he had his choice. He took up a seat down from Turk and ordered a rum and coke.

Turk placed his drink in front of him and stood still to catch a few plays of the game.

"What's up in here tonight? It ain't never this dead," Percy said craning his neck to catch a glimpse at the girl on the pole in the back.

"Yeah, I know, but I'm surprised you ain't heard."

"Heard what?"

"A war done started. Black boys killin other Black boys over some bullshit."

Percy suddenly lost all interest in the stripper and gave old Turk his full attention. "What? Was that corner shooting part of that? I heard about that on the news couple a days ago."

"Oh yeah. Damn shame dat was. They got that boy Blake in dat one, and I really liked him. He got chewed up so bad the lil nigga had to have a closed casket."

"Damn. Yeah, I heard about that too. Knew nothing bout no war though." Percy glanced around at the handful of quiet patrons. "I guess that explains the low turnout up in here."

"Hmph, don't nobody wanna get caught up in the middle a some shit and git themselves shot just cause dey wanted a drink or ta see some tits and ass. Know what I mean?"

"I hear that. I'm wondering what the fuck I'm still sitting here for actually," Percy said with a nervous chuckle.

Turk waved his hand in dismissal. "Don't be sweatin that. You safe here. Damn suicide to hit dis place. Sides, it's the last safe place left."

"Whatchu you mean?"

"All the safe zones there was? Hmph…not no more, not after that boy got shot at da barber shop tonight. Now everywhere be fair game," Turk said shaking his head. "Leonard prolly rollin over in his grave at this mess."

Percy frowned wondering if he should take his chances and head back to Chicago before this job for Florida got him killed. He took a casual glance around and then asked almost under his breath, "You hear anything?"

Turk's leaned against the bar to get a little closer and shook his head. "With all this damn drama, I ain't heard nothin but war plans. I'm listenin though," he said as he strolled away. "Gettin too old for this fool craziness. Too damn old."

"Fuck," Percy said to himself and took a long swig of his drink. "Me too."

35

Lily's head swam as she rang up another sale and glanced wearily at the long line of customers still waiting. Women of all ages had jammed Lady Foot Locker all day, and even though it was a late Friday afternoon, she still hadn't had her lunch break. She didn't understand the rush, but in the wonderful world of retail, she'd learned never to question the ebb and flow of the consumer. With a winning smile, she welcomed them in and helped them as quickly as she could before she sent them on their way. If she had a moment to step outside her store, she would have seen that the entire mall buzzed and was ready to burst at the seams.

As another co-worker took over cashier duties, Lily shifted back on the floor. Exhaustion dragged at her, but she kept the smile on her face and the pleasantness in her voice because she knew soon she would be out of there.

Seven more days and I will be out of this store, out of this mall, and out of Ohio. Those words were her mantra. The thought of New York City alone was enough to make her smile in the face of every obnoxious, spoiled princess that wanted to try on every running shoe on the wall before she settled for just one pair. Lily daydreamed about film school and working toward her goal of being the first female of color to win an Academy Award for Best Director.

"Was there a sale put out, and you didn't warn me?" Lily asked her manager, Marsha, when they bumped into each other in the storeroom.

"This is that 'end of school' slash 'beginning of too much free time' season America has come to know as summer. This is normal."

"Yeah well, it's more like madness," Lily said moving back out to the floor with her arms full.

Lily fixed her expression and smiled. *Seven more days and I will be out of this store, out of this mall, and out of Ohio.* She quickly set down her boxes for her three different customers even as a fourth woman approached, dragging her truculent pigtailed child in one hand and holding a sneaker in the other. Before Lily could say she'd be right with her, the unmistakable sound of gunshots ripped through the mall. The din of humanity fell silent in shock as every employee and shopper froze, their eyes wide. They held their collective breath as the rapid booms continued to hammer. Lily's eyes darted to the front of the store. *They're close!*

As one, the masses cramming the mall snapped from their stunned disbelief. Lily pushed her customers toward the storeroom and the store's back exit. "Go! Go! Go!" People pushed passed her storefront in a cacophony of screams and yells that echoed through the concourses. In seconds her store emptied, but Lily turned her back on the safe retreat and stepped towards the chaos in the corridor.

Moved by some unforeseen force, Lily clung to the wall and crept towards the gunfire as a river of panicked men, stumbling women with toddlers, and teens surged past her. People crashed into her, but she managed to stay on her feet. Though fear gripped her gut, her only thought was on those who could be hurt. Soon the frantic crowd thinned, and when Lily glanced around the corner she watched as two young Black men backed out of Pistachio's and fired indiscriminately into the store. The shooters then stuffed their guns into their waistbands and took off in the direction of the food court.

Silence fell, and Lily dashed into Pistachio's. Broken glass, spent shells, and strewn clothing littered the dark carpet. Lily struggled to make sense of the chaos. Display signs and racks, some splattered with blood, blocked the aisles, and gunpowder hung thick in the air. Moans and cries came from every corner of the store as Lily staggered into the battlefield and desperately searched for her friends. Several bodies lay lifeless, two young Black men, a white teenage girl. An older woman lay unseeing as her son sat silently next to her in shock.

Lily choked back a scream and dialed 9-1-1 with trembling hands. Then she saw her. A foot away on the other side of a clothing rack, Clarissa lay on her back. Heavy blood spurted from a neck wound, and her eyes blinked rapidly as if trying to focus. Lily dropped to the injured girl's side and snatched up a shirt. She pressed it to the neck wound, trying in vain to stem the blood flow, but Clarissa quickly bled through the makeshift bandage. Frantic, Lily did the one thing she could think of that might save Clarissa's life.

The operator finally came online, and with a blood soaked hand Lily put her phone on speaker. As she lifted the girl's head and placed it on her lap, Lily struggled to speak.

"Yes, help, we need help at…at the mall. Sh…she needs help. P…please. She's been shot!"

"We have people on the way. Are you hurt? Can you tell me where you are?"

"No, I wasn't…uhhh I wasn't here. I'm at Pistachio's. Please…just get here! She's dying!"

"We're on our way, sweetie. You hang on now. You hang on, okay?"

Lily never answered her. She focused instead on how Clarissa's eyes turned glassy and her blinking slowed until her eyes eventually closed.

"No, no, no. Clarissa! Come on. Stay with me," Lily pleaded through tears. "PLEASE STAY WITH ME!"

Amidst the whirling lights of a squadron of patrol cars and emergency vehicles, Lily sat on the back step of an ambulance, as an EMT looked her over. In a monotone voice she again explained that the blood on her clothes wasn't hers. The examiner warned her about shock and released her but routed her towards the police command center where eager investigators pushed for statements. Lily nodded and walked away wrapped in a blanket. With numb legs she stumbled over to the line of witnesses waiting to be interviewed.

Exhaustion crashed like a wave over Lily's body as her mind tried to recall the details of the last hour. The one thing she did remember vividly was Clarissa—beautiful, vibrant, strong Clarissa—had bled out and had taken her last breath in her arms. The experience had been nothing like the movies. The distinct metallic smell of blood had overwhelmed her senses.

Lily had shoved her finger into Clarissa's neck in the hopes that it would somehow save her life, but the relentless flow of blood continued to pulse until it simply oozed like slowly poured maple syrup. Starring sightlessly ahead, she moved forward a few steps in line. *It's a weird thing, hearing someone take their last breath, feeling their last heartbeat.*

Lily shook herself from her thoughts. Her body screamed to collapse. *Gotta get home soon.* She pulled out her blood-smeared phone and called the only person she could think to call. *He needs to know about Clarissa,* she thought. *Everyone does.* He answered on the third ring, but her heart sank, and a sob clawed in her throat. He was high again. She could hear it in his speech.

She coughed hard. "Charlie. It's Lily."

"I know, baby. Your cuteness comes up on my phone when you call me. You forget that or something? I know you think I'm a little slow and all, but I ain't that slow," he said before breaking out in a low chuckle.

She could hear Gavin and Chad's laughter in the background. She rubbed her head before pulling the blanket tighter around herself. "I…I have something to tell you."

"Is it important? Cause I'm kinda busy…I'm…kicking Chad's ass in this game and–"

"Yes, Charlie. It's important," she interrupted. Her calm voice barely rose above a whisper. "Clarissa is dead."

"Huh? What you say?" Charlie asked while yelling at Chad to get off of him. "Speak up, Lils. I didn't hear you. Sounded like you said someone was dead. Who's dead?"

"Clarissa." She took another step forward. *Just a little longer. A little longer.*

Charlie laughed again. "Clarissa ain't dead. She's at the mall. Wait…did she say something to upset you, baby. I thought we settled this. You know you're the President of my fan club."

Lily sighed and fought back another round of tears. "Turn on your TV, Charlie."

"Ummmmm…okay. Hold please," he said in the same tone an operator would use.

She heard Chad complain that the "rice and bean queen" had interrupted their game, but she was too numb to care. Charlie scuffling with his friend and ordering him to shut the fuck up only heightened her impatience. Then she heard one of the local news stations come across his television, and the boys finally shut up and paid attention.

"Five dead and many more wounded from a vicious shooting at the mall in Boardman this afternoon. Authorities are at the scene…"

This is definitely going to ruin their high, Lily thought. "Charlie, I have to go." She was next to talk to the police, and she finally thought to call her mother. "But I need you to come get me. I need a ride home."

"Lily…wait…are you okay?"

"Yes…no…Charlie, just come and get me, please."

"I'm on my way, Lils," he said.

She hung up and sat down in front of a rotund cop at one of the rickety dining tables in the food court.

"I'm Officer Blanton. Can I have your name please?"

"Lily. Lilibeth Fernandez," she whispered.

"How are you doing tonight, Lily?"

Lily looked at Officer Blanton and with dead eyes asked, "What do you think?" *Out of this store, out of this mall, and OUT of Ohio.*

36

Early Saturday evening, Hannibal and Monique stormed into The Wolf's Den. Their foul moods radiated off them like summer heat off pavement. They spoke to no one, and at a glance everyone knew not to speak to them. Monique peeled away towards the boxing ring, her heeled boots clicking a sharp staccato on the cement floor, while Hannibal stalked past the equipment to his office. Silas silently stood sentry, grim and waiting. Hannibal's second hadn't slept in days since his brother's murder at the barbershop, and he admired him for being there.

"You good?" Hannibal asked.

"Best I can considerin, you know."

"I feel you. You or your peoples need anything?" Hannibal asked quietly.

"Naa, we good."

Hannibal nodded to the office. "They in there?"

Silas nodded.

Hannibal's mood grew even darker. When he walked into his office to confront two young members of his crew, he was The Wolf. They both fidgeted in their seats, and one looked like he needed to go to the bathroom. The Wolf stood and glared as they gazed at their sneakers seemingly shocked that they were even wearing something on their feet.

"One of ya'll better tell me why," he said when he finally spoke.

The two boys looked at each other and then back at their feet.

The Wolf roared. "I know you niggas heard me! Ya'll better speak, dammit. SAY SOMETHING!"

The boys jumped in their seats, and one finally mumbled something barely above a whisper.

"Speak up. I can't hear you! Tell me why you two dumb asses shot up the fucking mall!"

"We…we was in the store see, and…," started the boy who had to use the bathroom.

"And…one a dem South Side niggas came in. He was talkin to da girl behind the counter," the second boy said.

"AND?"

"And she saw us starin and told him, and he turned and saw us and flashed us," bathroom boy said.

The Wolf growled. "And so because he flashed you his heat, you two dumb niggas shot up the entire fucking store and killed all dem people?"

Both boys noticeably began to shake. When they didn't answer, Hannibal sat and broke down what was next. "It's punishment time. You know that right? We don't go around shootin at mothafuckas while people, specially WHITE people are around. That bullshit ya'll did yesterday is costin me big time, so now it's gotta cost you. You got two choices, something you ain't give them people in that store. You can sit on the sidelines, see no action for three months, make no money for three months, get no ass for three months, nothing, you feel me? LOCK DOWN! Pelican Bay type shit. And you be lucky I don't cancel your fucking cable. House arrest, feel me?"

The two boys nodded like bobbleheads.

Hannibal got to his feet. "Or you can get in the ring with me for three minutes, and after that, it's business as usual. You got thirty seconds to decide," he said and left the room.

"Silas, bring em over to the ring in a minute," Hannibal said and climbed into the ring with Monique, who sat on a corner stool in silent fury.

"Well?" she asked.

"They scared shitless."

"Good, they should be. They tell you why they did it?"

"They saw some South Side nigga, and something jumped off. I don't know."

"So all of those people are dead because they saw someone from the South Side? I'm letting you know now, if they choose to get in here with you, I'm using the broken stopwatch."

Hannibal smiled down at his fiery chocolate hellion and kissed her. The broken stopwatch took rounds passed the standard three minutes and into the five to six minute range.

Silas marched the two boys ringside. Monique and Hannibal climbed out of the ring and sat on the apron. Bathroom boy chose lockdown, but the other chose the ring. Hannibal's surprise didn't register. He simply stood up and removed his shirt.

The boy swallowed hard and instantly changed his mind.

"Smart choice," Hannibal said. Suddenly and with blinding sped, The Wolf reached out and tried to snatch the soul out of bathroom boy. The vicious smack echoed through the gym like a gunshot, and the boy spun like a broken top before he crumpled to the floor. Hannibal pounced and pinned him face down to the cold cement. "Right or left, homie?"

"Wh...what?" the stunned kid asked.

"Right or left hand?"

With blood starting to trickle from his nose, bathroom boy answered with a whimper. "Right."

Hannibal looked at Monique who didn't hesitate. She began to stomp on the boy's right hand with her boot until they heard several bones snap. His screams fell on deaf ears. "No video games neither, bitch," Hannibal whispered in his ear. He then spun on the other boy Silas had by the shirt.

"You tryin ta run? Huh? Is that what you tryin to do?" Before boy number two could answer Hannibal slapped him as hard as he could sending the boy flailing to the floor and was on him the second he landed. "Right or left, nigga?"

"Right," he said as his face began to swell. Monique repeated her vicious dance, and the second boy's shouts mixed with the other's whimpering moans.

"Hand over them phones. NOW!"

They complied.

"Silas, take these two to the hospital and then home. You two fuck up again, next time I won't be so nice. Now get the fuck outta my face."

When they were alone, Monique spoke first. "They deserved it."

"I know."

"They deserved more honestly," she said.

"I know, Mo."

"That girl could have been me."

"I know. I know," he said quietly.

37

Dressed in their Sunday best, Charlie, Lily, Gavin, and Chad sat in the last pew of Clarissa and her family's Baptist church. Mourners pressed into the airy nave, lining the walls and standing in the back foyer. The church held a pungent sweet smell thanks to the many stunning floral arrangements, and the burgundy and gold clad choir sang a rousing rendition of *Goin' Up Yonder* that brought the entire church to their feet. Lily, however, stayed seated, clutching tissues and wondering why she had come.

As the good Reverend Dr. Powell dramatically approached the pulpit, Lily's eyes roved over the throng of people who had gathered. At times she'd catch someone looking her way and pointing, and her stomach would flutter uncomfortably. There was so much love in the room for Clarissa that Lily felt guilty having even light-heartedly marked the track star as competition.

During Reverend Powell's eulogy, he praised Clarissa and reminisced about her as a little pigtailed, scrawny, knock-kneed girl. "When I got the news that Clarissa, this wonderful blessing of a child, had been taken from us I didn't believe it. I thought it was a cruel lie. I thought it was some evil joke. And did something I find myself doing far too often these days. I cried."

Clutching his Bible and raising it to the ceiling, the portly preacher continued. "I broke down. I say. I broke down...and something broke in me," he said as he bowed his head, his voice barely above a whisper, "because she was what all the youngsters of my flock are to me...precious flowers in my garden." The preacher lifted his head as his sweat and tears mixed together, and when he spoke again his voice boomed. "And sadly someone snuck into MY garden and viciously cut this rose from the stem before she ever...got the chance...to fully bloom."

The Reverend wiped his face before he launched into an emotional litany of what Clarissa could have done had her life not been cut short from the Black on Black violence plaguing the streets.

When he came to the end, the only sounds that could be heard were the muffled sobs of Clarissa's mother.

Reverend Powell slowly searched the many faces in the sanctuary. Lily fidgeted still trying to ignore the pit in her stomach when the Reverend locked eyes with her. His piercing stare made it difficult to breathe.

"Now ladies and gentlemen, brothers and sisters, with us today…is an angel. A young lady who did everything she could to save our Clarissa's life."

Lily began to tremble at the unexpected turn in the eulogy and bowed her head so that her hair shielded her face. She wished she could disappear and instead grabbed Charlie's hand and held on as if it could save her life.

"This young lady, instead of running away when she heard the thunderous gunshots, walked towards them. Church did you hear ME? I don't think you heard me. I SAID…she bravely walked TOWARDS the violence to help those in need and almost saved…our rose." The Reverend somberly gestured to the casket. "This brave young lady put the lives of others…ahead…of her own. This angel is Lilibeth Fernandez."

At the mention of her name, Lily jumped as if she'd been hit with a hundred volts of electricity. Every eye shifted to her, and she buried her face in her hands as Charlie took her in his arms. She began to hyperventilate.

"I want Ms. Fernandez to know that Clarissa's family, I, and indeed this ENTIRE congregation are grateful for everything she did that fateful day to help our darling Clarissa. We will forever love you, Lily. Let the church say 'Thank you.'"

"Thank you!"

"Let the church say 'Amen.'"

"Amen!"

With the words of the Reverend ringing in her ears and the memory of that day still haunting her, Lily wrenched free of Charlie and blindly staggered from the pew. She pushed through those standing while Charlie gave chase. Together they burst outside into a bright quiet midday sun.

Charlie reached out and grabbed her before she wandered into the street.

She fought his hold. "I can't…I…I gotta…get outta here," she gasped.

"I know. I know," he said as tenderly as he could. "Come with me." Charlie gently took her hand and led her to his car. He helped her in and buckled her up before driving from the church as fast as he could. For long minutes he listened as Lily sobbed. His stomach clenched, and suddenly his suit felt too constricting. He'd never seen Lily like this. She was always so strong, so in control. He hurt because she did. He didn't know what he could do for her, but he knew where he could take her.

Eventually, she began to calm down and breathe regularly. "Where are we going?" she finally whispered after blowing her nose.

"I have a place in mind. Just relax, Lils," he said. For the rest of the ride Lily stared out the window in silence while Charlie drove as smooth as he could. Twenty minutes later Charlie had them at Lily's spot on the edge of Berlin Lake. He shut off the car, and the two held hands. A lone motorboat occasionally interrupted the calming sounds of the lapping lake.

After almost an hour without a word Lily looked at him and gave him a weak smile. Her red puffy eyes still held the echo of pain and sorrow. "You remembered."

"Of course. How could I forget, Lils?"

"Well kudos, Charles Jackson. Sometimes, buster, you boggle the mind, you know that?"

"What do you mean?"

She inhaled deeply before replying. "One moment you are the most charming, most compassionate, and most intelligent guy I know. The next you're a smoked out pothead whose biggest priority is a video game."

Charlie grimaced and broke eye contact. He didn't like that she was essentially right.

"I never know which Charles I'm going to get from one day to the next." Lily said through a sniffle. "That's so frustrating."

He swallowed his instinctive smartass remark and faced his own shame. "I don't mean to frustrate you, Lily."

"I know you don't. You're too stupid to get it, and I see that now."

"I'm not stupid, and what don't I get?" He watched a sad smile trace her lips.

"I love you, Charles," she said leaning her head back. "I am in love with you, but I am leaving this place behind, the place where I grew up, and you, who I love, because neither convinced me to stay."

"You...you love me?"

She stared off into the distance and smiled again for a moment softly. "I have loved you ever since I read that essay you wrote about your mother."

Charlie fell silent. He had known she liked him but never suspected she felt that strongly. *Fuck. Love? I like her and all but love? I don't even know what that feels like. Besides she's leaving.* Charlie shook his head and tried to re-focus. Lily's news was an unexpected surprise. "Look, Lils, you were leaving anyway to go to film school in New York."

She laughed mournfully. "You idiot. I could have gone to Ohio University or any of the other film schools in the area. Granted there is nothing like NYU, but I could have stayed in state and been just as happy."

"I doubt that seriously," Charlie said with a bite to his tone.

She pulled her hand from his. "You seriously don't get it. You know, if I could have called someone else to take me home from the mall that night I would have."

"Then why did you call me?"

"Because I wanted...no...I needed...sober Charles that night, not the high or baked or whatever you call it version. I don't like that Charles, the one that made picking New York so easy, but that's the one I got after I just had someone die in my arms and saw more blood and broken bodies than I'd ever thought I would. Dammit! I was so angry because when I needed sober Charles," she said as tears made their way down her face again, "he was nowhere to fucking be found. Instead I got smoked out Charles…and it broke my damn heart." She took a few deep breaths and calmed down. "You…you let me down."

Again Charlie fell silent.

"You actually disgusted me that night, Charles, and I didn't think I could ever feel that way about you. I was disgusted by those guys shooting into the store, disgusted that I couldn't stop her blood from pouring out of Clarissa's neck, disgusted that it took them so long to get to us, and then finally I was disgusted by you, by the way you were when I saw you in the parking lot. I wanted you to hold me close, hold me tight, because I was broken, but you were high as a kite, so that never happened. Instead I had to put myself back together."

"Maybe you should lower your expectations of me," Charlie said, still on edge.

"Obviously.

"I'm not perfect, Lily. I never claimed to be, so try to remember that, please."

"I get it. Too bad you don't. I never expected you to be perfect. I only ever hoped you would try to be the better than what you pretend to be." She turned her head away. "Can you please take me home?" she whispered.

"Sure thing." He sat up straight and started the car. In half the time that it took for them to get to the lake from the church, Charlie pulled up in front of Lily's house.

She turned and searched his profile before she leaned over to kiss his cheek. After she climbed out she turned back once more. "Thanks for getting me out of there. I love you, Charles, and I'm sorry your friend died."

Charlie nodded but refused to meet her eyes and tried to keep himself from exploding. He doubted she was sorry, but he kept that to himself. After she quietly closed the door, he made a U-turn and sped towards home.

As he drove away, Lily knew she would never see Charles Jackson again.

38

"There's no other explanation. You must be an alien," Seth said lounging against the extra large down pillows of his king-sized bed thankful that it was Tuesday and that they had the day off.

Marta laughed at him as she pressed herself against his side and traced his naked chest with her perfectly manicured nails. "What are you talking about?"

"How have you lived in this city for as long as you have and never seen an IMAX movie?"

Marta shrugged. "First off, I'm busy. I've been busy damn near my entire life, so I never got the chance to look up and see what was out there. Secondly, since I was usually fighting most men off me I rarely got around to seeing these little treasures. Men were interested in other things instead of dragging me around the town."

"Would you like to see this 'little treasure,' Marta? Let me know because I'd hate to feel like I'm 'dragging you around the town' against your will."

"Okay, maybe 'dragging' was the wrong choice of word, baby. I'll be happy to see a…what kind of movie is it again?" she asked while slowly kissing his chest.

"IMAX."

"Yes, that's right, IMAX. Sounds big."

"It's huge."

"Well, there you go. You know how much I love big things," she said seductively as she slipped her hand under the sheet and across his hip.

"Woman, you are insatiable," Seth said as he closed his eyes with a sigh of contentment. "I so love Tuesday afternoons."

"Mmmmm…You and me both, baby," she whispered as she began to stroke him back to life. "What time is our IMAX movie?"

"5:30."

"Well there's more than enough time for a treat," she said and slid below the covers.

"There you go, reading my mind again."

Later that evening, after they'd enjoyed *The Perfect Season*, one of the best of the summer blockbusters, Seth was still laughing as they waited for their entrees. The handsome, confident couple sat tucked in a corner both at his favorite seafood restaurant, *City Crab*, a comfortable place devoid of any serious pretension but whose kitchen always sated his taste buds.

"You could have warned me you know," Marta said as she cut her eyes at him.

"What? And miss out on you dropping your popcorn when you saw the size of that screen for the first time? I wouldn't have missed that for the world," Seth said with a laugh. "Did I or did I not warn you it was huge this afternoon while we were in bed?"

"Yes, but that's a horrible description. It's so much huger than huge."

"Huger?" he asked raising an eyebrow.

She pursed her lips and laughed. "You know what I mean," she said, buttering her bread.

Over Alaskan king crab and fresh Maine lobster the two laughed, flirted, and feasted, sharing their dishes. They talked music, movies, politics, and even work, but that topic didn't last long.

After Seth paid the bill he asked, "You coming back to my place?"

"No, I need to go home for at least a night. Can you give me a ride?" she asked as she rose from the booth.

"I do believe I've given you several of those today. Fine by me if you want another one," Seth said with a dark hooded gaze as his hand squeezed her thigh.

"Mmmm…yes, you insatiable man, you have," she said tossing his earlier accusation back at him. "But I have to work tomorrow, and the owner can be a bit of a tyrant sometimes."

"I hate that bastard," Seth said making Marta chuckle. "But I'm sure you do your best to drive him crazy at times, so he has my sympathies."

Marta laughed turning heads thanks to its husky tone. "Touché, boss. Touché."

When they arrived at Marta's condo she offered Seth a drink, which he politely declined. After pouring half a glass of cabernet sauvignon, she turned on her stereo and curled up next to him on the plush leather couch. Kenny Lattimore's *For You* softly echoed throughout her place. She kicked off her heels and tucked her legs under her and leaned into him.

"There's something I want to ask you, Marta," Seth said playing with her hair.

"Uh-oh, this sounds serious," she said looking up at him with a smile on her face.

"I'm thinking we should move in together. What do you say?"

Stunned, Marta's glass stopped on its way to her lips. She sat up and searched Seth's eyes. She tried to recover the smile she'd lost at his unexpected suggestion, but it was gone. "Baby," she said when she finally found her voice, "I don't think that's a good idea."

She took a long sip of her wine, but Seth had noticed a slight tremor in her voice. "Why not?"

Marta shifted away from him. "We work together...see each other almost every day. To move in together could ruin what we have. What if you get tired of me? What if I get tired of you?"

Seth was super glued to his seat. He contemplated her questions. "Do you love me?"

"Of course I do. Don't be foolish," she said before she gulped what was left in her glass.

"Then what's keeping you from doing this?"

"Experience," she answered tightly. She rose and walked to the bar. This time she poured a full glass and took a deep swallow.

"You're constantly at my place, so I thought moving in together made sense."

"Usually it would but not here not now," she told him as she crossed her arms.

Seth leaned forward. "You didn't answer my question, Marta. What am I not getting? What am I not understanding? We've been together for years. Neither of us is getting any younger."

She exhaled sharply and raised her chin in a show of strength and defiance. "Look, baby, I am the kind of woman that loves her independence and moving in with someone, even someone as sexy as you, Seth, removes that independence, and that's not something I'm willing to part with right now." She waved her hand at him. "Ask me in a few months."

Seth's anger flashed at her casual dismissal. "I think it's time I go," he said as he stood up.

With a shaking hand she set her glass on the bar. "I'm sorry, baby."

"Save it. But answer me this. You doing me dirty?"

Marta raised her eyes to his. "While I know I've recently given you a reason to think that, Seth, you are the last man on the planet I would ever do dirty."

"That's good to know. You care enough not to fuck around on me but don't believe in me and us enough to live together. Got it."

She flinched at Seth's harsh words but said nothing.

"I'll see you tomorrow," Seth said leaving her where she stood. The front door slammed behind him.

Marta closed her eyes and wondered if she'd just made the biggest mistake of her life.

39

Percy once again took his nightly trek to Romare's. His hands gripped the steering wheel, and he craned his neck left and right searching for any hint of trouble he should avoid. *The last thing I need is to get shot. Florida got me out here knowing a nigga ain't got no health insurance. I can't afford no bullet hole.*

He'd spoken to Florida earlier. The conversation hadn't gone well.

"Florida, this crappy ass town has been a damn war zone for the last week. I'm done. I been shot before, and I ain't a fan of the experience. The South Side is the front lines, man! And the only person I got any rap with is the craggily old barkeep. While the man makes a serious drink, what's he gonna know about some damn art? I been at this for two weeks and ain't heard shit. Hell who the hell steals art in the hood anyway?" He had hoped his argument was compelling enough that Florida would let him off the hook, but there had been nothing but silence on the line. "Hello?"

"Oh…you're done whining? You know, Evil and I were taking bets on how long you'd go on. She lost, so she's going to be pissed at you. Now…somehow, my friend, you seem to have mistakenly come to the belief that you have a choice in this process. You don't. You owe me your life, and it's payback time. Somebody in that forgotten little town knows something, so shut up, listen, and get me what I need or getting shot by a stray bullet is going to be the least of your problems. Understand?"

Percy had slumped in his tattered armchair, resigned to his fate. Florida was serious, and his reach was long. "Yeah, I get it, man."

When he finally made it to Romare's he craved a drink like a house craved a roof. He ordered a double shot of Jack from a bartender he'd never seen before. Gulping it down, he felt steadier, and his hands quit shaking. He glanced around and realized that a good portion of the usual crowd had returned. Just as he was going to ask where Turk was, two hands grabbed him by the shoulders, and a drunk Turk greeted him with a wide gap toothed grin and an unsteady stance.

"What's up, man? You not working tonight?" Percy asked.

"Hell nah! It's ma birthday," he said in his distinct drawl. "Hey, you want gets summa ma birthday cake? Lemme get you a piece a cake," Turk slurred and disappeared in the crowd before Percy could stop him. Two minutes later he stumbled back to Percy balancing a brick size chunk of cake that barely fit on the plate. "Here ya go. Ahh shit, you needs a fork. Hol on."

Percy eyed and smelled the good-looking cake. The gooey glaze and honey brown crust started to make his mouth water even though he wasn't much of a cake fan. Turk returned with two plastic forks and clumsily handed one to Percy.

"What kind of cake is it, man? Don't look like no damn birthday cake to me." Percy said.

"Crazy rum cake, and the shit's strong. Cuz I knows ya like some rum I gots you a big piece," Turk said, pleased at his flawless logic.

"Who made it?"

"One of da pole girls. Got a crush on me I think. She got some daddy issues I spose, but she can make a damn good cake, my man. Dig in!"

Percy cut off a conservative piece and could smell the alcohol. *Crazy rum cake is right.* He put it in his mouth. "Holy shit, this is good!"

"I told you! Girl's got mad skills," Turk said with a wink.

"I don't wanna know. Anyway, happy birthday, man," Percy said and extended his hand. Turk pulled him close and gave him an unexpected hug.

"I gots something for you," whispered the old barkeep.

When Turk backed away he could see the confusion on Percy's face. "Come on outside wit me right quick," he said. "And bring da cake!"

Percy grabbed the cake and followed Turk out the side door into the warm summer night. The two men walked around the corner of the club, and Turk lit up a joint.

"I didn't know you smoked."

"Hey, it's my born day, so why not, ya know?"

"I hear you. So whattup?" Percy asked scooping up another piece of cake.

"Dat info you been lookin for, about that art thing?" Turk asked before he pulled on his joint.

Percy nodded.

The old man squinted trying to hold in as much of the drag as he could. "I gotta name."

Percy almost choked. "Get the fuck outta here."

"Yeah, some kid named Charlie."

"That's it? No last name, huh?"

"Dats all I got, but I think he the DA's kid or some shit," Turk said leaning against the building as his high took hold.

"Woah."

"Yeah, ain't dat some shit?"

Percy nodded his head again and shoveled in more cake. "Damn. These cats are crazy."

Turk nodded. "Leonard muss be losin his ever lovin mind up dere."

For the rest of the night Turk partied with friends and patrons alike, even climbing on stage for some pole dancing.

Between his double shot, the crazy rum cake and his relief of having some bit of information to give Florida, Percy indulged much more than he'd planned and took full advantage of the open bar from ten to eleven in honor of the birthday boy. He celebrated with the mostly naked ladies of the pole, spent more money than he should have, and did more drugs than he'd ever done in his life. Around midnight Percy found a nice dark corner behind a fake plant away from the festivities and began drifting off to sleep, but before sleep grabbed a hold of him two men sat down at the table next to him.

"You havin' fun, Stone?"

"This isn't about fun, Frank. Not for me anyway," Stone said.

"I know. Looks like your party idea worked. The loot is flowing in."

"Cash rules…"

"Everything around me," Frank finished. "I feel you, nigga."

"Turk is damn near family. I had to show him love, so this is good. Anyway, what's it looking like out there?"

"That mall shit got everything on lock. Nothing is moving at all. Cops pulling motherfuckas over just because they drivin," Frank said.

"Then until this get's settled we shut it all down."

"That's what I'm thinking."

"Good because like I told you last night," Stony said, "I want to get back on that thing with the Charlie kid."

"That Basquiat painting shit again?"

"Yeah. The exhibit will be in town soon. I need to get back on that horse, so hopefully all this will die down before then."

Frank's reply took a minute in coming, but the last thing Percy heard was, "No promises."

40

The next morning, Percy found himself in his bed still in his clothes. He vaguely remembered a bouncer kicking him out telling him he "didn't have to go home, but he had to get the hell outta there." After that it was all a blur. His head ached, but the pain wasn't as bad as it could have been when he considered how much he had drank and smoked last night.

He stripped out of his clothes and did his best to scrub last night out of his skin under the weak but thankfully hot shower. He remembered Turk had given him a name, same name he had overheard from the guys in the booth talking about the painting with the odd name. However his mind sputtered like an old engine that refused to turn over. He tried not to panic. After making a cup of strong coffee, he turned on his TV to watch the morning news. When Chuck, the local anchorman, came on the air, Percy bolted from his kitchen chair and grabbed the phone.

"Percy, you best not be shot or callin to whine again, nigga," Florida said by way of greeting.

"I got a name for you about that art thing."

"Yeah? Good news then. Let me have it."

"Some kid named Charlie is involved. Your boy Turk didn't have a last name, but I also heard two guys, some guys named Frank and Stone, talking about the mall shooting and how they were gonna have to shut down cause of the heat. Then one of em mentioned some Basket painting, and he said the name Charlie too."

"That's not much to go on, but it's a start. You ain't got nothing else?"

"Oh Turk did say something about this Charlie being the D.A.'s kid, but he was getting baked when he said that, so I don't know." Only silence buzzed in Percy's ear. "Hello?"

"Repeat that last part. I don't think I heard you right."

"I said he's supposed to be the son of the district attorney out here or some shit."

Florida sighed. "That's what I thought you said. These fools think they have heat on them now. If they try to make this happen they could bring us all down with them."

"I know. I know. They crazy out here, man."

"Okay. I'll look into this, but if you got this wrong, I swear I will find you, and I will let Evil hurt you. She already doesn't like you. You hear me?"

"I hear you Florida, but this is solid, man. Bedrock!" Percy immediately gripped his exploding head.

"Okay then, we even. Get out of town for a while because what's about to go down out there could be a bit hazardous to your health. You feel me?"

"Yeah, trust me. I feel you, but I ain't got no money to be getting out of town. My money ain't long like that," Percy said, hoping for a little sympathy.

"I'm gonna put you on with Evil. Tell her how much you need and where she can send it to. This is for a job well done, understand?"

"Yeah, man. Thanks!"

"Good, and don't get stupid with the amount. Hold on," Florida said and put Percy on hold. "EVIL!" When his thick juicy woman came to his door, Florida was tempted to keep Percy on hold for a few minutes but knew he had much bigger issues to handle. "Percy needs to get paid. Send him whatever he asks for but no more than the usual cap."

"Sure thing, sugar."

He leaned back in his squeaky chair to stare at the ceiling. The bigger shit was something he needed to deal with and quickly.

41

Florida spent the rest of the morning researching the DA's office and the war in Youngstown. He made calls and spoke to as many people as it took while Ivelisse scoured the Internet and social media.

The foundation of Florida's power rested on reliable information. He was blind without it, and he relished fresh news. Even gossip sufficed when all else failed. Information kept him in business. It kept him viable. It had even kept him alive at times. If someone wanted to know about someone, they came to Florida. If they wanted to know where to invest their money, they came to him. However, he understood his power was tenuous at best. Anyone could do their own homework, but for the most part, the majority of human beings had one thing in common. They were lazy.

Once Florida had the details, data, records, news clips, and photos, he munched down the last of his BLT and gulped the rest of his tequila-spiked coffee. He cleared his throat, steeled himself, and made the call he'd been dreading since he hung up with Percy.

"The Pearl. This is Paulie."

"Hey, Paul. It's Florida. How you doin, man?" Florida swore he heard a slight growl. He never had been able to establish a smooth rapport with this half of Harlem's infamous duo.

"What's up, Flo?"

Florida clenched his jaw in annoyance, but unlike Percy, he didn't reprimand the notorious hothead about the use of his hated nickname. "Is Seth there?"

"Not right now. He had to step out. You wanna leave a message, or you wanna call back?"

"I'll call back," he said before changing his mind. "You know what, on second thought, Paulie, let me go head and leave him a message."

Paulie sucked his teeth. "All right, hold on then." He returned to the line a few seconds later with pen and paper in hand. "Shoot."

"Let him know that there's plans being cooked up if not already in the works for an unsanctioned felonious art theft in Youngstown. If these fools make a mess of it, which I have no doubt they will, it could potentially bring down the network and–"

"Slow down, negro. Art theft? Since when does Youngstown have art worth stealing? And why you callin us with this bullshit anyway?"

Florida sighed. He really hated Paulie sometimes. "Look, you guys are still the heavy hitters of the network," Florida said attempting to stroke Paulie's ego. "I need at least one of you to intervene, but it may be better if Seth went."

Paulie's brow creased in confusion. "Why, Flo? Fuck is going on? Speak to me, negro."

After Florida explained why, Paulie was stunned. "Are you serious?"

"Unfortunately I am, very serious. I got two sources, who both say the same thing. I then spent all morning confirming the details. Sadly this ain't no joke. Talk to your boy and let me know what's what, Paul, after you do."

"We'll get back to you," was all Paulie said before slamming the phone on the bar. He leaned back in his chair and wondered what the future held for his best and only real friend.

"You okay, sweetie? Did you break the phone?" Tamara asked when she walked passed him carrying a rack of clean tumblers.

Paulie nodded to the young woman. "I don't know about the phone, but yeah, I'm fine. It's just life can definitely kick you in the teeth or the balls at the damnedest times. Just depends on whether you're standin or kneelin. The thing is…a man, a real man, he always gets kicked in the balls cause only boys live on their knees." He shook his head thinking of the news Florida had smacked him with. *Seth about to get kicked squarely in the balls,* he thought as Tamara leaned in and kissed his head. "Stop breaking stuff, sweetie," she cooed.

When Seth came through the door an hour later, Paulie slid a cognac snifter across the bar.

Seth eyeballed his partner. "Is it my birthday?" he asked setting a package next to the drink.

"Nope."

"You hit the lottery?"

"Nope."

"You gonna be a dad?"

"Hell no."

"You dying?"

"Nope."

"Am I dying?"

"Nope, not that I know of," Paulie said.

"Then what gives?" Seth asked as he brought the glass to his nose. "The expensive stuff, huh? What's going on, Paulie?" Seth pointedly asked his friend. "Is there a body in the sub-zero?"

"Let's go up to the office, man," Paulie said with a smile.

"I got more shit I have to bring in from the car."

"It can wait."

"But–"

"Seth, look at me," Paulie said softly grabbing a second snifter and the bottle of Martell Creation. "It can wait. Come on."

As he headed up to their office with Seth in tow, Paulie poked his head in the kitchen and ordered Roscoe to unload Seth's car and handle things for a bit. Once upstairs, Paulie closed the door with a quiet click.

"That uppity negro, Sunshine, called for you a little while ago. You know he's the only one that calls me Paul?" Paulie said taking a seat. "I hate that shit. Anyway…there's a problem in Youngstown we need to take care of. Sit down, man. Lemme explain."

The two men holed themselves in the office for two solid hours.

"Youngstown is going down faster than a prostitute to her knees," Seth said, rubbing the ache in his forehead.

"I can go if you want," Paulie said. "I would probably just end up killing somebody though. You're way more diplomatic than I am, old man."

Seth arched an eyebrow at his friend. "You think?"

"No question. How many times did you pull me back from the brink of adding another body to the Hudson River count? And most of those fools deserved to go bye-bye."

"Yeah, I know," Seth said as he sipped his second cognac.

"I'm all about spoon-feeding someone bullets cause I ain't got time for excuses. You at least hear them fools out before you feed em to the fishes. You're a better man than me, Seth, always have been, always will be."

"Well if I am, which I'm not sure I completely agree with you on that, then it's only because you've always had my back. That being said, I have to be the one to go. Besides, it'll do me good to get out of town for a while. I need to get away," Seth said.

"Why? What's up?"

"Just some shit with Marta," he sighed.

"You two kids all right?"

"Yeah. No. Fuck, man, I don't know," Seth said as Paulie stared at him. "I need some space so maybe this Ohio mess is what I need right now."

"When you leavin?"

"Tomorrow morning. You'll be all right here?" Seth asked.

"Oh, I can handle this place fine for a bit without you. Just don't be gone forever, motherfucka. It takes the damn fun outta things, and you might come back to a burnt out building. You know how I am with stress…and people," Paulie said darkly as he got up from the leather armchair.

"Lean on Marta and Roscoe," Seth said. "That kid knows the ins and outs of this place damn near as well as I do. He's smart. Let him do the grunt work. Challenge his ass. He'll thank you for it. Hell, he's been here a minute, so it's about time we gave him a promotion or something."

Paulie nodded. "I'll get right on that. See…you're such a people person."

Seth laughed as his partner walked out of the office leaving him alone with his thoughts. *Should I say something to Marta or leave that mess alone and go? I thought she'd jump at the chance to live together. Can't believe I misread that. Whatever, we can talk when I get back.* He sighed and took another sip of the expensive amber liquid. *Ohio is the last fucking place I ever expected to be.* He sighed. *I should probably clean my guns.*

42

The alarm clock blared at precisely 6:00 a.m. shattering the silence of his tranquil bedroom. Seth glanced absently at the digital display, surprised to see an hour had gone by since he'd woken. Thoughts of Marta and Ohio had made restful sleep hard to find. He stretched and did his best to stop dwelling on his impending road trip. *There's nothing more to plan for. It'll be what it'll be.* Marta proved harder to let go of. He casually leaned over and shut off the obnoxious sound.

After a quick shave and shower, Seth headed down to his kitchen in a black tracksuit, white t-shirt, and black sneakers to toast a bagel and down a cup of coffee. His bag sat next to the front door like a dog itching to get outside, and as he chewed he debated whether he should bring his other pistol. A small .28 stayed stashed in the Cadillac. Living the life he'd led, he always kept a piece in the car, and while Seth held the belief that a gun only increased the likelihood of trouble, he'd decided to take both his 9mm Glock and his snub nosed .45 along with extra clips. *In case I need to blow a hole through something or someone. 'Sides, I didn't clean it for nothing, and it's better to have and not need than to need and be shit out of luck.*

Twenty minutes later after he'd locked his place up tight and put his car in drive, his cell phone rang. It was Paulie.

"Where you at?"

"In the car, why?"

"Up and out early, huh?"

"Why wait?"

"I hear you. Just callin to remind you not to worry bout a thing over here. Everything will be cool, jack. I got this," Paulie said.

"I know you do. Now why don't you tell me why you really called?"

Paulie paused and sighed. "I want you to be careful, Seth. I know you think these ain't nothing but a buncha kids, but if you get into any trouble, your stubborn ass better call me."

"Cavalry?" Seth asked.

"Cavalry, motherfucka," Paulie answered.

Seth chuckled to himself. 'Cavalry' was a saying from their childhood. One day the biggest, baddest kid on their block had decided to bully a young scrawny, bigheaded Paulie for his baseball cards. When he'd knocked Paulie to the ground, the smaller boy had curled up into a fetal position to protect himself from a pummeling that never came. Instead he had looked up and found Seth toothlessly grinning at him. Seth had come up behind the bigger kid and whacked him in the head with a stickball bat knocking the bully out cold. The first words out of Seth's mouth as he reached down to help his new friend off the dirty sidewalk had been "Cavalry's here." They had used it ever since whenever help was needed.

"Well, let's hope I won't need it, but it's good to know it's still there just in case," Seth said with a smile.

"You packin?"

"Yeah."

"Real heat or that little .28?"

"I got the real thing too."

"Good, let's hope your diplomatic shit does the trick and you don't need em," Paulie said. "I love you, brah. Be careful."

"I'm always careful. Hey, do me a favor, don't tell Marta where I'm off to."

"Will do if that's what you want. Just know she's already on alert. She said you were actin kinda funny and asked me what was up. I told her you had some business to handle and would be out for a day or two. Hope that wasn't too much to say."

"Don't sweat it. I love you too, man. See you soon," Seth said and disconnected the call.

Crossing over the George Washington Bridge, he punched an address into his GPS. His four or five hour trip to Ohio would run him along I-80, making it pretty much a straight shot through Jersey and Pennsylvania to get him into the buckeye state by early afternoon.

Seth found Marvin Gaye's *Trouble Man* in his music collection and settled in for the long ride.

It'll be what it'll motherfuckin be.

43

With only a single stop for gas and a bite to eat, Seth pulled into the Youngstown suburb of Boardman around 2:00 p.m. Youngstown couldn't claim a single respectable hotel, so he'd opted for a three day reservation at the Best Western on the outskirts of town, thinking what he had to do wouldn't take any more time than that. Once he freshened up, he grabbed his gun and set out to get answers.

In less than two miles, Seth had a much clearer perspective on the tension in the area. A local cop had trailed him almost as soon as he'd pulled onto the main drag. Not knowing if the attention was due to his skin color or his New York license plate, Seth took the cautious route keeping his speed below the limit and his pistol tucked under his seat.

When the patrol car flashed his lights and hit his siren, Seth pulled over to the shoulder and waited with his hands in plain sight on the steering wheel. He had never liked cops, and he could tell his opinion wasn't about to change as he watched the officer approach his car with his hand resting on the butt of his firearm.

"Good day. License and registration, please?" the young white officer asked.

Seth understood his rights and knew without some valid suspicion that he'd broken a law he didn't have to hand over his information. If he'd been in New York, he would have challenged the stop, but he kept his mouth closed. The last thing he wanted was to get into a legal debate with a small town cop who had yet to take his hand off his gun.

Keeping one hand on the steering wheel, Seth slowly leaned over and pulled the registration from the glove box and handed it to the officer.

"I'm only reaching for my wallet," Seth stated before he made another slow move.

"Are you a smartass?"

"If so, then I'm a cautious one," Seth said as he fished out his New York State license and handed it to the officer who had smirked at his answer.

The cop returned to his car to run the documents. Ten long minutes later, the officer was at his window again and handed Seth his information. "Thank you for your cooperation. Everything appears to be in order. You have a good day, Mr. Cautious."

"May I ask why I was detained, officer?" Seth asked. While he'd been waiting, he'd noted a heavy police presence for such a small docile retail area in suburbia, USA.

"Sure, there's been a rash of shootings in the area lately, and I was instructed to look for anything out of the ordinary. Your New York plate was definitely out of the ordinary," the officer said.

"Shootings? What kind of shootings?"

"It all seems gang related, so be careful, Mr. Cautious. Have a good day," the officer said, walking away.

Seth watched closely in his mirrors and noticed the cop still hadn't taken his hand off the butt of his sidearm. *These boys are wound up tighter than a first timer in gen pop.* He slid his car back into drive and went on his way. Following the GPS and the info Florida had sent him, Seth eventually found his way to the next town and a collection of mini-mansions that was nearly in farmland. He shook his head as he scanned the eerily quiet neighborhood. Each of the houses practically mirrored the other, offering a complete lack of personality and a strong dose of conformity. *How come the richer the folks the less fun they seem to have?*

He killed the engine and considered grabbing his gun but chose to leave it in the car. The neighborhood looked about as dangerous as Disneyland.

Seth knocked and braced himself for a variety of possibilities and emotions. He had no idea what to expect. *Hostility? Respect?* He smirked at the last one and waited. The shocked face that appeared in the open doorway stirred faint butterflies in his chest. Seth ignored the angst riding up his spine and got right to the point.

The smirk was gone, replaced by a look of cold determination. "Where the fuck is my grandson?" Seth asked Browning.

44

"Seth?" Browning asked, suddenly feeling nauseous.

"Yes, it's me. Where is my grandson?" Seth said again as he brushed past Browning and stepped into his son's home without invitation. He didn't bother admiring the surroundings. He focused instead on one goal. "Where's Charles?"

Stunned that a man he had vowed never to lay eyes on again had just stepped foot back into his life and barged into his house, Browning closed the front door to keep the imminent confrontation as private as possible. He followed Seth into the living room, both bewildered and irritated.

"You mind telling me what the hell you're doing here, in my house? I believe I made it extraordinarily clear to you the last time we spoke that I never wanted to see you again."

"Did you not hear me the first time?" Seth asked with his arms outstretched. "Where is my grandson?"

"I heard you. I don't recall inviting you in."

"You want me to leave, son?" Seth asked as he slowly lowered his arms.

Browning's anger spiked. He pointed at Seth and growled. "Don't call me that. You don't have the right to ever call me that."

Their glowering eyes bore into each other until Seth broke the silence. "I have more right to call you that then you can even imagine, but if you want me to leave," Seth said slowly as he walked towards his son until the two men were almost nose to nose, "Then I'll go, but not before you tell me where in the hell my grandson is."

"Why?"

"Because he needs my help."

"No, he doesn't. I can assure you of that," Browning said backing away from his father, his eyes wide with disbelief. "If MY son needed help, I would be the one to help him. Me! Not you! Now get out of my house! Go back to your precious Harlem, since it was the only thing you ever really cared about!"

Seth calmly looked at him for a long minute before he made his way to the door. "Look," he said, "I didn't say he needed help. I said he needed my help." When Seth crossed the threshold and stood on the quaint welcome mat he slowly turned and faced Browning. "Now if you care about your son, my grandson, then you will tell me where he is."

Browning tried to think, but his rage clouded his thoughts. He couldn't believe he was face to face with his father again. That was bad enough, but for him to demand an audience with his son was too much.

He was about to slam the door when he heard Seth say, "I'll sit out here all night, Brownie."

Browning reacted as if he had been slapped. He hated that annoying childhood nickname. He'd worked hard to move past it and make a name for himself that demanded respect. Throughout his career he had crushed anyone who dared called him 'Brownie' to his face. Yet with a word, his father reminded him of the clumsy child he had once been.

"I mean it. One way or another I'll see Charles. Look at it this way, the sooner I see my grand, the sooner I'll be back in New York.

Browning's jaw tightened. He knew first hand that his father's will was almost impossible to break. He knew his father would sit out in front of his house all night if necessary, just as he knew the sun would rise tomorrow. That spectacle was the last thing he wanted his neighbors to witness.

"He's at his friend Chad's house," Browning said feeling as if he'd licked a dirty boot.

"And where does Chad live?"

"Around the corner, second house on your right," Browning said before he slammed the door.

45

Seth was fuming as he walked back to his Cadillac. He'd known seeing his son would be emotional, but he was taken back by his own anger. *Nice to see you too, son.*

Minutes later Seth stood in front of another mini-mansion almost identical to his son's, and his heart pounded in his chest. He had only seen his grandson once, on a dreary rainy afternoon when he was about five. Seth did his best to slow his breathing and calm himself. When he felt ready he rang the doorbell.

A few seconds later a pale, blonde-haired blue-eyed teenage boy in a white t-shirt, blue denim shorts, and white ankle socks swung open the door with a broad smile. Seth thought he was a good-looking kid but in need of some serious color.

"Whattup, old man?"

Seth's facial features hardened, and his posture stiffened. "Excuse me?" Seth replied as he stared into the teen's red glassy eyes. Seth could see he was making this kid uncomfortable as he held his gaze. He enjoyed that more than he should have. Decades of experience gave Seth all the insight he needed into the boy's state of being. *No wonder my grandson is in trouble if this is who he hangs out with.*

"Uh…Can I help you? My parents aren't here at the moment."

"That's obvious. Is Charles here?"

"Oh, yeah," the boy said obviously relieved Seth wasn't there for him. "C'mon in. He's up in my room. I'll get him."

When the teenager dashed up to his room Seth knew he was truly in a different world. No child in Harlem would have let him into his house and then leave him alone. Seth instantly realized this trip was not going to be as easy as he'd initially thought. *God help Charles.*

"Can I help you?" a tall lean Black teen cautiously asked as he slowly came down the hardwood stairs.

Seth's heart swelled with unmitigated pride. His grandson was a handsome young man. His features favored Seth's. The broad lips, high cheekbones, strong jaw, and amber eyes had Seth feeling like he was looking at a much younger version of himself. "Charles," Seth said after clearing his throat. "It's good to see you…again."

The boy swallowed nervously. "Do I know you? Have we met? Did…did Stony send you?"

"No one sent me, Charles. I'm your grandfather."

Those words seemingly sucked all the air out of the room. The boy who had followed Charlie down the steps and sat at the base rose to his feet, mouth agape, while Charlie took a seat, never taking his eyes off Seth.

"Holy shit, dude!" Charlie's friend exclaimed.

"That can't be," Charlie finally said. "My dad told me my grandfather died before I was even born."

"Really? What did he tell you exactly?" Seth asked, back in control of his emotions and curious to hear how Browning had explained his forced absence from his grandson's life.

"He said you died how you lived, running the streets. He said…he said they found your body riddled with bullets and with a needle in your arm in some Harlem gutter."

Seth laughed openly. *A murdered heroin addict, shot dead in the streets? My son is a real dick.* "Well your father lied because I am happy to report that I am alive and well," he said as he approached his grandson. "I'd love to talk to you alone."

"I'm a bit busy right now," Charlie said, glancing at his friend. "How long are you in town?"

Seth scoffed. "That wasn't me asking, son. Get up and let's go," Seth said as he gave Charlie a look that meant business.

With a heavy sigh, Charlie reluctantly rose to his feet, told his friend that he'd see him later, and left with Seth. "How did you even know where I was? And what's your name?" he asked when they were outside.

"Your father told me where you were, and my name is Seth," he said. "Now get in the car."

Charlie looked curbside at Seth's gleaming black Cadillac. His eyes lit up. "That's you?"

"Well it damn sure ain't you, is it?"

"Rental?"

"All mine, son. Get in." When Seth was settled behind the wheel, he took a hard look at Charlie. The boy's crisp white t-shirt lay easily on his frame, as did his red and black plaid cargo shorts. His expensive looking black sneakers would signal him as a mark anywhere else except here. "How long you been gettin high?"

"I don't get high," Charlie said as he ogled the interior.

"Okay, because you obviously don't know how this works I'm going to let that one go. Lie to me again though, and I will beat you with this car. Let's try again. How long have you been getting high?"

Charlie leaned back in the leather seat and stared out the window, obviously reluctant.

"Look, I'm not going to tell your dad if that's what you're worried about."

The boy sighed and then mumbled. "Since fourteen."

"You do it every day?" Seth asked as he started the car.

"Almost."

"You high now? And before you answer me, again...make damn sure that the shit that comes out of your mouth is the truth, understand?"

"Yeah, and yeah I am."

"You hungry?"

"Yeah."

"You know a good place around here?"

Charlie nodded and directed his grandfather to Stymie's.

46

Once Charlie and Seth had placed their orders, they sat for a few minutes in silence. Seth took in the atmosphere while Charlie took in Seth. Charlie could tell that this man hated Stymie's and more than likely would never set foot in in the burger joint again. Eventually they locked eyes.

"You know you're an idiot, right?" Seth asked.

"What?" Charlie asked completely caught off guard.

"An idiot. I come knock on someone's door, tell him and you that I'm your grandfather, and you get in my car because I tell you to? I could have been anybody. Don't ever do that shit again, high or not, understand?"

Charlie's face flushed as he realized that was a pretty dumb thing to do. "Yeah," Charlie answered. "I won't do that again."

"Good," Seth snorted and sat back. "You know why I'm here?"

Charlie shook his head.

"It's respectful to answer someone when they talk to you or ask you a question. Head shaking is something babies do because they can't speak. Are you a baby?"

"No."

"Good. Once more, do you know why I'm here?"

"No," Charlie said.

"You sure?"

"Yeah," Charlie answered with a shrug enjoying the last floating effects of his high. "Unless you came for graduation I don't know why you're here."

"It has to do with a painting that will be arriving in Youngstown very soon," Seth stated watching Charlie closely. "Now, do you know why I'm here?"

Charlie's eyes went wide, not out of fear but curiosity. "Fuck, how do you know about that?"

"That's a question for another time, but now that I know it's true, would you mind telling me how in the hell you got yourself into this mess?"

Their food arrived, but at the thought of Stony and Frank Charlie's appetite faded, and he pushed his plate to the side.

Seth squirted ketchup onto his burger and fries. "I thought you said you was hungry."

"I was. Now I'm not. Now I feel sick."

"You eat that food. You're going to need your strength, every last bit of it, so eat up. Never turn down free food. You never know if that might be your last meal for a while," Seth said before he bit into his burger.

Charlie grudgingly obeyed.

Seth finished well ahead of Charlie. When Charlie finally swallowed his last fry, Seth picked back up where they had left the conversation. "So tell me, grandson, how in the hell did you get caught up in this? And remember, no bullshit. Always tell me the truth."

Charlie didn't answer. Instead he stared at the crumbs on his plate, wishing he could disappear.

"You hear me talking to you boy?" Seth asked. "How did this happen?"

Seth's grandson hung his head and said, "It's to pay off a gambling debt."

Seth leaned back in the booth and laughed loudly drawing eyes from the other patrons.

"What's so funny?" Charlie asked.

"You are, and it seems someone saw in you what I saw within minutes of meeting you. How old are you?"

"Almost eighteen."

"And you were gambling?"

"Only betting on sporting events."

"Yeah, that's still gambling, and apparently you're really bad at it, so bad in fact that the person who holds your marker wants you to commit art theft." Seth chuckled a little more. "How much are in you into him for?"

Charlie carefully eyed the man sitting across from him. "Why do you want to know? Why do you care?"

"You need to understand…if I'm hearing about this in New York, this whole thing is bigger than you. I need to know all this before we can move to the next step."

Charlie shrugged. He had no idea if telling the truth about what he owed Stony would spin his grandfather out of control and cause the older man to get violent. He was nowhere near his house, and he didn't have his car, so if things went south he'd be pretty much on his own. Chad was too high to pick him up, and Gavin was again out with Jennifer.

"Damn boy, is it that much?" Seth asked.

"Yeah."

"Is it more than fifty thousand?"

Charlie nodded.

"What did I tell you about nodding your head. Speak up."

"Yes, it's more than fifty thousand."

"A hundred thousand?"

Charlie wilted in his seat, refusing to meet his grandfather's incredulous gaze. "More," the boy said.

Seth's features darkened. "A hundred and fifty?"

"Closer," Charlie croaked.

Seth suddenly rose from the table and walked away toward the bathroom. When his grandfather finally returned he was humming some song under his breath.

Seth sat down and sighed. "I am doing my best not to tear your heart out of your chest. You know that, right?" Seth smiled menacingly. "You know what you are? You're what's known as a degenerate gambler. Meaning if had you a wife, kids, a car, a house, and a job, none of that would matter. You'd have pissed it all away chasing that winning high. Seems daddy never made the little prince accountable for any fucking thing, and the prince like a fool, thought it was okay to rack up a debt the size of which would make you a fuck up even in Vegas!" Seth yelled drawing all eyes to their table. "And how...what exactly was your brilliant ass plan to get you out from under this shit?" Seth whispered through clenched teeth.

Charlie stared wide-eyed at his grandfather. "I...I don't know."

Seth reached into his pocket and placed thirty dollars on the table. Then in what seemed like all one move, Seth snatched him out of his seat and walked him out of Stymie's.

47

Charlie's stomach was in his throat as he led Seth into his house. His grandfather hadn't said a word since they'd left Stymie's. He could almost taste the cheeseburger and fries as they rose to the back of his throat.

"Brownie!" Seth yelled, filling the entire house with demand.

"We're civilized here. There's no need to yell," Browning calmly said turning the corner into the expansive kitchen. "I thought I told you earlier that you are not welcomed in my house, Seth," Browning said with little conviction. He glanced at Charlie. "Go downstairs, son."

Charlie fought back the urge to run and hide and instead stood ramrod still.

Seth laughed. "Back on that crap again, huh? 'Get out my house, dad!' I see why my grandson is in such deep shit."

"What's that supposed to mean?" Browning asked his jaw tightening.

"With you for a dad, he was destined to fuck up," Seth said with a chuckle. "What kind of father are you that you don't know what's going on in your son's life?"

Charlie's eyes went wide. He'd never heard anyone speak to his dad like this.

"What kind of father am I?" Browning asked softly. "What the fuck kind of father are you? Don't walk in here all high and mighty like you raised me right, like you did a good job. You were never around. Your big bad ass was in jail the entire time I was growing up. You were locked away for more than years than I care to remember, and you think you have the right to come into my house and question the way I'm raising my son? Who the fuck do you think you are?"

"You're right," Seth said. "I was locked up, and I wasn't around, but look at where you are now. Look at everything you have. You think you would have any of this without me? You think I had no hand in any of this? In you? In him?" Seth asked pointing to his grandson.

"The size of your ego is massive, Seth," Browning said. "What role did you play in this? Where do you come in? From what I remember, where I am today is all because of mom NOT you, so please, enlighten me." Browning pulled out a seat at his dining room table and folding his hands like a fourth grader.

"Your mother, my wife, was a beautiful strong woman, and she had to step up and be both mom and part time dad when I wasn't around. This is true," Seth said softly. "Answer me this, though, son. Do you ever remember your mother working a day in her life? Was there ever a time when you came home from school, and she wasn't there to meet you at the damn door?"

"She was always there, Seth, always. Unlike someone else I know," Browning said cutting his eyes at Seth.

"Always there for her baby boy on the weekends and the weekdays, right?"

"What's your point?"

Seth's eyes tightened, but he casually leaned against the counter and crossed his feet. "How do you think your mother kept the rent paid or the lights on, so her baby boy could do his homework and read his books? How do you think your mother—who never worked—kept the fucking fridge full, so her baby boy didn't starve? How do you think your mother kept her baby boy dressed in the best clothes or sent him to the best schools? How do you think your mother was able to send her baby boy to goddamn college? A woman, the love of my life, who never held a job in her life, was able to do all of that how, Brownie? You ever wonder about that, or did that just never cross your narrow ass mind?"

Though Browning shook his head in denial, Charlie searched his father's face and could tell he saw the flaw in his own logic. "Uncle Paulie helped us," Browning said softly almost to himself.

"Yeah, my unofficial brother was there with money whenever it was needed. Who do you think he came to for the money? Me, Browning, he came to me to get the okay to pull out whatever she needed whenever she needed it. Even after your mother stopped coming to see me, Paulie came on her behalf, and I gave. He came to me to help take care of you and your mother in every way possible." Seth looked around the house. "No son, you didn't get here—in your cookie cutter mini mansion—by your own sheer will. You had help, MY help, and don't you ever forget it."

"Enough. Get out, Seth. Don't come back, or I'll call the police. Do you understand me?" he asked as he rose from his seat. "And you," he said pointing to Charlie, "I don't want you seeing this man again. I don't care if you see him on the side of the road on fire. You keep moving. Don't say a goddamn word to him."

Seth laughed, which only incensed Browning more. He pushed away from the bar and walked to the door. "It's funny," he started, "how the fruit never falls far from the tree." On his way out, Seth turned back and met Charlie's eyes. "Charles, I'm staying in Boardman. Find me because we both know you need to." With that, he politely closed the door behind him.

48

The next morning as Seth walked out of the hotel to grab breakfast, he found Charlie standing awkwardly next to his Cadillac. Seth looked his grandson over and stared into his clear eyes. "Took you long enough. I was about to head out to get something to eat. You hungry?"

"I could go for some pancakes," Charlie said.

"Me too. The receptionist, Marjorie, gave me directions to a little diner down the street. Hop in." Within minutes they were on the road with Dexter Gordon's rendition of *Round Midnight* playing through the Cadillac's premium sound system.

"There's some decent radio stations around here to listen to," Charlie said.

"What's the matter? You don't like jazz?"

"I'm not big on jazz."

"You can't even vote yet, so of course you don't like jazz. You like hip hop?" Seth asked.

"Yeah."

"Hip hop is pretty much jazz on steroids."

"Get outta here," Charlie said as they pulled into the parking lot of an unassuming eatery.

"Seriously. I'll tell ya what I mean while we eat," Seth said. As they headed in, Seth watched his grandson's walk. Charlie had a confident gait, not clumsy or sloppy like most kids his age. He seemed very comfortable in his skin, which made Seth smile. *At least that's one thing I won't have to teach him.*

After Seth ordered a plate of chicken and waffles and a short stack of blueberry pancakes for Charlie, he started with the easy questions. "So what was it like after I left?"

Charlie let out a soft whistle. "It was crazy. Dad lost his mind, going on and on about what a horrible father you were and what an evil man you are and how he should have you arrested because he's sure you're breaking parole by being here. You're not, are you?"

Seth laughed. "No, I'm not breaking parole."

"Okay," Charles said relieved. "Just crazy shit…oops, sorry. Just crazy stuff last night. I've never seen him like that. Not that I see him all that much anyway."

Seth raised an eyebrow at the last remark but tucked it away for later. "I can imagine. Sounds like it was quite the show, and you can say 'shit.' It's all right. What did you say to him?"

"I was like, 'Why'd you lie to me?' but he never answered. Actually I'm not even sure he heard me. He just kept railing on and on about you, about how he left New York and worked for everything he has without stealing or hurting people. How he built a good life in Ohio away from you because you're 'pure evil,' and everything you touch crumbles to shit."

"Pure evil, huh?" Seth said as their waiter placed their orders in front of them. "I don't think pure evil eats chicken and waffles, but if believing I'm pure evil motivated him, then I'll be that," he said as he doctored his waffles with butter and syrup, and Charlie followed suit. "Do you have any questions for me?" Seth asked before biting into his juicy fried chicken.

"Yeah, one really important one. What do I call you? Gramps? Seth? Old guy?"

Seth's eyes flew to his grandson's, and he squinted in amused annoyance. "Don't ever call me gramps, or I'll break your jaw."

Charlie snickered, and the sterner Seth looked at him, the harder he laughed.

Seth eventually cracked a smile. That was the first time he'd ever heard his grandson's laugh. His heart swelled, but in that moment he also realized all the years he had missed with the boy. It felt like Larry Holmes had shot a jab to his chest. His breath caught, and a deep ache bloomed beneath his ribs. He took a sip of coffee to recover. "Call me Pop. That's what I called my grandfather, so that's what you can call me," Seth said before taking another swig of coffee. "Now I have a question for you."

Charlie swallowed his mouthful of pancakes. "Okay, Pop."

"When you kept losing, what was your plan B, boy? How were you going to cover your losses and fix this fucking mess?"

Charlie stared at Seth's shirt as he swallowed thickly unable to meet his grandfather's gaze.

Seth watched the shame descend over the boy like frigid air "Well? Is it that bad?" he asked, setting down his fork.

Eventually his grandson looked at him. "It ain't good," Charlie said softly.

"Tell me."

Charlie inhaled deeply. "My dad has a thing for watches. He's got a massive watch collection. None of them are cheap, but he's got a few really, really expensive ones. I was going to steal a couple of those."

"How?" Seth asked, his face a mask of concern.

"I was going to have some friends help me. Make it look like a robbery."

"What were they going to take?"

"My stereo and laptop, my stepmother's diamond necklace and some other stuff of hers, and about five or six watches."

"Five or six watches wouldn't nearly cover your nut," Seth said. "What kind of watches are we talking about?"

"Four Patek-Phillipes and two Breitlings."

Seth let out a low whistle. "Nice."

"Yeah," Charlie said. "They're insured, so I figured he'd have gotten something back, you know?"

"So what happened?"

Charlie shrugged. "Changed my mind."

"Good for you," Seth said. "You made a decision, and you stuck to it. Most can't even do that. They need people around them all the time tellin em what to do and how to do it. You made a decision not to rob your dad, and you stuck to it. Good for you." Seth saw that his words affected his grandson.

Charlie cleared his throat and sat up straight. "I have another question for you, Pop."

Seth raised his eyebrows as he ate the last of his waffle.

"What were you in jail for?"

"Taking another man's life," he said with all the seriousness it deserved.

"You were in jail for murder?"

"Manslaughter."

"What's the difference?"

"Parole. You get none for murder. Manslaughter is a little different."

"No, I meant what's the difference between murder and manslaughter, not sentence wise but like definition wise, you know?"

"Manslaughter isn't premeditated. It's not planned. It happens almost by accident, a wrong place wrong time type of thing. Murder typically isn't by accident."

Seth watched the wheels turn in his grandson's head. "Okay, I think I got it," Charlie said. "So how is jazz hip hop on steroids?"

Seth wiped his hands on his napkin and smiled. "Okay, you know what a groove is?" he asked.

"Yes."

"Ya sure?"

"Yeah, Pops."

"The groove is the most important thing in music. Without the groove you don't have music. The groove is the foundation. If you listen to jazz say bebop and big band, even some of that avant-garde stuff, the groove is the thing that holds it all together, same for hip hop. The groove allows the saxophone and any instrument involved to have a solo. They can go anywhere they want musically, but in the end they come back to the groove and fall back into the pocket. Hip hop is the modern day take on jazz. The guy on the mic is soloing and either saying what comes to his mind or reciting something he's already written, right?"

Charlie nodded, seemingly fascinated.

"Eventually that guy stops soloing and allows the groove to continue until he's ready to go again or let someone else rap. Same thing in jazz, understand?"

Charlie blinked and Seth saw a lost look in his eyes.

"You all right?" he asked.

"Yeah. I'm thinking I need to listen to more jazz."

"Of course you do," Seth said with a nod. "Now, my turn to ask you something. Where is your mother?"

"My biological mother?"

"Is there any other kind?"

"I gotta stepmom."

"That's nice. Where is your mother, Charles?"

Charlie set his fork down on his plate. "She died, Pop."

Seth leaned back in the booth stunned. "Damn, son. I'm so sorry. When? How?"

"Cancer, about four years ago."

"Shit, I liked that girl. She was the best thing that happened to your dad. I'm sorry."

"You knew my mother?"

"Not knew but I'd met her once, and she left an impression on me. Your father brought you and her out to New York when you were about five years old. Of course you probably don't remember that, but it was the first and only time we ever met. Your father was busy doing something, I don't recall what, and your mother brought you to the back of the church and introduced you to me." Seth smiled at the memory. "I gave you some quarters to put in your pocket. It was only a few minutes, but the moment meant a lot to me."

"I don't remember, Pop."

"I know you don't. How could you?"

After the waitress collected their plates and the money for the bill, Charlie asked, "Why did we come out to New York?"

"For your grandmother's funeral," Seth said as they made their way back to his car.

"So you weren't yet shooting heroin and hadn't yet been shot dead in the streets?"

"Not yet," Seth said with a laugh.

"What was she like?"

Seth paused for a bit and a smile formed on his face at her memory. "You know, she was a lot like your mother actually."

"How?"

"She was the absolute sweetest woman I had ever met, selfless, caring, giving. I had no idea why she was wasting her time on me, but she loved me something serious, much like your mother loved your father."

"You miss her?" he asked.

"I miss her every day," he said as he looked to the sky. "She used to love Bobby Short to no end and his version of *Too Marvelous For Words*. I play it from time to time, and I can still see her smiling face."

"Pop, can we go somewhere?" Charlie asked after a quiet moment, pulling Seth out of his memories.

"Sure, get in," Seth said.

After a fifteen-minute drive, Charlie directed his grandfather through wrought iron gates into a small but serene cemetery.

"This is your mother's resting place?"

"Yeah," Charlie said in a hushed tone as he stared out the window at the sea of lush greenery and stoic tombstones.

"Do me a favor, yourself too. Stop saying yeah and start saying yes. You're an articulate kid, and only lazy people say 'yeah.' Don't be lazy. Understand?"

"I get you, Pop. Turn right over here. Okay…stop," Charlie said and then opened his car door. After a short walk they stood at the headstone of Iris Christine Jackson. Charlie knelt and started to pull a few weeds.

"We should have brought flowers," Seth said. "Next time." Silence fell over them as the scent of freshly cut grass hung thickly in the air. Seth saw Charlie quickly wipe a tear, and he gripped his grandson's shoulder. As he read the dates on the dark marble headstone, pieces of Charlie's puzzle quickly snapped together. His mother had passed when he was fourteen, and apparently Charlie had started to self-medicate with weed to numb the pain of his mother's loss. Yet, the boy was still a mystery to Seth. From what he'd seen so far, the boy seemed soft, and while he was a quick learner, his mind seemed dormant as if nothing had ever fully flipped the on switches. His grandson had potential but was missing one very key element in his life that every boy needed to become a man, leadership.

If Seth's guess was right, Charlie hadn't had any for quite some time. The problem was that Charlie was the son of a man who had been devoid of paternal leadership as a child himself, and Seth knew that heavy weight fell solely upon his shoulders. Now his rudderless ship of a grandson was in debt to sharks, and sharks never forgive a debt. They want their money, save the sob stories. Seth couldn't hate. He had felt the same way when he had been a shark.

Charlie stood and brushed off his jeans. "Thanks for bringing me."

"No problem. Remember she's always with you." Seth said as they headed back to his car. "The memories, the emotions, the love…it's all still there inside you."

Charlie thought about that for a moment and then nodded. "I know."

Seth smiled. "When is graduation?"

"Tomorrow."

"And you have everything you need for tomorrow?"

"I do."

"Good. Charlie, can we go somewhere?" Seth asked using Charlie's question.

"Sure, where to?"

"I want you to take me to the guys who want you to steal that painting."

Charlie stopped walking and stared at Seth wide-eyed.

"What's the matter?" Seth asked.

"Why you wanna meet them?"

Seth heard the fear in Charlie's voice, and he almost chuckled. *Sharks do have that ability to put the fear of God in someone.* "I want to see what they're all about."

"I don't think that's a good idea, Pop."

"No, you're right. It's not a good idea," Seth said and watched relief flood Charlie's features. "It's a great idea. Now get in the car, and let's go." When Charlie groaned, Seth looked at him "I won't let anything happen to you, son."

Charlie sighed. "Promise?"

"What are you, five? You wanna pinky swear or something? You'll be fine. Trust me."

49

Seth pulled his Cadillac up to the curb in front of a non-descript corner bar on the South Side of Youngstown. "This the place?"

Charlie nodded solemnly.

The bright afternoon sun sucked the life out of the somewhat colorful exterior. Romare's almost seemed abandoned, but Seth knew better. "Don't look like much."

Charlie grudgingly climbed out and took a long look at the place.

Seth reached into his glove box and grabbed his gun, a nickel-plated snub nose .45. He left the Glock under his seat and the .28 he kept as backup stayed in the door's side panel. When he climbed out, Seth slid the gun in the waistband of his trousers where it snugly fit in the small of his back. He closed the door and walked over to stand next to Charlie.

"I've never seen it during the day. Seems different at night," Charlie said.

"That's exactly how this kind of place is supposed to look. It's not supposed to attract attention. Go knock," Seth said as he leaned against his car.

Charlie swallowed and slowly approached the dark entrance. After a few raps, each louder than the last, the door finally cracked opened.

"We ain't open yet."

"Hey, you're the DJ. I'm Charlie. I was here the other night. I...I need to speak with Stony."

"He ain't here," the portly man said and slammed the door in Charlie's face.

Charlie looked like a man who'd gotten a governor's stay of execution as he walked back to his grandfather. "He's not here."

Seth smiled having heard the entire exchange and shook his head partly in annoyance but mostly in amusement. "And you believe that, son?"

Charlie thought a second and shrugged.

"Don't shrug. Only clueless dicks and children shrug. C'mon," Seth said as he strolled to the entrance. Without hesitation he banged on the metal door as if thunder demanded access.

Charlie cringed.

A few seconds later, the same chubby faced DJ yanked the door open wide. Before he could say anything, Seth threw a vicious punch to his throat. The DJ hit the floor gasping for air, and Seth sauntered in followed by Charlie who closed the door, staring in awe at his grandfather.

Seth knelt down and asked, "Is the man here?"

The downed man nodded emphatically, still struggling to breathe.

"Good, get on your feet," Seth said and helped up the rotund man.

"Whatchuwant?" he croaked.

"Shut up, and I'll tell you. Let your boss know we're here. Tell him it's Charlie and his associate."

The DJ walked off, still holding his throat but breathing a bit better. Seth looked around Romare's. He'd heard about this place from old acquaintances and Florida's network, but he'd never thought he'd be inside. Given the rumors, he had never wanted to be. Leonard's place had been notorious for the drama that went on in and around the South Side, but Romare's had always made money. The decor was simple enough, black on black except for the floor that was a sand-colored subway tile. *Expensive, not the smartest flooring,* Seth thought, *but it looks nice.*

The DJ returned still rubbing his neck. "This way," he said in a rasp.

As the trio headed deeper into Romare's belly, Seth continued to take mental notes of the setup, a few stripper poles in back, a small stage and off to the right, a sports book and gambling area further back. A craps table, two blackjack tables, and a few slot machines stood silent.

A lithe man of average height who carried confidence on his shoulders like the wind carried sound met them at the bottom of the steps. Seth immediately recognized that this man was dangerous and not to be toyed with.

"That's Frank," Charlie whispered standing close to Seth.

"I got it from here, Nellie," Frank said.

"Nellie, is it?" Seth asked.

Nellie stared daggers at Seth.

"Sorry about the throat."

"Fuck you, gramps."

Charlie flinched at the DJ's insult.

Seth's eyes went from compassionate to hard in a blink. "You want another one, fatso?"

"Nellie," Frank warned, prompting the DJ to leave.

"Sorry about that." Frank said, glancing at Charlie but focusing on Seth. "Had we known Charlie was comin, that woulda gone smoother. How you doin, Charlie?"

"Ummm...I'm fine."

"Yeah? Why don't you make some introductions? Who this you got with you?"

"Like I told your fat boy over there, I'm his associate," Seth said. He locked eyes with Frank for no longer than a few seconds, but he instinctly knew his grand was about to piss his pants. "Just to let you know, so there's no surprise. I'm carrying. Hope you don't mind."

"Carrying what?" Charlie asked.

Both men ignored his question.

"So am I," Frank said. "Hope you don't mind."

"Free country."

"There ain't shit free about this country," Frank said which made Seth smile.

"You've got a point." Seth's continued assessment of Frank told him that his grandson was in more trouble than he could even imagine.

"Follow me then," Frank said leading them both up the stairs to the office.

"Whattup, Charles," Stony said as he greeted Charlie when they entered the office. "Who's that handsome older cat with you?"

"His associate," Frank said.

"Associate? Well, isn't that interesting. Please, gentlemen, have a seat," Stony said motioning to the sofa. Frank leaned over and spoke into Stony's ear, and Stony shot a cold look at Seth. "I understand you assaulted my DJ. That's not a good first impression."

"He earned it," Seth said noting the low profile bulletproof vest under Stony's oversized Hawaiian shirt.

"How so?"

"He lied. I have no time for liars."

"What did he lie about?"

"He said you weren't here, and yet here you are," Seth said with a smile.

"Here I am." Stony smiled back. "But how did you know he was lying?"

"There's an Escalade ESV on what looks like thirty inch rims in the alley. Who's driving that, the help?"

Stony nodded agreeing with Seth's point. "I like you."

"Nice to be liked."

Frank stilled for a millisecond at Seth's reply.

Seth glanced at the younger man and knew he understood his response.

"So how can I help you?" Stony asked unaware of the message sent between the other men.

"I want to know exactly how much Charles here owes you," Seth said with a polite smile.

"Why is that any business of yours? You gonna pay his marker?" Stony asked and took a closer look at Seth. "I'm sorry, but I didn't catch your name."

"No need to apologize. I never gave it."

The room fell silent.

Stony barked an annoyed chuckle. "The suspense is killing me. Can we know your name?"

"Do you need it to let me know how much Charles owes you?"

Stony's smile vanished. "Yeah, I do, motherfucka."

Seth hardened, but he was in this man's house, so he smiled and leaned back. "The name is Seth, but motherfucka is close." His smile never left his face.

Stony then broke out into laughter and stood. "You's a funny dude," Stony said as he went to his desk and grabbed his ledger. He flipped a few pages. "Here we go. Charles Jackson owes the house approximately two hundred and four thousand dollars. I don't know if Charles told you, but we have found an alternative solution for him to pay his debt."

"Yes, he explained that you want him to steal a work of art valued at more than five times what he owes you, correct?"

"So he told you," Stony said studying them. "You know, you two share quite a resemblance."

"Yeah, we get that a lot," Seth said as he stood and snatched Charlie off the sofa with him. "Well we got what we needed. Thanks for the sit down."

"Leaving so soon?" Stony said getting to his feet as well. "I got lemonade coming."

"Yes, Charlie has things to do before graduation," Seth said.

"Ahhh yes, the big day is when, Chuck, tomorrow?"

Charlie nodded his head.

"Congratulations, wish I could watch you walk the stage and get your diploma," Stony said.

"Yeah well, ummmm...it's family only."

"That's what I heard. Is your associate going to be there?"

"Ye—"

"No," Seth interrupted.

Stony looked at them both with mock surprise. "You sure? You two don't seem to be on the same page. Wait a sec. Are you two family?"

Silence once again danced between the men.

"You ARE family. How cool is that, Frank? Chuck has fam who wears gators and drives a Caddy."

Frank smirked. "And carries a gun."

Stony's eyebrows rose in surprise. "You carrying, old-timer?"

"Told your boy I was. Told him I hoped it wasn't an issue. I like to lay my cards on the table."

Stony smiled and said, "Apparently not all of them. I can respect that."

Seth stared at Stony and Frank and slowly maneuvered himself between them and Charlie.

"Don't worry, old-timer, we don't intend to hurt him. He owes too much money," Stony said.

"Then we'll just be going. You boys have a great day," Seth said as he backed his way towards the door that led to the staircase and followed Charlie.

When they were gone Frank slowly shook his head. "Watch out for that nigga."

"Gramps?" Stony asked shrugging his shoulders. "What are you talking about? He may drive a Caddy and dress and carry himself like he's used to respect, but he's harmless."

"No, Stone. He's not."

"You're just mad he wasn't intimidated by you, unlike every other person who ever comes face-to-face with you. That's just old school. He reminded me a little of Unc actually."

Frank frowned. "He said, 'Nice to be liked.'"

"So?"

"That's a jail phrase. When guards try to cozy up to an inmate to get info, the C.O. usually starts with some shit like, "I like you." I've seen it happen. Once a nigga starts squealing on the cellblock, he's trapped. If he quits cooperating, the guards threaten to out the snitch to the block's shot callers. Smart motherfuckas tell guards who approach them to fuck off with the reply, 'Nice to be liked.' While civilians occasionally use that phrase, I know that the guy on that sofa, the one carrying a gun, was no civilian."

"Charlie didn't unearth some super thug. Please. Mr. Flashy Red Silk Shirt and Black Gators was just looking to pay his grandson's note.

Frank's frown deepened. "That old man is not to be taken lightly, Stone. Trust me."

50

"Where are we headed now?" Charlie asked.

"I'm taking you home," Seth said as he chirped the alarm on his car. "Get in."

Seth stayed silent as they made their way out of the South Side. He was pissed that Charlie had helped those two baby gangsters piece together who he was to Charlie. Now his advantage of being an unknown factor had been played far too early in the game, and it weakened their position significantly. He inhaled deeply. "Charlie, do you have the time?"

Charlie looked at his watch and gave his grandfather the time.

Seth shook his head. "You give up too much information, you know that?" The clueless look on his grandson's face only frustrated him more. "Dammit boy, don't you get nothing?"

Charlie shrugged.

"What'd I tell you about shrugging? Ask me the same question I just asked you," Seth instructed as the GPS calmly announced a right turn in fifty feet.

"Pop, do you have the time?"

"Yes, I do," Seth answered as he turned. He could see the bewildered look on his grandson's face. "You ask a question. I give you the answer, but I don't give you any more than you ask for, and even then I only give the most succinct answer possible after I've decided the information can't be used against me. When what's his name…Stony?" Seth asked looking at Charlie who nodded his head. "When Stony talked about how it would be cool to watch you walk across the stage and get your diploma, you shouldn't have said a word. He was baiting you, boy, and you swallowed it like a hungry puppy. His ass didn't need to know that it was family only, and he damn sure didn't need to know that I was going to be there. Stop spilling your guts trying to be liked. Don't give out more than asked of you. You got change for a dollar?"

Charlie plunged his hands into his pocket, before he realized Seth was testing him. He pulled his hand out of his pocket. "Maybe," he said and sat back against the leather seat.

"Better. But it needs to be second nature. Keep working at it."

Twenty minutes later Seth pulled in front of Charlie's house and laughed, snatching Charlie from his thoughts. "Who's car is that?" he asked nodding toward the driveway. An unknown vehicle in the vicinity would normally put him on alert. Instead he was amused. A glittering cotton candy pink Jaguar lounged in the sun.

"That is my stepmother's car. She must be back from her cruise."

"A pink Jag? Ain't that something. Never knew they offered that color."

"They don't." Charlie dragged himself from the Caddy just as his father pulled up. "Shit."

Seth looked in his review and saw his son rush out of his Mercedes and make a beeline for Charlie. Seth quickly moved to intercept him.

"I thought I told you to stay away from him!" Browning yelled pointing a finger in Seth's direction. "Get in the house. NOW!" He shoved Charlie up the stairs towards the house.

Seth stepped between his son and grandson. "He's not a dog. Don't talk to him that way."

"Mind your damn business. This is between me and my son, not you, so stay the fuck out of it," Browning stated with an icy stare before he moved around Seth and pushed again at Charlie.

"Not today," Seth said and grabbed his son's arm with his left hand. Browning pulled his arm away and threw a sloppy punch that Seth easily sidestepped and countered with a hard right to his son's nose sending Browning down to his knees.

"Dad!" Charlie yelled and ran to his father's aid.

"Goddamn it! Help me get him inside, Charlie, before any of your neighbors see," Seth said as he and Charlie lifted a stunned and wobbly Browning. They brought him in the house to the sofa. Seth handed his son his handkerchief and told Charlie to get a bag of frozen vegetables.

"Stop whimpering like a damn baby, Browning."

"You broke my nose," Browning said as Charlie handed him the ice pack of peas.

"No, I didn't. I barely touched you," Seth said.

"You damn near knocked me out."

"That was a love tap. Next time you swing at someone you better do it with bad intentions or don't even bother," Seth said as he clenched and unclenched his hand becoming acclimated to the pain. It had been a while since his hand had hit bone.

"What in the world is going on here?" came an airy voice.

Seth cracked a smile at the statuesque, brunette walking towards them. He met her curious hazel eyes warmly to try and put her at ease, but as Charlie and Seth turned toward her, they provided a view of Browning with a bag of frozen peas draped over his face.

"Hi, honey. Welcome home," Browning said to his wife. "How was your trip?"

"Oh no! Baby, what happened to you?" Bailey asked rushing over to sit next to her husband.

"Seth punched me and broke my nose." Browning nodded to Seth, lifting the bag as proof.

"What? Why did you hit my husband?"

"He took a swing at me, and I reacted," Seth replied before he looked again at Browning. "And trust me when I tell you your nose is not broken, son."

"Son?" Bailey searched Seth's features. "Oh my," she said softly. "What's going on here?"

"I told you," Seth said as he casually sat in the sofa's matching plush love seat.

"Don't get comfortable, Seth." Browning clumsily got to his feet. "It's time for you to get out of my house before I call the police."

"Don't be a pussy, son," Seth said which brought a chuckle from Charlie who had retreated to the kitchen counter to watch from a distance. "There's no need to call the police. Relax."

"Don't tell me to relax. You show up out of the blue, demand to see my son when all hell is breaking loose, and…" Browning looked hard at Seth. "What are you really doing here?"

"I'm here for Charlie's graduation," Seth lied.

"How'd you know when it was? Charlie had no way to get in touch with you."

"Lucky guess."

"Yeah, my ass lucky guess," Browning said.

Charlie chuckled again.

"And you, mister," Browning said as he spun to face his son, "are grounded. I'll be cancelling that graduation party of yours tonight too."

Bailey gasped and cut her eyes toward her husband.

Charlie chuckled again. "So what," he mumbled under his breath, heading to the stairs.

"What was that, Charles?" Browning asked, ready for another confrontation.

Charlie wheeled on his father and said, "I said 'So what.' I didn't want the stupid party anyway." Charlie then took the steps in twos followed closely by Bailey.

Browning whirled back to face his father still sitting at ease in his living room. "See what you've done? One day here and you've turned everything upside down."

Seth smirked. "You're putting this all on me?"

"I'm placing blame where blame is due."

"You should get your head out of your ass before it's too late, you know that?"

Browning stared at his father and finally said, "Please, just go and never come back."

Seth wasted no more time and showed himself out, leaving the ornate front door wide open.

51

Complaining of a headache, Browning had gone to bed early, yet hours later Charlie was still furious. The only person who'd shown any ability to help him through the worst drama in his life was his grandfather, and with each encounter his dad seemed to lose every bit of sense and reason the second he saw the older man. However, Charlie had yet to see anything that resembled the drug addict and thug his dad had described his entire life. In fact, Seth Jackson seemed to be one of the few men he'd ever met who understood life and cared enough to explain some of it to him.

Fuck this, Charlie thought and grabbed his phone. He considered calling Chad but changed his mind. This time of night Chad would be out of his mind high and in no shape to drive. He didn't know what his friend was getting high on these days, but it wasn't just weed, and that worried him. His fingers instead dialed Gavin who answered as if waiting for the phone to ring.

"What's up, Charlie?"

"Hey, man, I need a favor. I gotta get the fuck out of here. Can you give me a ride to my car?"

"Sure but where is it?"

"Out passed the mall at my grandfather's hotel."

"Okay but I won't be alone. I got Jen with me. We'll be over in five, cool?"

"No problem. I'll be out front."

Within minutes, Charlie was in Gavin's back seat and breathing a little easier. After quick hellos, Charlie closed his eyes and listened to the classical music sliding easily from the rear speakers as his friend drove across town. When they eventually turned into the hotel's parking lot Charlie caught sight of his grandfather reclining in his Cadillac.

"Thanks, G. You two headed back home?"

"I don't know. We might drive around some. Why?"

"If my father or stepmother asks if you seen me…"

"I ain't seen shit, homie," Gavin said finishing Charlie's sentence.

"Thanks."

Once Gavin left, Charlie walked up to his grandfather's gleaming black beast of a car. He was smart enough to know coming up unannounced to the window was a bad idea, so he rapped on the hood.

Seth opened his eyes to see his grandson's youthful face staring back at him. One look and Seth knew the boy was in a bad headspace. He motioned to the passenger door.

"Rough night?"

"I've had better," Charlie said searching Seth's face. "You all right, Pops? You seem upset."

"I'm good, son. Just sittin here listening to some music."

"More jazz? I told you that stuff wasn't that great."

Seth smiled. "I was actually listening to your grandmother's favorite song."

"The marvelous song by somebody short?"

"Close enough," Seth said with a chuckle and pressed a button on the steering wheel that muted the music.

"So when did you get into jazz, Pop?"

"When someone introduced me to a cat named Miles Davis. I was in my early twenties then and hard into disco, but a friend of mine told me I didn't know what I was missin and dropped Miles' *Bitches Brew* on me. I was blown away. It was ninety-three plus minutes of some serious music, and I've been hooked ever since."

"I'll have to check him out."

"After that," Seth continued, "It was Herbie Hancock, Roy Ayers, Pharoah Sanders, Charles Mingus, Thelonious Monk, Rahsaan Roland Kirk and so many others." Seth smiled at the memories. "Hell, pretty much anyone I could get my hands on. A good chunk of my money started going to my record collection," Seth said. "You do know what a record is, right?"

"Yeah, yeah…I've seen those. They're big black circles with a hole in the middle, right? Need a needle to get the sound and all that? Yeah, I'm hip, Pop," Charlie said with a smirk.

"Whatcha mouth, boy. Don't no one like a smartass…not even smartasses," Seth replied with a soft mush to his grandson's head.

"Yeah, yeah. So what was it about jazz? Why were you so into it?"

"Because it was new musical territory. It fascinated me, and I fell in love. Plus the best part was that it was Black music, and while I know a lot of greedy white boys got paid off the backs of those musical geniuses, I wanted to support them." Charlie nodded his head as if he understood, but Seth knew the child didn't. However he was encouraged at how his grandson asked questions and listened intently. "So tell me about Bailey. She seems nice."

"You're kidding, right?" Charlie asked. A look of disgust crawled over his face.

"Well she seemed nice to me, but I can see you aren't all that fond of the busty one. What's up with you and her?"

Seth's question bounced around in they boy's head for a bit before he answered. "I don't hate her or anything. I just don't like her."

"You look at her as if she was a roach that scampered across your plate of food. That doesn't jibe with 'I just don't like her.'"

Charlie laughed. "I guess."

"So again, what's really going on with you and stepmom?"

"It's not really her I'm mad at, I guess. She just gets the brunt."

"Who you mad at then?"

"Dad."

Seth nodded slowly as his suspicions were confirmed. "Why?"

"Because he married the 'busty one' less than a year after mom died. Bed wasn't even cold yet, and they was on their honeymoon."

Seth could hear the bitterness in his words and figured it was best to let Charlie relax a little on the topic of Bailey. After awhile he asked, "What kind of cancer did your mother die from?"

"Ovarian cancer but by the time they found it, it had spread."

"She was sick a long time?"

"Yeah, about a year and a half."

"I know that musta been hard on you. Watching anyone go through that, especially your mother, can't be easy."

"Yeah. It sucked."

"As hard as it was for you though, imagine how hard it must have been for your father to lose his wife so young. Losing the love of your life is absolute hell." Seth saw the moment his words registered with Charlie and continued. "Maybe your mother urged him to move on once she was gone, to not get in the grave with her. Maybe she wanted him to be happy and find a good woman to help raise you too."

"One day," Charlie started, his voice thick with emotion, "I come home, and mom is gone, and what feels like the very next day, Bailey's there. It was too fucking soon, Pops. Too fucking soon."

"If had been ten years later it was going to be too fucking soon, son."

"Whatever," Charlie said under his breath before he closed his eyes and leaned his head back in the leather seat.

"That's when you started smoking, right?"

Charlie nodded.

"You know, I'm all for a little self-medicating the pain and hurt away once and a while, but you ain't doing yourself any favors. I'm not saying you have to be nice to your stepmother, but she doesn't deserve your disdain."

"My what?"

"Your wrath, Charles. Your anger. She didn't take your mother away, and she won't ever replace her. She's only loving your dad, and from how she reacted to your dad cancelling your graduation party maybe you too."

Charles nodded.

"Anyway, you can't keep numbing your pain either. Sooner or later you're going to have to deal with what's eating at you, and the longer you put that off, trust me, the worse it'll get."

Charlie's stomach knotted because his grandfather's words reminded him too much of the things Lily had said their last night together. "What do you do in New York?" Charlie asked.

Seth went along with Charlie's blatant change in subject. "I own a bar and restaurant in Harlem."

"Really? What's she like?" Charlie asked.

"She's a nice little place, not too big, not too small…"

"I meant Harlem, Pops."

"Oh, Harlem is beautiful. There is no place like it on earth, and there never will be. Her streets have seen history, tragedy, comedy, and triumph. Harlem is one of a kind."

"Sounds like it. So what's the name of this restaurant?"

"The Pearl."

"Wow, you're serious? You own a restaurant? Get outta here. I thought you were joking or something."

Seth chuckled. "What did you think I did?"

"I dunno. Retired maybe, I hadn't thought about it. I did just meet you yesterday, and I know you aren't the average grandfather after watching you deal with Stony and Frank today. That's why I asked, Pops."

Charlie's words reminded Seth once again of all he'd missed in the boy's life and regret gnawed at the base of his skull. "Well, I spend most days at The Pearl."

"The Pearl? Huh, okay."

"What, you don't like the name?"

"It's all right. Could be cooler though."

"My partner and I named it that after your grandmother. Her nickname was Pearl."

"Well in that case, it's a great name."

"Damn right it is."

"So I'm gonna guess there are no stripper poles in the back?"

"Do I look like Stony to you?" Seth asked with an edge in his tone. He could feel a headache coming on.

"Nope. You sure don't, my bad," Charlie said with a smile. "What kind of food do you serve at The Pearl?"

"Soul food with some Latin dishes as well."

"I haven't had any of that in awhile."

"You too busy eating burgers from Pee Wee's."

"Stymies."

"Same difference."

"Seriously, why'd you open a restaurant? You like to cook or something?"

"Paulie came up with the idea of just owning a bar actually. I thought it made sense since we weren't getting any younger, and there's no retirement plan for ripping through the streets. Then we expanded, and that gave us the ability to help out a community that needed some help. The Pearl allowed us to give back a little and help heal a corner of Harlem at least in a different way than we had in our younger days. We bring in jazz musicians, offer people a place to eat and drink that's still true to the community, and give jobs to young people who've been in trouble and can't find work. We give em a trade that they can take with them wherever they go. Do for them what wasn't done for me or Paulie. And it was ownership. There is nothing in the world like owning your own, be it a house or a business. Knowing you're in charge, you call the shots, you make it happen, there is no greater feeling in the world, Charles."

Charlie was about to ask another question, but Seth cut him off.

"It's late, son, I'm tired and you have a big day ahead of you tomorrow. You need to head home and get some beauty sleep."

With a frown Charlie agreed. "Okay, Pops, but I've got more questions."

"Good. I admire an inquisitive mind. Oh, and here," Seth said pulling out a thumb drive from the armrest. "This is a collection of jazz standards by Charlie Parker, Monk, Mile, Dizzy and a few other cats for you to enjoy. I want it back, understand?"

"Cool. Thanks, Pop. See you tomorrow?"

"Of course but I won't be at graduation for obvious reasons."

Charlie paused. He was about to voice his disappointment with his grandfather's decision but kept that to himself. "Fine. I understand. Night, Pop."

"G'night son. Thanks for the visit and try to enjoy tomorrow."

"No promises."

Seth watched Charlie as he pulled onto the main road as John Coltranes's *In A Sentimental Mood* softly eased from the Cadillac's Bose speakers. For the first time since he'd been there, Seth felt hopeful that his grandson wasn't a total lost cause.

52

Charlie walked down the aisle amidst all of the pomp and circumstance of graduation with little enthusiasm. Despite the fact that this was one of the biggest days of his life, Charlie simply wanted the day over with as quickly as possible. As he neared his assigned seat, he caught sight of his dad and stepmom, who sat among the school board members and the other local dignitaries in one of the front rows. Even with his grandfather's words from last night still banging around in his head, he simply couldn't find it in him to smile or wave for Bailey's frantic picture-taking efforts. Charlie continued to ignore her and instead looked around for the one person he'd wanted most to share the day with, but she was nowhere in sight.

The second he'd arrived for the ceremony he had searched the cafeteria's sea of smiling graduates for Lily's face, but she'd never shown up. From time to time he habitually scanned the area, but deep down Charlie knew she was well on her way to New York if not already there, starting her dream to become a film director. He looked forward to the day when he could buy a ticket to see her first film.

When the class stood, Charlie snapped out of his own thoughts to watch the school principle and Clarrisa's parents hoisting a purple flag in Clarrisa's honor to fly under her state championship flag. Sniffles could be heard throughout the graduating class. When the principle requested a moment of silence for the memory of Clarissa Moore, Charlie could no longer keep the tears from welling up, and he made no move to stop them as they fell. His funny vibrant friend was gone too, just like Lily. However, he would never get the chance to see Clarissa again, hear her voice, or watch her burn up the track as she defeated her opponents with laughable ease. He clenched his fist. Her senseless death ate at him. It always would.

After everyone sat down, Charlie mentally checked out of the ceremony completely. When it was his turn to cross the stage his neighbor had to shake him awake. Charlie chuckled humorlessly as the valedictorian wound up her speech about not being afraid of the future, and when she said it was "theirs for the taking" Charlie fought back the urge to yell "bullshit!" As his cheering classmates tossed their caps in the air, Charlie simply stood stoic waiting for everyone to get out of his way, so he could meet up with his boys.

"Well, that was fun," Gavin said when the three friends finally found each other.

"I think an acid eye drip would have been more enjoyable," Chad said with a dry hostility that mirrored Charlie's mood.

Charlie looked closely at his friend. "Oh my God, are you sober?"

"Don't make a big deal out of it but yes. Thankfully, however, the day is young."

"What's with the purple flag? Why purple?" Gavin asked looking up.

"It was Clarissa's favorite color," Charlie stated.

"Well then that makes sense," Gavin said. "You seen Lily?"

"She ain't here. She's probably already in New York."

"Well then I hope you smashed that before she left, nigga," Chad said with a laugh.

"Shut the fuck up, Chad," both Charlie and Gavin said.

Chad shrugged. "Whatever."

Gavin looked around and spotted Bailey waving at them. "Come on. Mothers want pictures, and dads want to go home," he said.

"They aren't the only ones," Charlie mumbled before joining the group photo shoot.

On the drive home Charlie stayed silent and let Bailey fill in the awkward tension. Charlie would have loved some jazz at that moment, anything but her jack hammering, high-pitched inane chatter. Once home, he and his sour mood retreated to his bedroom. While Charlie felt a small sense of pride for graduating, he couldn't shake the feeling that it was for nothing since the likely outcome of summer would result in either years in jail or ending up an orphan. His stepmother interrupted several times urging him to eat, but he ignored her as usual and eventually fell asleep still in his dress clothes and robe.

Two hours later Charlie stepped out of the shower and changed, figuring his friends would be by shortly. While he waited, he visited the Facebook page set up in honor of Clarissa and left a comment before doing something he'd avoided since the day of Clarrisa's funeral. He checked Lily's status.

He'd been right. Four days ago she'd announced that she was on her way to New York and bid a fond farewell to Ohio, her friends, and family, promising to visit soon, which he knew she wouldn't actually do for a long while. He hated that she was gone but also envied her freedom. Lily was fearless in his mind, choosing to pick up and go, to chase her dreams, and follow her passions. He never thought about doing that himself. Chasing dreams sometimes seemed like too much work. He had started and stopped working on his "novel" claiming he hadn't done or seen anything yet. When in reality he had given up.

Charlie growled at the knock on his door but answered it. He'd expected his stepmother with her hands on her hips, wearing something clingy, and trying to get him to eat again, but instead it was Gavin and Chad. Charlie sighed in relief. He didn't want to think anymore. The effort was giving him a headache.

His friends' arrival quickly brightened his cranky mood. Both laughed about how much they'd hauled in at their "lame" parties as Gavin broke out a small dime bag and rolled a joint.

"Is that just for me? That's kinda small for all of us to be sharin, Gav," Chad said.

"Be easy, pasty. This shit will blow your mind. It's more than enough, trust me," Gavin said and lit up. Charlie opened his window and stuffed a towel at the bottom of his door.

"Holy shit," Chad said as he coughed and passed the smoke to Charlie. "Fuck is that?"

"It's called The Surge," Gavin said laughing. "Smoke up, man. We's officially ed-u-ma-cated."

Charlie shook his head at his friend's silliness and took a long slow drag. He needed escape, and he needed it fast. Within fifteen minutes all that was left of Gavin's powerful joint was ashes and a roach. The boys draped themselves around the room relaxed and content.

"Yo, nigga, was that really your granddaddy that came by the other day?" Chad asked, his voice thick.

"Yeah, fucking trippy."

"Your grandfather is really in town?" Gavin asked.

Chad lifted his head from the designer beanbag chair in the corner. "Isn't that what I said, chink?"

"Yeah, but I can't believe half the shit that comes out of your mouth anymore, white bread. Most of the time you so high I bet you don't know what you're saying or doing."

Chad dropped his head back again and spoke to the ceiling. "You make a convincing argument, sir."

The three of them fell out into laughter. "You kill me when you do your father's voice," Charlie said.

"You're an idiot, Chad," Gavin said.

"You make another convincing argument, young man," Chad said again in a false baritone.

Waving away Chad in dismissal, Gavin turned to Charlie. "Anyway, when you said your car was at your grandfather's hotel I thought that was like some kind of code for you getting laid," he said unable to contain his laughter. When he composed himself he asked, "Is this your grandfather on your mom's side?"

"Father's."

"I thought he was dead," Gavin said.

"Me too until two days ago."

"Charlie, that old man scared the piss out of me when I opened the door. I swear I thought he was some hit man or something," Chad said.

Charlie chuckled. "Yeah, Pops can be intimidating as hell when he wants to be. Other times, he's really cool. I can talk to him about almost anything."

"What's his name?" Gavin asked.

"Seth."

"Same last name as yours?"

"I guess so."

"Let's Google him," Gavin said whipping out his phone.

"Are you serious?" Charlie asked.

"Why not? What's the worse that could happen?"

"I could find out he's a wanted fugitive running from the law maybe."

"That'd be so cool," Gavin said as he launched his phone's browser. Charlie moved next to him, and a heartbeat after he typed 'Seth Jackson' into the search engine, their jaws dropped. A mug shot of a face almost the splitting image of Charlie stared back at them along side dozens of search results including news clips and bio information. They looked at each other and quickly moved to Charlie's desktop. Silence descended as the boys clicked on the first link.

> The NYPD once considered Seth Jackson to be one of the most dangerous men in Harlem along with his partner Paul "Paulie" Johnson. In the seventies, they led one of the area's most ruthless gangs, The Known Men. Because of their ferocity, the NYPD and the FBI coordinated their efforts to take down the gang's leadership and dismantle The Known Men. While the two law enforcement entities tried numerous times to tie the gang to various crimes, especially a rash of armored car hijackings in New York and New Jersey, they were never able to secure convictions on any of the charges brought against the gang. Authorities suspected the members of money laundering, extortion, racketeering, armed robbery, murder, and numerous cases of assault with a deadly weapon.

> The original version of The Known Men formed in the 1930's to fight the Italian mob's attempt to take control of the numbers racket in Harlem. However with the rise of the Nation of Islam and the Civil Rights movements in the fifties and sixties the earlier Known Men dissipated. In the seventies, Seth Jackson and Paul Johnson reconstituted the Harlem-based group to

combat the rise in drug crimes and other gangs' attempts to move into the area and expand the lucrative Harlem drug market. Rumor had it that Seth Jackson gave an impassioned speech in front of hundreds at the Alhambra Ballroom of New York. That speech is believed to be what lead to the resurrection of The Known Men. While no recordings or notes exist, most in Harlem believe the urban legend that Seth Jackson was the author of these words. "It is time to rise up again, bear arms again, and be willing again to defend Harlem at any cost from police brutality and the onslaught of heroin that has flooded her streets and torn at the soul of the once treasured stronghold of Black strength and pride."

Eventually the new Known Men, whose territory extended from the East River to the Hudson River and as far north as the Audubon Ballroom on 165th Street and as far south as 110th Street and the tip of Central Park, began fighting a two pronged enemy, Harlem's crumbling deindustrialized economy and the escalating violence from police-protected drug kingpins. With Harlem's slow downward spiral, in the late seventies and early eighties The Known Men were engaged in an all out war as established drug sellers branched out and turf battles with Puerto Rican and Italian gangs increased. Unable to combat the on-going drug epidemic that exploded due to crack cocaine, and with Seth Jackson's manslaughter conviction, the vigilante group dissipated in the mid-eighties."

"Holy shit, Charles!" Chad whispered. "Your grandfather was a bad ass gangster."

"A big one apparently," Gavin chimed in. "Look. It even says here that he was convicted for manslaughter in 1974. Can I meet him? I've never met a felon."

"No, chink, can WE meet him?" Chad corrected.

Charlie shook himself out of his awe. While he knew from the visit to Romare's yesterday that his grandfather was no punk, he'd had no idea Pops was once a man feared and hated. "Sure. I don't see why not."

"Cool, let's go," Chad said quickly, grabbing his keys and tugging on his shoes.

The three boys immediately took off down the stairs. Charlie glanced at his father scooping up a spoonful of ice cream as he went over yet another stack of papers at the kitchen counter, but he didn't bother to say a word to him. While Charlie's father may have grounded him the night before, he rarely enforced his punishments, and Charlie dashed out the front door followed by his two friends.

Chad was still too high to drive, so Charlie got behind the wheel of his friend's graduation present that he'd already had for two weeks, an Audi A8. When Charlie hit the ignition button, the stereo rumbled to life under them pounding out Chad's favorite song of the moment, *Wth* by Jhene Aiko. Charlie backed out of the driveway and threw the car in drive. Wearing a mischievous smile, his first genuine smile all day, Charlie gripped the wheel, hit the gas, and the three boys tore off across town to visit a legend.

53

After slowly making his way through Saturday evening's traffic, which clogged nearly every road in Boardman that held a restaurant or bar, Charlie steered the Audi into the space next to Seth's Cadillac. Charlie sent a quick text, and minutes later he proudly introduced his larger than life grandfather to his friends.

"A threesome, huh?" Seth asked quickly assessing that all three of the new graduates were stoned. He hid his disappointment, understanding that nothing was going to change the state of the three young men tonight. "You boys hungry?"

"I could eat," Gavin said.

"Seriously, we could all eat," Chad said rubbing his stomach and grinning.

"Okay, get in my car then. Where do you boys want to go?" Seth asked as he got behind the wheel. "And if anyone of you says Stymie's, you get a punch in the throat," he said glaring at each of his passengers.

"What are you hungry for, Mr. Jackson?" Gavin asked.

"Call me Seth, kid. Mr. Jackson was my grandfather, and I haven't had a good steak in a while."

"Then you might like this place called Fire. They've got the best steaks between Cleveland and Pittsburgh," Gavin said.

"You know how to get there?"

"We all know how to get there, Pop," Charlie said with a wide grin and glassy eyes.

"Well?" Following Charlie and Gavin's instructions, Seth jumped on the highway and headed north.

"Pop, tell Gavin and Chad what you told me about jazz and how hip hop is actually jazz on steroids."

"Why don't you tell em? They might buy it coming from you."

Charlie attempted to explain the relationship between jazz and hip hop and how rap songs merely mimic the patterns of jazz tunes. When Gavin or Chad asked questions Charlie couldn't answer Seth jumped in and cleared up any confusion. The conversation was lively and stayed that way even after the hostess seated the foursome at an oversize booth.

"Since all of you boys graduated this afternoon, this is my graduation gift. The meal's on me. Get whatever you like."

"Ummmmm…thanks, pops, but can I get a real present?" Charlie asked.

"Depends."

"I want to drive your car."

"You enjoy that steak, okay?" Seth said which amused Gavin and Chad.

As they looked over the menus Seth asked, "So how was graduation by the way?"

"Maudlin," Chad said.

"Well that's a first? Why so?"

"First the crying because of Clarissa and then the cheers that high school was finally over then more crying because 'I'll never…sniff…see you…sniff…again so take…sniff…a selfie with me' nonsense. Like I told these two clowns earlier, an acid eye drip would have been more enjoyable."

Seth shook his head at the white kid's description and saw beyond the caustic façade to the boy trying way too hard to appear unaffected by everything. "Who's Clarissa? And why did she make everyone cry?"

Seth instantly felt Charlie stiffen next to him when he asked about the girl, but it was Gavin who explained that Clarissa was their classmate who had been gunned down recently in the mall. "Yeah, I remember seeing that on the news. They claim to still have no leads or a clue as to who is responsible. Damn shame. I'm sorry to hear about your friend, Charlie."

"How'd you know she was my friend?" he asked.

Seth gave his grandson's back a quick rub with a knowing smile.

After the waiter took their orders, Gavin dove in. "Okay, I can't contain myself any more, sir. Can I ask you something, Mr. Jackson?"

"Sure, Chad," Seth said.

"That's Gavin, Pop. That one's Chad."

"My apologies, Gavin. What's on your mind?"

"Were you a gangster?"

Seth smiled. "You been talking to Charles' dad?"

"No, we Googled you," he said.

Seth laughed and leaned back a bit surprised. "Really? That's a first. I've never Googled myself. What came up?"

"Your mug shot from the seventies and bunch of articles about you, Paulie Johnson, and your gang, The Known Men," Gavin said.

"We weren't a gang, son."

"That's what the Internet said," Chad replied.

"And the Internet has never been wrong?" Seth asked the young man. "Look, The Known Men were protectors and defenders of Harlem dating back to the days of Dutch Schultz and Murder Inc. You know about Murder Incorporated, right?"

All three boys shook their heads.

"Go home and Google them and Dutch when you get the chance. In the thirties and forties the mafia moved into Harlem wanting a piece of the numbers racket, and Dutch Schultz was the main pain in the ass. Murder Inc. was like his enforcement. They came up into Harlem doing whatever they could—robberies, brutal beatings, murder—to get in on the millions of dollars running through the streets of Harlem back then. The Known Men stood up and fought back against Murder Inc. and the mob alongside Madam St. Clair and Bumpy Johnson to get them bastards out of Harlem."

"Were they successful?" Gavin asked.

"That's all relative."

"What do you mean it's relative?" Charlie asked.

"First Murder Inc. killed Dutch, and then a member of Murder Inc. turned rat on them. He exposed them to the world which was the end of them for the most part," Seth said as their waiter brought their appetizers.

"But you weren't a part of that crew, right?" Chad asked.

"No, that was way before my time. After the mob turned their attention to other areas in New York and Murder Inc. fell apart, The Known Men went their separate ways. The Mob never really left Harlem, but they were no longer in the streets gunning us down, especially once the Nation of Islam gained strength. Anyway, some thirty years later in the early seventies, my partner, Paulie, and I brought The Known Men back," Seth said shaking his head. "We was real young then and a whole lot of stupid, but the beautiful vibrant gem that had been Harlem, our home, was crumbling around us. Parasites sold nasty shit like heroin and PCP out in the open like kids trading baseball cards. The police and the government stood by and did nothing. Soldiers back from Nam and kids were getting strung out and dying of overdoses while addicts mugged old folks in broad daylight for whatever little bit of money they had. We had to do something. We couldn't just sit around and bitch.

"Everything Malcolm and King had stood for and fought so hard to win was being flushed down the sewers as Harlem became overrun with hardcore drug pushers and addicts, so we fought like hell to get that shit off the streets when the 'authorities' refused to help us. We robbed dealers, dirty cops, mob associates, you name it. We used any and all means available, but no matter what we did, we couldn't get rid of it. I like to think we stemmed then flow some though at least for a while, but then LSD came, and when crack hit, all we could do was save what and who we could."

Charlie's face scrunched in concentration. "Why wouldn't the police help, Pop?"

Seth's hand stopped midway to his mouth, and he stared in shock at his grandson. Knowing how Charlie grew up, he immediately understood the boy's naiveté on matters like this, so he couldn't be mad at him. No one had taken the time to educate the boy.

Seth inhaled deeply and slowly explained. "Charlie, they didn't care. Harlem was a Black community, and the lily-white New York City police department and the government of this country wasn't worried about the crime or the death toll of the Negros up in Harlem. We were on our own. I'm sure to some, we were getting exactly what we deserved considering the shit storm Black folk had caused during the Civil Rights Movement."

Confusion swam across his grandson's face while the other two boys sat silently.

"Son, you do know about the Civil Rights Movement don't you? Malcolm X? King?"

"Yeah, I learned some in school. King marched on Washington to get Black people the right to go to white schools and not have colored sections on the bus and stuff. Malcolm X was an extremist and hated all the white people," Charlie said pleased with himself.

Seth cocked his head in surprise. "That's all you know, son? Didn't your dad teach you anything about the history of your people?" Seth asked as the waiter placed four heavy platters of seared red meat around their table.

"Ummm…no, Pop," Charlie said with a humorless laugh, tucking his napkin into the collar of his shirt. "Dad works. Dad's always working."

"I see. Well first off, Malcolm didn't hate white people. He just loved Black people more. He believed from his childhood and the way his parents and his family had been treated at the hands of white folk that we shouldn't trust anyone over our own, and that went especially for whites. His sole focus was on uplifting his people and giving us a sense of pride. His parents were Garveyites. Do you, do any of you know who Marcus Garvey was?" Seth asked the table.

All three boys shook their heads as they chewed, and all Seth could do was shake his head right along with them in frustration.

"You kids have access to all kinds of information today right at your damn fingertips, but if it's not staring you in the face you don't care. I want you to remember this one thing if you never remember another damn thing in your life, Charles. Whenever you see a Black person in this country, know that the only reason that person is here, like you are here, is for one reason and one reason only. White people saw us as nothing more than an economic opportunity. Our ancestors were free labor, chattel that maximized plantation owners' profits by at least a thousand percent. Slavery created cottage industries. Businesses cropped up, and even men without land or crops became wealthy because of us. That's the only reason why we are here."

All three boys had set down their forks as the considered Seth's words. Their meals forgotten, they simply stared quietly at him.

"Wow, I had never thought of it that way, Mr. Jackson," Gavin said. "I'd simply considered it a part of history. I never thought about it in today's world."

"There's no other way to think about it, Gavin."

"Yeah but…ya'll are free now, right?" Chad asked.

"What's free look like to you?" Seth asked.

Chad glanced nervously at his friends for help as he tried to answer. "The ability to come and go when you want and to go where you want. Free means getting to eat what you want, say what you want, wear what you want, you know what I mean…freedom and shit."

"Chad is it?" Seth asked staring at the pasty yet good looking young man. Chad nodded. "Keep this in mind, Chad. I know you may think that everything was solved fifty-some years ago, but the fact is, everything the Black man has is either through the benevolence or the reluctance of the white man. We wouldn't have gained what little we have without whites, and we'd have more if whites didn't continue to hold us back. You say freedom is the ability to come and go when you want, but other than Charles here, how many Black people live in your gated community? If Charles didn't live there, could he waltz in and visit you whenever he wanted? Or would the Canfield police stop him on his way through your gates?"

"You waltzed in," Chad retorted.

"You've seen my car, right?"

The boy fell silent.

"What is a Garveyite?" Gavin asked.

"A follower of Marcus Garvey."

"And he was?" Charlie asked.

"I could sit here all night and talk to you about Marcus Garvey and other Black men like him, but we don't have that kind of time. Ya'll need to eat up before your food gets cold."

Charlie cut another piece of steak. "How'd you learn so much, Pop?"

"By having meaningful conversations with people smarter than me and doing something that seems is a lost art these days."

"What's that?"

"Reading, son. Last lesson of the night, Charles. Hear me and remember this. The most dangerous person on this planet is an educated Black man. They can take away everything you own—all of your possessions, your money, even your family, but the one thing they can never take from you is your smarts. Once you have that, it's yours for life, son, and they fear that kind of Black man more than anything else. Remember that."

"What's to fear?"

"Because then you see the distractions for what they are. Then you can no longer be lied to. You suddenly realize that those Jordan's everybody is clamoring for isn't the end all be all. You understand that latest phone ain't nothing but a damn phone, and the one you already have is fine. When you get educated, when you become well read, your eyes open. You see everything differently. The veil is lifted, and you can finally discern what matters from what doesn't."

"If you're so smart, how'd you end up in jail?" Chad asked.

"That's a long story."

"Don't mean we don't wanna know," Charles said.

"Some other time, boys. The history lessons are over for the day, but feel free to do some more Googling. It's almost closing time, and you boys should start heading home. I don't want your parents to worry, especially yours Charles," Seth said as he placed a credit card in the tray that held the bill.

On the drive back no one said a word, and the sound of Charlie Parker's *Parker's Mood* filled the Caddy as the boys continued to digest everything they'd heard. Once they were back at the hotel, Gavin and Chad thanked Seth for dinner and got in the Audi to wait for Charlie.

"This is for you," Seth said as he handed an envelope to Charlie. "I wanted you to know...I'm proud of you for graduating today. I know you probably think it's small potatoes and that it was no big deal, but a lot of great men in this world never did what you did today, so what you've accomplished is pretty special. I...I wish I could have been there, son."

Charlie swallowed the emotion that suddenly swelled in him. "Thank you, Pop. I...I really needed to hear that today."

"Don't go spending that all at once, or I'll punch you in the throat, you hear me?" Seth said with a smile. "Remember what I said about distractions." Charlie hugged his grandfather and got a kiss on his head in return for good measure.

As his grandson drove away, Seth knew he would cherish that hug for the rest of his life.

54

"Yo, it's dead over here too. I'm tellin you, this beef is killin the summer for real," Ripper said after he puffed and passed the blunt to the backseat. "It's Saturday night, and ain't no body out this motherfucka, man. No bitches, no homies, ain't no house parties poppin, nothin."

Ripper and his boys cruised through the wrong side of town with the bass of Yurhonor's *Hands Up* at a low thump. "This that real shit right here, nigga," he said as he bobbed his head to the beat. In the passenger seat, his younger brother Kay-Kay rattled off the lyrics with ease as he also nodded to the rumbling rhythm. Behind them slumped a stoic Manny and a nervous Petey.

High and restless, the four young men had searched all night for something to get into. When Ripper had jumped on the highway and taken one of the east side exits, he'd known this stunt would make Frank's head explode when word got to him, but he didn't care. He was itching for a fight. Ripper rolled his 98 Cutlass Supreme slow and easy through the quiet streets of Wolf's territory. The danger and arrogance fed his high. His boys all had pistols in their laps, and Ripper caressed his AK 47 as they puffed and passed blunts laced with PCP.

The manic laughter and hardcore rap that spilled from their open windows didn't go unnoticed. Anyone who saw the Cutlass quickly passed the word that something was up.

Eventually Ripper pulled into the parking lot of a tired stone church and eased out of the Olds and into the night. He cracked open a forty-ounce of malt liquor and poured a long swallow onto the uneven pavement. "For my homie, Blake. Rest in peace, nigga," he said before he took a swig and passed the bottle to his brother.

Kay-Kay swayed on his feet and leaned against the front fender, laughing as the world spun to a slow stop around him. Before he could take a sip, he caught sight of a black truck with heavily tinted windows pulling into the opposite end of the lot. It came to a stop and idled quietly in the distance. Kay-Kay put the bottle on the ground, gripped the butt of his pistol, and gestured to the other car. "Yo, who dis?"

Ripper glanced over his shoulder and with a broad grin sauntered towards the SUV with his arms outstretched. For a few long minutes he stood in defiance while the three other boys tightened their grips on their guns waiting to see if anything was about to jump off.

Slowly the Explorer backed out of the lot and took off. Ripper sucked his teeth and spat in disgust. "Punk ass East Side niggas. You can't even call them niggas pussies cause you'd be dissin pussy if you do." His boys doubled over in laughter as he settled on the hood of his ride to finish off the rest of the drink and smoke. "Yeah, these East Side bitches know what's up," he said as he brushed ash from his clothes.

Suddenly, as if on cue, the quiet night shattered as the black truck roared back into the parking lot with guns blasting. The two cars in tow also had their windows down, unloading round after round. Ripper jumped off the hood and returned fire with his semi-automatic. His boys followed suit.

Bullets flew in all directions with Ripper's AK punching a trail of holes into the cars as they skidded to a stop. Despite the additional cars, Ripper's chopper and the Mac 10's the three others were firing completely overwhelmed the East Side crew. They swallowed their pride and tore off after only seconds.

"Go home, bitches!" Ripper yelled. In the distance he could hear faint sirens and knew it was time to leave the scene as well. With more laughter he and his boys piled back into the car and tore out of the lot themselves.

Alistair Conrad got to his feet after dropping to the kitchen floor when the shooting across the street started. He'd been washing dinner dishes after he'd put his four-year-old son to bed. Making a note to sweep the kitchen floor before he went to bed that night, he brushed his clothes as he called his son's name.

"Kenyatta!"

When silence answered him he made his way to his son's bedroom. "Kenya, don't you hear me calling you, boy?" Alistair said as he flicked on the overhead light. The growing dark stain across his son's back stopped him in his tracks. "NO!"

Alistair rushed to the bed and turned his little boy's lifeless body over as blood coated his fire engine sheets and teddy bear pajamas. He felt for a pulse. Finding none, he snatched his son into his arms and ran for his car.

"Daddy's here, baby. Daddy's got you, Kenya. Hold on, baby. Be strong for Daddy. Can you do that? I'm gonna take you to see mommy at the hospital, okay? She's gonna be so happy…so happy to see her baby," he said as tears momentarily blinded him. "Please God, please. Please don't take my boy. PLEASE!"

55

"I want his fucking ass in here, now!" bellowed Stony as he paced his office.

"You need to calm down, Stone," Frank reasoned. "The kid tried to play you. He ain't do nothing new there, so don't let your pride fuck witchu. We got bigger shit on the table than this boy's grandfather, know what I'm sayin?"

"Fuck that. This kid and his family are mine, and one way or another they are going to suffer. I don't give a damn who his grandfather is. I want him here, face to face, and I want to hear what he has to say. Go get him right the fuck now."

Fury flashed in Frank's eyes at the order. "Who you talking to like that?" he asked calmly.

Stony spun to stare at Frank but realized he'd crossed the line. He inhaled deeply and pulled himself together. "My bad, could you do me a favor and bring Charles here tonight, please?"

"You got it, but remember who you talking to, Stone. We boys and shit, but don't forget exactly who and what I am." Without another word Frank disappeared down the stairwell.

Stony took a seat at his desk and stared at his laptop screen. Sundays were typically quiet for Romare's and by early evening, Stony had killed some time researching Charlie's unknown "associate." When the face and intimidating mug shot and bio of a much younger Seth Jackson had appeared on his screen, Stony had nearly thrown his laptop across the room.

Stony's hands ran across his face. *What the hell is going on? That fucking kid has more connections than Cleveland airport. His father, the District Attorney, isn't going to save himself or his clueless son, and there is no way his grandfather, the one time leader of the motherfuckin Known Men, is going to save either one of them.* Determined that his plans would go forward, Stony poured himself a small tumbler of whiskey and waited for little Charlie Jackson.

Stony hid his fury behind a fake smile when Frank escorted a nervous Charlie into his office.

"What's up high school graduate? Had a good day yesterday?" Stony asked.

"Yeah, it was one of my better ones," Charlie said as Frank pushed him towards Stony's desk.

"Good. Sit down and lemme holla at you for a bit. How's gramps?"

Charlie was about to respond, but remembering his grandfather's words about giving up too much information, he stayed quiet. He knew Pop would be proud of him but pissed that these "baby gangsters" now knew about their connection.

"Yeah, we know who he is, mothafucka," Stony said easily. "What was all that 'my associate' bullshit? Why couldn't you be honest with me, Charlie? And here I thought we was friends."

Frank cracked a tight-lipped smile.

"I...I was following his lead," Charlie said.

"Yeah, he was hoping to gain and keep the upper hand. That whole 'I know who you are, but you don't know who I am' dance. I get it. I respect it, but it ain't gonna help you," Stony said, emphasizing his words by his finger hitting his desk. "Is gramps gonna pay your way?"

"I don't know."

"Well he may have the money you need, but if he doesn't, our deal still stands. You remember our deal, right?"

Charlie nodded his head.

"Lemme hear it."

"You want me to steal a painting, or you'll kill my dad."

"You owe me ten dollars, Frank. I told you he would remember." Stony leaned forward. "He thought you'd forget, but I told him you would remember," he whispered to Charlie before he pulled a Cuban Montecristo out of his uncle's antique nickel-plated humidor.

"You want a cigar?"

"Sure."

"You promise not to make a blunt out of it?"

"Never mind then," Charlie said.

"Yeah, that's what I thought. So how was graduation?" Stony asked.

"It was cool."

"Be proud of that, man. Be proud. Not everyone graduates high school. Hell some don't know what a high school even looks like. Remember that, Chuck. You accomplished something special yesterday. You're going to college, right?"

"I want to, but you know…" Charlie said, his voice trailing off.

"No, I don't know. Know what?"

"Ummmm…if I don't pay you back and you kill my dad, I ain't gonna be able to afford college, so I don't know."

"Don't let set backs hold you back, Chuck," Stony said as he reclined his chair.

"Yeah, but that's a lot of money," Charlie said.

"True, but I'm sure you'll find a way to make it happen. So how well you know your grandfather?"

"Not all that well, only what he's told me so far. He says–" Charlie stopped talking.

"He says what?" Stony asked.

"He says we met before, but I don't remember."

"So as far as you're concerned this is your first time meeting him?"

Charlie nodded.

"Ain't that some shit. You've had quite a week, haven't you? You know about your gramps?"

"A little. He told me and some friends of mine some stories last night."

"Yeah, what did he say?" Stony asked, leaning on his desk.

Not wanting to give Stony and Frank any details they could use against his grandfather, Charlie relayed some of the least important information Seth told him yesterday. "He just told us about what things were like back in Harlem when he was coming up, why they reformed the Known Men after they ran the mafia out, stuff like that."

Stony and Frank laughed. "The Known Men didn't run the mafia out of Harlem. Their greed and Thomas Dewey did. Not saying them boys didn't have a hand in it or play a part, but they didn't run the mafia out of anywhere, believe that."

Charlie shrugged.

"What else he tell you?"

"He said the cops and the government allowed drugs to be sold openly in Harlem back in his day which is why he reformed the group, to push back," Charlie said.

"'Push back' sounds a lot cleaner than what truly went down. Don't get it twisted. The second chapter of The Known Men was far more ruthless than the first. Don't let your grandfather downplay shit. That man is a legend in certain circles, respected. Ain't that right, Frank?"

"Respected and feared." Frank's voice came from behind Charlie.

"That's right, and I can't help but wonder why the hell that man is here. Any ideas, Chuck?"

"No," Charlie said and shrugged.

"He seems to know a hell of a lot for him to show up out of the blue and no one to have said anything to him. Frank, you tell him anything?"

"Nope." Frank's disembodied voice again rang out from the dark.

"I ain't tell him a thing, which leaves you. You sure you didn't call in the troops?"

"I just met him," Charlie reasoned. His stomach knotted, and despite the central air working overtime, Charlie began to sweat. "All my life I was told my grandfather was dead, that he was a junkie who was gunned down in the streets of Harlem with a needle in his arm. How could I have called him and told him anything when I didn't even know he was alive?"

After a long silence, Frank said, "Kid's got a point."

"Yeah, maybe he does. Mr. Graduate, you thirsty?"

"Sure," Charles said about to shrug when Seth's words came to him again.

"Frank, take our graduate down to the bar and get him anything he wants. Since he's not driving, he's cool. Whatever you want, tonight it's on the house, all right?"

"All right," Charlie said and nearly fell off his chair when Frank put his hand on his shoulder.

When Frank returned Stony stopped pacing his office and asked, "You hook Charlie up?"

"Yeah, Sadie's got him. She's cozied up next to him at the bar with Turk playing chaperone. Last time he was here she couldn't take her eyes off him, so he's in good hands," Frank said as he sat confidently on the sofa. "Whatchu pacin for? You still stressin over gramps?"

"None of this adds up. If Charlie didn't call him, what brought Seth motherfucking Jackson to Ohio? Someone must have heard what was in the works for that kid."

"You gonna wear a hole in the damn floor the way you going. Remember when you told me about chance and coincidence and shit?" Frank asked rubbing his head. "Look we don't know what brought the old nigga out here, and we may never know, but we need to focus on what we need to do. We'll deal with gramps when the time comes."

Stony nodded. "Yeah, yeah...I'm just trippin."

Frank was about to respond when the roar of automatic gunfire thundered through the bar and screams shattered the normal hum of Romare's. Frank jumped up and yelled for Stony to stay put before rocketing headlong into the war zone downstairs. With a second wave of gunfire Stony smashed his cigar in the ashtray, grabbed his gun, ignored Frank's orders, and headed clumsily downstairs.

Screams and yells echoed off the walls as bullets continued to tear through the exterior. Mirrors, fixtures, and bottles at the bar exploded one after the other. From a crouched stance, Stony took in the chaos that had once been his comfortable stronghold. Customers ran for their lives, ducked for cover, or lay injured and bleeding. Some made a run for the side and back exits thinking the streets were a safer bet. The more he watched his place, the place he grew up in and at times wanted nothing to do with, resemble a shooting gallery the more outraged he became. He gripped his gun tighter, willed himself to his feet, and started making his way to the front.

Stony searched for Frank, but with all the confusion he was nowhere to be seen. Stony hoped like hell he wasn't somewhere dead. Another volley of shots rang out as tires squealed. Stony struggled towards the front entrance, but when he caught sight of the bar, pure dread stopped him where he stood, and icy fingers gripped the back of his neck. Destroyed liquor bottles left growing puddles of liquid as shards of glass reflected the colored lights. Standing alone in the middle of the mess, frozen stiff and covered in blood, was Charlie.

The kid didn't duck. In fact, he wasn't even blinking. His eyes were wide amber pools filled with terror and shock. Warm blood and brains dripped from his smooth cheeks and chin, and his once grey polo shirt was stained a deadly dark red.

Stony moved toward Charlie just as Frank walked in from outside looking disgusted. He calmly assessed the entire bar in a swooping glance and headed over to Stony and Charlie.

Stony gripped Charlie's shoulders, but the kid didn't flinch. "Fuck! Is this his blood?" Stony asked as an eerie silence descended.

Frank shook his head. "It's Turk's."

"Turk's been hit?"

"Yeah."

"He okay? Where's he at?" Stony asked as people started to get themselves together.

"Turk's dead," Frank said, nodding to the bartender's body on the other side of the bar. "The kid's wearin what's left of his head."

Stony leaned over the bar to find Turk's small wiry body crumpled on the floor with the side of his skull missing. Stony swallowed to keep his dinner down. "Fuck! The kid can't be here like this. The cops will be here any minute, so he can't be."

"Well, he can't go the fuck home looking like this," Frank said as they led Charlie to the back.

"Take him to Harlem. Let him handle the kid. I need you back as soon as you can."

Frank handed Stony his gun. "In case they double back before five-oh show. I got another."

Without another word, Frank slid out the back exit pushing a catatonic Charlie. "Just hurry the fuck up, Frank," Stony said as he slammed the heavy back door closed and locked it.

56

Frank had the car pulled over on a little side street in a neighborhood that understood not to pay too much attention to what happened outside their doors. He leaned against the passenger side front fender with his arms folded as Charlie threw up in the scrubby weeds. Frank had known it was coming. He'd seen people in shock before and knew this was part of the ritual. His cell buzzed for the fifth time, but he ignored the call.

Frank had taken the dark, quiet streets instead of the heavily trafficked and patrolled main roads knowing they'd need to stop at least once. He was glad Charlie vomited before they got into Boardman. He'd have a hard time explaining to the cops, who acted like border patrol between Boardman and Youngstown, why Charlie was soaked in blood. Frank had tried his best to clean up the kid, but there was only so much that could be done with some bottles of water and the paper towels Frank kept in the trunk.

After a swig of water to wash out his mouth and a piece of gum, Charlie mumbled that he thought he was done.

"You sure, nigga?" Frank asked as he again ignored another call. "I can't have you throwing up in my whip."

"Yeah," Charlie croaked.

"Good, now get the fuck in the car. I've got places to go, and people to hurt. I don't have time to be babysittin your ass all night," Frank said before he stuffed Charlie back in the car and seconds later threw the car into drive, impatient to dump the kid on grandpa. Frank's phone buzzed again. This time he answered. "Yeah?"

"Where are you?" Stony's voice boomed throughout the car's cabin.

"About five minutes away from dropping the kid off. Whattup? Any more drama?"

"It's a madhouse, police, coroner, ambulances. It's crazy, man."

244

"No doubt. I'll be back in about twenty."

"They hit my fucking place, Frank!" Stony yelled which made the kid flinch.

"And we'll hit back, believe that. Trust me, them niggas gon pay," Frank said and disconnected the call. A second later, another came in, but Frank ignored it.

Charlie closed his eyes, swallowed hard, and tried not to think about Turk's head exploding like a cantaloupe. The only time he had seen anything remotely close to tonight was in the movies, but no one yelled, "Cut!" and Turk didn't get up off the floor smeared in phony blood. Another wave of nausea hit him again as he recalled brains and blood rushing at him in an unavoidable wave. The old bartender had been there one second, talking and smiling a toothless smile, and the next he was gone, smeared all over Charlie. Charlie cracked the window, but the hot, humid, summer air didn't help.

"Fuck. How ya feelin, kid? You want more air?" Frank asked. When Charlie didn't answer, Frank immediately cut the tires and quickly slowed to a stop.

Charlie pushed open the door as dry heaves broke through the silent night.

Minutes later Frank glided his BMW into the hotel lot and dragged a dazed Charlie into the thankfully empty lobby. "What room, kid?" Frank shook him when he didn't get a response. "What room?"

Charlie blinked rapidly and finally choked out the room number.

Seth was lounging on his bed as he clicked through late night TV shows when pounding on his door startled him. He snatched his Glock from under his pillow. Through the peephole he saw a haggard and bloodied Charlie accompanied by Stony's hammer. Seth yanked open the door.

"What the fuck happened?" When Charlie only stared blankly back at him, Seth grabbed his grandson and carefully led him to the bed.

"He was at Stony's when we got hit," Frank said standing in the threshold.

"Hit? Was he hit?" Seth asked tucking his gun into his rear waistband and quickly searching Charlie's torso and arms.

"Nah, unless you talking about getting hit by bone, brains, and blood. He be all right. He just saw his first dead body for real tonight, and he's still in shock."

Satisfied Charlie didn't have any physical injuries, he turned around to confront Frank. "Who's blood is this?"

"Our bartender's. He was standing next to Turk when he took one to the head. Glad it wasn't Chuck. Kid just graduated. Turk done lived his life, ya know?"

"Yeah, I know. Smart of you to bring him here, but how'd you know where I was?" Seth asked, eyeing the blasé killer on the other side of the doorframe.

"You don't think we know all about you, Harlem? You think we stupid? We knew where you was after that first sit down."

Not as stupid as they look, Seth thought and smiled.

"Yeah, we know exactly who you are, old timer."

"Fair enough, but answer me this. What the fuck was my grandson doin at your place?"

"Relax. We just wanted to talk."

"Relax? Your place got hit with my grand inside," Seth said. "Let me make this clear to you, youngin. You want to fuckin talk to Charlie, I better be there when you do, period!"

"Temper, temper, old man. That's fair. You got this?"

"Yeah, get the fuck outta here," Seth softly said as his hand went behind his back and gripped the butt of his gun.

"Watch your blood pressure. They say it's a killer." Frank said quietly before he turned his back and headed to the elevators.

Seth slammed the door and locked it. Seth sighed as he glanced at Charlie. *What are you doing to yourself, kid?* Heading into the bathroom, he turned on the shower and made the spray as tepid as possible. "Come on, son. Let's get you cleaned up," With a quick rub on the head, Seth took Charlie by the arm and led him into the bathroom, where he undressed him down to his boxers and ushered him into the shower. The water seemed to pull Charlie out of his haze. "You okay, son?"

"Yeah."

Seth didn't have the heart to correct him and simply lathered up a washrag and cleaned the blood, bone fragments, and flecks of flesh from his grandson's skin. Leaving his grandson under the therapeutic spray, Seth left the bathroom, keeping the door ajar in case the boy needed him.

Seth turned off the TV and stared out the window, past the lights of Boardman into the giant void of inky blackness in the distance. *The child is clueless. He's not wired to deal with any of this shit he's gotten himself in. Good thing I am.* He'd come close to losing Charlie tonight and was more determined than ever to see safely him through this mess. When Charlie emerged from the bathroom wrapped in a towel, Seth abandoned his morose thoughts. "You nothing but bones, boy. You could put on some weight."

Charlie looked at himself and shrugged.

"How are you feeling?"

"I…I don't know, Pops," Charlie answered. "What…what I saw tonight I won't ever forget."

"I know," Seth said as Charlie sat on the bed.

"A friend of mine…she was at the mall shooting a couple weeks ago. She tried to save Clarissa," Charlie said staring out the window at the same darkness that had moments before called to Seth. "Even stuck her finger in the hole in her neck trying to save her. She didn't even like Clarissa. I didn't get it, Pop. I didn't get it at all. Now I do. Now I understand."

"What do you understand, Charles?" Seth asked as he pulled out of his bag a pair of nylon shorts and a t-shirt.

"Why she was so angry. It could have been her that was shot that day easily and for nothing, not a damn thing, Pop."

"I remember the first time I saw a dead body. It messed with my head for a long, long time too, so I have a pretty good idea as to how you feel, son."

Charlie shook himself from the view to tug on the t-shirt and slide into the shorts under the towel. "When was that? When you saw your first body?"

"I was around your age, coming home one night from hanging out. I had some cats looking for me, and whenever I was rolling alone, I took the rooftops to avoid any nonsense on the streets. Anyway, a few months before that night, me and this new cat, Checkers, who'd just moved from Chicago, were on the basketball courts. Check had fouled me hard, and things got pretty heated.

"Paulie grabbed me, and others stepped in to break it up. Checkers had a mouth on him that was almost as big as he was, and he was big. He said something about how I should stop wearing panties when I played ball. I smiled but said nothing, so everyone though Checkers got the best of me. Truth be told, I ain't want no parts of Check, so fast forward back to me walking across the rooftops. Right before I almost get home, I find Check laying on my neighbors' rooftop, dead, choked out, eyes wide and unblinking, and a pair of pink panties shoved in his mouth."

"So what did you do?" asked Charlie.

"I sat up there for hours, staring at that boy. I couldn't take my eyes off him," Seth said. "It scared the shit out of me, but I couldn't stop looking at him. I may not have liked that boy, but he was someone's son. He must have brought pride and joy to someone at some point in his life. There had to be a point in his life where someone loved him more than they loved themselves, but that was done. He was gone."

"You know who did it?"

"No, but to this day I think Paulie did it," Seth admitted. "He's never copped to it, but I think it was him."

"Why?"

Seth took a long look at his grandson before speaking again. "He knew I was scared. He knew I was scared of that big Chicago boy and wanted nothing to do with him, and he wanted to send a message to me and everybody else in the neighborhood too."

What message, Pop?"

"For me, there was nothing to be scared of—ever. The message for everyone else was don't ever fuck with me," Seth said darkly.

Charlie swallowed hard. He'd seen that even though his grandfather was in his mid-sixties, he was still not a man to take lightly, not even a little bit, and he also knew people who were as dangerous as he was. "I think Stony and Frank know that too now."

"What'd they say to you?"

Charlie inhaled. "Stony told me that they knew all about you, who you were, where you came from, what kind of man you were, all that. They seemed to respect you a lot, but what they didn't get was why you're here, how you knew what was going on."

"What kind of man I am?"

"Yeah, when you were in the Known Men. They said the second chapter was way more violent than the first." When Seth said nothing, Charlie asked softly "What put you in jail Pops?"

Seth chuckled to himself and took the seat at the desk to face Charlie. "What landed me in jail was when I took a life for the first time. I had seen a number of dead bodies after Check, but none I ever had a hand in. Guys came back from the war. Many of them strung out on that shit, walking around like extras on *The Walking Dead*. Not eating, not sleeping, they simply moved from one high to the next until their bodies couldn't go anymore and gave out on the streets looking like a lump of dirty rags. Like I said last night, I was in my early twenties when Paulie and I regrouped The Known Men to fight the flood of drugs into Harlem. We wouldn't have had an issue if it had stayed amongst adults, but kids got caught up in it as well.

"So our crew of concerned Black men pushed back against the dealers. We also ripped them off. We definitely weren't angels, but we weren't peddling poison. We ripped off shipments, hit stash houses, burned down shooting dens, any and everything we could think to do to get that shit off our streets. Not only were we driving the dealers crazy, we were driving the cops crazy too. Both them and the dealers came at us hard, but they couldn't stop us.

"Pretty soon, though, one of us got caught and gave up me and Paulie as the leaders of the 'notorious gang.' They felt like with any organization, if they took off the head, the body would die, so they focused on Paulie and I."

Charlie moved to the edge of the bed, listening intently.

Seth continued, "By then your grandmother had already had your father. I was about twenty-three, and we still lived in the same place I grew up in. One night I was taking the rooftops home, keeping a low profile. It was late, so I was trying to be quiet as possible because when your dad got to cryin, gettin him quiet again was almost impossible. When I unlocked the door that led to the steps I knew something was off. The house didn't feel right. I closed the door and stood silent in the dark. Then I heard it. The window that led to the fire escape in the nursery made a particular noise when it opened, so when I heard the window come open, I waited.

"This figure silently slid out of the room into the hallway, heading my way. There wasn't a light on in the place, so he couldn't see me, but I saw him. He made his way into the living room and clicked on a flashlight. That's when I hit him with everything I had. We fought long and hard and loud. We broke furniture, shattered glass, and damn near woke the building. I eventually choke the fucking life out of him," Seth said as his trembling hands wrapped around an imaginary neck. He stopped and sat back, avoiding his grandson's stare.

"Once he was dead and I'd pushed him off me, there was a knock on the door. I'd told your grandma to call the police in the scuffle, so I went to unlock the door thinking it was them, but they kicked it in. Before I could say anything, they threw me to the floor and cuffed me.

"Come to find out the man I killed that night was a dirty cop, and the other cops found him with enough drugs on him that would have sent me away for decades. He was supposed to plant all that shit in my place while I was asleep. The cops that banged on my door already had a warrant to search the place and expected to arrest me for distribution. It's deeper than that, but you got the short version."

Charlie sat speechless.

"They still arrested me but charged me with manslaughter instead and tried to bury me under ten years of hard time. Then they added on an additional five for bad behavior."

"Bad behavior?"

"Fighting and shit. A lot of the guys we ripped off were in jail with me, and they all had beefs they wanted to settle, so we settled them."

"How old was my dad when you went to jail?"

"He was three going on four. A daddy's boy," Seth whispered.

"Why couldn't you defend yourself with some shit like self-defense or something. That guy was in your house. You had a right to defend yourself."

"Son, I was a Black man that killed a white cop. There is no self-defense in that situation, then or now. You gotta stop believing that justice sees no color. It always has, and it always will."

"Does dad know that they set you up?"

Seth laughed humorlessly. "To my knowledge, he don't know, never cared to know, and doesn't want to know. So no, he doesn't. It is what it is, Charles," Seth said rising from his chair. "How are you feeling? Better?"

"Yeah, I mean yes. I can breathe again."

"Good. That's good. What you saw tonight may keep you from getting some sleep, but do me and yourself a big favor. Don't light up tonight, deal?"

Charlie gave it some thought. He'd had every intention of going home and getting baked, but when he looked at his grandfather, he promised himself he wouldn't. "Only if you agree to come to dinner tomorrow night, Pops."

"You think that's wise?"

"Sure."

"Well, I don't," Seth said. "But fine, it's a deal."

"Great, dinner's at six."

"Yeah, yeah," Seth said rubbing his head. "Come on, let's go. You need some sleep."

"Okay," Charlie said then stopped. "Pops…thanks for tonight. For taking care of me."

"Son, that's what families do."

57

When Hannibal awoke that Monday morning Monique wasn't in bed beside him. He didn't smell her cooking either, so he threw on a pair of sweat pants and headed downstairs. He called her name a few times and checked the outside deck, figuring she had a book in her hands and headphones in her ears, but she wasn't there. He started to worry a bit as he walked into the empty kitchen until he noticed a note hanging on the fridge in her neat cursive handwriting.

Gone for a drive. Had to clear my head. See you at the den. Love, Mo.

He frowned at her words and snatched the note off the door. "She done lost her damn mind." The clock on the kitchen wall read 7:45. Stomping up the stairs, Hannibal tossed on a shirt and shoes and was out the door minutes later.

With a quick squeal of tires, he made his way to the gym a couple miles away, muttering under his breath. "She know we in a damn war. Fuck is on her mind driving around without me?"

When he spotted her car parked outside the gym he exhaled a sigh of relief. Hannibal sat in his truck for a moment as he calmed down. His woman was riled up. While they had gotten payback for Appleton's death, his war with Frank and Stony had been costly to the community, and Monique had grown frustrated at the long line of bullet riddled young Black bodies in its wake, including that little boy shot in his bed. Monique understood the game, how it had to play itself out, and that collateral damage was the unfortunate risk. Soldiers had to be soldiers, and a civilian catching a bullet was bound to happen, but the death of a civilian who hadn't even reached elementary school had scarred her heart permanently.

Hannibal knew she had a soft spot for the babes. Unable to have children herself, Monique did everything she could for the little ones in their neighborhood. As soon as she had asked, he'd given his blessing for her to take all the food his truck could carry and a purse full of money to Kenyatta's parents. The donation hadn't calmed her soul though.

Maybe some time in the ring will help, he thought.

The Wolf's Den had been a second home to them since Appleton had handed the keys for the empty warehouse to Hannibal four years ago. Monique had wasted no time and put her talents to work. After just a week, she'd done her homework and started to recommend equipment, layouts, and proposals to help her man put a profitable business together. She'd made him so proud.

After The Den's one year anniversary barbeque, Ike had teased her of being too "prim and proper" to be in the gym. Monique hadn't been able to resist the subtle dig from the old man and had challenged the ex-boxer for lessons after hours. Whatever Ike had told her to do, she'd done. She'd put in serious work and after a couple of months, she'd surprised everyone and jumped in the ring with The Wolf wearing sparring gear.

Hannibal had laughed and warned her. "Between these here ropes, ain't no time for games, Mo." She'd smiled and shot a stiff jab to his face. On instinct, he'd dodged and telegraphed a vicious wild right that was never meant to land, just to scare. She'd easily ducked out of the way, slid to her left, and playfully attacked his ribs. In seconds, everyone, including The Wolf, had seen that she had done her homework once again. Ike had smiled at his beautiful student like a proud father. When Monique survived the two-minute round Hannibal grabbed her wrist and raised her hand in victory.

Since that day, they had begun every week with a few light rounds in the ring. It was a ritual they enjoyed, and while Hannibal did his best to avoid rituals because they could get you killed in his world, neither of them could resist the power of their beautiful and violent dance in the squared circle.

Today was no different. He inhaled deeply as he climbed out of his truck and made his way into the gym. He couldn't wait to see Monique in the ring, eager and raring to go with that mischievous glint in her dark eyes rather than the sour frown she'd held for days. He said his hello's to the regulars and the kids in Ike's boxing program before he walked to the ring in the back and stood on the apron next to Ike as two young men went at it under the trainer's watchful eye.

A local icon, Ike "The Spike" Perry had once been a feared middleweight who had possessed hands like a heavyweight, feet like a lightweight, and a smile like a movie star. He had been on his way to the title, and his biggest fan had been a young kid named Hannibal. When Hannibal had seen Ike in the news winning fights, he'd had proof that being from Youngstown's East Side hadn't meant you couldn't make something of yourself, and he'd worked harder in the gym and on the field in hopes of realizing his pro-football dream.

However, a detached retina had ended Ike's boxing career and triggered his downward spiral into addiction, first with booze and painkillers before progressing to coke and eventually heroin. Between the drugs, bad business decisions, and fast women, the one-time superstar had quickly lost everything.

Three months into the gym's opening, Hannibal had overheard someone say they had seen Ike talking to himself and shadowboxing down near the Rescue Mission. Hannibal had immediately tracked down his childhood hero, who had been living on the streets. Over the best meal Ike had eaten in months, he and The Wolf had shared a few laughs and reminisced about his fights and the good times. Without a second thought Hannibal had offered Ike an apartment and a job as manager of The Den. Once Ike had gotten clean and sober, the ex-fighter's gap-toothed smile had quickly become the gym's signature trademark. Before long he had found a couple of kids with real potential, and Hannibal had added "Scout" to Ike's title.

When the bell ended the sparring Ike turned to greet Hannibal. The caramel-colored old man looked and spoke to Hannibal as a son. "Before you say anything, she in the back with Tracy."

"She all right?" Hannibal asked.

"Nah, she ain't all right. Hell no, she ain't all right," Ike replied in his usual slow deep gravelly baritone. "What'd you do? Kill her dog or somethin? That girl a yours is mad bout something, something serious, and she wantin to work through it, but I think today ain't that day for it, you understand?"

"I hear ya, old man," Hannibal said as he climbed down from ringside, "but today is that day."

"Go on and don't listen to me. We both know what happens when ya don't, don't we?"

Hannibal laughed and walked into Ike's office. Monique sat with her eyes closed in Ike's chair as Tracy, Ike's assistant, massaged her well-toned shoulders. He smiled when he saw her in full gear minus headgear and gloves. Hannibal could stare at her all day, and that would be a good day to him.

"Don't you know how to knock?" asked Tracy with an eye roll.

Hannibal leaned against the doorframe. "I know how to knock you out, Ms. Mouth. That's what I know how to do."

"In your dreams, fat boy. Don't forget that butt kicking I gave you once and don't make me do it again."

"So you beat me up in grade school that one time. So what? And who you callin fat, Slim Jim?"

"Sent you home cryin and shit."

Monique chuckled.

"Yeah. I'll pull your skinny ass apart now though, arms first, then them sorry excuse for legs, you keep messin with me…toothpick."

"All right you two, that's enough," Monique said. "What's up? Why aren't you ready?" she asked Hannibal.

"Cause I just got here." Hannibal nodded toward the parking lot. "What I tell you bout drivin alone?"

Monique looked away and waved away his concern. "I know, but I had to get out of the house, and I didn't want to wake you. You didn't get in until late."

"Don't do that shit again, Mo. It ain't the time for you to run off by yourself, specially after the shit we did last night."

Monique eyes snapped back to his. Slowly she got to her feet and asked, "What exactly do you mean by 'shit we did last night'?"

He winced. He hadn't yet told her about the attack on Romare's, and given her mood, he wanted none of the drama that was sure to come with an explanation. "Nothin, don't sweat it," he said grimly. "I'm a go get changed. Hey, toothpick, where's ya boyfriend? I ain't seen him in here this morning."

"I don't know where Bobby at," she said throwing a towel at Hannibal's head. "And I keep tellin you that damn fool ain't my man.

I don't like light-skinned niggas. Gross!" she said with an overtly dramatic shiver.

Hannibal watched Monique smile for the first time in days at her friend's histrionics.

"Girl, quit your stupidity. Ain't nothin wrong with that boy's smooth skin," Monique replied with a playful push.

"Yeah, if you like freckles."

Maybe she ain't all that mad, he thought as he watched her head to the ring before going to his private locker room. Within minutes he stood in the ring, bouncing lightly on his feet.

"You sure bout this, son?" Ike asked.

"She needs it. We both do," Hannibal said with a shrug as he cracked his neck and tried to stay loose.

Usually everyone in the gym gathered around to watch The Wolf and his "Little Hellion" go a few rounds. The couple's smack talk always brought laughter from the throng, but today Ike cleared the ringside. At Hannibal's questioning glance, he said, "I know my kids, and you two need some time alone time to work out whatever it is that's botherin her, and that ain't no one's business but your own."

"I think she all right, a little cranky maybe. Don't be so worried, Ike. I'll go easy on her."

Ike rubbed his salt and pepper covered chin. "It ain't her I'm worried bout." He sighed as Monique climbed between the ropes at her corner.

Hannibal's heart rate ratcheted up as he watched her prep. "Don't make me knock you out, now. You hear me?" he said from across the ring.

Monique rolled her eyes. "Don't make me punch you in your dick!" she yelled with no sense of mirth.

Ike cracked his trademark gap-toothed smile at her retort.

"Now, you know doing that just hurts us both, right?" Hannibal replied as he pounded his gloves together.

"You more than me, pinky," Monique said in a low growl before she clamped her teeth down on her mouthpiece.

"Yeah…let me get the hell out the way of you two. Good luck, son," Ike said as he slipped in Hannibal's mouthpiece. With a pat on the shoulder the old man scrambled through the ropes.

The Wolf drank in the sight of her. Her shimmering onyx complexion reflected the overhead lights as her sinewy form bounced in place awaiting the bell. Hannibal thought Ike was overstating his woman's mood. They'd had their talk about her driving around alone, and he had even made her laugh. While the delicate features of her face looked ready for combat, it wasn't a look he hadn't seen. His heart always swelled seeing her eager to go toe-to-toe with him. He loved her like he had never loved anyone or anything else in his life.

When Ike rang the bell rang, she charged him, catching him by surprise. Usually they bobbed and weaved towards each other and shot jabs when they met center ring, but today she brought the fight directly to him. Hannibal quickly stepped to his left and threw a lazy right jab that she easily maneuvered to avoid.

She set her feet and fired a low left hand to his midsection that he barely felt followed by a hard right to his jaw that for a moment buckled him at the knees. Before he could respond, she fled to the corner.

"Keep your hands up when you retreat, Moni," Ike said. "And remember, no dick punchin allowed either."

That right cross told Hannibal all he needed to know. Monique had never hit him like that. Maybe Ike was right. "You all right, baby?" he asked as he stalked her.

Her eyes squinted hard. "Shut up and fight."

Hannibal eyebrows rose at the vicious anger he heard.

"Told you," Ike said with grunt of disapproval.

Hoping to get answers, Hannibal bore down and cut off the ring, trapping her in a corner. Her triple jab right cross combination thwarted his impending attack and put him on his heels. He blocked her punches with ease, but she slipped out of the corner and bounced to the center of the ring before he could counter.

"Very nice, Mo. Very nice," Ike shouted.

Hannibal followed swiftly. He moved in close and lowered his voice. "You mad, huh?"

The fire in her eyes seemed to jump even higher. "You noticed."

Hannibal bobbed and weaved as he danced around her, intermittently firing a light jab at her. "A lil bit, yeah. Hard to miss with you trying to take my head off. What's your problem? As far as I know I ain't piss in your Fruit Loops this morning."

"I'm sick of it, Han," she growled and slowly lowered her hands. "Sick to my stomach of hearing about another dead boy, dead friend, dead son, dead…soldier every damn day."

"You know the game, Mon. This is the life. They killed App," Hannibal said and followed her lead dropping his hands at his sides.

"Yeah, but it's a bit harder to swallow of late, especially with drunk, high dumbasses carelessly waving around automatic weapons with extended clips. That little boy didn't deserve to die!" Both gloves hit him full force in the chest, knocking him back a step even as he caught the pain and teary gaze in her eyes.

Understanding struck Hannibal like her vicious right cross. "Ahhh…baby."

Monique pushed him away from her. "Don't fuckin 'baby' me. Fight, dammit!" Once again her face contorted with anger as determination settled like concrete in her eyes.

"I get it, Mo. You need to punch something, kick something, scratch, claw. You wanna hurt something. I know that like I know my name. I get it, baby. I'm right here, ain't going nowhere. Let it out. Let me have it." Hoping to give her an outlet for her aggression he never raised his hands. Instead he held his arms out wide in invitation. She stayed low and slowly circled him.

"GIVE IT TO ME!" he bellowed, his voice booming through the gym making heads turn. With no hesitation and a howl all her own she fired off a patented Ike left hook to his ear that almost snapped her wrist before she darted to her left off the ropes.

"Time!" Ike shouted.

Hannibal blinked through the ringing in his head and watched carefully as she walked to her corner and sat.

"All right, gods dammit, that's enough," Ike said rushing into the ring. "Whatever's goin on with you two this damn sure ain't da place to work it out at. I told you that. Tracy, get me a bucket of ice, and you," he said to Monique, "You wanna tell me what's up witchu before you do some real damage to your pretty hands?"

"Nothin a little more sparring won't help," she said as Ike pulled up a stool and plopped down in front of her.

He was removing her gloves when Hannibal walked over with the bucket of ice and tapped Ike on the shoulder. Ike glanced up and rose. "Good luck, son. You may wanna put your mouthpiece back in."

Hannibal took Ike's seat. "How's your wrist?"

"Fine," Monique replied too quickly.

Hannibal's suspicions were confirmed when she winced as he gently tugged off her glove. With a tenderness that belied his strength, he slipped her hand into the bucket. "You still mad?"

Through clenched teeth she said, "I'm more than mad. I'm pissed! This damn beef with those South Side pussies got a little boy killed in his motherfucking bed while wearing his motherfucking Spider Man pajamas, Han!"

Hannibal hung his head. "So you beat up on me?"

"Yeah, I do. It helps me feel better. You got a problem with that?" she asked trying to find his eyes.

Hannibal chuckled and smiled. "Oh so you wanna go one more round then, sprout?"

Monique rose and squared her shoulders. "Let's go, big boy. Put my damn glove back on. You know I'm not scared."

"Hell no! You two is done for the day," Ike said from his ringside bench. "She damn near broke her wrist already. What more you want?"

"Can we get some privacy, old man?" Hannibal said with a smile. Ike didn't move a muscle.

"Psh…You just got saved by Ike," Monique said.

"Is that how you see it?"

"That's how it is."

"You keep telling yourself that, and you may believe it someday, baby," Hannibal looked up ready to call it a day. "Yo, Ike, where's

Bobby? Have him dump this bucket while I get her dressed to go home."

"I got it. Bobby called in this morn. Said his moms was sick or some shit."

Hannibal's brow furrowed in confusion and a sharp chill ran up his spine and his shoulders tensed. He stood up slowly.

"Are you all right?" Monique asked him softly. "Baby?"

"What'd you say?" Hannibal asked Ike.

"He said his moms wasn't feeling well, and that he'd be in tomorrow. Why?"

"Ike, his moms is dead."

"Yo! Wolf! Trouble!" shouted one of his younger crewmembers as the squeal of tires cut through the thumping rhythm of leather hitting leather. Hannibal was about to jump out of the ring but froze mid-step as three masked men burst through the front door and bullets from automatic weapons pierced the musky air of The Wolf's Den. Unarmed as they worked out with guns tucked away in lockers, everyone scrambled for any cover they could find.

Two of the gunmen fired at everyone and everything while one shooter quietly stalked towards the ring and Hannibal. They shot down light fixtures, destroyed heavy bags and equipment, and added to the war's body count. When the main gunman took aim at the ring, Hannibal turned to jump through the ropes, but seeing Monique curled on the canvas he threw his body over her. Gunfire rang out but missed him as return fire began to target the invaders.

They retreated, scattering dozens of rounds as they covered their exit. The attack was over in seconds, but it felt like twenty endless minutes. An eerie quiet descended as the assailants tore out of the parking lot as quickly as they appeared, their message delivered.

Wolf rose off Monique's lithe frame and scanned the gym. "They're gone, baby. You okay?" When she didn't answer Hannibal looked down to see Monique unmoving as her blood stained the ring. His stomach dropped, and for a moment he couldn't move or breathe. "Moni!" On instinct, Hannibal scooped her up and ran to his truck, uncaring if the gunmen were still close.

The Wolf was no longer the fearless leader of the East Side. He drove her like a madman to the hospital, blaring his horn and dodging traffic, even as he did his best not to panic. Less than five minutes later he slammed to a stop in the emergency lane and carried Monique's limp body through the glass doors, shouting for a doctor. Almost as soon as they had her on a stretcher, they hustled her into a trauma room before they whisked her away to emergency surgery.

Some of his crew showed up and for hours they waited. He paced the bland colored hallways and lobby like a caged animal. His muscles rippled with rage. They'd violated his sanctuary and shot his woman. Someone had to pay, and he promised to unleash hell on the cowards. This conflict had been personal since the beginning, but now he vowed to scorch the South Side to get whomever was responsible for hurting Monique.

Finally the doctor came out and met The Wolf's dark gaze. Hannibal's throat nearly closed as he waited for the news. "If she hadn't gotten here as fast as she did, she would have bled out. She's very lucky to be alive."

Hannibal tried to slow his pounding heart as the doctor told the gathered crowd that despite the massive blood loss, Monique would live. One bullet had shattered her clavicle and missed killing her by centimeters. The second bullet had grazed the back of her head with only a superficial wound.

Hannibal thanked him, and then the hulk of a man leaned against the taupe colored hospital wall and passed out, hitting the floor with a bone-crunching thud. Exhaustion and fear had taken their toll. Three orderlies and two of his boys lifted him onto a gurney. They wheeled him into triage and ran an IV into his massive forearm. Hannibal slept through the evening with the nursing staff monitoring his vitals.

When The Wolf awoke briefly, feeling like he had been hit by a semi, Silas gave him an update. Ike Gamble had been killed but not before killing the gunman that had Hannibal in his sights. The old man had saved his life. That was his last thought as he drifted back to sleep.

58

Seth never made it to Charlie's for dinner yesterday, and he hoped his grandson would forgive him. He'd had too much on his mind to sit and break bread with his son who detested everything about him. Seth had known he wasn't going to take Charlie up on his invite, and deep down he was sure Charlie understood that too.

Seth had one question, and it pestered him, bounced around his head, and demanded attention. He glanced at his watch. It was almost noon, so he grabbed his phone and headed outside into the cloudy, blustery day, which was a relief after spending the night in his stuffy hotel room. Taking a deep breath of fresh air, Seth hit the speed dial on his phone and waited for a pick up on the other end.

"Whadup, partner?" Paulie's raspy bark asked.

Seth closed his eyes and smiled. He hadn't realized how much he'd missed his friend the last five days until that moment. "That's how you answer the company phone? I knew we shoulda gotten a receptionist."

"When it's you callin? Hell yeah, that's how I answer the phone."

"How you know it was me?" Seth asked.

"I got this psychic, right. In fact she's sitting on my lap right this minute. Chick's got curves for days, and tits you have to see for yourself. They're amazing, soft and big like those expensive down pillows you like. Anyway, when the phone rang, she waved her pretty little hand over it and told me it was your crusty old ass."

"Tell her I said hi," Seth said with a chuckle in his throat.

"She knew you was gonna say that too. Anyway, how you doing? How's lovely and boring Ohio treating you?"

"This place is crazy."

"Crazier than here?" Paulie asked.

"Not quite, but they trying."

"How's the grand?"

"Up shit's creek, no boat, no paddle, don't know how to swim, and for whatever reason he seems hell bent on tying boulders around his damn feet whenever I'm not around."

"Well then it's a good thing you went and not me. If I had gone, everyone would prolly be dead already."

"Yeah, what you lack in diplomacy, you do make up for in ferocity."

"You damn right," Paulie said. "That's my motto."

"Since when?"

"Since now," he said bringing them both to laughter. "So how bad is it really?"

Seth took another deep breath and sighed as he gazed at the traffic on the busy side street. "It's like Florida said. They want little man to steal some priceless work of art, and I can't wrap my head around it."

"Ohio has priceless works of art? Who knew?"

"Well if they don't they will soon. It's on its way, some kind of tour or some shit."

"A tour means a short window of opportunity, there and gone. Who's the artist?"

"Does that even matter?"

"It can. Picasso, forget it. Pollock, forget it. Van Gogh, forget it. Basically if the artist is white and dead then forget it. Security will be deep and heavy."

Seth chuckled. "This from a man that's never stepped foot in a museum."

"I may have never stepped foot in a museum, but that doesn't mean I haven't read a damn book. Besides, I'm a criminal and a crook, and the art world is full of criminals and crooks, so it was a perfect match!"

"Your old ass never ceases to surprise me. It's a Basquiat."

After a few seconds of silent contemplation Paulie said, "That's actually doable. While his work is seminal, he's Black, well Haitian, so security might not be as tight. That's a great investment for whoever pulls it off. His shit sells."

"What books are you reading? What you know about Basquiat?"

"More than you apparently. I actually met the young man."

"Get the fuck outta here. You never told me that."

"Never had a reason too, and you don't need to know all my damn business."

"So when was this meeting?"

"Hmmm…eighty-six, around the time they was talking about letting you out early. He used to come up to Harlem and score once and a while. I ran into him one night, helped him out of a jam, and he invited me to a show of his someplace downtown. You know how much I hate it down there, so I never went. Wish I did though. He was twenty-eight when he OD'd a year or so later. Fucking tragic, man."

"It always is with that shit."

"Anyway, not to get morose. You know, I almost bought one of his pieces to hang above the bar, but them art cats wanted way too much money, damn criminals. You cased the place yet?"

"No. I've been getting the lay of the crumbling asphalt out here, so I can decide how best to get the grand out of this mess."

"Be that as it may, I'm calling the Preachers. Keep them on stand-by. What's the name of the museum?"

"No clue yet," Seth admitted.

Paulie let out a huge sigh. "What the hell, man? Is your head in the game?"

Seth sighed. "Honestly? No. I'm foggy as hell."

"Why? What's got you all befuzzled?"

"Befuddled?"

"Whatever!"

"You just asked the magic question. 'Why?'"

"What do you mean, Seth? You startin to scare me. What you talkin bout?"

"Why have a wet behind the ear seventeen-year-old kid try to pull off this kind of job?"

"Because he can? The guy's got the kid by his baby black balls."

"Yeah, but why, Paulie? That's what I can't understand. There are a million other ways to have my grandson pay this note off."

"How big is the note? Fifty large?"

"Try two hundred," Seth said with a sigh.

"Damn! Who the hell let's a kid get in that deep of a hole?" Paulie asked. After they silently mulled over the implications and possibilities for a minute, Paulie broke the silence. "Let me ask you this, Seth. If your grandson—a boy that I'm guessin never had to steal a thing in his life—fails at getting this painting, what's the penalty?"

Paulie's question stopped Seth cold. "Shit, Paulie, I have no fuckin idea."

"Well it sounds to me like you have some diggin to do, so you won't be all befuzzled."

"Very true. You cleared the tracks for me."

"That's cause I'm the brains in this outfit. Seriously though, how's things goin out there for you? You need the cavalry?"

"Well, my son hates me, my grandson loves me, and these baby gangsters have started a war with each other that's leavin Black boys in coffins no matter what part of town they in. That pretty much sums it all up. And I can take care of myself."

"We heard about the little boy catching a stray, unreal."

"Tragic is more like it. How's the place?"

"She's hummin right along like a hooker with an iPod. What we got here is a fine, well-oiled machine, my friend."

Seth shook his head. "Yes…yes, she is. Who woulda thought you and I would have ever become restaurateurs?"

"If the me today traveled back in time and told the young me this shit, I probably woulda shot me, so there ya go. And before you ask, Marta's fine. She asks bout you, and I tell her you're okay. I am not about to get into your business, but whatever the hell went down between you two must have been serious. You might want to give her a call sometime."

Seth's stomach clenched at Marta's name. "I will, just not yet," Seth said. "Not yet."

"Okay, well it was good talking to you. Call again soon, will ya?"

"How'd you know I was about to get off the phone?"

"Psychic in my lap, remember? We bout to head to The Met. She said to tell you goodbye too."

"Fuck you, Paulie," Seth said with a smile.

"Love you too, man. And look, whatever you do, don't be careful. That shit will get you killed," Paulie said and hung up leaving Seth with a good feeling and a clear sense of direction for the first time in days.

59

When The Wolf had awoken chilled and alone at 4:30 a.m., he'd yanked out his IV and left his hospital bed to search out Monique. Within minutes he'd found her room, gotten the update from the floor nurse, and settled uncomfortably into the tiny vinyl chair next to her bed. For hours, he had quietly held her delicate hand and listened to her every breath. As the minutes ticked by, he barely held in check his terror that he'd almost lost her.

The flinch of Monique's hand snatched him from his thoughts. Her long dark lashes fluttered, as he squeezed her hand. Her eyes opened weakly and immediately sought him. With a faint smile and a soft sigh, she closed her eyes, still groggy from the heavy pain meds. Somewhat reassured, Hannibal gently placed a kiss on her forehead.

"What are you still doing here?" Monique whispered.

"Making sure you're okay."

"I am high as a cloud," she croaked. "I am so good, babyboy."

"You sure bout that?" he said softly.

This time she blinked open her eyes with conviction. "When do I lie to you?"

"Neva and you betta not start."

"Don't be threatening me," she said slowly. "I'm thirsty." Hannibal turned a cup of water up to her lips, and she drank slowly. "So, what are you planning?"

Hannibal thought for a second unsure on how to answer. He wanted revenge, he wanted blood, but he wasn't sure if that's what she wanted.

"I was gonna go home and get some sleep."

Monique slowly turned her head and allowed her eyes to focus on her man's face and a smile came to her lips. "You know you full of shit, right?" she said groggily.

"You callin me a liar?"

"No. I am calling you a damn liar. Don't forget the damn. That's very important." She leaned back and closed her eyes.

"Mo?"

"Get outta here and do what you have to do."

"You sure, Mo? You know this won't end things."

Her eyes opened and met his with an intensity she mustered from somewhere deep within. "They violated. They shot me," she said slowly. "Now they have to deal with you."

He smiled slightly, "I'll be back soon as I can."

"Please be as careful as you can."

"I'm always careful."

"Still full of shit apparently. I love you anyway," Monique said quietly and closed her eyes again.

He squeezed her hand. "I love you back, Mo," he whispered.

An hour later The Wolf walked into his house still clad in the same bloody clothes from the day before. With none of their usual banter Silas and his other captains huddled around the dining room table to discuss their "get back."

The Wolf leaned his fists against the tabletop and took a moment to meet the eyes of each of his men. "This gon be short and sweet. I want information. I want names, hangouts, hideouts, where they eat, sleep, shit, shower. I don't care what it costs. Make it happen. It's already been more than twenty-four hours."

Silas was grim. "We've been on it since it happened. We lost three crew and Ike. Plus there were like a dozen injuries with two cats and Monique still up at St. E's. They hit hard and fast. Our borders are on lock down, but we got calls into every one of our connections. There were three shooters inside and two out, and we're guessing at least one cat acting as the driver and lookout. Ike shot one of the shooters before he caught a bullet and bled out his damn self."

Silas glanced around the table before he continued. "Ain't no one seen or heard from Bobby's bitch ass, but we lookin. We guessin he was tipped off which means he was workin for them. He's prolly outta town by now. No one's heard shit, but we huntin that freckled fuck too." Everyone at the table nodded their heads.

The Wolf grumbled low and deep. "Look, ya'll let it be known that there's a price on his light-skinned ass same as Rippers for killing that kid, a stack. That should shake their worlds up some, and I wanna hear something by sundown." Hannibal once again met the eyes of every one of his captains. "Ya'll understand me? No excuses!" His fist slammed the solid oak dining table, and a hairline crack splintered across the smooth dark finish.

"Yo, can I say something?" asked one of the captains.

"Speak," ordered Hannibal as he sat down at the head of the table.

"Honestly, we should have seen this coming. We shot up their place hard the other night. Word is we took out the ole timer behind the bar and four or five others, not to mention Romare's looks like it should be condemned. I didn't think anyone over there would have the balls to come back on us after that. I thought it was a wrap. Now we know something we didn't."

"What's that, Shep?" Silas' brow furrowed.

"We know we not dealing with some regular dudes. What we did would have put the fear of whatever God they pray to in the hearts of some regular niggas," Shep said. "These South Side cats didn't flinch. They swung back, and not just at us, Si. They swung back at you, Wolf. They came at YOU! We need to think about this."

"Think about what, nigga?" Silas argued. "They came at our chief and tried to take him out the picture. They already brought down App. We need to hit these bastards back with everything we got!"

Shep rubbed his chin. "And then they'll do what, Si? They'll just come back at us and maybe go gunning for your head next, and we can't afford to lose someone else. There's one dude we need to focus on and one dude only, and that's Frank, you feel me?"

"That midget rat bastard?" asked Silas.

"Yeah!"

Hannibal focused hard on Shep and considered. "Why?" he asked already knowing the answer.

Shep leaned back in his chair and met his Alpha's gaze. "Because everyone at this table knows that Stony is straight up punk. He ain't got the heart for this, and without Frank he ain't got no spine neither. Frank is the head of that snake, not Stony. Get Frank, and this is over."

A short humorless chuckle slipped from Silas' lips. "You ever seen Frank by hisself?"

"Nope."

"You ever seen Frank period?"

"Nope."

"Exactly. Frank is like a damn ghost, the fucking boogeyman."

"I never said this shit was gonna be easy, Si."

"Then how the hell do we do it?" asked a frustrated Silas.

Silence met Silas' question.

"We hunt him," Hannibal finally said as he locked eyes with Shep. "And make sure we there when he pops his head up out his hole. For now find out something, anything, and bring it to me no matter what it is."

As his captains left Hannibal's, they jumped on their phones, getting the word out that retribution was coming if info wasn't in hand soon. "You want me to stay?" Silas asked.

"No, I'm headed back to the hospital, but keep your phone close."

When Silas closed the door behind him, Hannibal slipped down to the basement to his weapons safe. Bypassing the vicious precision of his AR-15 assault rifle, he chose the brutal power of his AA-12 automatic shotgun. He loved the Tommy Gun look of the weapon. The coal black finished mini-canon was more effective at close range, and more than anything Hannibal wanted to look into the faces and soak up the fear and pain of the ones who brazenly had come at him and his people.

With a disquieting calm fueled by rage, he broke down the weapon, cleaned it, oiled it, and reconstituted it, before meticulously loading 12-gauge shotgun shells in its 20-round drum and locking it firmly in place.

"Come on out and play, Frank."

60

After a late lunch at what had become his favorite Ohio diner, Seth pulled up smoothly to Romare's. What had once looked like a modest unassuming bar stood like a casualty in a war torn country. Seth shook his head and wondered how long these baby gangsters were going to keep up their slaughter and chaos. Seth slid his snub nose .45 into his ankle holster and retrieved his Glock from under his seat, tucking it into the small of his back. While Romare's wasn't officially open, the black Escalade in the alley told Seth the "man" was in. He banged hard on the front door.

The portly DJ once again greeted him with a sour look. "Not yo fucking ass again."

"What's happening, fat boy? I'm here to see your boss."

Warily and with a suck of his teeth the DJ moved back, letting Seth into the dim establishment where several people were working on clean up and temporary repairs. "Wait at the bar."

Seth glanced around. "Fuck happened in here? You wanted a snack, and they told you no?"

The DJ fisted his chubby paws and closed his eyes as if counting to ten. He then pointed at the bar. "Just wait there."

"And here I was waiting for a reason to punch you in the throat again. You learn quick. I see why they keep you around, fat boy," Seth said as he walked to the battered bar, which looked like it had taken the brunt of the battle. Dozens of liquor bottles were missing. Bullets had riddled and splintered the once smooth grain, and unmistakable stains marred the dark wood. Instead of seeing his reflection in a mirrored backsplash, plywood stared back at him. Seth shook his head in sympathy, imagining how he'd react if his place had been a victim to violence. The Pearl was as much of a home to him as his Harlem brownstone.

"What the fuck you doin here, nigga?" Frank said coming up behind Seth.

Seth's compassion vanished. Slowly he turned to face the young criminal and met the shorter man's cool gaze with one of his own. "Apparently you don't know how this works, so let me explain some ground rules to you. First one being, don't call me that again, short stuff."

An amused smile tugged at the corner of Frank's mouth. "You think I give a damn what you want, gramps?"

Seth settled back on his heels, understanding this face-to-face had been inevitable from the moment they had met. "Not really, but you will if you call me that again. I am not your nor anyone else's nigga. You understand me, junior?"

Brooms froze mid-sweep, and hammers stilled. The inside of Romare's became quiet enough to hear the fat DJ breathing in the corner. Instinct nudged the workers toward the exits while they waited to see what might happen next.

Frank chuckled darkly. "Yeah, I get you, old man" Frank said taking the two steps toward Seth invading his personal space. Frank cocked his head and rubbed his hands together as if preparing for a fight, but Seth stayed loose. "Yeah...I understand you one a dem other kinda niggas," he said as he slowly began to circle Seth. "You one of dem kinda niggas that hates being called nigga. Gets ya panties all in a bunch and shit, but see you need to understand that I'm that kinda nigga that don't give a fuck about the feelings of sensitive, over-emotional, and touchy niggas like ya self." Frank came to a stop in front of Seth.

Seth held the younger man's challenging gaze without hesitation. "Yeah, you right," he said as he calmly slipped his hands into the pockets of his silk slacks. "I am one of those kinda niggas that hates being called a nigga, especially by dumb ass young niggas like you, the kind of niggas that are too fucking stupid to live because you carry around your neck with pride the very ignorant bullshit others fought so hard for us to be free of. You and your little sycophants wallow like stupid dogs in that negative, destructive shit that smarter Black men learned to leave behind, too busy killing each other instead of building something. But let me break this down in words someone like you will get."

Seth moved closer to Frank and held a tight leash on his vicious temper that begged to spill blood. "What YOU need to understand, nigga, is that I'm the kinda nigga that is more than capable of ridding the world of ignorant niggas like you for calling someone like me a nigga ever again. Got it? Or do I need to draw you and all the rest of these little mothafuckers running around here kissing your ass a picture?"

For long seconds, no one dared breathe as the two dominant males stared each other down. Despite their casual stances, the threat of certain violence hung heavy in the air. No one blinked until Frank smiled and backed away with a short laugh.

"I like you, gramps. You gotta set on you that hangs. You wanna soda or somethin?" Frank asked as if he was talking to an old friend.

"No, thanks," Seth answered in an equally pleasant tone, pulling back from his instinctive urge to draw his gun and be done with this. "I'm good. Your boy here?"

Everyone heaved a collective sigh and tentatively made their way back to work on the various areas of the bar.

"Yeah, c'mon up," Frank said leading the way to Stony's office.

At that moment, staring at the younger man's back, Seth knew someday he would have to kill Frank. *Stony may be pulling the strings around here, but Frank likes this gangster shit too damn much. He's too dangerous to my grand and Brownie to leave breathing. When all this is handled, he's a problem I'll need to solve.* Seth let go of his thoughts as he took the last step into Stony's office.

Stony looked up from the stack of papers and rolled his eyes. "Old man, why is it you always show up uninvited? You here to pay your grandson's knot? If not then you can leave." Stony motioned to his desk. "As you can clearly see I'm a little busy."

Seth casually took a seat without invitation. "No, but I did want to ask you a question about the alternative option you gave my grand."

"Hit me with it then, so I can get back to work. Time is money, and you fucking with my money," Stony said coldly eying the older man.

"My question is 'Why?'" Seth asked.

"Why what?"

"Why would you give a seventeen-year-old snot-nosed kid a job like this? A kid that ain't never stole even a pack of gum...what the hell makes you think he can pull off felony art theft? Why?"

Stony's eyes locked with Seth, and his face contorted into confusion. "Because I want to. Does that answer your question?"

"Okay, and if he fails?"

"You don't know?" Stony reclined in his chair and laughed. The sound chilled the fine hairs on Seth's neck. "You should talk to your grandkid, pops, and stop wasting my money."

Seth tried to stamp down his rising frustration with these wannabe gangsters, who were too busy fighting over territory filled with empty lots and crumbling sidewalks. "Why not make him a drug runner, a janitor, a stripper's assistant, anything that would help him work off the debt. Why not give him something he could actually do? Art theft? Do you truly think that's the answer?"

Stony shrugged. "What can I say? I really want that painting."

Frank stifled a chuckle.

Seth threw his arms out in exasperation. "And when he can't get it, and you don't have nothing but a kid spilling his guts to a prosecutor and sending heat your way? What then? What then, Stony?"

"His word against mine. Ain't no proof of a thing. You're an OG. You figure the rest out on your own, gramps. It's time for you to go," Stony said as he walked from behind his desk.

Seth stood and grabbed the younger man by the arm when he walked passed, but Stony wrenched out of Seth's grasp and exploded like a firecracker on a hot dry night in early July.

"Don't fuckin touch me!" Wide-eyed the short-tempered young man stepped nose-to-nose to Seth as Frank silently maneuvered behind him. "Don't you ever put your hands on me again, New York. You hear me? We ain't family, and this ain't Harlem, motherfucka! You may be respected, but you damn sure ain't feared. Now get the fuck out of my office...while you can still walk."

Seth nearly pressed Stony one more time until he caught a glint of steel. Glancing down he spotted Stony's Desert Eagle firmly gripped in his hand. Seth's eyes met Stony's and saw something he'd seen in other men who had suddenly found themselves in bad situations they'd never planned. He saw fear. The events of the last few days had pushed the young man to the breaking point. Instinct told Seth this wasn't the time or the place, so he choked his temper down once again, slowly raised both hands, and backed away to the stairway with his hands open at his sides.

"Later, nigga," Frank said with a smirk.

"Fuck you, junior." Without hesitation Seth turned his back on them both and left the office, vowing to himself that he'd make good on his earlier promise.

61

Almost a half an hour later Seth rang Charlie's doorbell hell bent on getting the answers he needed. When Charlie opened the door Seth immediately knew the boy hadn't handled the aftermath of Romare's well. The bags under his grandson's eyes told of sleepless nights.

"You all right?" Seth asked, his voice full of concern.

"Yeah, just tired, Pops" Charlie said, closing the door behind Seth.

"Not sleeping much?"

"Not since the other night, no."

"Self-medicating?"

Charlie looked away unable to meet Seth's eyes and shrugged. "A little, yeah."

"It can be that way after seeing your first shooting."

Charlie wiped his hand across his haggard face and sighed. "I don't want to talk or think about that. What's up, Pop?"

"Charlie, I need you to answer a question for me," Seth said as Charlie grabbed a stool at the kitchen counter. "If you don't deliver this painting what did Stony tell you he was going to do?"

Charlie's shoulders drooped further, his eyes fell to his lap, and his head lowered.

Seth stood there and watched his grandson fold. Seth wished he could spare the boy this anguish, but he needed the information if he was ever going to make sense of this mess. Eventually Charlie's shoulders began to shake, and fat tears dropped onto the bright red fabric of his pressed shorts.

"Charlie," Seth said softly, "talk to me, son."

Charlie lifted his head. "They…they said…they'd kill Dad." The words were strained and sounded almost alien.

Seth went cold at the unexpected direction the situation had taken. His mind raced as he walked into the kitchen and returned with a paper towel for Charlie. "Don't cry, son. Dry those tears," Seth said as he rubbed Charlie's back. "It'll be all right. Ain't nothing gonna kill your dad but old age. I'll see too that."

"I don't even know why I'm crying," Charlie said, wiping the tears in anger and annoyance. "It's not like we love each other and shit."

"Your tears tell me you're lying. If you didn't love your dad, you wouldn't be crying. Some of your anger toward your dad is justified, but that doesn't mean that deep down you don't love him, even though my son is a complete idiot."

Charlie smiled and nodded his head.

"I'm sure your friends feel the same way about their own parents too. Hell, I used to wish my mother would get hit by a bus when I was young."

Both Charlie and Seth laughed.

"Look, thank you for telling me, and I hate to do this to you, but I have to run. Are you gonna be all right?" Seth asked.

Charlie nodded his head and stood.

"Sorry, I didn't make it to dinner."

"Don't worry about it," Charlie said with a smile. "I didn't think you'd come anyway, Pops, but I'll keep tryin."

"I'd be hurt if you didn't."

"I'll wear you down. You'll see."

"Oh, you might be waitin a good long while then. My stubbornness is world renown. Ask your Great-Uncle Paulie about it if you ever get the chance." Seth turned back to his grandson before he walked out the door. "Try to get some rest, son, and lay off the chemical assistance."

Once Seth had retreated to the solitude of his car, he rubbed his face and growled low before shifting into gear and pulling away from his son's idyllic neighborhood.

So, the baby gangsters aren't just stupid. They're cruel. My boy's been walking around with the burden of ten men on his shoulders and no possible solutions or help in sight. They gave that boy a task that will more than likely get him arrested and destroy his future, and if he doesn't do it it'll get his father killed. This sounds more like a damn vendetta, almost…personal.

The more Seth thought, the more questions that popped into his mind. As he pulled into the parking lot of his hotel, he called Florida, who answered on the first ring. "You answering your own phone? Where's Evil? Don't tell me she finally got smart and left your nosy ass."

"Whatchu talkin about? She ain't goin no damn where. She runnin some errand or somethin. There's always some kinda emergency she gotta take care of. Now what can I do for you?"

"For starters you can tell me everything you know about what's going on out here in Ohio and how it leads back to my family."

Florida sighed heavily. "Okay, how much time you got?"

"How much you need?"

"I don't know everything, but the details I've pieced together…. Well, you better sit."

"I ain't some old biddy, negro. Speak."

"Before Leonard died, the DA's office was on him like corns on a pinky toe. Every time he woke up they were dragging him into that circus court for some bullshit violation or trumped up charge they had no solid evidence for. It was one of those throw-everything-at-the-wall-and-see-what-sticks kinda things. They were trying to pin anything they could to his ass, drugs, illegal gambling, prostitution, weapons, hell even illegal parking and noise ordinance violations. They drove him damn near crazy. The strain…well he wasn't in the best of shape or as young as he use to be, and the aggravation got to be too much, ya know. One day on his way to court he ended up in the hospital instead. Those assholes held him in contempt and issued a warrant."

"Florida, hold on man. What does any of this have to do with what I asked you?"

"Word on the street was that the DA's office went after him because a young assistant was trying hard to make his bones and wanted a big fat win to make his name. That whole damn town thought Leonard was a criminal mastermind instead of the just getting by, smart, pain-in-the-ass hustler you and I knew, but it didn't matter to them what the truth was. The guy went after the old man with both guns blazing."

"This assistant DA, you gotta name?" Seth asked even though he was sure he knew the answer.

"What?" Florida asked incredulously. "Seth, you're a smart man, one of the smartest I know, so I'm damn sure you can put two and two together. Can't you? Asking me for a name? You have to be kidding me. I didn't do all that talking for no reason, baby."

Seth let out a long sigh. "That's what I was afraid of. Thanks for the info, Flo."

"That's why you pay me, man."

"Yeah, me and everybody else."

"Hey baby, you take it easy and don't go underestimating them fools out there."

"I'll try not to," he said and disconnected the call. He needed a number and fast, so he dialed Paulie again at The Pearl. When Marta answered he almost dropped his phone. Seth cleared his throat. "Hey, Marta. It's Seth."

A silence dragged between them for a heavy minute.

"Hey," she finally said awkwardly. "How are you, baby? Where are you?"

Seth smiled at her "baby" which was vastly different than Florida's. He ignored the sweat that formed on his brow and the pigeons pecking in his stomach. "I've been better, but it's too much to explain. I need the number to Broome and Crowe."

"All right, I'll text it to you," she said. A few seconds later Seth's phone buzzed with his legal team's contact info.

"Thank you, I appreciate it," he said.

"You're welcome. When are you coming home?" she asked quietly.

"Hopefully in a few days. I have some loose ends to tie up here, and I'll be back."

"Where's here?" she asked innocently. Getting no answer she shifted gears. "Well I'm glad you'll be home soon cause I miss you," she whispered.

Seth swallowed his unkind remark. "I've gotta go, Marta," Seth said instead. "Thanks for the number." Without waiting for her reply, he disconnected and pushed away the riot of emotions and thoughts her words sparked.

He tapped his phone's screen and called his lawyer. Enemies and friends alike referred to Jonathan Washington as "The Black Hat" because he took no prisoners and didn't care what anyone thought. The brash, reviled, talented, and not-yet-thirty-year-old attorney intimidated everyone including fellow lawyers and even some judges. Seth had loved the kid the moment they'd met.

"Seth, my man! What's going on? Long time no hear from. I thought you forgot about me."

Seth grinned at the confident legal wunderkind. "You never take advantage of the open invite to eat at my place, so it's a two way street."

Jonathan laughed. "Touché, my friend. Touché. So then what do I owe the honor of this call?"

"I need you to look into some things for me and confirm what I know and what I've heard."

"Okay, shoot."

Seth explained quickly what information he needed and about who.

"Yeah, I can do some digging. I should have something for you by the end of business tomorrow."

"Lives may depend on it, so make it a priority."

Jonathan sighed. "Will do."

62

Sitting behind his desk Browning Jackson he scanned the afternoon's headlines. The entire front page of *The Vindicator* featured how the conflict between Youngstown's South Side and East Side was reminiscent of the early nineties when Youngstown had earned the ominous moniker, "Murder Town, USA". With a grimace, Browning slammed the newspaper down. *As if the damn political pressure isn't already at an all-time high. Front page headlines are the last thing I need*, he thought. He took another forkful of his favorite salad, but he couldn't savor the tangy homemade raspberry vinaigrette dressing his wife made, the delicate watercress, or the tender chicken grilled to perfection. The number of bodies stacking up on his watch had squelched his appetite days ago. Now he ate only because his body needed fuel.

Since a handful of nosy kids playing in an abandoned house had found Appleton Harris lying dead in women's underwear a few weeks ago, Black bodies had piled up in the morgue almost daily. The frantic mayor had called that morning comparing the apparent gang war to a biblical apocalypse. "Browning, do something! It's like the end of days, like the rapture itself has descended on this goddamned town. I'm getting a damn ulcer. I hate ulcers, Browning! I do!"

Browning rolled his eyes remembering the conversation. At least the man finally took a position on something. The balding, chronically sweaty, overweight mayor was officially anti-ulcer. Browning tossed down his fork and snatched up his cell phone when the police chief finally returned one of his numerous calls.

"Mac, what in the hell is going on? We need to shut this shit down. My phone is blowing up with media calls, and the mayor's bleeding ulcer has him riding my ass."

"Everything that can be done is being done."

Browning had never heard anyone talk as slow as Mac Johnson. The police chief's casual cadence always sounded as if he didn't have a care in the world. Each syllable oozed out of the pinkish man's mouth like a dark, rich molasses on a cold winter day. "And before you say it, more cops on the streets won't do a damn thing but destroy this year's budget."

"Yet gunshots ring out day and night, and now innocents are paying the price. That little boy who died in his Dad's arms sparked media frenzy! Mac, you have to get a toehold, something other than 'Everything that can be done is being done.' Do you understand me? All that does is make us all look incompetent."

"Browning, we're guarding the suburban neighborhoods and are stopping anyone suspicious on the borders. Look…if the savages would stop being so savage we might be able to get somewhere, but they seem hell bent on killin each other, so why not let em?"

Browning's swallowed the bile rising in his throat. "What did you just say to me, Mac?"

"No offense meant, Browning. You know I wasn't talking about you."

"Offense taken, and that's not how your job description reads, Mac. You aren't paid to allow people to kill each other. You read me? This city will NOT be the reason the murder rate in this country heads north this year. The people pay us to stop crime and quell the fucking madness not sit idly by on our hands and wait until both sides destroy each other. You're the police chief. Do your damn job and get some traction on this!"

"Well if the Governor hadn't cut the damn budget, maybe I could, Brownie. Maybe I could get some traction on this. Maybe I could get a damn handle on things and do my job, but those Black sonsabitches out there have us outmanned and outgunned, not to mention the backwards loyalty of their people who refuse to help and choose instead to go deaf, blind, and mute the second my men show up. Maybe when those people wake up and realize we are the good guys and when the idiots in Columbus get their heads out of their asses and realize that we don't have the manpower or the firepower to do anything against these lunatics or about little boys dying in their daddies' arms, then maybe I can get some traction over here."

Browning took a deep breath. Mac had a point. It's hard to fight a war like this let alone win when you didn't have the resources or the community backing you up. "I'll make some more calls and see what I can do. In the meantime, work on making some legitimate arrests of those responsible instead of trapping them in the inner city so they can continue to kill each other off, get me?" Browning said then hanging up before Mac could. He didn't want to hear anymore of the man's thinly veiled racism.

Browning rubbed his temples and threw the rest of the lunch he couldn't taste in the trash. He wondered if the boys on either side of this slaughter even saw each other as human beings. *What do they see when they look at each other? Don't they see someone else's son, someone's brother, best friend, or father? How in the world can they not care about or see that when a bullet hits one of them boys, that's exactly who they are killing? How does that thought not even enter their minds?*

He gulped the last of his coconut water and crumpled the container. *How did shit get like this?* Then he remembered what an original gangster had once told him off the record a few years back during a grisly multiple murder case that had involved one of the old timer's soldiers.

"It's a game, and the game never changes. Those who play, pay the price—their souls. The young bucks, like my boy on trial, they find safety and acceptance, something they don't usually find or can't find at home. It's hypnotic. Their new fam listens to them, teaches them, praises them, puts money in their pockets, food in the bellies, and the moment we know they'll do anything for their new fam, a gun goes in their hand. The game turns boys into soldiers, and soldiers die on the battlefield—on both sides—every day. If a 'civilian' happens to catch a stray, well that's just collateral damage. We can't show no sympathy cause sympathy don't never feed, clothe, or protect us. When those young cats survive a clash…when they come out the other side alive…they celebrate. Liquor. Pussy. Drugs. Whatever. Don't matter cause they still livin. They defied statistics, fate, the damn Reaper hisself. There ain't no time to be wonderin if they clipped the mailman deliverin a social security check or if they shot some kid on the playground. They can't let themselves feel. They can't afford too. If they do, they die."

Browning had shaken his head but understood. "How'd it get this way?" he'd asked the gnarly older man.

With tired hard eyes he'd answered. "This is what the white man left us, nothin but scraps. We just tryin to make the best of it, boss."

The OG's words had chilled his blood and forced him to see his childhood through a different lens. While his mother, Uncle Paulie, and a host of other neighborhood guys had protected him, he had understood that the impoverished areas were breeding grounds for the game, especially cities that were economically withering on the vine and where decent work was next to impossible to find. He finally understood how well that protection had shielded him. The game too often was one of the few choices facing Black youth, enticing them to turn on their own. A lucky few outran it, some got sucked into it with no other choice, and others ran to it and embraced it. A very lucky few even survived it. But no matter how or why they got in the game, they all eventually realized that there was really only two ways out—death or prison.

Browning hated the game. After growing up the way he had, with his father behind bars for most of his life, he had been hell bent on making sure his son never ended up tangled in anything remotely resembling street life. He'd worked long hours, earned the praises of his superiors, gotten promoted, made a lot of money, and though he wasn't there for everything, he lavished his boy with almost anything his heart desired. He only wanted Charles safe and as far away as possible from those involved in the life and death struggle of the streets, including his own father.

Popping four ibuprofens, Browning scrolled through his contacts for the numbers of a few political friends in Columbus. Lunch was over. He'd use any connection he had to help Mac get whatever he needed in order to find those responsible. Once the police found them, he would put these criminals with complete disregard for human lives behind bars for as long as he possibly could. He hoped his efforts would save a crumbling city from tearing itself apart, maybe save some innocent lives in the process, and keep the ulcer-suffering mayor off his ass.

63

Late Tuesday night after spending the day at Monique's bedside Hannibal's phone finally rang. Within seconds he had a name and location. "Stay where you are and keep ya eyes open. Call if there's any movement. We comin."

The Wolf grabbed his freshly oiled weapon and within minutes he, Silas, and Shep climbed into Silas' black SUV and quietly left the neighborhood. Silas kept it just under the speed limit, but with the adrenaline coursing it felt like they were doing eighty. A half hour after the call, they pulled up slow and smooth to a dimly lit corner, and a lean short teen in a dark hoodie emerged from the shadows to climb in behind him.

The new passenger's low raspy voice broke the silence. "Go straight up da block and make a left. He's up in da second house on da left."

"You sure about this, AJ?" Hannibal asked as they sat idling quietly next to the curb. The light-skinned boy with hard eyes nodded. Hannibal wasn't convinced. "Who you hear it from?"

"My cousin and his boy, Lemon, found out this where Ripper's layin up. Ripper was bragging over at the barber's bout how he and his tore up The Den. My cuz said they followed the fucker back here, and he climbed out actin like he ain't have no worries and shit. Don't know if he live there, but dats his ragged ass Olds out front, and he ain't come out dat house yet."

"And you trust your fam and this Lemon, nigga?"

"They ain't never lie to me."

"First time for everything," Silas said cutting his eyes in the rearview mirror to AJ. The air in the car was heavy. The only sound was when shifting weight caused the leather interior to moan.

Hannibal finally growled. "Fuck it. Some is better than none. We go. We light the bitch up, his car too. I kick in the door, find this little nigga to make sure he dead, and then we out."

"Han…you shouldn't be anywhere near this, man," said Shep.

"He right, fam," agreed Silas. "You too visible. One witness see you, they can damn sure pick yo big ass out a line up, for real. You should sit this one out. Feel me? You too important."

Hannibal's hands tensed. He knew his boys were right, but he wanted blood. He longed to be the one to extract revenge for Monique and Ike, but he was no longer App's second. He was their Alpha and the direct link to their supplier. If he went down, so did the resources that paid rent, put food on tables, clothes on backs, and money in pockets of so many.

The Wolf sighed. "Fine, I'll drive," he said, opening the passenger door to switch sides with Silas. In less than a minute they stopped in front of a tired but well kept little one-story house that even had a few flowerpots lining the concrete steps that lead to the wooden porch.

Without hesitation his three-membered crew exited and opened fire, littering the lawn with shells. As bullets tore through the car and the house, the muscles in Hannibal's forearms rippled, and his shoulders tightened to the satisfying echo of gunfire.

Silas and Shep kicked in the door and entered the little house as AJ stood watch. Lights flipped on as nervous neighbors started checking the streets. *We're runnin out of time before five-o shows.* But before he could get anxious, his team rushed out of the house and back into the truck. Hannibal let off of the brake and quickly pulled away from the bullet-riddled house.

"Ya'll get the fucka?" Wolf growled.

Silas clenched his teeth. "Just drive, Wolf."

"DID YOU GET HIM?"

"Drive, man. Drive."

"What the fuck happened, Si?"

"He wasn't in the house."

"WHAT? Wasn't that his hooptie out front?"

"Yeah, but he wasn't in the house."

"Fuck. I wanted that nigga's blood spilled!"

"Wolf…we got blood, just not his."

"Whatchu mean? Who we get, Si?"

"Drive, Wolf. We can sort it out back at the crib."

Hannibal's eyes left the road and looked over at his second's grim face. "Who we get?"

Silas looked up, and his dead gaze shocked Hannibal. "Looked like a mother and her little girl. They was on the sofa. Prolly fell asleep watchin TV."

"We need to call 911 or somethin? They all right?" Hannibal asked.

"No," Shep said solemnly, "they ain't. They won't ever be all right."

Hannibal's hands tightened on the steering wheel as anger raged within him. Without warning, the Wolf howled, and the steering wheel buckled in his hands.

64

The next morning after watching the grim morning news about another fatal drive by on Youngstown's South Side, there was a knock on Seth's hotel door. He grabbed his gun and cautiously moved to the peephole. After a quick glance, he tucked the weapon and opened the door to confront the three faces smiling back at him.

"Well, if it isn't the trust fund trio," Seth said to Charlie, Gavin, and Chad. Seth glanced at his watch noting that it wasn't yet 8 a.m. They reeked of pot. "Kinda early for a social call, huh fellas?"

"Breakfast call," Gavin said.

"Yeah, we were cravin pancakes, and you were on the way." Charlie bounced on his toes almost giddy. "You in, Pops? Our treat."

Seth looked them up and down. "Long night, boys?" he asked assessing their glassy eyes.

"Just an all night bender, no biggie," Chad said with a shrug and an arrogant smirk as he grabbed his crotch.

"Uh-huh," Seth was about to tell them to go home, take a shower, and sleep it off when he thought feeding them first was a better idea. He didn't want to send them back on the road in this condition, and he didn't want to think about what the ride over had been like. *Fucking kids*, he thought. *They have the whole world in front of them, and what do they do all night? Get high.*

"Wait for me outside and keep it quiet," Seth said shutting the door. Already dressed in tan slacks and an undershirt, he slipped on his brown leather loafers and threw on a blue, short-sleeve, button-down shirt before he grabbed his wallet and adjusted his gun.

On the drive over to the tiny diner the trust fund trio giggled and tossed around inside jokes. His frustration with the boys grew, and he made no attempts to hide it. "Sit up straight, Charlie, and what's with all the giggling? Something funny? Tell me. I want to laugh too." His question quieted the three, and they rode in silence for the duration of the ride.

Seth ordered four coffees as soon as the waitress seated them in what had become his table.

"I don't like coffee, Pop," Charlie said.

"Yeah well, you need some, so you're drinking it today. Hopefully it'll sober your asses up."

"You know, Mr. Jackson, coffee and caffeine don't really sober you up," Gavin chimed in from behind his menu.

"Yeah, how you know?" Seth asked.

"Dad's a doctor, and I've sat through more than enough epic lectures on the myths of modern society's chemical dependency on sugar to gluten to caffeine," he said making the other two trust funders laugh.

"Apparently he must have failed to touch on a few key chemical dependencies in his lectures, or are you an extremely poor student?"

"Besides," the pretty Asian boy continued as if he didn't hear the question, "I've done some research on my own about the coffee myth. All caffeine does is make you feel like you're more alert. When in reality you're still as drunk or high as before. You're just a more alert drunk or high person."

"Thanks for the lesson, doc, but you're all still getting a cup," Seth said before he turned to face his grandson sitting next to him. "So what's the plan?"

Charlie and his friends looked at Seth and then at each other completely confused. Charlie shrugged. "Plan?"

"Yeah, boys. What's the plan? You guys have a plan, right?" Seth asked as he glanced at both Gavin and Chad. "I mean you guys hung out all night and got high, right?"

They all sheepishly nodded.

"Right, so I'm guessing you guys crafted a plan that's gonna get Charlie out of the mess he's in. Or did you blow the entire damn evening smoking, playing video games, giggling like a bunch of schoolgirls, and doing whatever else you do when you get high?" Seth asked as he eyed each sternly and finally settled on his grandson.

Each boy suddenly found his lap utterly fascinating.

Seth leaned in towards Charlie and whispered in the boy's ear through clenched teeth. "You are wasting your time, and you don't have time to waste, son. I am out here to help you, but if you would rather smoke your life away I will go home—back to my life, my friends, and my responsibilities—and let you work this out all on your own. Is that what you want?"

Fear flooded Charlie's eyes, and he shook his head emphatically.

"Then get your shit together, and why can I see your drawers, boy? Are you wearing a belt?"

"I was. I think I was. Wait, yeah I was, but then something happened, and it came off, and…. I don't know what happened. It should be back at the house."

Seth shook his head as their coffees arrived with a small carafe of milk and container of sugar. Chad and Charlie went for the sugar at the same time, and the white grain spilled across the table.

"What the hell?" Seth said exasperated.

"Damn, nigga! What the fuck?" Chad said laughing.

Seth's temper snapped like weak tinder. "What did you just say?" he asked, his eyes wide with fury. Seth watched the little white boy's face flush crimson red, which told Seth this kid knew it was wrong to use that word, but he'd used it anyway and with a comfort level that incensed Seth. The boy looked like he was about to piss himself, but Seth didn't care or relent. "What the fuck did you just say?" Seth asked again leaning forward to catch the eyes of the young white teen.

"C'mon, Pop, he was playing. That's how we talk. He's cool, settle down," Charlie said as he tried to defend his friend.

Seth slowly tilted his head to Charlie and with a hard glare asked, "Was I talkin to you?"

Charlie fell silent.

"Don't you ever tell me to 'settle down' again." Seth turned his attention back to Chad. "Let me tell you something, white boy. If I ever hear that word come out of your mouth again, I will beat you to within an inch of your life. Do you hear me?"

For long minutes, all three of the boys stared at the sugarcoated table in silence.

Gavin swallowed. "It's just a word," he said quietly. "We joke all the time calling each other names. We call Chad 'pasty.'"

Seth stared at Gavin incredulous. "Yes, because 'pasty' carries just as many years of hurt, anger, and fear. This coming from the smartest kid at the damn table?" Seth shook his head as if coming out of stunned stupor, but his anger remained white-hot. "Shut the hell up, genius."

Gavin fell silent.

"Do you know that for generations Black boys that looked like you were strung up from trees and hung until their necks snapped? And were tarred and feathered just for being Black while that word rained down on them by boys that looked like him?" Seth asked gesturing to Chad.

"Boys your age, younger than you, and older than you, were called that word as they ran for their lives, as they were set upon by dogs, cut open, set on fire by white people simply because they were Black. I'm sure Chad is a nice kid, a 'cool dude' who loves hip hop, and would maybe even date a Black girl if given the chance, but if he or anyone else for that matter—whether they're Black or white—ever calls you a nigger, you better try and knock them the fuck out.

"Since you dumb asses like Googling so much, when you get home today, Google Emmitt Till and guess how many times he was called that word as he was dragged down to the river before having his head smashed in. Look up James Byrd or Michael Donald and guess how many times they heard that word before they were murdered. Maybe instead of getting high you can spend an hour reading about how for hundreds of years the white folk of this country used the word nigger to belittle Black folks and keep us in our place," Seth said before taking a sip of his cooling coffee. "Charlie, don't ever let another person call you that or refer to you as that for as long as you live. You're more than that, son. You're better than that. We are better than that. Always have been. Always will be."

"Black people say it all the time though," Charlie said still gazing at the sugar.

"Is crack a bad idea?" Seth asked.

"Yeah."

"And if a Black person lit up a crack pipe in front of you, would you take a hit?"

"No."

"Exactly. Just because some ignorant Black folk don't know any better doesn't mean you should follow their damn lead, does it?"

Reluctantly Charlie answered with a timid, "No."

"Exactly, don't let it happen again," Seth said as he motioned for the waitress who wiped their table clean before delivering their food.

They all ate in silence. Seth eyed the boys closely as they tore into their breakfast and wondered what it must be like growing up in a world with no real supervision or responsibility. He thought about what it must be like never knowing what it felt like to go to bed hungry or having to use the heat of the oven to make sure you didn't freeze during the night. He looked at his grandson and then over at his two friends. They were clueless, and that was mostly their fault, but it wasn't entirely. Their parents dropped the ball on these young men, and for a moment he pitied them for that.

There was no excuse for cluelessness in today's world, and that's what had already gotten Charlie in trouble—ignorance and arrogance. He'd thought he was smarter than Stony. Stony had played into that, and Charles had fallen right into Stony's hands. Seth couldn't allow his grandson to grow up without knowing strength and a stern hand. He wasn't responsible for his grandson's friends, but Charlie and his friends damn sure needed some tough love.

Seth shook his head and finished his pancakes. He looked at Chad and Gavin again as he wiped his mouth. "You boys hear about the woman and the little girl that was shot and killed in their house last night?" Seth asked before he finished off his coffee and nodded to the waitress for a refill.

"Yeah," Gavin said. "It's the war."

"What war?"

"The one between some guy named Apple and Stony," answered Charlie.

"Apple?" Seth asked with a smirk on his lips. "Who names their kid Apple?"

The waitress refilled Seth's cup, but as she'd listened to their conversation her usual smile had disappeared. Without its magic, her beauty went with it. "Your young men have that wrong. It's between Frank and the Wolf. Frank and his South Side crew killed Appleton, the Wolf's cousin, and they haven't stopped fighting since," she said.

"Yeah, the one between Frank and his people and the Wolf," Chad said acting as if he'd won some competition. Seth shot him a look that shut him down again.

Seth turned his attention back to the waitress. "The Wolf?"

"Hannibal Wolf, he runs the crew over on the East Side. Since Appleton was killed there's been no peace," she said.

"So that's what all this is about?"

"Revenge, territory, ego, take your pick," she answered with a slow shrug. "Does it matter anymore?"

"Suppose it doesn't."

"Ya'll ready for the check?" she asked resting her hand had on her ample hip. Seth nodded, and she sauntered off.

"That's not what I heard started it all," Gavin said once they were alone again.

"Really? What'd you hear genius?" Seth asked.

Gavin leaned in and whispered. "I heard one of Frank's boys got beat down coming out of a movie or something. It was bad. They put him in the hospital. Frank and Stony found out the East Side crew was responsible, and they decide to take out Appleton and The Wolf as payback. They killed Appleton but never got to The Wolf," Gavin said as he sat back triumphant.

"This coming from the guy that thought 'nigga' was just a word," Seth said as he and Charlie leaned back in unison. *That explains a lot.*

The waitress returned and placed the bill on the table.

So who's winning this war?" Seth asked her.

"If I had to guess, I would say The Wolf," she replied, sliding the bill in front of Seth.

"Why?"

"Cause he has a bigger crew. Plus he's crazy," the hefty cinnamon colored woman answered. "They're the ones who shot up Romare's last Sunday."

"Yeah, word is he ain't wrapped too tight," Charlie confirmed. "Took too many blows to the head or something."

"He's a boxer?"

"No," she said. "He was a star football player in high school and got too many concussions. They said it was his knee, but everyone thinks it was too many blows to the head."

"What's your name?" Seth asked her.

"Alice."

"Well thank you Alice for the hospitality and the information," Seth said as she walked away carting their dishes with an extra swish of her hips. He smiled for the first time all morning and left a twenty-dollar tip on the table before he headed up front to pay for their tab.

"I said this was our treat," Charlie said.

"Keep your money in your pocket. Use it to buy a damn belt," he snapped at his grandson, who once again dragged at his sagging pants.

The ride back to the hotel was far more subdued than the ride to the diner. When the boys exited the Cadillac and headed back to Chad's car Seth took hold of his grandson. "Look, I'm glad you wanted to have breakfast with me, but if you ever come to me high as a kite again, I will hurt you. Do you understand me?"

Charlie nodded.

"Good, because I love you, but I won't hesitate to beat the snot out of you. You need to get your shit together, Charlie. You're no longer a little boy living in a world where your dad can protect you every minute. This ain't no video game, son. Out here the bullets are real. Or have you somehow forgotten what it was like at Romare's? You need your wits about you now more than ever. Go home and take a shower. Tell your friends they need one too, and I'll see you later," he said as he headed into the hotel leaving the trust fund trio to their own devices.

65

When Hannibal walked into Monique's hospital suite, her clenched jaw and furrowed brow were a clear indication that she was not at all pleased. The large bouquet of flowers he'd brought had little effect on her mood, but he hoped she was simply aggravated with being stuck in the hospital. He did his best to get past her cold gaze and leaned over to kiss her. While she didn't turn her face away, she didn't turn into his kiss either.

"How are you?" he asked as he set the flowers by the window. He took the small chair next to her bed and reached over to caress her hand.

"I'm fine," she replied flatly keeping her eyes on the elevated TV. "See what I'm watching?"

Hannibal looked up to see the local news anchor show the same footage he'd caught an hour before he'd left the house. He hung his head and inspected the linoleum-tiled floor. Her reaction wasn't a surprise. He'd known the little girl's death would inspire her wrath once again. He lifted his head, and her angry brown eyes pierced through him. He was furious with himself as well, and regretted not listening to that little voice that said he should wait and see her tomorrow. He swallowed hard and wondered if she'd kick him out of her room or even out of her life. "What do you want me to say?" he asked her quietly.

"What can you say?"

"I can say we fucked up," he whispered. He hated uncontrolled environments where he wasn't sure if extra ears were listening.

"I can see that," she whispered through clenched teeth. "What happened?"

"Bad info. We was told the dude that…painted the den was there, and we went to see him about the cost. We thought the nigga was alone, babe. I swear to you."

"Were you there?"

"I stayed in the car," he whispered. "Silas and one a his rang the doorbell."

Monique closed her eyes and sighed. "I know you didn't mean for it to go down like that, but the payment was too high, baby.

Hannibal's head rested on the bed, and Monique touched it softly.

"I feel somewhat responsible. I told you to do what you had to, but I had no idea this is how it would end up."

Hannibal looked up at her tear-soaked face. "No, Mo…"

She put a finger to his lips. "Can you get me some water from down the hall?" she asked, interrupting him. When he got back to the room, Monique sat with her feet dangling over the side of the bed. A fine sheen of perspiration covered her forehead as she grimaced.

"Where you going?"

"I need to get out of this room, please," she said.

The two left her room and slowly began to walk the hallways of her floor. Her left arm was in a sling, and her right was wrapped tightly around Hannibal's tree trunk of an arm.

"Hey, who taught you that double jab?" he asked.

"Ali."

"Been watching his fights again, huh?"

"Can't help it. That's my porn," she said with a soft smile. He loved her smile but missed her throaty, contagious laugh. When Monique laughed, everyone around her laughed too. They couldn't help it. Even on the dreariest of days, her laugh brought out the sun. He couldn't imagine having any kind of existence without her in his life. It would have killed him if he'd lost her to bullets meant for him.

"What's wrong? You're tense," she asked as they got to the end of the hallway and made a slow U-turn.

"Thinking how I almost lost you."

"But you didn't, so calm down, baby."

"I got lucky."

"We both did," she corrected him. "Which is why it's time to bring this mess to an end."

"What?"

"It's time to call a truce," she said.

Her delicate features hardened anticipating push back, but he had none to give. Deep down he knew she was right, and to argue the point would have been a waste of time.

Monique stopped walking and gazed into his light brown eyes. "There's only us dying out there, and if it was just soldiers I would still feel horrible, but civilians…children are getting caught up in this now. It's time to make peace," she said as she squeezed his arm. "Appleton would tell you the same thing, and you know it." They started walking again and made it back to her room. Instead of getting in bed, Monique took one of the seats by her window.

Hannibal took the other. "They killed Ike," he said thickly.

She winced in pain at his words but mumbled, "I know."

"How you know?"

"He's the only one who hasn't visited me yet," she said wiping at tears. "Promise me you'll stop this, Han."

"I will. I'll put the word out that I'm looking for a sit-down the second I leave."

Monique left her chair and climbed into Hannibal's lap. "Thank you, daddy." She kissed him, and he wrapped her in his arms.

"So when you gettin paroled?"

"Maybe tomorrow if everything looks okay. Doc said it wasn't as bad as they initially thought." She yawned and closed her eyes.

Hannibal's eyes drank her in. Her dark chocolate complexion and full lips mesmerized him. She had eyes that could look into a person's soul and see all of their weaknesses and shortcomings, something she had done to him and yet still she loved him. This beautiful, smart, intelligent Black woman loved him. That knowledge still took him by surprise. He knew he would have been either in jail or dead if it weren't for her. He owed this beautiful woman his life, and he knew that like he knew the sun rose in the east and set in the west.

"Daddy, carry me to bed, please?" she asked softly, her eyes still closed.

"Will that hurt your shoulder?"

"I don't know. If I scream then put me down, okay?"

"Okay," he said with a chuckle and lifted her with ease. Once he'd tucked her in and kissed her on the lips, he told her he'd come by tomorrow to pick her up.

With another yawn, she whispered, "You better."

Minutes later, Hannibal walked out of the hospital and climbed into the passenger seat as Silas started the car. "Put the word out when we get back. I wanna sit down with them niggas. It's time to stop this shit."

Silas paused and searched his Alpha's face before he slowly nodded his head. "I feel you," Silas said. He was about to throw the car in drive when the driver side window imploded, and buckshot shredded Silas' head, spraying the interior of the truck with blood, skin, and brains. Hannibal stumbled out the truck and pulled his gun.

"Fuck!"

Drenched in Silas' blood and with his ears ringing, he crouched and made his way to the rear of the truck. When he came up from behind back bumper, he was ready to shoot, but no one was there. A car fishtailed out of the parking lot and disappeared.

"FUCK!"

66

"You happy now?" Frank asked Ripper.

"Hell nah, I ain't happy, not by a long fucking shot!" the slim killer screamed as his fists clenched and his body shook.

"What else you want, nigga? We got the shooter. We was told he was the shooter of your babygirl and your ex, and we got his ass. What more you want?"

"I want his family!" Ripper yelled.

Ripper, Frank, Stony, and a few others had gathered around the bar after the successful hit on Silas. Frank had wanted to get The Wolf too, but the way the car had sat in the hospital's lot, there had been no way to set up on the passenger side without being seen. Frank had told them to go with the scattergun and hit the driver side door in the hopes that they'd get lucky and get Hannibal too. They knew Silas had fallen, but Hannibal was still breathing.

"Hell no," Stony said pinching the bridge of his nose. "You out your fucking mind? Be happy with him. There will be no going after his family. You can forget that shit."

Ripper quickly went from Stony to Frank. He looked at Frank with a crazed pleading in his eyes, seeking permission for payback.

Frank locked eyes with Rip for what seemed like an hour but was mere seconds and with no change in his body language shook his head with regret. "Normally I'd be with you, but Stony's right on this one. There's too much heat to take that shot. When senators start pledging to clean up the streets you know it's hot. Let's let shit die down before we make that move. Feel me?"

"Nah, nigga, I don't feel you. What you tellin me is I should just be happy we got one of the mothafuckas that killed my family? Is that…is that what ya'll are saying to me? IS THAT WHAT YA'LL ARE SAYIN TO ME?" Ripper screamed as every muscle in his sinewy dark form tensed.

Frank braced himself. "Rip, calm down, man," he said softly in warning.

"No. No, Frank. You calm down," Ripper replied before pointing at Stony. "And Stony, you calm the fuck down too. Me...I think I'll lose my fucking mind if that's okay with ya'll," he said as he pulled his gun.

With the speed of a black mamba, Frank lashed out, snatched Ripper's wrist with his left hand, and his right connected with Ripper's jaw putting the crazed boy down and temporarily out of his misery. He looked at his young soldier sprawled on the bar's dusty floor.

"Kay, get him up, and you and Manny take him home. Get him high, get him drunk, whatever. Just don't let the lil nigga get near his guns. He starts losing his mind again, hit me up," Frank said. The two boys nodded, lifted Ripper from the floor, and hauled him out of the bar. Frank wrapped some ice in a towel. Swollen knuckles made pulling a trigger difficult, and he couldn't afford to be slow.

Frank and Stony looked at each other, and they both shook their heads. Frank picked up a beer and took a stool next to his partner. They drank in silence, listening to the passing traffic. Both men were on edge after the Silas hit. They had no idea when they were going to feel The Wolf's blowback. It wasn't a question of if but when.

Stony's Desert Eagle sat in his lap. He no longer went anywhere without it. Its heft and power comforted him in a way nothing except for Frank's presence could, but he wanted this madness over with. When he'd had Frank take out Appleton in a demonstration of strength, he'd never imagined that the retaliations and bloodshed would escalate to this point. Their actions had started a fire that now raged out of control, and they needed to put a stop to it before it burned them and everything they had to cinders. He was nervous about bringing up the possibility of a truce to Frank since he seemed to be having the time of his life.

Stony leaned back and sighed. He couldn't put off the conversation any longer. "You know this shit is killing business, right?" Stony asked him. Frank stared at the plywood where the mirror used to hang but said nothing. Stony went on undaunted. "I mean, we can do all right without the corners for the moment, but you and I both know this place makes money hand over fist, and this shit with the East Side is putting all that in jeopardy. This place...it's like Wally World for adults, liquor, bitches, music, gambling, a veritable smorgasbord."

"A what?" Frank asked.

"Never mind."

"What's your point?" Frank asked.

Stony could feel Frank's frustration mounting, but he pressed on. He turned in his chair to face Frank. "My point is shit has slowed down considerably since we got hit, and that ain't good. People don't wanna go to Wally World if the coasters fall off the tracks, you feel me?" he said throwing is arms out, pointing at the repairs still needed. "People—no matter how desperate—don't wanna come out if they feel they might catch a stray in the noodle. This beef is slowing our money down," Stony said before he finished off his drink.

"I'm tired, Frank. I'm tired of looking over my shoulders wandering if a round is coming for me. I'm tired of cleaning up blood and brains, and most of all I'm tired of losing money. I got the police knocking on my front door with their questions and subtle accusations, looking into my licensing and shit. I lose my liquor license, and I might as well shutter the place," Stony said from behind the bar as he grabbed himself a beer and handed Frank a new one. "Remember what they did to my uncle, all the harassment, all the unnecessary bullshit? If shit don't start to settle down, they will be coming again. Could be on their way here now for all we know. Closing this place is bad business for us but especially you. I lose this place, and I lose a part of my uncle, and it'll hurt. I still have the real estate and shit, but Romare's was his dream...his baby. If you lose this place though, you lose your Laundromat. Your money will stay dirty, and we both know you're too smart to not give a damn about that."

"So what the fuck you wanna do, Stone? Get to the damn point already."

"I think I made my point, Frank." When Stony rose he gripped Frank's shoulder. "Think about what I said."

Stony dragged his weapon off the bar and headed up to his office. War was bad for business unless you were the United States. Then war was a boon. Romare's wasn't the US. It was a neighborhood spot that was limping along after being a casualty of this mess. Frank was no fool. He understood loss to profit margins, and he had to realize this beef with Hannibal was bad business. The only way to stop losing money was to end this, quickly.

Stony took a long swallow of his beer, stared at his fish, and hoped Frank could see reason.

67

Seth's phone buzzed on the night table early Thursday morning. He wasn't in the mood to talk, so he debated whether to let the call go to voicemail. At the last second he answered. "Yeah?"

"Seth, I hope you're sitting down, my friend. Are you sitting down? Tell me you're sitting down," Jonathan Washington said in a rapid-fire barrage.

His young lawyer's early enthusiasm before Seth's first taste of anything caffeinated felt like the roaring surf crashing against his eardrums. "I'm laying down. What is it?" he asked as he attempted to reign in his aggravation.

"You're still sleeping? Shit, I heard small towns can have that soporific effect on people. I've never believed that myself. I figure, hey, if you're tired then you're tired regardless where you are. Know what I mean, Seth?"

"Jonathan, exactly how much coffee have you had this morning?"

"Why? Am I talking too fast? I get that. People tell me that all the time in the morning. I have no idea why they say that or what they're talking about, but everybody asks that for some reason."

"Did you spike your coffee with adrenaline?"

"HA! That's a good one, Seth."

The Black Hat was excited about something, so Seth attempted to calm the younger man down enough to find out what he had. "I thought you were going to call me last night."

"I said end of business day tomorrow. It's tomorrow, and I'm calling."

"Get to the damn point."

"Don't be so touchy, Seth. Anyway, what I dug up…well, more what my assistant and the paralegals dredged up…was a significant history with Leonard Carmichael and the authorities there in Ohio, and it seemed that a Browning Jackson, related I'm sure, targeted

Leonard for destruction and applied the screws to the old man, seizing assets, freezing accounts, police raids. All to make a name for himself." The kid seemed to take a drink and finally paused for a moment.

"For some reason he was given carte blanche to go after Leonard Carmichael and did so with reckless abandon until the old man dropped dead of a heart attack. The family blamed the acute myocardial infarction on the District Attorney's office and filed a wrongful death suit, which went nowhere. They named your son in the suit as well. I haven't dug into Leonard's will yet, but it looks like his estate was left to his nephew. Who knows what kind of drama that caused in the family. I remember this one estate case, and man, I gotta tell you. The vultures were flocking and this one chick. Seth, she was so hot she was like human Viagra and...."

"The entire estate?" Seth asked interrupting his lawyer.

"What? Yeah, everything down to the last nickel. I hope that helps you in some way."

"In more ways than one, Jonathan. You corroborated what I've heard and gave me some other things to chew on."

"Good, the bill is in the mail."

"I'm sure it is," Seth said.

"Anything else I can bill you…uhhh…do for you?" Jonathan asked making both men chuckle.

"No. Thanks, you gave me what I needed."

"I don't feel like I did anything."

"Then don't bill me," Seth said.

"You must be out yo mind, Seth. Shit, I'd bill my own kids for helping them with their homework if my wife didn't stop me," the lawyer said bringing genuine laughter out of Seth as he made his way to the bathroom.

"Talk to you later, Black Hat. Try not to burn someone's world down today."

The young lawyer chuckled. "Don't cloud my joy, old man."

"You know that's not my style, junior."

"That's what I heard. Be easy, Seth. Be easy," he said as he hung up the phone.

68

Monique was already dressed, her left arm in its sling, and waiting patiently when Hannibal arrived pushing an empty wheelchair into her room. Her breath caught. He had told her about Silas, but she hadn't prepared herself for Hannibal's appearance. Flying glass had left the side of his face scarred, pockmarked, and swollen, and an eye patch covered his left eye.

"Oh my God, baby, are you okay?"

"I'm good, but I'll be a lot better once I get you home, Mo."

"Did you get any sleep? You look exhausted," she said as she caressed his face. "How bad is your eye? Did they get all the glass out? Will there be permanent damage?"

"One question at a time girl, damn," he said with a chuckle.

"I'm sorry, baby. It's…seeing you like that scares me," she said and stood up to gently place her hand on the good side of his face.

"C'mon," he said moving his face away. "In the chair with you."

"I can walk."

"Hospital regulations stipulate that you must be wheeled out of the building, so sit."

Monique grumbled but sat in the chair. "Stipulations, huh?"

"You know how many times I heard that shit back when I was playing ball and ended up in the hospital?" he asked as he grabbed her bags.

Hannibal slowly pushed her into the elevator after sincere thanks and a warm goodbye to the nurses at the station. Just before they made it to the front door, Monique bounded out of the chair eager to get outside and feel the sun on her skin again. Hannibal smirked at her impatience, and with speed that belied his bulk he was outside and quickly by Monique's side.

"Want me to carry one of those bags?" she asked.

"Look, one arm McCoy, I got it, okay? Let's go."

"One arm McCoy? Is that a new one?"

"Best I could do on the spur of the moment." He pointed to a black Chevy Suburban sitting curbside. "Now please get in the car," he said with a sense of urgency in his tone.

"And whose car is that?"

"For as long as we need, it's ours," he answered trying to hide the edge in his voice.

"Why?"

"Bulletproof," he answered.

"Ahhhh," Monique said. "That's smart. So who's is it?"

"Get in the goddamn car!" he bellowed. Monique froze. Hannibal didn't mean to snap at her, but she was being playful in the parking lot where he'd almost lost his life two days ago. He'd apologize later and make it up to her someway.

Hannibal's outburst caused every eye milling around the entrance to look his way. "We can talk about that once we all buckled up," he added in a calm but firm tone while he scanned the area.

Realization dawned in Monique's eyes. "I'm sorry," she said and quickly climbed up into the truck and closed the door.

On their way home, he didn't break the speed limit, but he pushed it as far as legally possible. "To answer your question, it's Cane's truck," he said.

"Cane? You two talking again?"

"Not really, but he heard what happened and had this delivered to the house this morning."

"How in the hell did he know what happened? Isn't he playing for the Dolphins?"

"Cowboys, and I have no idea how he heard, but he heard."

"So did you make the arrangements?" Monique asked as Hannibal smoothly pulled up to a stoplight.

"What arrangements?" he asked as he continued to check his mirrors.

"To bring this to an end."

Dumbfounded he said, "Are you serious? Look at me. I've got another funeral to go to because I wasn't driving. If I was drivin then that would be my Black ass going in the ground," he said pounding the steering wheel for emphasis. "Hell nah, I ain't make no arrangements. Fuck dem niggas. They can all eat a bullet."

"Pull over," Monique ordered him.

"What? For what?"

"Cause I fucking said so," she answered.

Reluctantly Hannibal pulled to the curb. He didn't like being so exposed, but he had faith in the truck. He shifted into park and sat back in the black leather seat.

"I know you're mad," Monique said slowly in a calm voice while looking straight ahead. "I know it. I can feel the heat coming off you, but you have to understand something. You have to see that the most important thing is not revenge. Revenge doesn't pay a damn bill, it doesn't buy any food, and it damn sure doesn't keep a roof over someone's head.

"They came at you yesterday, and I almost lost you. Do you see that?" she asked, her emotions rising. "I almost lost YOU after YOU almost lost ME!" she said as her voice wavered. "We've been lucky so far, but luck runs out, and pretty soon, they won't miss, and while you may be able to live without me, I can't make it without you. So you get on the damn phone, call whomever you have to call, put the word out on the streets, and let the world know that you want a cease-fire. And if you're worried about what some motherfuckers are going to think about you, whether or not you're bitching out, who gives a shit? All that should matter is what I think about you. That and the fact that there are too many kids dying, too many tiny caskets going in the ground."

Monique wiped at her eyes with her free hand. "I love you. God knows I do, but if you don't try to bring this shit to an end then I will leave town, and I will hope and pray every hour of the day that you are still breathing when I return. I've been shot once. I don't want to be shot again. Now take me home."

Hannibal wordlessly and slowly sat up, shifted the truck into drive, and did what he was told.

69

After four days of non-stop repairs, Romare's was in full swing Thursday night. Regulars along with those craving air conditioning came to drink, hang out with friends, gamble, and forget about the world at large for a few hours. The music thumped, and the girls gyrated and danced with the pole to the delight of the men who surrounded the stage.

Upstairs, Stony went through expense receipts and orders and counted the take so far. He was finding it hard to breathe. The past week had been horrible money wise. Between the labor, materials, and lost revenue, Romare's would end the month in the red.

The conversation with Frank the day before kept reverberating in his head. Romare's had already been hit once. The last thing he needed was another drive-by, and he hoped Frank understood that business was far more important than winning some war against a washed up football player on the other side of town.

Stony's uncle had explained to him long ago how important Romare's was to the community and that with few viable jobs in the area and next to none on the South Side the best way for anyone to make a living wage in the hood was to hustle, trick, or hit the stage and dance on the pole. "It's not like anyone wants to do shit like this," Leonard had explained. "They don't have no real choice in the matter. Romare's gives people a place to put some money in their pockets both legally and illegally, it gives some people a reason to get out of bed in the morning, and it gives them purpose." This war if it continued would take away that purpose.

A loud thump from downstairs caused Stony to grab his Desert Eagle that rested next to his MacBook. Every unfamiliar or unexpected noise signaled possible danger and bloodshed. Where Romare's had once felt like a safe haven, it now felt like a ticking bomb, a place where he could potentially die. Every bone in his body warned him that it was only a matter of time before The Wolf paid them back for Silas' murder.

"I can't take much more of this shit!" he yelled at the ceiling. As if on cue, his cell phone buzzed. It was Frank.

"Yo, you sittin down?" Frank asked.

"Yeah, what's up?" Stony asked taking a hard pull of his cigar, trying to calm his nerves.

"He wants to call a truce."

Stony coughed out cigar smoke. "What? Say that again?"

"The Wolf is calling for a truce. You believe that shit?"

"No, so stop fucking with me Frank. I'm not in the mood, man."

"Real talk. I just got word that muscle bound freak wants a sit down as soon as possible."

Stony shook his head in confusion. *Frank just had that 'muscle bound freak's' second murdered, but he wants a truce?* It didn't make sense at all, but he wasn't about to complain.

"When you wanna do this?" Frank asked.

"Tomorrow," Stony said. He didn't want too long of a wait and risk anyone or anything changing their minds. Another incident could heighten tempers again and dash any hopes of a cease-fire. No, he had to keep that from happening at all costs. "Where does he want to meet?"

"That soul food spot on Rayen."

"The Kitchen? Downtown?" asked Stony.

"Yeah, it's a smart choice. It's neutral territory, jail right across the street, university not that far away, cops up the block."

"Sounds good to me. What time is he talking?"

"We set the time since he set the place, so you tell me," Frank said.

Stony thought about it for a second. He was sure The Wolf would have someone scoping the place out hours before the meet. "Tell him two. That way the lunch crowd should be gone, and there can be no surprises."

"Aiight, I'll call you when I hear back," Frank said and disconnected.

Stony ran his hands across his face in relief. He eyed the gleaming hand cannon on the desk and shook his head. He had never been a fan of guns. Leonard had once explained that they were tools and a necessary evil in his world, but his uncle had done his best to keep them out of his nephew's life. With the sit down coming, Stony opened his desk drawer, put away his Desert Eagle, and hoped he would never have to wrap his fingers around the molded rubber grip again.

After a moment he walked to the liquor cabinet and poured himself a glass of Blue Label Johnny Walker. As the warmth spread across his chest Stony could finally breathe a little easier and again turn his focus back to Charlie and the Basquiat.

70

At first Charlie didn't know why he woke up that Friday morning with a dark cloud hung over his mind, but in the shower it hit him like a bolt of lightning. The Basquiat arrived at The Butler today. He slid down the wall of the shower as the dark cloud morphed into a cloak of fear that shrouded him from head to toe.

He suddenly regretted everything in his life. He regretted getting involved Stony. He regretted not taking his debt seriously enough, thinking he could laugh it off and it would magically disappear. He regretted the madness that he considered stealing from his dad and stepmother. He regretted getting high all the damn time. His habit had cost him so much time, but most of all it had cost him Lily. He had refused to sit and stew over her in the immediate days after she'd left, refusing to even think of her, but he wished more than anything that he could talk to her right now.

His grandfather was right. He needed to get his shit together. *No one stays seventeen forever.* He pulled himself up and wiped the water from his face. Charlie wasn't sure what he wanted for his future, but he desperately wanted to get past this moment of his life and hoped there was a future out there somewhere for him.

He shut off the shower when the water finally started to grow cold and slowly slipped into his robe as if his entire body hurt. Part of him craved to get high, crawl back into bed, and curl into a ball. Instead he hit speed dial on his phone.

"Hello," Seth answered.

"Pop?" Charlie asked, his voice betraying him.

"You all right, son?"

"The painting comes to town today. The one by the guy with the funny name."

"It's not a funny name. It's Haitian. Say bas-key-ot."

Charlie repeated his grandfather's pronunciation.

"Very good, so it comes today?"

"Yeah," Charlie said.

"Okay, so what's the problem, youngin?"

"I was hoping it wouldn't show, so I wouldn't have to go through with this. I don't know anything about stealing any art."

"Charlie," Seth started, "You and your friends know nothing about nothing if you want to get right down to it. Smoking a blunt? Yeah, you guys got that down to a science. Video games? I bet you guys could win some tournament somewhere. How to deal with life? How to think steps ahead? How to critically think and problem solve? Sadly, you and your boys don't have the slightest clue how to do any of that. You've turned your brains into mush, and honestly that frightens the hell out of me." Seth sighed. "Look, don't worry about the Basquiat, Charles. I am going to do what I can to help you. You just have to show me the museum. Do you know where it is?"

"Yeah, it's downtown right by the university and the library."

"Good, that's good. Relax, son. Get dressed and get out of the house. Take a drive somewhere, clear your head, and I'll be in touch, okay?"

"Okay, Pop, thanks." Charlie disconnected the call feeling significantly better. He had someone in his corner, all the way in his corner. There was someone not simply paying lip service or lying to him about how they'd be there when things got tough. This was someone who was connected to him by blood, and that made all the difference.

Charlie threw off his robe and rifled through his closet. He decided to take his grandfather's advice and go for a drive. He knew just the place.

71

Between college students, the professors, and the employees from the hospital and various banks, Rayen Avenue tended to reach frenetic levels between the hours of 11 a.m. and 1 p.m. A few eateries dotted Youngstown's downtown, but The Soup Kitchen was ground zero when it came to lunch destinations. The local landmark had a casual dining room, a back bar with a "to-go" counter, and the best menu in a five mile radius, delicious authentic soul food for a more than reasonable price. Many restaurants had come and gone thanks to Youngstown's ups and downs, but The Kitchen had thrived in the good times and withstood the hard ones.

Patrons milled in and out of the brick two-story restaurant to place their order, pick up their food to go, or eat on the patio in the warmth of the bright midday sunlight, but they never noticed the eyes spying down on them. Hidden in the shadows of a tattered billboard on the roof of the dilapidated building across the street was a man on his stomach, trying to stay cool and invisible. He'd been there for a few hours armed with a pair of binoculars, a burner cell phone, a fully automatic Mac 10, candy bars, extra clips, and a warm bottle of Pepsi. His primary task was to watch and alert Hannibal if anything about this sit-down felt or looked out of place. His second task was to shoot anything that moved should this thing go to hell.

His job was all part of the game, to set up on your enemies before they set up on you. He'd already spotted Frank's few lookers, each parked a few blocks down the cross streets, but they were distracted by their cell phones. He sneered. They stuck out like oil stains on a white shirt.

The crow checked his watch. It was 1:50 p.m. when he spied Stony's black Escalade cruise down Belmont Avenue and roll to a stop a few feet in front of The Kitchen's front door. Through his binoculars, he took note of Stony's gators and Frank's boots. "The wannabe pimp and the thug. It's hot as hell out here, and that nigga, Frank, in Timbs," he said with a low chuckle.

As expected, the duo wasn't alone. The truck carried extra muscle. With the number of casualties each side had suffered, back up made sense. They were all dressed in black, wearing body armor and sunglasses. "Them niggas look like background singers," the crow said with another chuckle. As Stony walked in followed by Frank, their boys fanned out to cover every possible angle, but none raised their eyes to search the rooftops.

He took a bite of his melting candy bar, confident he had every South Sider dead to rights. *If that's all the muscle Stony brought then maybe this shit might actually happen,* he thought.

He felt the bass before he saw the truck. Turning onto West Rayen off Belmont cruised a gleaming black Suburban. The music died as it wound its way into the parking lot, past Frank's sentry, and stopped.

The crow pulled out his burner and texted "ALL CLEAR" to Hannibal. Seconds later the doors of the SUV opened and out came Hannibal followed by familiar faces.

Hannibal was dressed like he was about to attend a backyard barbeque in dark denim shorts and a white tank top covered by an open ochre-colored, button-down, linen shirt. His crisp white sneakers clashed brightly against his dark skin. Despite his casual dress, every fiber of muscle seemed tense and ready to spring into action. He clenched the phone in his hand as he searched the area and glanced momentarily up at the rooftop. A knowing smile formed on his lips.

Taking The Wolf's bicep, Monique looked equally casual. Her lavender spandex top, black yoga pants, and purple sneakers made her seem as if she was on her way to a workout. After coming close to losing her life at The Den she had decided to do something she'd always wanted and cut her long dark mane pixie short. Her purple sling finished her outfit.

As The Wolf and his hellion strode confidently into the restaurant, two East Side crewmembers took up positions outside.

"Here we go," mumbled Crow as he took a bite of a melted candy bar and scanned the area for any surprises through his binoculars.

72

"Hello," the hostess said in greeting. "Two for lunch?"

"Hello. We're here for a meeting," Monique replied with a polite smile that didn't reach her eyes.

"Ahh yes, right this way," the hostess said, leading her guests to the back of the establishment.

A weathered, tall—taller than Hannibal—Black man stood like a Sequoia outside one of the private rooms. A scar ran down the right side of his face from temple to jaw, and the look in his eyes told Hannibal that the man was a survivor and not one to take lightly. Once the young hostess had retreated, the hefty old man gestured for Hannibal to lift his arms.

"Who you?" Hannibal asked the guard who's potbelly proved he rarely missed a meal.

"Insurance," the onyx-colored man answered, stepping closer. Though he outweighed The Wolf by at least fifty pounds, his muddy-brown irises were surrounded by pools of tinted yellow, which spoke on how his health was no longer what it had been in his youth. "The owner wanted to make sure you boys don't do anything foolish like shoot up his establishment, so here I am. Like I told them boys in there, I hope you're not gonna cause me any problems."

Hannibal sucked his teeth but raised his arms.

"Good. There's food already in there, compliments of the house. Enjoy," he said as he patted Hannibal down and then checked Monique's sling. Satisfied, Mr. Insurance knocked on the door and opened it. Already eating were Stony and Frank.

Monique sent a pointed look back at the insurance guy.

"Don't worry. They clean too," he said with a wink.

Hannibal saw Frank reach for a napkin and noted Stony's empty plate. A small mountain of barbeque wings, cheese fries, and cornbread sat in the center of the table. Hannibal's mouth watered, but he had every intention on keeping negotiations short and sweet.

Though they tried to hide it, both Stony and Frank were taken aback by Monique's presence. With a slight smirk she didn't bother to hide, Hannibal's fearless better half took the seat closest to the door, directly across from Stony, while Frank and Hannibal sat across from each other. When the door softly clicked shut, the room fell dead silent.

Monique had no time for false bravado. "Well, here we are gentlemen."

"Yes," Stony said with a nervous clearing of his throat. "First off, are you all right?" he asked motioning to the sling.

"Like you give a fuck," Hannibal snapped. Monique shot him a look, and Hannibal inhaled deeply before speaking again. "Look, I don't wanna be here any longer than I have to. I'm here to settle this shit. I'll agree to a truce, but I have one demand."

"And what's that, fatso?" Frank asked after taking a bite of a wing.

Under the table, Monique touched his leg to make sure her man stayed cool, to remind him why they were there. Hannibal leaned forward and rested his powerful forearms on the table. The table squealed in protest.

"I want the name of the shooter who did my cousin," he said as calmly as he could through clenched teeth.

"I'm sorry. Say that again," Stony said.

"You heard me," Hannibal snapped.

"What we are looking for," Monique interrupted with her best smile, "is the name of the person or persons responsible for taking the life of my dear friend and Hannibal's cousin, Appleton. Give us that, and this conflict is over."

Stony glanced at Frank and leaned back in his chair in an attempt to hide his nervousness. "We have some demands of our own," he informed them.

"And what would those be?" Monique asked.

"They're more assurances than demands. First off, the safe spots are back on the map. That includes the barber shop, the mall, and the movie theater, deal?"

Monique looked at Hannibal, and with an imperceptible nod they agreed.

"Secondly," Stony continued, "we want mutual commitments that not only those places but our bases of operations will never be hit again. That's my bar and your gym. They're off limits as well."

Frank tossed several more wings onto his plate. "In other words, keep your dogs on a tighter leash."

Hannibal's eyes tensed. "I will if you keep your pussies from pissing all over the place."

"Look, fat boy, it was your niggas that started this shit in the first place, so tighten the leash, or I will. Feel me?" Frank asked.

"Try it, nigga!" Hannibal shouted which prompted a sly smirk from Frank.

Stony leaned forward. "A while ago you and your cousin came to us and wanted a slice of our pie. We said no and to celebrate that moment, a crew of your boys sent one of ours to the hospital. Let's put all this to bed right here and now. There will never be a partnership of any kind between us. Cool?" Stony asked.

"It was Appleton that wanted to move on you and work together or some shit, not me, so don't worry cause that shit ain't never happening, so yeah, we cool," Hannibal said. "Now back to my one demand."

Frank grabbed another wing from the mountain as if they were discussing the latest summer movies. "What was that again?"

The Wolf gnashed his teeth. "The name of the fucka that killed my cousin."

Stony turned his attention to Monique. "And what if we don't?"

"Come again?" Monique asked raising one perfectly manicured brow at him.

"What if we decide not to snitch on the shooter of your dear friend and his cousin?" Stony asked. "Would that mean we continue gunning down each other and fucking up our money?"

Monique's grip on Hannibal's leg tightened before she answered. "There is no need for any more bloodshed or for any additional innocents to be caught up in our…differences. We all know we need to stop this. That being said, whoever this person is that defiled

Appleton by dressing him in women's under things and dumping his body in an abandoned house like a dog," Monique said still smiling, "is someone we would like to speak with to find out if all of that was necessary."

"I like your girl, Wolf. Not only is she fine, but she talk real pretty too," Frank said. "Now we see who the brains is behind your operation." With a cold smile Frank searched Monique's face. He took a sip of his beer and then met The Wolf's eyes. "So is all that true, Hanny? All you wanna do is talk to this 'person'?"

Despite Frank's easy tone, everyone in the room tensed.

"You heard what the brains said, short stuff," Hannibal said as calmly as possible grabbing a couple of wings for himself.

"You full of shit, and no disrespect to your pretty mouthpiece here, but she full of shit too. I can sit here and think of a few things I would like to do to someone who did that to my fam. Talking ain't high on that list. So why don't you cut the shit and get to the truth, nigga?"

Hannibal leaned back in his chair and licked his fingers as a broad smile appeared on his face. "Honestly, you right. There won't be much talking when I get my hands on the bitch ass. He'll probably shit his pants and beg for mercy," Hannibal said with a distinct edge in his voice as he stared unblinking at Frank. "He'll prolly talk about his kids and how he can't leave em, maybe even offer to work for me against you two. I won't pay that no mind, and just before I break that nigga's neck, I'll make him put on a lacy thong. What's ya favorite color, Frankie?"

With every word, Frank grew more and more coiled.

Stony spoke up again in the hopes of keeping negotiations from falling apart like a pair of ten-dollar sneakers. "Okay, so let's say we agree to give up the shooter. How long do we have before we give you his information?"

"Twenty-four hours," Hannibal said.

"And what would you say if I told you that you already got the shooter of your dear friend," he asked looking at Monique, "and cousin?" he finished with a look at Hannibal.

"Whatchu talking about?" Hannibal asked.

"I'm saying…you or whomever it was that shot up the corner and took the package already got the shooter."

A thin smile formed on Frank's lips.

Stony nodded. "So are we done since that was your only demand? Can we all agree to get back our quiet little lives before the Feds show up and shut us both down?"

"Yeah, but one last thing before we go our separate ways," Hannibal said to his two nemeses. "What was this faggot's name?"

"Does it matter, nigga?" Frank said quietly.

Hannibal's patience shattered like a wine glass. "Yeah, motherfucka, it does! What was the bitch ass nigga's name?"

"Blake," Stony replied. "His name was Blake."

Monique tilted her head back and laughed at the ceiling.

"Something funny, miss thing?" Frank asked.

Hannibal answered. "Yeah, ya'll are funny. You two should take your little act on the road, you know that?"

Stony stole a quick look at Frank. "What are you talking about?"

The Wolf cracked his knuckles. "I'm talking about the two of you being some lying ass bitches. That's what I'm talking about. You think you were the only ones smart enough to have a spy? Of course there's someone in your crew working for me, and he gave up a list of names you might say was the shooter. Guess which name was on that list. We don't know who the shooter was, but we DO know it wasn't some nigga name Blake."

"I can't believe you actually said THAT name," Monique said seemingly amazed. "That was the first name on his list because Blake was killed on the corner and would have been convenient, but I never thought he was going to be right."

"He who?" Stony asked.

"Do it matter? Just know we know you lyin."

Frank knew it was time to go and stood. "We done here, Stone."

Stony followed Frank's lead.

"Wherever you two get your information, it's suspect," Stony said as they made their way to the door.

Before they exited, Frank turned to face Stony. "No, it ain't, Stone," Frank said and then looked directly at Hannibal. "Wolfie's info is dead on. You wanna know who did your cross-dressing cousin, fat boy?"

Hannibal sat up in his chair, "Yeah, give him up, midget, and then say goodbye to him."

"Frank," Stony said and then shook his head, but Frank wasn't paying his partner any mind.

Frank opened his arms and smirked. "I did your faggot cousin, nigga. Now what?"

Monique was on her feet in a flash, but Hannibal was already rushing the door as she did her best to stay in front of the runaway freight train that was her Alpha. She grunted in pain as her shoulder made contact with his bulk, and Hannibal immediately tried to move around her, but she refused to get out of his way.

Stony grabbed Frank and yanked him through the doorway of the back room as Frank continued to holler, "Now what, nigga? What you got for me, huh, bitch ass? My favorite color is blue!"

Finally, with the help of Mr. Insurance, Stony pushed Frank through the restaurant and out of The Kitchen's entrance.

Monique stood firm in front of Hannibal.

With a growl Hannibal turned back to the table and slumped in one of the chairs. He clamped his hands onto his head and rocked back and forth as fury burned white-hot within him. Monique approached him slowly and gently caressed his head. She whispered to him that everything would be all right.

"How!" he yelled, flying out of his chair. "How is everything gonna be all right?"

"Because we got what we came for," she calmly informed him.

"Fuck you talkin about?" he asked as the veins in his neck became engorged and formed a pulsing roadmap.

Monique stepped up to him and rested her head against his chest. "Not only do we have a cease fire, we also know who killed Appleton. All we have to do is figure out a way to get him, baby" she cooed.

After a few seconds of thought Hannibal realized she was right and sat down again. Monique resumed her light massage, and he relaxed under her touch.

Just then Stony popped his head back in the room.

"Whatchu want, nigga?" Hannibal asked.

"Peace. What happens between you and Frank is between you and Frank. Agreed?"

Monique's eyes were menacing slits. "Yes," Monique said. "We agree to the terms. There will be peace, but we are done talking to you two. Go! This meeting is over."

Stony nodded and vanished.

With a sigh Monique turned back to her man and placed her free hand on her hip. "Can we go home?" she asked. "I'm hungry."

"Have a wing or somethin. They ain't bad."

"Fuck a wing. Besides I'm a better cook then anyone they have in that kitchen," she said with a wink.

Hannibal smiled and kissed her. "Since you the brains around here, let's go home."

73

Later that night, down the street and around the corner, a black-tie reception was in full swing. It was receiving night at The Butler Institute of American Art, and their elegant atrium was at capacity for the unveiling of Jean Michael Basquiat's powerful painting, *The Boxer*.

The bold painting of the victorious Black boxer in front of a white graffiti-filled backdrop was on prominent display, as the champagne flowed freely, compliments of the open cocktail bar. The abundant professional wait staff acquiesced to the whims of area congressmen, the governor, and other elected officials. The president of Youngstown University presided over the festivities alongside other influential faculty members and museum board members.

The local dignitaries, especially those with deep pockets, milled throughout the gallery and plastered on their best smiles every time the press cameras flashed. Most made inane chatter over the university's upcoming football season or fended off the power elite's subtle political donation requests. They glad-handed, back-slapped, and gave out congratulatory embraces in front of the six-foot-tall seminal piece that few recognized let alone admired. They were simply there to be seen.

When the mayor finally arrived and addressed the press, he dropped words like revitalization, re-energize, and renewal when asked about Youngstown's future. He discussed how hosting the painting for the next two weeks fed into those grand plans. However, after another reporter asked about the spike in violence and the number of young Black men dying in the streets, he conveniently snagged Browning as he and Bailey were making their way into the museum.

"Mr. Jackson, as the District Attorney, do you have any comment about the spike in violence lately?" asked one persistent reporter.

Browning shot daggers at the mayor before turning to face the cameras with his face shrouded in solemn seriousness. "It's tragic, and I'm working tirelessly with the police chief to do everything we can to bring a stop to the senseless slaughter happening in our streets."

"Do you know what the cause is?"

"A severe lack of opportunity is one of the main contributors to the spike in violence sadly."

"And do you feel this party tonight is somehow going to aid any of those with a severe shortage of opportunities?"

Bailey squeezed his hand in warning, but Browning knew the question was a set up.

"At this gathering tonight are some of Youngstown's best and brightest, and I'd like to believe that the people here will be willing to come together and search for answers to the unanswered questions. I'd like to believe that we can think outside the box and find viable solutions that will enable those in this community to strive for more, to reach for better, and to obtain it. Thank you," he said with his brightest smile before turning to enter the museum with his wife.

His answer momentarily silenced the gaggle of local of reporters until one of them shouted one final follow up question.

"Mr. Jackson...Mr. Jackson...Are you planning to run for mayor?"

Browning turned back and slyly smiled to the cameras. He paused to look up at the starry sky before returning his attention back to the reporters. "I don't know. The mayor is a good friend of mind, and I love what I'm doing, working on the community's behalf to create safer streets, but I'll put it in the hopper, and we'll see." With that, he and Bailey slowly walked into The Butler ready and eager to navigate the shark-infested waters.

"I'm proud of you...Mr. Mayor," Bailey whispered in his ear.

"Don't you start too," he said as they both laughed.

74

Unhappy with his meal, Seth tossed what was left of his General Tso's chicken into the small hotel garbage can. The Chinese food was far superior in New York in his opinion. He turned up the volume on his TV and watched the museum coverage on the local 11 p.m. news while chatting with Paulie on the phone.

"Can you believe this shit is the lead story?" Seth asked.

"Hey, it's Youngstown," Paulie reminded him. "What were you expecting?"

"And there's my clueless son and his busty Bailey."

"What's a 'busty bailey'?"

"His wife."

"Sounds like a drink, the kind that gets an umbrella."

"I swear the woman has more cleavage than Dolly," Seth said.

"More than my genie?"

"Yes, significantly more than your imaginary friend."

"That's impressive because I've got a pretty imaginative mind."

That made Seth laugh. He'd had no idea why he'd called Paulie, but he was suddenly glad he had. Youngstown and its uppity suburban neighbors were wearing on his nerves like a leaky faucet, and he craved to be back in Harlem's warm and sometimes chaotic embrace. Paulie was the closest he could get to that right now.

"Marta asked about you," Paulie said.

"Yeah?" Seth asked, somewhat embarrassed by the curious tone of his voice.

"Yeah, but she don't ask as much as she used to. Maybe she's coming to grips with things."

"What things?"

"That you two ain't gon make it."

"That's what you think?"

"That's what I know, ass pimple."

"How you know that?"

"You call her yet?"

"No."

"The prosecution rests."

"Whatever," Seth said with a quick suck of his teeth while listening to the last seconds of the news clip. "Oh give me a break."

"What happened?" Paulie asked concerned.

"Can you believe they asked him if he was gonna run for mayor?"

"Who, Brownie?"

"Yeah."

"Wha'd he say?"

"He'll put it in his hopper," Seth said derisively before he slammed his thumb against the TV's power button.

"Wow, he is just like his daddy."

"Shut up," Seth said as they both laughed. "I tell you what though. If he is gonna run then he definitely has the right kind of woman on his arm."

"Whatchu mean?"

"She white."

"Good choice," Paulie said as they laughed again. "Hey, I gotta run, Seth."

"Hot date with what's-her-name?"

"No, the place is on fire."

Seth was about to respond, but he hesitated for a second, refusing to take the bait and then said, "You know you not funny, right?"

"Yeah, but what I would have given to see that look on your face."

"Fuck you, Paulie."

"Love you too."

75

With his feet up Stony reclined on his oversized leather couch and relaxed for the first time in weeks. His eyes swept the room, and he realized how much he'd missed home. He'd essentially lived at Romare's during the war because the bar had given him some measure of safety.

Despite today's debacle at the sit down with Hannibal, he refused to worry about Frank's fuck up. It was time to focus on his plans with Chuck. Since Harlem was unwilling to pay his grandson's note, Stony was confident everything he wanted would be in his hands very soon. He took a satisfying puff on his cigar and flipped on the late evening news hoping for a glimpse of the painting.

He'd been just eleven when Leonard had first introduced him to Jean-Michel Basquiat during a quick trip to New York. His uncle had explained to him that the young man had once been one of the brightest stars in the art world. Transfixed by Basquiat's unconventional and daring style, Stony had dug into the Haitian artist with abandon and had fallen in love with the energy, the colors, and the unabashed power of his works.

After the lead in of a murder on the North Side, the news coverage flashed to the façade of The Butler before cutting to the Basquiat. He drank in the images of the imposing canvas and tuned out the reporter as she rambled about the black tie affair. His heartbeat increased as his eyes followed the bold lines and curves. He'd never seen *The Boxer* in person and couldn't believe it was so close. Seeing it would be one of the most thrilling moments of his life.

The reporter droned on about the bigwigs mingling under one roof, but Youngstown's socialites and friends were irrelevant to him until the District Attorney's face filled his TV screen. Stony's fist clenched, but he raised the volume to catch every word the bastard said. As Browning Jackson praised the Basquiat's stop in Youngtown as a step in a new direction for the community, Stony erupted in laughter until tears streamed down his cheeks.

You have no idea what's coming do you? You sowed the wind, and now, you will reap the whirlwind, motherfucka. No mercy will be shown. No quarter given.

After he calmed himself, he re-lit his cigar and rewound the segment to the Basquiat again. He smiled like a child on Christmas morning.

76

The echoes of gunfire and explosions vibrated through the man cave as Charlie and Gavin unleashed a relentless fusillade of virtual violence against one another in their favorite video game. Within minutes Gavin's forces had Charlie's in retreat. "Fuck, I'm bored," said Charlie, tossing down his controller.

"Nah, you're just pissed cause I got YOU on the run for a change," Gavin said as he took a long pull of a tightly rolled joint. "Sure you don't want some of this?"

"Nah, I'm trying to stop."

Gavin squinted at his friend. "What? Why?"

"Because it's time, man."

"Not for me it isn't. Tell you what, I'll smoke for the both of us."

Charlie laughed. "You already are."

"Good point, young man," Gavin said as he took another hit. "Hey, your grandfather…he is one intense man."

"I know, but with the shit he seen and been through, I guess that would make anyone intense."

"Yo, no lie…he scares the shit outta me."

"No lie, he scares the shit outta me too," Charlie said with a chuckle. "Like, he can be so calm one moment and then punch someone in the throat. I seen him do it."

"To who?"

"The DJ at Stony's place. I go to the door, and the DJ, this fat guy, tells me Stony's not there. Pop asked me if I believed that. Then he strolls up, knocks, and before the guy even got another word out…BOOM! Pop hit him right in the neck!" said Charlie, his voice painted with awe. "Sent the guy to the floor, and he walked in like he owned the place. I swear to god, I never saw that coming. I almost passed out."

"That's that crazy gangster shit right there." As they clicked away again on the controllers to start another game, Gavin asked, "Hey…Where the hell is Chad? I'm starving."

"Seriously, he should have been here already. Pause this and call him," Charlie said.

"And do what? Leave a third message?"

"If need be. What? You scared of bugging him?" Charlie asked.

"Ain't no fear here, nig–" Gavin stopped short of finishing his sentence.

Charlie said nothing, but gave him a wide-eyed look as if to say 'you know better.'

Without saying another word, Gavin grabbed his cell phone and called Chad. When no one picked up, Gavin didn't bother leaving another message.

"Maybe we should go over there," Charlie said.

"You just wanna stop the game because I'm beating you."

"After all the times I wiped the floor with you? Fine, you can have this one," Charlie said as he dropped his controller. "You comin?"

"Nah, I'll wait here because while you're over there, he may come here, so I'll wait here. Either way, we need to get some food…here." Gavin lifted his shirt and patted his flat abs. "Stomach want food."

Charlie shook his head. "How high are you?"

"Stratosphere and climbing," Gavin replied with low chuckle.

"Whatever, I'll be right back," Charlie said and left through the sliding doors. Charlie took a deep breath of fresh air. Not taking a hit of the blunt had been harder than he'd thought it would be. Turning his back on weed was not going to be easy, but he knew it was necessary.

As Charlie got closer to Chad's house, he frowned when he walked passed Chad's car in the driveway. *If he's home then why isn't he answering his damn phone?* Charlie rang the doorbell but got no answer, so he clicked open the front door and immediately heard Chad's upstairs TV blaring and headed up not worried about Chad's notoriously absent parents. Charlie and Gavin practically considered Chad's parents urban legends, the Yeti parents. Their existence was known of, but very few seldom laid eyes on them, which usually also included Chad.

At Chad's room he tried to open the door, but it didn't budge. Charlie put some muscle behind it and shoved. It opened enough for Charlie to yell through the crack. "Yo, dude! What's up? We've been calling you. Gav's whining because 'stomach need food.'"

When he still didn't get an answer, Charlie pushed his way into the room. Immediately the odor of vomit assailed his nostrils, and on the other side, pressed against the door laid Chad. His bathrobe was covered in vomit, and he had pissed himself.

"Dude, what the fuck? It reeks in here!" Charlie knelt and sighed. "Chad! Chad! C'mon man time to wake up!" Charlie grabbed the remote and shut the TV off. "Damn, dude…you are out," he whispered. "Chad!" he yelled with a shake to his shoulder and light slaps at his friend's face. The smell of the room overwhelmed him and made his eyes water.

Charlie started to rise to open the window when he saw an open bottle of pills roll out of Chad's hand. Fear and panic began to claw at Charlie. He slapped at his friend's cheek harder, but Chad's head lolled left to right. Charlie quickly felt his friend's wrist for a pulse. "Chad?" Not feeling anything he jumped up as fear viciously punched him square in his chest.

"No…no…no…tell me you didn't do this. TELL ME YOU DID NOT FUCKING DO THIS, CHAD!"

With shaking hands, Charlie snatched his phone out of his pocket and dialed his grandfather.

"Hey, Charles, what's…?"

"I think he's dead. I think he's dead. I can't feel a fucking pulse. Shit, Pops, shit, I think he's dead."

"Charles, slow down. You think who's dead?"

"CHAD!"

"Chad? Your little white friend?"

"Yeah, I…I came over to his house," Charlie explained wiping the tears from his eyes, "and found him lying in his own piss and vomit, and I can't feel a fucking pulse."

"Stop. Turn him on his side, Charles. Listen to me. Turn him on his side. Then hang up and call 911, Charlie. Hang up and call them, and I'll meet you at the hospital," Seth said firmly. "Understand, son?"

"Okay...okay," Charlie said, turning Chad on his side. A sob escaped Charlie's chest.

"Hey, stay strong, son. Call 911. I'm already on my way to the hospital," Seth said and disconnected.

More vomit dribbled out of his friend's mouth. With trembling hands he dialed 911. "I...I need an ambulance. My friend...I think he OD'd...I...I think he might be dead. Hurry...you gotta save him!"

77

Charlie wiped his tears from his face with the sleeve of his arm and found a seat in the crowded waiting area. He had no idea what to do, but he was pretty certain he had lost one of his oldest friends.

Shit, he thought, *Gavin*. Charlie fumbled for his phone and dialed.

"I thought you bitches forgot about me," the Asian boy answered with a chuckle.

"Gavin, dude…I'm at the hospital. Chad OD'd. I think he may be dead. They're working on him," Charlie said trying to make sense out of the last thirty minutes.

After a few seconds Gavin laughed and said, "Stop fucking with me, dude. You know how high I am."

Charlie grabbed his head in frustration. "Listen to me, dammit! You think I would say some shit like Chad OD'd as a joke? I'm not fucking with you. I am sitting here in the waiting room at the damn hospital as we speak, so snap the hell out of it!"

"Holy shit, holy shit, holy shit," Gavin said. "What the fuck man?"

"Just get here as soon as you can."

"Where? St. E's?" After Charlie confirmed his location Gavin told him, "I'm on my way, dude. Should I leave your dad a note or something?"

"Yeah. You sure you can drive?"

"I drive better high than I do sober. I'm on my way. See you in a few."

Charlie leaned his head back against the bright orange colored wall in the waiting room and closed his eyes.

"Yo, that's a nice phone, little man," came a voice from Charlie's left.

Charlie turned to see a dark skinned, bald headed man a few years older and a whole lot bigger than him. He was wearing a bandage around his head. A bright red stain stood out prominently against the bright white gauze wrap. Several other young men lounged around with him and also eyed Charlie's phone. "How much was that?"

"I don't know," Charlie answered trying not to sound intimidated.

The big man held out his hand. "You mind if I make a call? I gotta call my baby mama. She don't know I'm down here."

Uncertainty dragged at Charlie.

"C'mon, lil man. I'll give it right back," he said.

"Don't do it, man," said one of the guys standing off to the side.

"Shut the fuck up, Tre," the bald man said.

"Leave the kid alone, Van," Tre said.

"I just need to make a call. My phone is dead. C'mon, lil man. I'll give it right back. I swear," Van urged.

Charlie didn't trust the man but handed his phone to him anyway.

A Cheshire cat smile broke across the bald man's dark face. With a wink he said, "Thanks for the phone, podna," and slid the latest iPhone into his pocket. "Good lookin out."

Charlie quickly got to his feet.

The three others only laughed. "Told you not to do it," Tre said with a shrug.

Van slowly rose as well. His eyes danced with delight at the thought of violence. He towered over Charlie by a good four inches and outweighed him by at least a hundred pounds.

Before Charlie could muster the courage to say anything, a familiar voice interrupted.

"Give him back his fucking phone, or so help me God you'll need a lot more bandages before this night is through."

Charlie spun. His grandfather stood behind him like a one-man army. His eyes sparked with the same violent delight as Van's. Seth and Van stared each other down.

"You're thinking you can take me, aren't you big man? You're thinking I'm old, so I'm probably slow, way slower than you are, and I'm outnumbered, so you might be able to get the upper hand. Understand this though and listen very carefully," Seth said as people slowly moved away from the area. "You are in the hospital, bleeding from your head. Your luck ain't all that good tonight, so you can try me if you like, but I'm in a bad mood, and I'm looking to get bloody. Give the boy back his goddamn phone, and I won't rape you of your soul."

Seeing his boys back away from the old man, Van swallowed hard, pulled the phone from his pocket, and handed it to Charlie.

"Smartest move you'll ever make," Seth said as Van turned toward his boys.

"Did you just get punked by gramps, Van?" Tre asked.

"Shut the fuck up, Tre. Somethin bout that old man ain't right," Van explained as the four skulked away to the far side of the waiting room.

Once they were gone, Seth and Charlie sat down.

"Are you okay, son?" Seth asked.

"Yeah, I'm okay."

"What about your friend? Is he still alive?"

"Yeah...I think. They were still working on him last I saw."

"That's a good sign. What did he take?"

"Oxy," Charlie said.

"Shit."

"Think they'll be able to save him, Pops?"

"I don't know, son. They're probably pumping his system to get him to throw up some more. Then they'll give him doses of Narcan to help ease the effects of the overdose. After that, all we can do is hope for the best."

"Man," Charlie said staring off into space.

Seth nudged Charlie's arm. "The other trust funder is here."

Charlie looked up to see Gavin wave and head over to them. "How is he?" he asked as he flopped into the seat next to Charlie.

"Don't know yet, so I guess that's good news."

"What did he take?" Gavin asked.

"Oxy."

Mark Eric

"That motherfucker," Gavin said under his breath.

"Yeah," Charlie whispered.

"Yeah," repeated Seth.

78

It was nearly 1 a.m., and Browning and Bailey were returning home from The Butler in high spirits. Throughout the evening Bailey had flashed him cleavage, and once they had gotten in the car she'd become more brazen, showing him as much as her dress allowed of her tanned, toned thighs. He loved when she drank. She was a lightweight, so when she got tipsy, the wildcat in her purred to life, and tonight that frisky feline was baring her claws. He couldn't wait to get her home and out of that dress.

"You know the mayor couldn't take his eyes off you," Browning told her in the car, glancing once more at her ample cleavage. He gently grasped her knee and squeezed.

"The mayor AND the governor kept an eye out on yours truly," she replied with a giggle as she slowly slid his hand up her inner thigh.

A sly smile broke across his face. "Stop before you make me crash this damn car."

"Get me home, Daddy. Mama wants to play," she said. Her breath caught when Browning's fingers moved across her warmth.

"Does she now?"

She nodded, bit her bottom lip, and closed her eyes with a whimper.

Browning estimated they'd be home in another five minutes and all over each other in six as he steered his Mercedes Benz S550 through the gates of Covington Falls without stopping to chitchat with the guard. He gunned the engine and soon came to a quick stop in their garage.

Putting the car in park, he turned and kissed his wife deeply letting his hands roam over her flat stomach and ample breasts. Out of breath, he broke free, shut the car off, and slowly got out the car to come around to her side and carefully helped her into the house. Her legs were unsteady, and her face was flushed. Her strappy stilettos, while amazingly sexy, didn't help matters any. Another few steps and Browning would have those sexy shoes pointed towards the ceiling.

Once inside they pounced on each other. With a wicked laugh, Bailey shoved Browning against the door, stepped back, and then turned. With practiced moves, she slowly stripped out of her dark teal beaded dress and let it fall to the floor with a sexy shimmy. Browning swallowed thickly. Only a lacy thong the same color as her dress and stilettos graced her bare skin.

She seductively climbed the stairs, swaying her hips as Browning loosened his bowtie and removed his jacket never taking his eyes off her.

"Daddy? Will you bring up a bottle of wine? Mama's thirsty," she purred before she crawled up the last remaining steps and disappeared down the hallway.

Browning smiled and rushed to the wine fridge and yanked out a chilled Pinot Grigio, Bailey's favorite. When he snatched two wine glasses from the cupboard he spotted a flash of yellow out of the corner of his eye. He snagged the bright paper off the refrigerator.

The note wasn't in Charlie's chicken scrawl handwriting. This note he could actually read, yet he had to read it three times before the words finally penetrated his lust-addled brain.

"Are you kidding me?" He pulled out his phone and dialed his son's cell four times. Each time the call went directly to voicemail.

What in the hell is going on? he thought frantically as he grabbed his jacket and car key. In less than ten seconds he was back in his car.

"Brownnnnnning," Bailey cooed as she lounged on their bed still adorned in her thong and heels. "Where's my daddy?"

When she got no response she sat up.

"Browning?"

When she heard the familiar roar of the Benz' V8 engine and the tires squeal, she teetered to the window as fast as she could in her heels.

"BROWNINNNNG!"

79

After more than two hours in triage, Chad finally was in a private room resting. Charlie and Gavin sat next to the hospital bed in silence watching Chad's sallow face and glancing nervously at the monitors surrounding him.

"Okay you two, be honest with me." Seth said from the back of the room. "Neither of you saw this coming?"

The two boys looked at each other and shrugged.

"Well, I hadn't seen him lately," Gavin said. "Last time I did though he was floating. I knew he was on something stronger than weed, but I just figured it was Chad experimenting again."

"Again?"

Charlie ran his hands over his baldhead and sighed. "Chad liked to try different types of stuff to see what the trip would be like. He'd try to get us to go along with him, but we never did, so he'd go off and try it and come back and tell us what it was like."

Seth wrinkled his brow with concern. "How long has this sort of thing been going on?"

"Since we were about thirteen, maybe fourteen."

"And his parents never did anything? Never tried to get the boy some help?"

"No, sir," Gavin gravely said.

There was light rap on the door, and in walked Chad's doctor, five-seven and slim with a head that seemed far too large for his neck to support. He had a solid chin and full mop of unruly brown hair. Seth sized him up and thought looked too young to be a doctor.

The short man glanced around the room at everyone. "Uh, who are all of you?"

"Who are you?" Seth asked.

"I'm Doctor English, and I'm sorry, but if you're not family then you can't be in here."

"Doc, these boys are family," Seth said in a way that clearly explained no one was leaving.

The doctor cleared his throat and moved to Chad's bedside to check his chart and monitors.

"Is he gonna be all right?" Charlie asked.

The doctor glanced at Charlie. "Time will tell. Are you the one that found him?"

Charlie nodded and then looked at his grandfather. "Yes."

"Well he's lucky you found him when you did. You guys can stay a little longer," he said turning at Seth, "but not much longer."

Seth nodded, and the doctor motioned to talk to Seth in the hallway.

The doctor ran a hand through his thick hair and exhaled. "I didn't want to say this in front of the boys, but the next twelve hours will tell us what the long-term effects will be, whether he'll be in a vegetative state or not. Right now, we need to get in contact with his parents. Do you have any idea as to how we can reach them? We've left messages but aren't getting anywhere."

"Ask the boys, doc. They're the ones that would have that information, but if you can't reach them I doubt they'll be able to. From what I understand that boy's parents are hardly ever home."

"Then it sounds like your son's friend may be dealing with some abandonment issues," the doctor said heading back into the room. After asking the boys to do their best to get in touch with their friend's parents, the doctor asked Charlie, "Any idea where he got the pills?"

Charlie sighed heavily. "I think I saw his mother's name on the bottle."

The doctor pinched the bridge of his nose. "We're seeing a lot more kids overdosing on their parents' prescription medications looking for a new high. We're talking everything from antidepressants to blood pressure medication. They treat their bodies like science experiments."

Seth nodded his head. "I don't understand it either, doc."

Dr. English peered at the boys. "Does your friend suffer from depression?"

Gavin shook his head, but Charlie nodded. "It's rare, but when he does, it can be pretty dark."

"Does he have a counselor or a therapist? If he doesn't he may just end up here again."

"Not that I know of," said Charlie.

"We'll find him somebody, doc," Seth promised.

"Well, keep trying his parents. They need to be here. Now, if you'll excuse me, gentlemen, I have more patients to check before I call it a night," he said and left them standing at Chad's bed.

"Guess I'll try calling again," Gavin said.

"Leave them a message," Seth instructed.

"I can email them. Maybe they'll check that," Charlie said and pulled out his cell phone, but when he tried to power it up nothing happened. "Shit! My battery is dead."

Seth gently took Charlie's phone from him. "You've done enough." He glanced over at Gavin who'd hung up again with a quick shake of his head. "Look, you two relax. I'll be right back."

Seth headed down to the hospital's waiting area and the vending machines that lined the wall. The boys' adrenaline had faded long ago, and they needed something in their systems. Candy bars, drinks, and chips were on the menu. With pockets full, Seth turned and saw his son rush to the information desk still in his tux.

"Brownie!" Seth called. Browning spun in Seth's direction, his face a mask of confusion.

"What in the hell are you doing here? Is Charlie okay?"

"Hello to you too. I know your mother taught you better than that," Seth said.

"Answer my damn question!"

Seth looked his son up and down. "My grandson called me a few hours ago in a panic. He—"

"Is he all right?" asked a frantic Browning grabbing his father's arm causing a can of soda to almost crash to the floor. "There was this note on the fridge, something about St. E's and an overdose. Did

341

my son OD?" Browning screamed, fear blazing in his eyes. The two men stared at each other, and once Browning realized what he had done he quickly removed his hand.

Seth steadied himself and calmly explained the situation. "Charlie is fine, a bit freaked out, but he's good. The OD was his little white friend, Ch–"

"Chad?" Browning asked. "What? That makes no sense at all."

"It makes a lot of damn sense when you think about it," Seth said in irritation. "You parents today, you guys are never home. You leave these kids to their own devices while you're climbing the corporate ladder or hobnobbing with the mayor and the governor. What that boy did was a cry for help. He took his mother's Oxy for God sakes. What does that say to you?" Seth asked, trying to reign in his anger. "And what exactly does it say to you that your son thought to call ME instead of you tonight when he found that little white boy unconscious and alone at his own house?" Seth paused to let his son digest his words. "Let me help you out. It means that he knows you don't have any time for him, so why even bother calling you?"

Browning stared at his father then slowly broke eye contact.

"You got a number to reach that white boy's parents?"

Browning nodded his head as he pulled out his phone. "How's he doing?"

"He's not out of the woods yet, so call his parents and fucking get them here. Go home, Brownie. I'll make sure Charlie gets home safely."

Seth made the move to walk past his son when Browning grabbed his arm again. Seth stopped but didn't look at his son. "Take care of our boy, okay? I don't know what you're doing here or why you're here, but you take care of him."

Seth shifted and slowly pulled his arm away.

"Please?" Browning pleaded.

"Of course I will. You do your job. Get that boy's parents here." Seth punched the elevator call button. "Nice tux by the way," he said and boarded the lift without a backwards glance.

80

The following morning, when there had been a knock on Seth's door, he'd had a pretty good idea who it was. Charlie's red eyes and sullen gaze clearly indicated his grandson had gotten very little sleep after he'd dropped him off a few hours ago. Seth opted to keep things light. The last thing the boy needed today were sermons on how to live and what not to do.

As Seth finished getting dressed, he watched his grandson sort through the troubling thoughts in his head. He pawed through the morning news channels blankly and without any of his usual sarcastic comments. Yesterday Charlie's little bubble of perfection had been deflated even more. Real life with all its relentless viciousness had caught up with his grand this summer and showed very little signs of loosening its grip from around the boy's neck.

"You know, seeing your friend almost die would be hard for anyone to handle, but you showed a lot of strength yesterday, Charlie. You're a true friend. You didn't run and hide. You fought for your friend. You grew up some more yesterday, and I'm proud of you. I want you to know that," Seth said as he slipped on his loafers.

Charlie caught his grandfather's eye, and Seth saw a storm of pain and confusion roil across the young one's face as the boy attempted to piece it all together.

"Pancakes?" Seth asked knowing the boy likely hadn't eaten a thing except for the junk he'd bought last night.

Charlie gave a quick nod, and they made their way to the car. Neither spoke another word until they were seated and waiting for their breakfast.

"How was things when I dropped you off last night?" Seth asked, doctoring his coffee.

Charlie, who had been looking out the window, slowly turned his bloodshot gaze towards him and shrugged. "It was crazy. Dad and Bailey were still up and in a full-on fight when I got home."

"Fight? What kind of fight?"

"It was weird," Charlie said. "She was screaming something about how he should never leave her hot and bothered like that again if he had no plans on taking care of business."

Seth chuckled. "What did your father say?"

"He kept repeating 'It was an emergency. It was an emergency.'" Charlie was quiet for a moment, playing absently with the silverware.

Seth tried his best to maintain his decorum, but he couldn't contain his laughter and was on the verge of tears. "Well apparently it seems the party at The Butler was a smash, and it sounds like your parents had hoped to cap the night off right when they got home."

Charlie rolled his eyes. "Yeah, well, Dad's in one of the guest rooms," he said as the waitress placed his steaming pancakes in front of him.

Seth cleared his throat and tried to find his composure as she set down a generous plate of chicken and waffles as well. "Thank you, Alice. As always, it looks delicious."

She smiled and walked away adding a little extra sway in her hips.

"Pops, I think Alice might want to give you more than some chicken and waffles."

"You caught that, huh?" he asked as his thoughts went to Marta, and he wondered what she was she doing. Despite his anger and frustration, he missed her. He couldn't deny that fact, which shook him a bit because the only other person he had ever truly missed had been his precious Penny, Browning's mother. Seth didn't know what his future with Marta might be, but at that moment he wished it were her and not Alice who had set down their plates. "Eat up youngin. We got a busy day ahead of us."

81

Forty-five minutes later Seth was piloting his Cadillac out of the parking lot and headed uptown to the hospital.

"Do you think Chad will be awake?" Charlie asked.

Though Charlie tried hard to hide it, Seth could hear the boy's faint nervousness. "I hope so. Can't get much better news than that, but it may take another day or two," he cautioned. Seth knew better than anyone how strong the bonds of friendship could be. There wasn't a thing on this planet he wouldn't do for Paulie. He knew his grandson felt that way for Chad, but he didn't want to get Charlie's hopes up that his friend would snap back to normal after taking a short nap in the hospital. Life was rarely that kind or simple.

"Did you hear me, Pops?"

"What? No, son, I didn't. What'd you say?"

"How did you know to turn him on his side?" Charlie asked.

"Oh, that was something I learned a long time ago from some dope fiends I used to know."

"Knew a lot of dope fiends?" Charlie asked as he climbed out the car.

"I knew enough to know I never wanted to be one. Learn from someone else's mistakes. That's a vital part of growing up," Seth said as he chirped the alarm.

Since it was still fairly early on a Saturday morning, the hospital was as quiet as a library. When they reached Chad's room, they could see two people in his suite through the glass windows.

"Are those the parental units?" Seth asked motioning to the silver-haired man and blonde woman who sat by Chad's bedside. Dressed in matching shirts, khaki pants, and boat shoes, the couple had a windswept and refreshed look about them, as if they had come ashore from being out to sea.

Charlie nodded.

"Nice of them to finally show up," Seth said with a distinct edge to his voice. *Well done Brownie, you came through and did your job*, he thought as he watched them through the glass windows of the suite.

"Yeah," Charlie said as he pushed open the door. All eyes went to the door, and almost immediately Chad's father got to his feet, hugged Charlie close for a few minutes, and then held him at arm's length.

"The doctor told us what you did. You gave us our son back. Thank you, Charles," the silver-haired man said as his wife joined him and placed a big kiss on Charles' forehead. "If you hadn't checked on our child when you did, we'd be making funeral arrangements."

Charlie looked over to see Chad still asleep.

"Chad's breathing on his own, and they ran more tests this morning. They're optimistic that he'll wake up soon," Chad's mom explained.

Charlie moved to his friend's bedside and took a seat. Seth was surprised how small Chad looked. The kid who once seemed larger than life now appeared to have shrunk under the stark white sheet and horde of equipment. Seth's annoyance flamed hotter, and he turned his attention to Chad's parents, introduced himself, and asked to speak to them privately.

Seth leaned against the door to Chad's room, assessed the couple, and tried to grab the reigns on his temper. "I'm going to get right to it. It's nice you're here today acting all concerned. I'm happy for that little white boy that his parents finally decided to make an appearance and pay him some damn mind."

"I'm sorry, but who are you again?" Chad's father asked.

"I'm the one that made sure Charles got your boy to this hospital in time to save his life. Now, I know you're both very busy people with businesses to run, projects to check on, shit to do to pay for that fancy house and your nice cars, but you two brainless fucks have all but abandoned that boy in there. Honestly, you're lucky he's still alive."

Chad's mother gasped and covered her mouth with her hand as the father quickly threw his arm around her shoulders to steady her.

Seth was glad his words had struck a nerve, but he wasn't finished. "He's seventeen. Did you really think he could take care of himself for the entire summer while you two went off and lived your lives? If I thought it would help even a fraction, I'd call whatever child protective agency you have here and report you for child endangerment. You abandoned him. I can't even imagine how long this has been going on, but you need to know this isn't that boy's first cry for help."

"What are you talking about cry for help? Who are you? How dare you talk to us this way," Chad's father said.

"You need more than a talking to. You both deserve to have your asses kicked and your heads examined. Chad's cry for help this time is what landed him in here last night after taking too much of mommy's Oxy," Seth said looking straight at the blonde-haired woman who buried her face into her husband's chest.

Seth looked back at the father. "What kind of parent gives a seventeen-year-old an Audi A8 and then isn't fucking there to enjoy it with him? To make sure he's being responsible with it? Here's a word of advice, dumb ass," Seth said closing the distance between him and Chad's father until they were almost nose-to-nose. "Try being parents to that kid in there instead of just being providers. Cause if you don't, my grandson may not be around next time to save your boy again."

Despite his tanned skin Chad's father turned a dark crimson, his hands balled into fists, but he said nothing. Seth reasoned this man had rarely been spoken to like that in his life and very likely never by a Black man. As far as Seth was concerned though, they had gotten off easy.

The father looked like he wanted to take a swing at him, and Seth almost wished he would. Instead the man cleared his throat. "While I do appreciate your concern for our son, you don't know us, and I don't appreciate you speaking to us in this manner. You don't know what we have sacrificed to give our son the life he lives. Maybe we can do better, should do better, and we will, but we don't need you to tell us that."

Seth looked into the window of the suite and watched as Charlie rocked back and forth in his chair. He turned back and met the teary pale blue eyes of Chad's mother and strained face of his father's and simply said, "Apparently someone needed to."

He glanced at his watch. "Now please go back in there, be with your son, and kindly send my grandson out here. We'll come back when you two self-involved fucktards aren't here. You both make me nauseous."

Both parents stumbled back into their son's room and sent Charlie out to his grandfather.

"You almost done in there?" Seth asked.

"Yeah, let me say goodbye."

On their way downstairs Charlie asked, "What did you say to Chad's parents?"

"Why you wanna know?"

"Cause I do."

"Well, you don't need to know."

"Whatever you said made his mother cry."

"Yeah, well she's lucky she's not picking up her husband's teeth."

82

Within minutes of leaving the hospital they were on the Youngstown State campus, home to The Butler. Seth pulled into the museum's tiny parking lot and shut off the car. "I'm gonna ask this even though I already know the answer. You never cased a place before, have you?"

Charlie shook his head.

"Of course you haven't. Why would you need to? When we get out I want you to count the number of security cameras you see, okay? Do your best to not look obvious."

Wide-eyed and scanning the building, Charlie nodded his head.

Seth could see Charlie's mood hadn't improved much since that morning. Seeing Chad hadn't helped like he'd hoped it would, but Seth knew he had to pull Charlie out of his emotional pit. "Look, I know all you'd like to do is go home, get high, and hide, but you ain't got time for that. You think I'm in Ohio because I missed my son? You think we at this museum because we like art? Your ass is still on the fishhook of some very ignorant and very dangerous motherfuckers. I know you're sad about Chad and seeing him that way, but it's time to man up and do what you have to do to get on the other side of this. Can you do that? Can you man up, son?"

Charlie was going to nod again but remembered his grandfather's earlier lesson. "Yeah...yes, sir. I can man up, Pops."

"Good, let's go."

Once in the lobby, Charlie glanced at Seth. "I saw three."

Seth smiled. *Not bad for a virgin.* "Actually there were five," he said as he paid their entry. They strolled through the exhibit areas, and Seth recognized some of the art from the newscast. For a small town museum, The Butler surprised Seth. The American Art collection was somewhat impressive, and the layout was spacious. The recently lacquered hardwood floors reflected the dim overhead lights as well as the natural light coming through the large windows. *Most likely done for the gala*, Seth thought to himself.

However Seth wasn't there to appreciate the place but to assess its security. Docents wandered the various wings, and video cameras monitored the more high-end pieces. Eventually they found their way to the Grand Ballroom, where Jean Michael Basquiat's *The Boxer* towered in all its discomforting glory.

"Oh shit," Charlie whispered before he ducked behind Seth.

"Boy, what are you doing?"

"Stony is here," he whispered.

"What?"

"Stony is here."

"Where?"

"Over there," Charlie said motioning his head toward the painting.

"Well, look at that."

Stony sat perched on the edge of a bench, completely transfixed by the Basquiat. His eyes hungrily devoured every line, choice of color, and brush stroke. Stony had found his church, his place of worship. He noticed nothing and no one around him. Everything else had faded away from view the second he'd entered the room. It was just him and *The Boxer*. He absently brushed a tear from his cheek.

The Boxer and every other painting and sculpture housed within The Butler represented a life he had been forced to leave behind, a life he still loved, a life he'd once shared with his Uncle Leonard. Stony's hands trembled. He still wanted that life. He wanted it back so badly he would sell his soul to the devil for it.

Instead he had to deal with ignorant motherfuckers like Hannibal and the violent unpredictability of Frank. Due to uncontrollable and unforeseen circumstances, he'd had no choice but to run the business to keep the family afloat, and the resentment he lived with had damn near given him ulcers. Being in the presence of the Basquiat, however, brought his uncle and their time together back to life so vividly that it felt as if Leonard sat on that bench next to him. He missed that man more than words could ever say.

Seth watched the wannabe gangster wipe tears from his face completely immersed in the painting. Seth eyes quickly scanned the room and noted two guards posted not far from the painting along with several recently installed rudimentary motion sensors on the floor under it. In all he spotted six guards, none of them armed. He saw no one with Stony—not even Frank.

Seth rapidly calculated odds and potential outcomes. For the first time since he'd arrived in Ohio, the man responsible for his grandson's situation was alone. Seth felt the weight of his .45 at the small of his back like an encouraging friend. *Maybe it would be easier this way. I could take Stony out of here, drive him somewhere secluded, and be done with him and his bullshit. Then I'd just have to deal with Frank. Fuck it*, he thought, *I'll climb that mountain when I get there.*

Seth took two steps towards him when Stony's muscle strutted into the room. Their laughter shattered the gallery's dignified serenity. Like a trio of yipping children they were oblivious to the cutting looks from patrons and staff as they casually took up positions around Stony. The leader of the three leaned in to say something, but Stony waved him off and told them to "shut the fuck up" before he settled back into the comfort of the painting.

Seeing Stony in that gallery, realization hit Seth like a lightening bolt. *Stony's not the biggest threat to my grandson or his father. It's Frank and has been from the start.* Seth removed his hand from behind his back and headed to another wing with Charlie at his heels.

83

Later that same evening, after Charlie and Seth had visited Chad, who was finally conscious although quite lethargic, Seth drove them back to his hotel. Charlie was in better spirits and seemed more at ease after seeing that his friend wasn't going to die.

"Come to dinner, Pops," Charlie said before climbing into his car. "We can eat down in the basement. Dad and Bailey hardly ever come down there. Hell, they might not even be home. Bailey's probably munching on some weird salad at her favorite restaurant with Dad footing the bill."

Seth rubbed his head. "I need to think about that, okay?"

"Fair enough, but I'm gonna keep asking."

Seth laughed. "I hope you do."

Back in his room Seth called Paulie. After the pleasantries the two men got down to business.

"Did you call Preacher?" Seth asked.

"Of course I did. You know his price went up? He talking about some 'cost of living' shit. I don't curse him. I curse that damn CNBC shit," Paulie said.

"How much he want?"

"Ten thousand simply for him to keep his schedule open. He wants another fifteen after the job's done."

"Pay him," Seth said as he pinched the bridge of his nose.

"Already did, kemosabe. How does it look?"

"Like a Sunday afternoon."

"Thirty-five large for a walk in the park? Don't seem right."

"It is what it is," Seth said. "Answer me this. Grandson wants me to come by for dinner tonight. Think I should go?"

Paulie laughed hysterically, which confused Seth. After composing himself his best friend asked, "Why are you there, Seth? Honestly, why did you drive those four hundred plus miles?"

"To help my boy out."

"Exactly, to help your boy out, but that's not all, Seth. You wanted to meet and get to know that boy, and hopefully—even if it was just in passing—you wanted to make a difference in his life somehow. What I want to know is why you haven't gone over there for dinner with him already? You've been there how long?"

"Well I've been kicked out of that house more times than I can count."

"So? When has that ever fucking stopped you before? Someone tell you you can't? You turn around and do just out of spite. That's what I love about you, man," Paulie said. "Don't go changing on me after all these years. Get off your ass and go have dinner with your grandson. You hear me?"

Seth knew Paulie was right. He drove all that way not only to help his grandson out of this mess but also to hopefully get to know him, be near him, and let his grandson get to know him in return. The best way to do any of that was to break bread with his kin in his own home. "I hear you. I hear you. Thanks for the advice," Seth said.

"No problem, you know I'm the bright one out of the two of us anyway," Paulie said, making both men laugh.

"Anyway, genius, book a flight for the Preachers to Pittsburgh. Give me the details when you do."

"When you want them there?"

"The next day or two. There's no rush since the damn thing is here for the next two weeks. Let me go get ready for dinner. I'll call you later."

"Call me after. I wanna know how things went."

"Yeah, yeah. Don't nag," Seth said and hung up to dial Charlie. "I'll be there in an hour. Order some pizza. Extra cheese and pepperoni."

"Woo-hoo!!! You got it, Pops! See ya in a few."

The excitement he heard in Charlie's voice made him close his eyes and smile. *Yeah, this is why I'm here.*

84

When Charlie answered the door an hour later, his face wore a look of apprehension as Seth stepped inside the house. "What? Am I late?" Seth asked, hoping to lighten the boy's mood.

"Not exactly, Pops."

As they turned the corner and walked into the dining room, Seth understood. Bailey was setting the enormous mahogany table while Browning unpacked cartons of Chinese food. Seth looked at his grandson who shrugged. He knew Charlie hadn't known about this.

"Care to join us?" Bailey asked politely with a smile of overly white teeth.

Without missing a beat, Seth grabbed the closest chair followed by a reluctant Charlie. *Fuck you, Paulie*, Seth thought. "You guys got any ribs in one of those bags?"

"Yep, we got ribs, pepper steak, General Tso's chicken, egg foo young, egg rolls, you name it," she said.

"Yeah, we thought it was going to be the three of us, but when we spoke to Charles he explained that unbeknownst to us he had invited you over for dinner, so we ordered more food," Browning said as he alternated between opening containers and licking his fingers. "We know what Charles likes, but you're a complete mystery, so we got a little bit of everything."

Something in Browning's tone felt odd to Seth. It was a subtle cross between nice guy and asshole. The kind of attitude Seth had very little patience for, and a little red flag popped in his mind tugging at him to leave, but he ignored it and remained seated. His grandson had invited him to dinner, and Seth was determined to honor that invitation.

"Well this sure is quite some spread," he said hoping to gauge Browning's reaction.

Browning filled a plate with ribs and passed it to Seth. With a snap of chopsticks and an arrogant smile, he sat back in his chair. "Yeah, you know, sitting down to dinner as a family is all a part of being better parents, right? I mean, isn't that what you told Chad's parents to be, those two 'fucktards' that made you nauseous? Didn't you tell them to try being better parents and not just providers because next time maybe my son won't be there to save theirs?" Browning smirked and let his sarcasm spread like a bad odor through the room before popping a piece of General Tso's chicken in his mouth.

Seth put a rib down and wiped his hands. "Yes, that's pretty much what I said to them." He turned to face his son. "They're lucky that's all I said."

"Yeah? Tell me, Dad. What else would you have said to them?"

"Pop, can I get you an egg roll?" Charlie asked trying to diffuse the situation.

"You know, I never liked those things. I will have some fried rice and duck sauce though."

"You got it," Charlie said scrambling to find the container of rice.

"Seth…what else would you have said to the fucktards?" Browning asked again.

Seth took in the table. Bailey began to grind her teeth so hard that a shattered molar wasn't out of the realm of possibility, and Charlie mindlessly kept piling a mountain of rice on Seth's plate. Seth turned back to Browning. "Don't do this, son. Don't lawyer me."

"Do what?" he asked feigning innocence. "What am I doing? I'm only asking a question."

"Browning, baby, leave it alone, please?" Bailey asked.

"But I'm curious, baby. Because I gotta tell you, if some stranger had gotten in my face," Browning said his voice raising with each word, "after my son had just overdosed and told me I needed to be a better parent as I waited to find out if my child would be a vegetable or not, I would have gone upside his fucking head!"

"Would you really?" Seth asked sarcastically after biting into a rib. "You would have gone upside someone's head?"

"Absolutely."

"When was the last time you went upside anyone's head, son?"

Browning hesitated and tried to recover. "That's not the point, Seth. I want to know what else you wished you would have said since you were so good at being a parent and all."

"You damn right I was a good parent. I did what I could, and look at where you are now. Look at this house, the car you drive, the clothes you wear. You think I didn't have a hand in that?"

Browning tossed his chopsticks on the table. "Hell no, you didn't have a hand in a damn thing! I did this all on my own! How can you possibly believe even for a second that you had a hand in this?" Browning asked enraged.

Seth leaned forward toward Browning. "Who you think paid for college, boy? Who paid for your room and board? Your books?"

"Mom did."

Seth laughed as he shoved away his still full plate. "Your mother? Really? Like I already explained to your dense ass, where do you think your beautiful mother, who never worked a day in her life, got the money to pay for your college education? The very college education that got you the job that allows you to live this fucking bourgeois lifestyle you luxuriate in today?"

"I get it all right," Browning said with a humorless chuckle. "Your dirty, illegal money helped me get here, but it's funny how I never saw you hand mom any money. It was Uncle Paulie who was at the house. He was there when I had trouble and needed a man to talk to. He was there eating dinner with us, laughing with us. Him. Not you."

"And who you think sent Paulie to your mother whenever there was a bill that had to be paid or to you when there was a bully that had to be dealt with? You really think your Uncle Paulie didn't come back to me and tell me what the hell was going on with my own family? Are you really that stupid?"

Browning shot to his feet, knocking his chair over. "Did you tell Uncle Paulie to sleep with my mother too?" yelled Browning, his fists balled in fury.

Seth slammed his hands on the table. "YES!" Seth screamed. "Yes, goddammit, I did!"

Seth's admission slapped a look of disbelief on Browning's face. The silence felt like an aftershock. Neither Charlie nor Baily moved unsure of what to say or do.

Seth lowered his head and tried to stop his hands from shaking. He wondered how Browning could have assumed he hadn't known about his wife and his best friend. He watched Browning set the chair back on it legs as Seth's stomach soured. His son had hoped that little bit of news would crush him. Seth stared at the table remembering how hard those days had been.

"What kind of monster are you?" Browning slowly asked sinking back into his chair.

After another minute of silence, Seth softly said, "I knew your mother, knew her like the back of my own hand. She was one of the strongest women I knew, but she was weak in areas where she needed to be stronger. She shouldn't have married me. I was no good for her, and I knew that. To this day I don't know why she said yes. I had vicious ruthless enemies, the kind who would firebomb a house and kill everyone inside just to get their target.

"Your mother wasn't someone who could handle that. She tried though. She tried so hard to pretend that my lifestyle didn't bother her and that she was strong. She even went so far as to carry a gun around in her purse," Seth said with a defeated chuckle.

"It was when I went to jail," Seth said as tears welled up in his eyes. "My going to jail broke her. Something cracked deep down inside her. She hid that from you and tried to hide it from me. She acted as if there was no problem and kept things moving, but Paulie would come to see me and tell me how she was doing. He would tell me how scared she was and how she lived in this dark place. She wouldn't smile or laugh anymore, and your mother's laugh..." Seth sighed. "Your mother's laugh was the sweetest sound in this whole world, boy," Seth said finally looking into his son's moist eyes, his voice trembling.

"Time after time, visit after visit, Paulie would tell me how bad she was and how he didn't know how to help her. I didn't either, and it was that pain of knowing she was out there scared that ate away at me like acid til one day I told Paulie to take her out on a date. He refused, told me to go fuck off. I loved him for that, but I wore him down until he agreed. I'm not a dumb man, Browning. I knew exactly what I was doing. I knew exactly where that would lead, but I told him to do it anyway. I told him if he loved me he would do this for me, and he did.

"He came back and told me everything after their movie date, told me how she'd had a good time and almost smiled during the show. The pain I felt in him taking my Penny out was nothing compared to the pain of thinking about her being too scared to leave the apartment, so I asked him to do it again. He refused again of course and cussed me out some more, but I urged him to, and he did.

"Then I got hit with more years for killing an inmate who'd tried to kill me. After awhile I started wondering if I was ever gonna get out of there alive, so I told him to make her happy, just make her happy, and keep her safe for me and for you." His hot tears dripped freely.

"That was the hardest decision I ever made," Seth said as he got to his feet, "but it was one of the best I ever made too." Seth stood and took in the elaborate home his son had created. "So you look around this mini mansion of yours, Browning, and you think about the sacrifices people made to help you get you to where you are today, cocktail parties and rubbing shoulders with the Mayor." Seth wiped his face and politely pushed in his chair. "Thanks for dinner," he quickly said to Bailey. "Walk me out, Charles."

At the front door Charles hugged his grandfather, and Seth almost buckled from the sudden show of love. He didn't want it to end, but he let go first, kissed his grandson on the cheek, and walked out beneath a breathtaking star-filled sky.

85

Once back in his room Seth paced and debated whether or not to call Paulie. He wasn't in the mood to explain what had just happened. The day had been emotional, the evening exhausting. Something he certainly hadn't expected. He'd expected pizza and maybe a beer, not an ambush over Chinese food.

The truth he'd revealed was something he had thought he'd take to his grave, but Browning had pushed his buttons, and he'd completely lost control. Neither he nor Paulie had ever brought that time up once since Seth had been released. It was over, and it was Seth's cross to bear.

He dialed Paulie.

"Damn, dinner was quick," Paulie said.

"Dinner never quite happened."

"Fuck does that mean? At least tell me there was food. That's the one thing that usually makes an appearance at dinner."

"There was a ton of food. Food wasn't the damn issue even though no one really ate."

"Then what happened, negro?"

"My son happened."

"You mean Charlie, right?"

"I wish. No, Browning happened. He wanted to know what else I would have said to the parents of the boy who overdosed."

"Wait! Someone overdosed?" Paulie asked confused.

"Yeah, one of Charlie's friends. Kid's a royal fuck up. Privileged white boy who thinks it's okay to use the N-word."

"The heavyweight champion of slurs, and some white kid thought it was okay to use it?"

"Yeah, anyway this kid took way too much of his mother's Oxy and damn near died. I laid into his idiot parents for never being there, and word got back to Browning. He wanted to know what else I would have said to those two fucktards since I'm such a great parent. He kept pushing, and I lost it, Paulie. I fucking lost it!"

"Seth," Paulie said softly, "what did you say?"

"It wasn't what I said, Paulie. It was what he said." Seth paused looking down at his shoes. "He brought up you and Penny."

"Shit."

"Yeah, and I told him everything, Paulie. I thought 'fuck it, he brought it up then let's talk about it' and spilled my guts." Seth rubbed his pounding temples. "Dammit, Paulie, I coulda sworn I told you to be discreet."

"I was, Seth, and you know it. Don't put this on me. He's a smart man, and he was a smart kid. He was gonna figure it out, man, no matter how discreet we were."

"Yeah well, he threw that shit in my face. It was like he had been waiting all his life for the right moment to hit me with it."

"And so you told him everything?"

"Yeah," Seth said sitting wearily on his bed.

"How you feeling?"

After a good minute of reflection, Seth answered his best friend. "I feel unburdened to tell you the truth, like the gorilla climbed down off my back."

"That's a good thing. I know you carried that shit around with you, refusing to put it down, but it's long past time you did. Now maybe you can move on."

"Maybe," Seth said.

"You think Browning can or will forgive you?"

"First I didn't do anything to forgive, and two…you think I care?"

"Yeah, deep down I think you do, and it's okay to admit that man. It's probably the other reason you ran out there. Because you care," Paulie said.

"Maybe. Stop acting like you know me."

"As my brother from another mother, it's no act."

"Yeah, yeah. Look I'm gonna turn in, so I'm a let you go."

"Bullshit, you ain't about to go to bed. You ain't even eat yet, but I understand. I wouldn't be in the mood to talk either, so you have a good night, partner."

"Cut it out," Seth said. "Hey…thanks for listening."

"Anytime for you. You know that," he said before they disconnected.

Seth smiled as he slid his phone into his pocket and headed out to find something to eat.

86

After his grandfather's abrupt departure, Charlie had retreated to the man cave. Two hours later he still sat in front of the TV screen screaming instructions into the mic as he clicked away on his game controller. Focusing solely on the game allowed him a small outlet for his festering anger and a chance to ignore reality, which was why he was caught off guard when his father sat down next to him. He hadn't even heard his father walk into the basement.

Charlie looked over at his father and wrinkled his brow but said nothing. Instead he turned his attention back to the game, barking more instructions. His father watched as Charlie and his team systematically eliminate one enemy soldier after another. After Charlie's company secured the refinery, Browning tapped his son on the shoulder. When Charlie glanced over, his dad mouthed 'hungry?'

"Hey, guys, I've gotta go. I'll be back if I can." He disconnected his game before anyone could mount any displeasure, dropped the controller, and yanked off his headset. Unwilling to sit next to his father, he walked over to the fridge to grab a soda. He wanted to be left alone.

Browning cleared his throat. "You didn't have to stop, Charlie. In fact, I enjoying watching you and your friends kick ass. The graphics were amazing, and you guys were impressive. I have no idea how you keep track of everything. This is a far cry from *Pac-Man* and *Frogger* from my day." When Charlie didn't say anything and just stared at him, Browning continued. "So were those classmates you were playing with, whoever you were talking to?"

Charlie didn't blink. Instead he gulped down half his soda and belched in his dad's direction. "What's going on, Dad?"

"Nothing. You didn't eat much at dinner, so I wanted to see what you were up to and to see if you were hungry. That's all. Are you going to excuse yourself?"

"That's not all, and you know it," Charlie said with a distinct edge in his voice. "And excuse me," he added sarcastically.

"What makes you say that?"

"Forget it. No, I'm not hungry, Dad. Okay? Can you leave me alone?" Charlie snapped.

"Charlie, talk to me. What do you mean 'that's not all'?" he asked in his most sincere concerned voice, a tone Charlie hadn't heard in years.

"Well you never come down here, and I can't remember the last time you cared if I was hungry. Since you've done both tells something's up. So…what's going on?"

"Why does something need to be going on? Why can't I check to see if my son is hungry?" Browning's eyes narrowed as he rose. "Are you mad at me? If so don't sit on it, son."

Charlie laughed. "Yeah, Dad, I'm mad. Well…actually more pissed off than mad, but why get into it?" Charlie asked and slumped down on the couch. "What's the point?"

"Because I'm curious as to why you're pissed at me."

"Tell me why you're here."

"This is my house."

Charlie shrugged. "That's nothing new. I've been reminded of that my whole life, Dad. Tell me why you're here now."

Browning sat back down looking confused, which only incensed Charlie more. "Honestly, I just wanted to see how you were doing. I know you found Chad and saved him. I wanted to know how you were feeling about what happened and see if you wanted to talk."

Charlie laughed coldly again and wiped at his face. "Don't ya think it's a little late to throw your name into the hat for Dad of the Year?"

"Look, Charlie, you're about to leave for college soon, and…"

Charlie laughed sardonically. "You mean your college, don't you?"

"Is this about the college thing?"

"That's part of it, but it's so much more than forcing me to go to Ohio State."

"Why don't you tell me all that's on your mind, Charlie?"

Something snapped in Charlie. "Ya know what? You've had three major fuck ups, Dad."

"Watch your mouth, boy. It's still my house."

"Whatever. You want to know what your three fuck ups are? I'll run em down. First was telling me I had to go to the college of your choice or else you weren't paying and never asking me what I wanted. Second was marrying Bailey only six months after mom died, and the last was how you flat-out lied to me."

"What? I've never lied to you. I told you from day one what the deal was with college. Second, Bailey and I came to you and asked how you'd feel about us getting married and even asked your permission. You said you were okay with it, so what is it I'm not getting here?"

"I won't even get into the college thing with you again, but to ask me if I'm okay with you marrying someone barely six months after mom died was pretty foul, Dad. I was fourteen and fucked up after mom died, and you ask me if I'm okay with you getting married before my mother's perfume had even faded from the house? If you still can't see how bad that was then I don't know what to say to you. And what do you mean you never lied to me? You told me my grandfather was dead, and you knew that wasn't true. So why, Dad? Tell me why you lied to my face my entire life."

"Is that what all this is about?" Browning stood and started to pace. "I told you what I told you about your grandfather because Seth was and still is no angel. He's a bad man, Charles, the worst kind of man. Did he tell you he's killed a man?"

"Actually, he's killed two men."

Browning stopped pacing. "Two? See, he's not a good man, son, and I was trying to protect you. I don't even know how he knew where we were, but that's beside the point. I didn't want him in your life. Was that the wrong or right decision? Maybe, I don't know, but it was my call, and I made it. I felt you didn't need that kind of person in your life."

"What exactly were you trying to protect me from, Dad?"

"Men like him. Look, I told you he was a bad man, and when I was growing up he was never there for me. He was behind bars for killing a cop, so instead I got Uncle Paulie who I knew wasn't my real uncle, but he was all I had."

Charlie slammed his soda on the counter. "Dad…you're never here for me! Should I not know you? Should I be protected from you?" Charlie wiped his wet hand on his shorts. "You aren't in prison, but I hardly ever see you, so what's the difference?" He thought of how many times his grandfather had been there for him in the last two weeks, and his anger exploded. "You know what! You don't have a fucking clue about what's going on in my life! Not one! So spare me your sob story about Pops not being there for you. He had a good reason why he wasn't, but at least he made sure his best friend looked out for you and grandma. Who've I had looking out for me, Dad? Bailey? You're no better than Chad's parents!"

For the second time in one night, Charlie's father stood in stunned silence. He sat and put his head in his hands. "Charlie, I had no idea you felt this way. I mean I'm working and busting my ass to give you anything you could want or need."

"Did I ask for any of this?" Charlie asked as his arm swept around the basement. "When Mom died you had Bailey, and I got nothing. I lost not only a mother but a father too. Thanks for not being here, so you can buy me all this shit."

"Watch your mouth, Charles, please. Don't let me tell you again."

"Or what Dad? You're gonna hit me? That'll be a first. Do you have any idea what…" Charlie paused and stared at him. "Ya know what…never mind."

"Any idea what? What were you going to say, Charles?"

"Nothing. I've already said everything I wanted to say to you. Good night, Dad," Charlie said and left Browning in the man cave speechless.

87

Seth woke at the crack of dawn. In truth he hadn't gotten much sleep, and his brain yelped for coffee. Scenes from last night's dinner flashed across his mind, and he sighed. *What a fuckin mess that was*, he thought. *But the truth is rarely pretty, and it's about time Browning and Charlie knew the truth rather than believing in some bullshit fairytale.* Seth rubbed the sleep from his eyes and set about his day.

Over breakfast and coffee, he mulled over the situation with Charlie and sifted through everything he knew looking for the best plan of action. Having a plan calmed him unlike Paulie, whose motto was "Motherfuck a plan!"

Where Paulie got off on being spontaneous, Seth was almost meticulous in his approach, which is why the two worked so well together. An old friend of theirs likened them to a jazz duo. Seth wrote the music, and Paulie bided his time until his solo when he could play whatever the hell he wanted. When he was done, he would fall seamlessly back into the groove of the song right back in line with Seth.

This plan wouldn't include Paulie, and for that Seth was grateful. He didn't like the odds he kept calculating. While Stony wasn't Charlie's biggest threat, the wanna-be gangster was driving the deal that was more likely for revenge rather than profit, and Stony's irrational logic was driving the snake that was Frank, which made the whole situation dangerous as hell. Seth rubbed his temples and knew he had to try one last time to confirm his suspicions. Once he had the truth he could pick a final course of action. Seth chuckled. *Revealing truth seems to be my mission lately.* He threw two twenties on the table for Alice and left without his customary goodbye.

He checked his watch and pulled out of the lot. *The baby gangsters should be up and moving by now.* He ran through how he needed the conversation to go to learn the truth. The cold calculating approach Stony had taken to this entire saga impressed him. *I must be getting slow not to have picked up on this earlier.* Merging into traffic he prepared for what was coming, whatever it may be.

A half an hour later Seth pulled up in front of Romare's and assessed his surroundings. A black and gold Camry sat across the street halfway down the block. The driver was smooth, but Seth was no fool. He wasn't a cop, but he was definitely watching the place. Seth considered various possibilities, but none affected his plans. He again slipped his Glock in his waistband and his snub nose into his ankle holster.

The overweight DJ met him at the door.

"Tell your bosses I'm here."

"Yeah, yeah, hold on. I'll be back. Oh and don't punch nobody in da throat, okay?"

"You got it, Rerun," Seth said with a wink and a smile.

The DJ sighed and walked off to the office.

Seth grabbed a barstool in front of the petite cinnamon-colored young woman prepping for business.

"You the new bartender?" Seth asked as she dried a glass. She had such delicate features she seemed almost fragile. Her tight braids were bound together into one long one that fell down past her shoulders, and she wore a tight t-shirt that had "Romare's" emblazoned in shiny gold across her ample breasts. He couldn't resist her frozen, pouty, lip-gloss smeared lips and suspicious gaze. "I thought bartenders talked to their patrons."

"You ain't bought nothin yet. That's what makes someone a patron," the pretty girl said to him dismissively.

Her quick wit gained his approval. "Fair enough," he said and slapped a twenty on the bar. "Give me a Heineken, please."

With a flip of her braid and a suck of her teeth, she pulled out a beer, popped the top, and placed it in front of him on a napkin before she snatched the twenty off the bar.

Seth felt someone slide up silently behind him and figured it was Frank. "What's your name, darling?" Seth asked.

"China," she replied as she rolled her eyes and dropped Seth's change on the bar.

"The name suits you." He mentioned to the change. "Keep it, China," he said with a smirk as he took a casual swig of his beer. "It's yours."

China's mouth didn't crack a smile, but her big brown eyes did.

Seth winked and took another swig of his beer. "You gonna stand behind me all day like a stalker, junior, or are you gonna take me to see the man?" Seth asked still looking at China.

"You one brave nigga, Harlem. Follow me," Frank said and headed towards the back of the building.

Seth slid off the barstool and ignored the slur. He had bigger goals to achieve today, and he was outmanned and outgunned here anyway. He left his half empty bottle on the bar and gave China a sly wink that finally put a hint of a smile on her face.

Stony greeted Seth at the door to his office and offered him a seat. "I'm glad you stopped by. I wanted to apologize for the way I acted the last time you were up here," Stony said. "I was tense, and I threatened you. My apologies. We cool?"

Surprised, Seth locked eyes with the wanna-be gangster who seemed more relaxed than he had ever seen him. "I didn't take your words as a threat, but I accept your apology. My mistake was grabbing your arm. I might have reacted the same way."

"Still, my reaction was over the top, so again I'm sorry."

"Apology accepted."

"Great, with that out of the way, what can I do for you?" Stony said as he walked back to his desk and sat while Frank left the office.

"I'm here of course about my grandson," Seth said trying to tear his eyes away from the door Frank had just closed behind himself. Something was definitely different. Frank no longer felt the need to guard Stony's every breath.

"What about him?"

"Are you certain there's no other way he can pay his nut other than this Basket-guy's painting?"

Stony's jaw tensed at Seth's blatant slaughtering of the artist's name. "Not unless you got 250 large on you," Stony said as he looked over Seth.

"What if I had a hundred?" Seth asked. "You could have it tomorrow, cash, and I can get the rest to you in a few days."

Stony's eyes widened a hair in surprise, and Seth knew the wanna-be gangster recognized the business opportunity. Cash spoke volumes no matter what type of industry you were in or lifestyle you lived. In the next breath though, the younger man's eyes tightened. "Did I stutter? One hundred is not a quarter of a million, is it?"

"I need more time to liquefy assets. That shit takes a minute, Stony."

"I'm not interested in more time or partial payments." Stony grabbed his ledger and flipped through pages to Charlie's history before laying the long list in front of Seth. "He's owed me that money for a good minute, Seth, and the only thing he's ever brought in here is you. As it stands, it's either the full note or the Basquiat."

Seth met Stony's hard gaze. "You're passing up one hundred K in clean cash? From what I've seen around here it looks like you could use the money."

"Do I need to repeat myself, old timer?

Stony's refusal confirmed everything for Seth. He didn't need to hear anymore. If Stony had made the smart business decision, Seth's instincts would have been wrong, but Leonard's nephew hadn't even considered his offer. This was all personal, and Seth knew exactly what was coming. Even if they handed over the painting to Stony or Frank, he and his grandson would be dead seconds later. No loose ends.

Seth leaned forward, his elbows on his knees. "You must really hate my son."

"You mean your grandson? Naaaa...I don't mind the kid," he said with a hint of a smile.

"No, Stony. I'm talking about my dickhead son who destroyed your uncle."

Stony's eyes immediately grew dark and cold. "Watch your step, old man. You have no idea what you're talking about."

Seth held up his hands and strategically back-peddled, content with triggering Stony's tell. "Not trying to offend at all, youngblood. I'm not particularly fond of my son either. He seems to have forgotten where he came from and is only worried about sucking on the tits of who's who in this town. I was only trying to understand the lay of the land. I think I got it now. You'll have the Basquiat soon enough. Hopefully that will repay the debt you think my family owes yours."

Stony slammed the ledger shut. "I seriously doubt that, New York. I seriously doubt that."

"Then there's nothing more to say is there?"

"Not really."

Both men got to their feet. Seth looked around Stony's office for what was probably the last time. "Hey, no Desert Eagle today? What gives?"

"That's no concern of yours. Is it?" Stony asked pointedly. "Don't you have some work to do, New York?"

Seth heard the edge in Stony's voice and knew it was time to leave. "Catch you later, youngblood," he said with a smile before he left Stony's office and the bar without a backward glance.

When Frank re-entered the office minutes later, Stony was at the window watching Seth's Caddy pull away from Romare's.

"What was that all about?" Frank asked.

"I may have shown my hand," Stony answered.

"What do you mean?"

"You know the problem with that man is he's too damn smart, yet he doesn't let on that he is. He doesn't have that snotty attitude most people from New York have," he said as he sat back down in his desk chair.

"Well, whatever you told him, nothing changes, right?" Frank asked.

"Right," Stony said with a dark smile. "Not a damn thing changes."

88

When Seth got back to his hotel his cell phone buzzed as the elevator doors dinged open.

"Hey Paulie, what's up?"

"How'd you know it was me?" Paulie asked.

"I have this fortune teller sitting on my lap–" Seth started to say.

"Hey, get your own damn material."

"Why when yours is so readily available?" Seth asked as he unlocked his room door.

"Anyway, I'm calling with the flight information for the Preachers. Write this down. You know how bad your memory is, old man," he said.

Seth ignored the crack about his memory and grabbed the pen on the nightstand and a piece of paper.

"Flight 1025 tomorrow. It gets in at 2:20. Please be there on time. You don't need any extra drama or nonsense, and you know how touchy they can be. By the way, Preacher Sr. is looking forward to seeing you again."

"I'm sure he is."

He and Preacher went back almost as long as he and Paulie. The two had been good friends until their late teens when Preacher had had eyes on the same girl as Seth. The two rivals had come to blows at one point, and even though Preacher had won the fight, Penelope had walked off with Seth. Despite Seth's denials, most felt— especially Paulie—that Seth had let Preacher beat him so he could limp off with Penny.

The friendship between Preacher Sr. and Seth had never been the same. Preacher had opted out of being a member of the Known Men, but they'd continued to work together from time to time when it was mutually beneficial. Many were surprised how they were able to keep business above pride.

Seth sighed. "You didn't bring up any old shit, did you?"

"Would I do some shit like that?"

"Yeah, you would. I know it, and you know it too."

Paulie laughed. "You right, but trust me, nothing was said. He's cool. Besides, you're paying him thirty-five large, and I told him to play nice."

"Or?"

Paulie hesitated and then blurted, "Or I told him I'd burn his shop down."

Seth sighed again and chuckled. *Always looking out for me.* "A little dramatic but thanks. Tomorrow. 2:20. Got it."

"Still can't see why we just can't pay off the note," Paulie said.

"I tried to negotiate that option. They said no."

"WHAT?"

"Yeah, this is a vendetta, and they're backing us into a corner, so it might get a little messy out here," Seth said throwing his hand in the air.

"You know I don't mind getting messy. I can be there by midnight."

As tempting as that sounded, Seth declined Paulie's offer to come out and kill everyone.

Paulie growled unhappily. "You know what this means, right?"

"Yeah, it means they plan to kill us the second we hand over the painting."

"You gotta plan?"

"I'm working on one."

"Good," Paulie sighed. "All right, old man, I need to get back to work here, but you call me if you need me."

"If I need you I will."

"Seth?"

"Yeah?"

"Watch your back, Black man."

"Always do."

89

After spending most of Monday at the hospital with Chad, Charlie sat in his darkened basement and stared off into space, wiping hot tears from his face. So much had happened in such a short time that he felt like the weight of it all was crashing down on him, and he didn't have any clue how to make things right.

He grabbed his phone and immediately tossed it down as he swiped at more tears. *How had everything turned to shit, he wondered. Clarissa's dead, Chad tried to kill himself, Lilly's gone and never wants to talk to me again, and I have to steal a fucking painting. What the fuck happened?* For days, he had fought the overwhelming urge to get high, but tonight he had no more strength. *Fuck it,* he thought. He snatched up his phone.

"Yo, man, what's up?"

Charlie leaned back on the sofa and closed his eyes. "Can you bring me some of your best shit?"

"What? You sure?" Gavin asked, "I mean…I thought you were done."

"I was done, and now I'm not." Charlie hung up, uncaring if he was rude.

Minutes later Gavin arrived with a fat blunt already rolled. Without any hesitation, Charlie flicked the lighter and puffed. The wonderful familiarity filled his lungs, and instantly he felt some of his anxiety fade.

Gavin sat down and began rolling another one. "You go see Chad today?" he asked quietly.

Charlie nodded and took another toke.

"He talk to you?"

Charlie shook his head, holding the powerful smoke in his lungs for greater effect. He passed the blunt to Gavin.

"Yeah, he won't talk to me either. All he does is stare out the window." Gavin took a drag. "I think he's depressed."

Charlie finally exhaled. "Yeah…yeah, I know. His demons, they almost got him. I don't know. I guess he's embarrassed or something. Scared." Charlie pushed his palms into his eye sockets. "I wish I knew how to help. Fuck, I don't even know if he wants help."

"I don't know, man. I just keep stopping by, so he knows I'm there." Gavin shrugged and grabbed the remote to zone out on the most recent J.J. Abrams flick.

Charlie swallowed the desperate scream inside him. Everyone was slipping through his fingers, and he felt helpless. He took another long pull of the blunt and surrendered.

About an hour later Charlie's mind was adrift in a cloud of blissful numbness. The worries, fears, and angst that had plagued him had become hazy and distant amidst the O-rings of smoke he had exhaled from his mouth. His eyelids felt heavy, and his vision was blurred, so he closed his eyes and tried to focus on something good. Lily's face immediately flamed to life, and Charlie shot to his feet, even as Gavin sat droning on comparing the original Star Trek to the movie versions. Charlie stumbled to the bathroom. Dropping the toilet seat, he sat down and yanked out his cell phone to swipe through the pictures of Lily that had survived the purge. On impulse, he dialed her number, knowing she wouldn't answer. She hated him, but he wanted to hear her voice and maybe leave her message.

"Charlie?" she asked sounding suspicious.

Charlie almost slipped off the seat when she answered. He coughed. "Hey…hey Lils. Ummm…how are you?"

"I'm fine. What do you want, Charles?"

The sound of her sweet voice caused him to sweat. "I'm just calling to see how you're doing in the big bad apple."

"Charlie, everything is fine here. What do you want? Why did you call?"

"I was…wondering if you heard about…uh…about Chad?"

"Yes, I did. It didn't surprise me at all, but congrats on saving your friend's life. Way to go. Look, I have to go."

"Waitwaitwaitwait a second," he said getting to his feet.

"What, Charlie? I'm busy."

Charlie stared at himself in the mirror and swallowed. "I…I miss you, Lily," he said with a nervous laugh.

"Charlie…Are you high?"

Charlie broke eye contact with his reflection and chuckled. "Jussa little. Not much."

"Typical," she said away from the phone. "Goodbye, Charlie."

"Why you so mean to me?" he asked.

"Because you're a fucking disappointment. Nothing has changed, has it? How does Charlie cope with his friend almost killing himself by overdosing on drugs? He get's high of course. Figures. You were a pothead when I was there, and no matter what happens you'll always be one."

"This is the first time I smoked in like two weeks!"

"And you threw all that right out the window. One step forward. Two steps back, Charles. You're a dumb ass. You know that?"

Charlie's anger spiked through his haze. "No…You…You're the dumb ass!"

Lily sighed. "Goodbye, Charlie."

Anger and fear swirled within Charlie's gut, and he began to pace the small bathroom. "Waitwaitwaitaminute…" he said his words slurring. "You know what? You know what? You're not a dumb ass," he said with a pause, "You're a dumb ass biiiiitch."

The quiet click of her hanging up sounded like what it was, the last nail in the coffin of their friendship.

"Hello? Hello? Lily? Lily?" Realizing she was gone again and that he'd fucked up he screamed at his phone, "Fuck you, bitch!"

He returned to the sofa. Gavin was still talking as if he had been there all along. "Shut the fuck up, dude," Charlie said. "I'm hungry. You hungry?"

"Yeah man, stomach need food," Gavin said and then burst into peals of laughter.

Charlie laughed along at his friend's stupid joke. "Good, whatchu want on your pizza?" he asked, and he lit up another blunt. Fuck it.

90

After watching the late night news report on the dramatic decrease in gun violence over the last weekend, Seth settled down on his bed and finally called Marta. He'd avoided it as best he could, but he missed her voice, her laugh, and her smile, and he hoped she was home. Sundays were typically light at The Pearl once brunch was done, so he figured she might be out. Thankfully she picked up on the second ring.

"I was beginning to think you had forgotten about me," Marta said.

"If there is one woman in the world that is impossible to forget, you are her," Seth retorted with a smile.

"You were always that silver-tongue, smooth-talking devil."

"Was or is?"

"Pick one."

"Well since I am still breathing, I'm gonna go for is."

"Smooth talker and smart. The ladies need to watch out for you."

"You mean I need to watch out for them," he said with a laugh. He'd missed their banter too but hadn't realized how much until that moment.

"Seriously, how are you, Seth?" she asked, her voice dripping with concern.

"I'm well, baby. Honestly, I'm fine. How are you?"

"Worried sick over you," she said. "Where are you?"

"Boardman."

"Where the hell is Boardman?"

"Ohio. Outside of Youngstown."

"And what are you doing in Ohio?"

Seth sighed. "Getting to know my grandson and helping him out of a big mess," he said as he leaned back on the hotel's fluffy pillows.

"Oh my God, you met him? After all this time? How was that?"

"His father told him I was dead."

"Are you serious, Seth?"

"I wish I was lying."

"Well his father is an asshole then," she said with a suck of her teeth.

"Yes, he is. I can't argue with you there."

"So what's this mess that has my man in bumblefuck Ohio?"

Seth weakened a bit at her "my man" reference. "My grandson has gotten himself into some trouble with some dangerous people."

"Guppy swimming in the shark tank kinda thing?" she asked.

"Exactly."

"I overheard Paulie saying something about a gambling debt. What does he owe?"

"They suckered him into being in the hole for $250 grand."

"Oh baby, I can pay that no problem. Tell me how to get it to you."

Seth smiled at her open generosity. "I know you can, and I love you for the offer, but I can pay it too, and then some. Unfortunately this isn't about money. This trouble goes deeper than that, way deeper than that."

Seth explained the history between his asshole son and Leonard Carmichael and how Stony had designed the whole scheme to destroy his son and grandson. He told her about the painting and what he suspected would happen to the Jackson family should they hand over the painting to Leonard's nephew.

"So that's where the Preachers are going. They were in for brunch today with Paulie. They're headed to you aren't they?" she said.

Seth shook his head at how quickly the woman could put two and two together. "Yeah."

"So you're going to steal this painting?"

"Yeah," Seth said.

"Be careful, Seth. Please."

"I will, baby."

The two of them shifted to small talk to lighten the mood. They talked about her kitchen and how well Roscoe was doing. The young man was becoming indispensable. Seth smiled knowing he had been right about him.

Then Seth took a deep breath and addressed the eight hundred pound gorilla on the line with them. "Marta, why didn't you want to move in with me?"

She sighed. "See," she said, "here we are having a nice conversation, and you come out of left field on me like that. You know I hate that."

Seth remained silent.

"I…I tried to explain that night, Seth. I need my independence, baby. I can't be living up under another man, no matter how good he treats me. I've lived with men before, and once I got out from under the last one I vowed to never do that to myself again. It's nothing against you personally. If any man asked me, he would have gotten the same answer. It's not you, baby," she said, "It's your gender."

Marta hadn't said anything she hadn't said that night, but now that the wound to his pride had scabbed over, Seth finally understood. He had heard the stories both from her and her friends about all the shit she had been through because of her abusive last husband, the visits to the ER and the reconstructive surgery. Seth had tried to hunt down the monster once he'd gotten his name, so he could show the ass what it was like to need plastic surgery, but after the divorce settlement, her ex had vanished.

"Seth…I love you, and I hope you know how hard it was…to say no to you."

"I do," he said. "And I understand, Marta. I'm just sorry that your past continues to dictate your present and future. Maybe some day you'll be able to move past what happened. But I love you too."

"Good, so when are you coming back to me?" she said in a seductive and playful whine.

Seth raised an eyebrow at her desire. "I hope to be back in New York as soon as I'm done here."

"You swear?"

"That's my goal. Cross my heart and hope to die."

"Good," she said softly. "I miss the fuck out of you."

"And I, you, baby."

"Say goodnight to me and meet me in my dreams," she whispered seductively.

"Goodnight, baby. I'll see you soon," he said. Seth pressed "End" on his phone. With a loud exhale he closed his eyes and vowed that he would do whatever he could to see her again.

91

A half an hour later as Seth stepped out of the bathroom to head to bed there was a knock on his hotel room door. On instinct he silently grabbed his gun.

Seth clicked off the safety. "Who is it?"

"Pop, it's me," said Charlie.

Seth sighed. *Looks like my pleasant dreams will have to wait.* He slipped the gun back under his pillow before he checked through the peephole and let in his grandson. When Charlie walked past him, Seth smelled the weed.

"Are you fucking high?" he asked grabbing the boy by his shirt and ramming him against the wall.

Charlie winced. "Yo, Pops! What's up? What are you doin?" he asked with a nervous giggle.

"I asked you a question, boy," Seth said, shaking Charlie against the wall. "Are. You. High?"

Charlie shrugged. "Slightly."

"Fuck I tell you about coming to see me when you're high?" Seth asked as he smacked his grandson on the side of his head, wiping the smirk off the boy's face. "What did I tell you, huh?" Another blow rained down on Charlie who raised his arms to protect himself. "Didn't I tell you I'd hurt you?" he asked as he grabbed one of the boy's arms with his left hand and began to swing in earnest on his grandson.

Charlie twisted his head from side-to-side, trying to avoid Seth's relentless blows. "Stop, Pops! Please!"

With one last shove, Seth released the boy and backed away. Completely disgusted, he tried to get a grip on his temper.

Charlie slumped to the floor and wept.

"Charles," Seth said grinding his teeth.

Charlie didn't move as his he slowly composed himself. He simply sat with his back to the wall and stared straight ahead at nothing.

"Charlie, look at me, boy. Don't make me say it again," Seth sternly said.

Charlie grudgingly looked up at him.

"What in the hell are you crying for and why are you high?"

Charlie wiped his face, clumsily stood, and headed for the door.

Seth stepped in his path.

"Please move, Pop," Charlie said wiping his face with the hem of his t-shirt.

Seth stood his ground. Experience told him this was about to get even uglier.

"Please move," the boy said again. When Seth didn't move Charlie screamed, "MOVE!" and tried to push Seth out of the way.

Seth swiftly grabbed his grandson's hand and bent it down. Intense pain shot through Charlie's wrist the likes of which he knew the boy had never felt before. His defiant grandson dropped to his knees. "You ain't going nowhere, not until you tell me what the hell is going on with you," Seth said before he let go of Charlie's hand.

Charlie quickly pulled his hand into his body, folded his arms, and again found the wall with his back. "What do you want to hear? Huh?" he screamed. "You want to hear how fucked up everything is? How in less than two months my entire life has fallen apart? Is that it? My best friend tried to kill himself. My girl couldn't wait to get a million miles away from me. I had to bury another friend. I got to watch a guy's head get blown off and have his brains all over me, and the whole time I owe more money than I can count to some South Side fuckers." Charlie pounded his head against the wall. "You want to hear that I'm scared, that I'm stressed the fuck out, that I don't know what the fuck to do? Is that what you wanna hear?" Tears bathed both his cheeks as he rocked back and forth, but Seth could find no compassion.

"You're stressed? Really?" Seth grabbed a hand towel from the bathroom and tossed it at Charlie's head. "Wipe your damn tears. You know, anytime a pampered baby starts whining about how stressed they are, about how hard or unfair it all is for them, my ass begins to itch and all I want to do is tell them to shut the hell up. You sleep in a bed all your own, you got clean clothes on your back and brand new shoes on your feet, you have hot and cold running water, and you never go to bed hungry, do you?"

Charlie said nothing.

Seth began to pace back and forth. "Answer me this, little man. What the fuck did you think was going to happen to your little white friend? You and the Asian kid both knew he was getting into some hard nasty shit, but you didn't step up and step in to save him until it was almost too late. Your girl ran away? Well, after what I've seen the last few weeks I can't say as I blame her since you don't seem to have a goddamned thing figured out. She's apparently way smarter than you are. That's for sure. As far as witnessing that bartender's death, what the fuck did you think would eventually happen if you kept hanging out on the fucking South Side, son?

"You want to know what real stress is? Go live over there. Go live on the South Side for a month. Leave your dad's McMansion and try to live in the hood for a month. Then maybe you'll have a pretty good idea of what it means to be stressed and scared when you don't know if a stray bullet is gonna cut through your window or your wall while you sleep or when the only food you can afford is greying meat or some shit that comes out of dented cans. You talking about you scared," Seth said under his breath. "What the hell you know about being scared? What you so damn scared of?"

"I have to steal a fucking painting, Pops!" Charlie yelled.

Furious, Seth leapt to where his grandson still sat and towered over him. "First off, lower your goddamn voice," Seth said through clenched teeth. "Secondly, you ain't stealing shit, so get that out of your head. You think I would have you—YOU—go in there and try to steal a painting? You, who can't count five damn cameras in front of the museum, really?"

"It was my first time counting cameras," Charlie mumbled.

"Exactly, your first time. You don't know shit, so don't be foolish," Seth said moving back to his bed. He pinched the bridge of his nose trying to stem the pounding in his head and figure out a way to get through to his immature grandson. "How long have I been here, Charles?"

"I dunno. Like two weeks or something."

"Yeah, I've been here almost two weeks. Do you have any idea what I'm giving up to be here, Charlie? Did it sink through your thick skull that I have a somewhat successful business to run? That I have friends who depend on me? That I have a woman who misses me?"

The look on Charlie's face told Seth the self-centered boy had never once considered any of that.

"But instead I'm here. With you." Seth pointed at him. "Trying to get your ass out of the fire. You don't hear me whining about what I'm sacrificing because men don't whine. They handle their business, and that's what I'm doing here. I'm handling business. I'm taking care of my family. That's how it's suppose to be." After a few seconds he sat on the edge of the bed and asked, "What the hell are you doing here, Charlie? Why did you get high and knock on my door tonight?"

Charlie almost shrugged his shoulders, but he glanced up at Seth and thought better of it. "I don't know, Pop. I got in my car and started driving," he said through sniffles. "Next thing I know, I'm pulling into the parking lot, and here I am."

Seth thought about that. He was looking at a boy with no direction and no motivation. "You got a plan, Charlie?" he finally asked.

Charlie stayed silent.

"Did you hear me, boy?"

"I don't know what you're talking about. A plan for what?"

"For your life."

"What the fuck do you think?" Charlie shouted as he got to his feet faster than Seth ever thought he could. "HUH? Do I look like I have a damn plan, Pops? My life is falling the fuck apart. NO, Pop! I don't have a plan. I don't know if I'm coming or going, and maybe that's why I'm here. Maybe I figured you're the only one who could help me. Maybe I thought you could fix shit, but maybe I was wrong!"

Seth watched his distraught grandson slump to the foot of the bed with a tear streaked face and snot dribbling from his nose. *Maybe it's time to put the stick away.* Seth sighed. "Charlie, you need a plan, son. You are going to grow up and become an adult. That's inevitable.

Whether or not you become a man or you stay a child depends on your attitude and your plan. Do you understand me? Time is up, and you're gonna have to learn to stand on your own two feet. I'm not always going to be able to see you through shit or save you. You're going to have to do that for yourself, and you can't do that getting high every time shit don't go your way or life busts you in the mouth. Life is a battle, son, and no one—especially a Black man—should ever enter a battle without a plan, understand?"

Charlie nodded.

"Good, good," Seth said grabbing the desk chair. "You're a high school graduate now. What's the next step? Sit in your dad's basement, get high, and play video games until he kicks you out?"

"College." Charlie said. "I want to go to college."

"That's a great start to a plan."

"Yeah, but if I don't go to Ohio State Dad said he wasn't paying for college," Charlie stated.

"What? Wait, say that again."

"Dad's not going to pay for it unless I go to his old school."

Seth rubbed the ache gnawing at his temples. "So let me get this straight. You want to go to college, and you don't want to go to Ohio State, but your dad said 'no Ohio State, no money.' I got that right?"

Charlie nodded sadly.

"That's some bullshit," Seth replied and leaned back in his chair. "Where do you want to go?"

"Michigan."

Seth laughed and shook his head. "Of ALL the schools in the world, you had to pick that one?"

"So what if they're rivals. I want to study English and get the fuck away from here." Charlie exploded and jumped to his feet again which prompted Seth to do the same. "I'm so sick of him! When's it gonna be my turn to run my life!" he yelled. "When, Pops? I get bullshit from home. I get you coming down on me. I got Frank and Stony breathing down my neck. Then I call the best person I know in the world a fucking bitch tonight." Charlie's voice cracked as pain and fear overtook him again. "I...I just want it all to stop. I just want to catch my damn breath!" Charlie growled while he pounded his chest in emphasis.

Seth wrapped his arms around his grandson and pulled him close. Charlie's sobs broke over his shoulder, and Seth wished more than anything he'd been in Charlie's life sooner. "Your time is coming soon, son. I promise you. It's coming soon if you reach for it, but this is the last time you cry over something like this, you hear me?" he softly said in Charlie's ear as Charlie continued cry.

"You stub your toe, you can cry. You break your arm, you can cry, but this crying over your life…this is the last damn time you cry over your life. You wanna to know why?" Seth asked grabbing the boy's face and forcing Charlie to meet his eyes. "Because you haven't stood up and taken control of your life yet. You don't act. You only react. That's gotta stop. It's your life, and there can be only one driver. From this point on don't ever let someone else drive your life. You got me?"

"I…got…you," Charlie said.

"Good." Seth kissed him on his forehead, and Charlie sat down on the bed and wrestled to catch his breath. "Lay down, son. Get some rest. We'll talk more tomorrow."

In minutes his exhausted grandson was in a deep sleep. Seth pulled off his sneakers and slipped Charlie's phone out of his pocket. With a few quick strokes, he called Browning.

"Charles, where are you? Are you okay?" Browning asked in a panic.

"He's fine. He's sleeping in my bed tonight, son," Seth said and heard Browning's relieved sigh. "I'll bring him home tomorrow, and then you and I need to talk." Seth quietly disconnected the call and turned off the ringer before he settled in next to his grandson with the TV remote.

92

When Charlie awoke the pressure in his head was borderline paralyzing, and his pulse roared in his ears. Sensing he wasn't home, he sat up a bit too quickly. His eyes snapped shut, and his hands immediately gripped his head as the pain forced him to slowly return to his pillow.

Once the pounding subsided, Charlie rose more slowly than his first attempt. With blurred vision, he took in what he could of his surroundings and finally remembered where he was. His grandfather wasn't there. As his memory of last night trickled back, Charlie was grateful he had a few minutes alone to pull himself together before he had to face him.

Charlie stumbled into the bathroom, caught a glimpse of himself in the mirror, and grimaced. The slight bruising and puffiness around his eye and the cut on his upper lip were painful to the touch. Charlie sighed. *Pops told me what he would do to me, and he did it. I deserved it.* Charlie splashed cold water on his face and head hoping that would help his appearance some. His smelly, rumpled clothes, however, were a lost cause.

Charlie sat on the edge of the tub for a minute and weeded through everything that had happened the night before. While he remembered Gavin coming over and remembered everything after he'd got to his grandfather's hotel room, there was a whole section of last night he couldn't remember. It was gone, and something about that time scratched like a cat at the door of his memory. When he came out of the bathroom, his grandfather lounged at the desk leafing through the morning paper.

"Good morning," Seth said without glancing up from the newsprint.

Charlie meekly waved.

Seth looked him over and smirked. "You feel like you got hit by a building, don't you?"

Charlie rubbed his temples and nodded.

"I brought you some aspirin, a toothbrush, and some deodorant. Why don't you jump in the shower? You'll feel a thousand times better," Seth said. "I also bought you some clothes. Nothing fancy, but they'll do."

"Thanks, Pops." Charlie took the items and returned to the bathroom. Twenty minutes later, Charlie stepped out feeling more like himself.

Seth took in his grandson's physique. "Well, look at you. Almost a man you are with muscles and everything," he said before he returned his attention back to the paper. "Hungry?"

"Yeah, can we get breakfast, Pop?" he asked as he laced up his sneakers and then looped his belt into the shorts.

"Let's go," Seth said. In seconds Seth had his wallet and keys and had tucked his gun into the waistband of his slacks.

On the elevator ride down to the lobby Charles asked, "Do you take a gun everywhere you go?"

Seth looked at him for a second. "Yeah, when you've seen the things I've seen and come across the people I have in my life, you'd be a fool not too, son. Hopefully you won't ever have to know about living like that."

Charlie thought about his grandfather's words as they crossed the parking lot. *I've seen a lot this summer, and I want nothing to do with guns,* he thought. Once they were buckled up in the Caddy, Charlie steeled himself. "Pops?"

Seth looked over at him and paused before starting the car. Charlie swallowed and then met his grandfather's eyes. "I'm very sorry for last night. I know you told me what not to do, and I know words don't mean much after what I did, but…" Charlie blinked and looked out at the sky trying to find the right words. "I want you to know I'm sorry, and I swear it'll never happen again."

"Charlie, I can tell you're sorry, and normally I'm usually pretty quick to forgive, but as you said you not only did something I told you specifically not to do and came around me high as a cloud last night, but you promised me that you wouldn't get high again. You promised, and you did anyway. Understand this one very important thing, Charles," Seth said as he started the car. "Boys do what moves them while grown men keep their word. Never forget that."

"I won't, Pops. I won't."

"Good, but we'll see," Seth said as he pulled out of the hotel's parking lot.

Minutes later his grandfather pulled up to the familiar diner. On their way in Charlie asked if his dad knew where he was.

"I called him last night and let him know you were with me," Seth said as they wound their way to his table. "Hey, you want to go to Pittsburgh with me?"

"When?"

"Right after we eat. I need to pick up a few friends from the airport. Their flight gets in at 2:20, so I need to head out as soon as we're done here."

"Sure," Charlie said, smiling at the prospect of a quick road trip with his grandfather.

Seth cracked a small smile as well.

Once they'd made a small dent in their food, Seth looked up curiously at Charlie. "So what did you mean last night when you said you called the best person in the world a fucking bitch?" Seth asked before sipping at his second cup of coffee.

Charlie's face froze in mid-chew. *Shit.* That was what had been gnawing at him all morning.

"Charles, are you all right?"

Charlie barely heard the question. The memory of every dreadful second of his phone call debacle with Lily slammed into him with the strength of a swung sledgehammer, and his heart sank. Suddenly his pancakes weren't all that tasty, and his breathing became labored. Charlie gripped his head and groaned. *Damn! I destroyed that bridge, blew it right up*, he thought.

"Charles?" Seth asked.

Inhaling sharply, Charlie pushed his plate away. "I called this girl last night. Best person in the world I know. She's the one that introduced me to the lake off 224. I called her last night–"

"While you were high?" Seth interrupted with a look of skepticism.

"Yeah. I know. Not smart. For some reason I didn't think she'd answer."

"Why did you call her then?"

"I wanted to hear her voice, maybe leave a message. If I told her how I'd saved Chad, I thought maybe she'd find that impressive enough to let me back in her life a little. I don't know, Pop," Charlie said. "Just me being a clueless dick I guess."

"Hmm…ego. One of our biggest problems is trying to keep that beast caged."

"Mine apparently escaped last night and lost its damn mind."

"I am glad I'm not a teenager in love." Seth took another bite of waffle. After a few seconds he asked, "Why don't you go to her house and apologize? Throw yourself on your sword."

"I wish I could, but I can't."

"Why not?"

"Because she's in New York."

Seth looked at his grandson. "Ain't that something?"

Charlie offered up a little lopsided grin.

"She from here?"

"Yeah."

"What's she doing in my town then?"

"Escaping and going to NYU."

"Impressive," Seth said as he put a twenty on the table for the small tab. "You ready?"

"Yeah…I've lost my appetite." Charlie stood after wiping his mouth.

The ride to Pittsburgh was enjoyable. Despite the dramatic evening, the events of the last twelve hours had bridged an emotional gap between them, and brought the two men closer than ever. Quickly crossing the Ohio-Pennsylvania line, they dove into new topics.

"Tell me about The Pearl, Pops."

Seth smiled before speaking. "That's my pride and joy, Charles."

"Why?"

"Mainly because I never imagined me and Paulie would someday own a restaurant. We were a bunch of knuckleheads, but we were smart and determined to work for ourselves. We'd done our best to keep drugs from tearing Harlem apart, but we were quickly getting too old for that game. Then an opportunity fell into our laps. We had a good amount of money, so we jumped. Mind you neither one of us had any experience running a bar let alone a restaurant, but we learned quickly, surrounded ourselves with people who knew the business, and lightly applied what the streets taught us," Seth said as he easily handled the Caddy through traffic.

"I gotta tell you, Charles. There is nothing better than owning something. Being one of the only two people on this world that has the keys to the locks is empowering. Add to that the ability to give someone a job, so they can take care of themselves or their families. That is the most amazing feeling ever. We have some of the best people working for us, great people. Our head chef, Marta, works magic with food and keeps people coming back. We got a young man, Roscoe. He's a little older than you. We gave him a job a while back as a favor to his mother to help keep him off the street, and he's doing a fantastic job learning the ins and outs of the business. You should come out to visit sometime. Meet Paulie and the whole Pearl crew. Maybe while you're there you could look up that girl you were talking about and apologize."

Charlie smiled. "I don't know if she would want to see me, but I'd love to see your place."

"Then we'll make it happen. So tell me…why English?"

Charlie paused. Most who asked that question were only making polite conversation, so normally he tossed out a well-rehearsed answer, which usually ended things. However Charlie understood that his grandfather deserved more than small talk. "It's like this, Pops. With just twenty-six letters, man has the ability to reduce people to tears, start a revolution, inspire the stagnant, and add fuel to dreams. Numbers are infinite. They go on and on forever, but words…words are powerful beyond measure."

After a few minutes of silence his grandfather glanced over at him. "There is no way you aren't going to college. Your ass is going to college, dammit."

Charlie smiled basking in his grandfather's praise.

93

They pulled into short-term parking at two on the nose, and Seth told Charlie to stay in the car. Content to spend a few minutes alone, Charlie turned on the stereo and punched buttons until *The News* by Anthony Hamilton softly rumbled around him. He was already impressed with his grandfather's Cadillac, but the sound system made him drool. He couldn't help but turn up the volume. Even though he had never heard the song, he quickly began to bop his head to the track and made a note to himself to download it when he got home. When Anthony's song *Soul on Fire* came up next and thundered from the speakers, Charlie found a whole new respect for his grandfather's taste in music.

Around 2:30 p.m. his grandfather emerged from the airport with two short men. One looked to be around his grandfather's age with very fair skin, a close fade of salt and pepper hair, and bright green eyes. The other had a darker complexion with eyes like the older man's but a baldhead and looked to be around his own father's age.

"I see you found my music stash," Seth said when Charlie climbed out to meet them.

"Jesus, Seth, he looks exactly like you did at that age, same eyes and everything," said the older man with a distinct but not quite recognizable accent. "How you doing, good sir?" he asked Charlie, sticking out a hand that belied his stature. Not only was it large, but the man also had the longest fingers Charlie had ever seen. "I am Seamus Preacher, and this is my son, Junior."

"It's nice to meet you," Charlie said. Once they had stowed their gear in the trunk, Charlie offered the older man the passenger seat.

"No thank you, son. The backseat is fine with me. Junior and I plan to catch some shuteye anyway. The damn flight was bumpier than a wagon wheel on cobblestones. I won't even mention how bad the service was. That's why air travel is dying a slow and painful death. No one wants to put up with being trapped in that kind of misery for ten minutes let alone hours."

Seth chuckled. "Seamus, it was either that or a long ass bus ride."

"Yeah, yeah. I know. I know," Seamus said with a smirk.

Charlie noticed that Junior didn't speak which he found slightly odd.

"Hotel first or straight to the museum?" Seth asked as he buckled himself into his seat.

What? The museum? Charlie thought. *Why do they need to go to the museum?* Despite the sudden flutter in his gut, Charlie said nothing.

"Museum first," Seamus said as he settled in for the ride.

Within minutes both Preacher Sr. and Jr. were asleep, and Seth turned down the volume on the stereo. Since the ride back had little in the way of conversation, Charlie settled back in his soft leather seat as well. Soon he dozed off too.

When Seth gently shook him awake they were across the street from The Butler, and the Preachers were no longer in the backseat.

"While they're inside the museum, I wanted to catch you up on a few things. You good, son?"

Charlie yawned and shook his head quickly trying to get the blood moving. "I'm good, Pops."

"Preacher Sr. is one of the best thieves I know, and his son is equally as good. They're here to get the painting for us. I've known Seamus going all the way back to elementary school, and the man is as talented as they come. Hell, he could probably steal a Blackhawk helicopter for the right price."

"So they're in there now doing what we did?"

"Yeah, but they're better at it than you or I will ever be. They'll see things we missed and never thought to look for, so sit tight. They'll be out in a few."

"Why are we over here and not in the parking lot?" Charlie asked.

"Cameras, remember? That painting gets stolen, and they're going to review all the footage from those cameras in the last few days. They see a black Caddy pull in twice in two days, the second time with four people, only two of which get out and stay ten to fifteen minutes? They're going to deem that suspicious and run my plates. They'll then bring us in for questioning, and I'd like to avoid all that."

"Me too," said Charlie. "Hey, why doesn't Junior say much?"

"A while back the Preachers robbed someone who wasn't appreciative of their talents. They caught Junior and cut out his tongue. They sent it to Senior and demanded he return the merchandise, or he'd continue to get his boy back in pieces until there were no more to send."

Charlie's stomach churned. *No tongue?* he thought. *How do you even eat with no tongue?* Charlie swallowed, completely uninterested in knowing any more. "Ummm…what kind of name is Seamus?"

"Irish, Seamus' mother was Creole. His father was Irish," Seth replied. "He grew up with me and Paulie in Harlem. As we got older, we worked together when our interests were…mutual."

About fifteen minutes later the Preachers emerged from the museum and headed towards the street. When they got to the curb, Charlie watched them say their goodbyes and part ways. One went south while the other turned north and started walking up the hill. Senior soon made his way to the car and climbed in behind Seth. Without a word Seth put the car in drive. Halfway up the block, he pulled over, and Junior slipped in behind Charlie. Seth quickly found the entrance to the highway and sped away from downtown.

"Well?" asked Seth.

"Like you said, it's a walk in the park," Senior said with a smile.

"So when can you get it?"

"When you want it?"

"Tonight?"

"No problem," replied Senior. "Hotel, please. I need to shit, shower, and plan."

"You got it," Seth said.

Charlie swallowed again. *That's it?* He thought to himself. *We'll have the painting tonight? They make it sound as easy as ordering a burger.* He was suddenly very nervous.

94

"You got news for me, Crow?" asked Hannibal as he and the jet-black man walked through the repairs in progress at The Wolf's Den towards the back office. Jimmy Crowder a.k.a. Crow had an uncanny talent at staying in the shadows and not being seen. That's what made him Hannibal's most valued asset and an effective triggerman to boot.

Crow leaned against the frosted glass of the office door while Hannibal took a seat. "I've shadowed your boy for four days," said Crow, "and so far he is never alone. I'm beginning to wonder if he'll ever be."

The Wolf slammed his palm against the desk in frustration.

Crow didn't even blink. "Relax," he told Hannibal "He's being extra careful, extra cautious since the meeting. He either rolls with two or three guys or with Stony, but the fucker has to roll solo eventually. This won't last forever."

"He know he wearin a bull's eye. He know he a marked man, so he gonna roll deep. You right though. That ain't gonna last forever. All that shit he was talkin at The Kitchen, and now he scared to even go to the bathroom by hisself, the punk ass. Yo, C, I'm tellin you, the second you see that nigga alone…."

"I know. I got you on speed dial. You my first call."

"Exactly," Hannibal growled. He reached into his back pocket and pulled out an envelope and handed it to Crow. "For expenses and shit."

Crow pocketed the money and shook Hannibal's hand before slipping out the back door to his awaiting black and gold Camry.

"I'm comin, Frankie," Hannibal whispered as the back door closed. "No matter how long it takes. I'm coming for you."

95

After dropping off the Preachers, Seth and Charlie had gone back to pick up Charlie's car, so Seth could follow his grandson home. Seth anticipated another round of turbulence when he brought up Charlie attending Michigan to his son, so before heading in Seth did some breathing exercises.

When Seth and Charlie walked inside they found Browning in the kitchen, fixing himself a bowl of ice cream with chocolate syrup and nuts. There was a pile of paperwork stacked on top of the breakfast bar.

"Hello, gentlemen," Browning said.

"Hey, Dad," Charlie said.

"Hey you, next time you leave a little Asian in the basement, let me know. Okay?" Browning chuckled.

Charlie cringed. "Sorry about that."

"Don't sweat it. I like Gavin," he said as he locked eyes with his father. "Charlie, do me a favor and head down to the cave, so my dad and I can talk. Okay, champ?"

Seth wore his best poker face and refused to show his shock that Browning had willingly called him dad. That may have been the first time in Browning's adult life that he had ever used that word in relation to Seth. Even Charlie looked stunned, but the boy quickly snapped out of it, eyed Seth, and smiled before disappearing downstairs.

Browning asked, "You want some ice cream?"

Surprised, Seth didn't know what to say. He looked at his son and eventually uttered, "Uhhh no, I'm good. Thanks." Glancing at the large stack of reports and briefs, Seth asked, "Working from home today?"

"Yeah, the climbing murder rate has suddenly dropped off a cliff for some reason. I figure whatever conflict there was has come to an end, but we still need to find the parties responsible for this bloody summer, which is a damn near impossible task honestly." Browning sat on one of the barstools. "But enough about all that. You said we needed to talk. You wanted to talk, right?"

"Yeah, we do," Seth said as he walked further into the kitchen, still unsure about being called dad and Browning's unexpected welcome.

"Before we get into whatever you want to discuss, there's something I want to say," Browning said.

"Okay," Seth said, braced for another asinine sermon about his relationship with Charlie.

"I want to say I'm sorry," Browning said ignoring his ice cream.

Seth reached out to grip the bar stool as his legs almost gave out beneath him.

Browning continued, "I'm sorry for everything, from not understanding and not realizing all the things you did for me and mom even when you were behind bars to telling Charlie that you were dead and pretty much everything in between." Browning took a deep breath and then raised his eyes to Seth. "I am sorry, Dad, truly, and I hope you can find it in your heart to forgive me."

When Seth was able to find his voice again he said, "Brownie, I was nowhere near the best parent or husband, and I understood your disappointment and hard feelings towards me. We both made mistakes, son, and I can forgive you if you can forgive me."

"Done, Dad," Browning said as he put down his bowl and embraced Seth.

The last time Seth had hugged his son, Browning had been a child. Up until the point of contact he'd vigorously convinced himself that moments like this were past them and that they didn't matter, but now standing in his son's house he realized he'd done nothing but lie to himself. This embrace would be one Seth would cherish for the rest of his life.

Browning stepped back, cleared his throat, and smiled. "Now, what is it you want to talk about?" he asked scooping up a spoonful of ice cream.

Seth took a few seconds to compose himself. He didn't want to break the fragile truce they had finally found, but he had to fight for his grandson. As gently and as sincerely as he was able, he asked, "Son, what is this I hear about you not paying for college if Charlie doesn't go to Ohio State? Did you really say that?"

Browning sighed. "Yeah, I did."

"So let me get this right. You have a kid that WANTS to go to college and apply himself, but won't be able to unless he goes to the school of your choice. One he has no interest in attending whatsoever?"

Browning took another bite of ice cream even as his shoulders sagged. "Yeah."

"Why, son?"

"Because I want him close, Dad, even more so after seeing what happened with Chad and his parents. In the last week I've even thought about sending him to Youngstown State. I want Charlie close, so I can see him more often than I'd be able to if he goes somewhere else hundreds if not thousands of miles away."

"You blew that chance, son."

"What do you mean?"

"I mean over the last four years, when you had the chance to build that bond with Charlie to where he would never want to go anywhere BUT Ohio State, you pushed him away. Much like I was wasn't physically in your life, you haven't been emotionally in his. Sure you provided him with a nice roof overhead, a car, clothes, and an expense account, but you weren't around when he needed you or wanted you."

Browning said nothing and just spooned ice cream into his mouth.

Seth continued, "Son, there are little Black boys and girls all over this nation who would kill to go to college, but they can't. You have one of those little Black boys in this very house, and because he has the audacity to want to go to Michigan, you say you aren't going to pay for it? That makes no sense to me, none."

"Dad, I don't expect you to understand, but I think this is in the best interests for him, me, and his step-mother," Browning argued.

Seth took a seat on a barstool next to his son. "When you wanted to go to Ohio State, you broke your mother's heart, you know that? Broke her right in two. We both hoped you would stay in the city. Hell, even Syracuse would have been fine, not ideal, but we would have been fine with that. I eventually came around though and told your momma, 'Penny, you got to let that boy go sometime.' I told her that if you wanted to leave home and go to a school all the way out in Ohio, who were we to say no? I told Paulie to cut the checks. Your mother hated you and me for a while. Thankfully she made peace with the whole thing before she passed. What I'm saying, son, is you got to let him go. He ain't eleven or twelve anymore. He's a young man, and he should be able to go to school wherever he wants on his parent's dime. You did. Give him the same opportunity."

Browning had set down his melted ice cream, and he was wiping at his eyes. Seth squeezed his shoulder, and Browning nodded his head. "Okay," he said. "He can go wherever he wants, but only if he comes home for the holidays."

"I will, Dad. I promise," Charlie said from the top of the basement stairs. He walked over to his dad, and father and son embraced.

"Michigan, huh?" Browning said in Charlie's ear.

"I guess."

When they let each other go, Browning looked Charlie square in the eyes and said, "Just don't wear those damn colors in this home, you understand me?"

Grandfather, son, and grandson laughed together for the first time ever.

96

"Why can't I go with you, Pops?" Charlie asked walking around the sectional to stand in front of the cave's TV with Seth.

"Because it's no place for you," Seth said still marveling at the size of the TV hanging on the wall. "How big is this thing again?" he asked.

"One hundred and ten inches. Look, Pop, what's going on tonight is because of me, right?"

"Yeah, in a way."

'C'mon, Pop, in EVERY way! This is my fault, so not only should I be there, I want to be there."

His grandson's logic was somewhat sound. Seth played his one last card. "What if the police roll up, stop us, check the car, and find the painting? Your future is screwed, no Michigan, no nothing. Is that what you want?"

Charlie crossed his arms and gave him a skeptical look. "Nice try, Pop. You told me, 'No man goes into a battle without a plan,' and I know you got one. I know you got plans on top of plans."

Damn kid's right, Seth thought. *Seems he was listening last night after all.* Seth shook his head. "I'll think about it," he said as they walked back upstairs where Browning was loading the dishwasher with Bailey.

"How much was that TV, Brownie?" Seth asked.

"About three grand if I remember correctly," he said.

"She's impressive."

"Yes, I am," teased Bailey.

"Yes, you are Bailey," Seth said with a light-hearted smile.

"I don't have the time to enjoy her like I used to," Browning said.

Seth eyed his son and said, "Make the time."

Browning looked at Charlie before he met Seth's eyes again. "I will, Dad."

Seth smiled. "Good, I'm glad to hear it. Well, thanks for dinner you two. Charlie, walk me out?"

"Hold up, Dad," Browning called. "You never did say what you were doing out here," he said as he walked towards Seth rolling down his sleeves.

Seth took Charlie by the shoulder and said, "Someone who means a lot to me needed my help. That's all."

"Is everything okay?" Browning asked, concern written on his face.

"Not yet but soon. I promise you, son. I'll set everything right."

"You two want to tell me what's going on?" Browning asked his father and son.

"It's all under control, Brownie."

Browning inhaled deeply. "Okay, Dad. I trust you. But before you leave for back east, make sure you stop in and say goodbye, okay?"

"Of course," Seth said as Charlie headed out the door. "You two have a good night."

"You too. And Dad…I love you," Browning said.

Seth smiled, hugged his son, and said, "I have been waiting damn near forty years to hear those words again. I love you too, son," he said as he kissed his son's cheek before walking out the door.

Seth found Charlie leaning against his Cadillac. "When are you going to let me drive this beast?" his grandson asked.

"On the tenth of never. Now get your ass off my car and give me a hug," Seth said. He hugged Charlie goodbye and whispered in his ear. "Meet me at my hotel around ten, okay?"

Charlie nodded. "Will do, Pops."

As Seth pulled away from the curb, he saw Browning join Charlie in his rearview mirror, watching him go. For the first time since he'd arrived in Ohio, he thought everything might be okay.

97

It was midnight, and for the last ten minutes Seth and Charlie had sat in tense silence as the Cadillac idled quietly in the darkened semicircular driveway across from The Butler. The atmosphere hung thick with nervous anticipation. When Charlie reached for the stereo, Seth stopped him.

"No noise. No distractions. Stay focused," he whispered.

Charlie nodded.

Ten minutes turned into fifteen, fifteen turned into twenty, and that's when Seth began to get a little nervous. In all his time working with Senior it had never taken him this long to get in and out of a job. *Maybe they couldn't get the painting off the wall, ran into a guard, or something.* He recalled the conversation he'd had with Senior earlier.

"So how are you going in?" Seth had asked.

"Why you want to know?"

"Because I do."

"Like I would tell you," Senior said.

"Why not?"

"Two words, plausible deniability."

"Oh please." Seth said in disgust.

"In other words…"

"I know what it means."

"In other words if I don't tell you anything, and someone asks you something, you have nothing you can tell them. However, should I tell you what, when, where, and how, and then someone asks you something, then I've put you in a position where you have to lie, and I would hate myself for that," the elder Preacher had said.

"Fuck you, Seamus."

The short man had simply cackled in self-amusement.

Fucking Senior, Seth thought with a smile. *Sarcastic smartass.*

Suddenly two police cars zoomed passed the museum heading downtown with sirens blaring. Seth had no idea what that was all about, but as soon as they were gone, two dark figures emerged from around the corner of University Plaza and crossed Wick Avenue. Junior was carrying a large duffle bag, and they were coming straight for them. Seth unlocked the trunk and the doors and then shifted into drive.

Senior climbed in while his son placed the bag in the trunk. Once Junior slid in behind Charlie, Senior asked, "Can we get the hell out of here?"

With a satisfied grin, Seth rolled the Caddy onto Wick Avenue away from downtown, and they disappeared into the night.

98

After dropping off the Preachers again at their hotel and telling them he'd be by in the morning to get them to the airport, Seth drove Charlie back to his hotel.

Seth was about to climb out of his car when he noticed Charlie wasn't moving. "Hey, you all right?"

"What just happened?"

Seth closed his car door. "What do you mean?"

"I mean what just happened, Pops?"

"We settled your debt, Charles. That's what just happened."

"Just like that? No shootout? No car chase? No helicopter flying overhead with a spotlight on us?"

"You watch too many damn movies on that big ass TV in your basement, boy, you know that?"

"That was some *Ocean's Eleven* type stuff though, Pops. Won't someone get in trouble for what we did?"

"First off, you did nothing but sit in my car. Secondly, that painting is insured for way more than it's worth, so sure, someone may lose their job, but you and your dad get to keep on breathing. What's more important, son?"

Charlie sat still for a few minutes before slowly turning to look at him. "You saved my life," Charlie softly said.

Seth reached over and put his hand on the back of his grandson's neck and gave it a reassuring squeeze. "That's what grandparents do, Charles. We save our children from themselves. C'mon," he said as he climbed out from behind the wheel and chirped the alarm.

"Swing by tomorrow night for dinner, son," said Seth as Charlie climbed into his Jetta.

"Okay, Pops."

"And do you have Stony's number?"

"Yeah." Charlie gave it to him. "What time should I be here?"

"Around seven. Get yourself home safely. It's been a long day," Seth said with a smile.

As Charlie drove out of the lot, Seth thought, *Now comes the tricky part.* He grabbed the duffle bag and headed up to his room. Tossing the card key on the dresser, he went over and closed the drapes. Then as carefully as he could he unrolled the massive canvas across his king-sized bed. Without the frame and the dramatic lighting, the artwork looked even more like a child's drawing to him. Seth chuckled at the million-dollar price tag and punched Paulie's number on speed dial.

"Did you get it?" Paul barked.

"I'm staring right at it," Seth answered.

"Is it amazing?"

"Not in my opinion, but what the hell do I know about shit like this?"

"Yeah, I swear Basquiat was only fuckin with those white artsy fartsy folk, and they ate it up," Paulie said. Both men laughed at that. "So how long did it take them thieving bastards?"

"A little longer than I thought. I remember Senior being in and out a lot faster, and at one point I thought we were done. Cop cars went screaming past us. I ain't gonna lie. When I heard sirens I damned near shit myself," Seth replied.

"That was Seamus' new toy. He calls it the Tripper. When activated, it trips every alarm in an almost mile and a half area. That way they can break any window, smash any door, open any safe, and pull anything off a wall they want without having to worry about alarms."

"Ain't that something?" Seth whispered.

"So I'm guessing they're worth every penny?"

"Every last one," Seth agreed.

"So what's next?"

"The hand off."

"You come up with a plan yet?"

"I think so."

"Is this a plan where you make it out alive?"

"I hope so, but if it's not promise me that you'll look out for my boys," Seth demanded.

After a pause, Paulie finally said, "You think I wouldn't? They your boys which makes them my boys, and I'll make damn sure they are okay. You have my word, Seth."

"I know. I was just checking," Seth said with a soft chuckle.

"You ever wonder why I would do anything for you?" Paulie asked quietly.

Seth sat in the desk chair and closed his eyes. "Same reason I would do anything for you, because I love you."

"It's deeper than that. It's because you knew what kind of evil, dirty, grimy motherfucka I was, and you stuck with me anyway. Without you, I don't know where I'd be. You did an amazing job of civilizing this beast," Paulie said, emotion flooding his voice. "So whatever you need, old man, this old man's got your back."

All Seth could say to that was, "I know."

"If you don't make it back, I know you tried, right?" Paulie asked.

"Know that I did my best."

"That's what made it fun," Paulie said on the verge of tears. He gruffly cleared his throat. "Anyway, flight reservations have been made for the Preachers. They fly out tomorrow at 10:30 a.m. with a layover in Chicago."

"Good, good. Hey, last thing, I want to say thank you. When I had my head in the clouds or up my ass, you opened my eyes. You made all the difference for me out here. You kept me sane, Paulie."

"I knew being out there was going to be difficult for you, man. I'm glad I was able to help."

"You did good, my friend," Seth said. "All right, man, I'm gonna try to get some sleep. It's gonna be a busy day tomorrow."

"All right, take care, Seth. I love you, man," Paulie said.

Seth ended the call and whispered, "I love you too, Paul. I always will."

99

Later that morning, after a vigorous bout of morning sex, Monique was in the kitchen making breakfast. Hannibal strode into the kitchen and smacked her ass on his way to the fridge.

"Don't start nothing you can't finish," she warned him, waving a spatula in his direction. He grinned and turned the orange juice carton up to his mouth when Monique smacked his broad shoulder, the highest point she could reach in her bare feet.

"Get a damn glass," she ordered.

"Freakin germaphobe," he said under his breath as he pulled a glass down from the cupboard.

Monique smiled to herself and ignored his accusation. "I want to go out tonight," she said.

"And do what?"

"I don't care, and it doesn't have to be anything fancy, but it appears the ceasefire is real, and we haven't been out in awhile. How bout a movie? You know how much you're missing your big bucket of popcorn."

"True, true. Aiight, find a movie, and we'll go. Just no damn chick flick," he warned.

"Shit," she said with a knowing smile, "you'll see anything if you can get your killer popcorn."

"Stop acting like you know me," he said as he slapped her on her ass again on his way out of the kitchen.

"What did I tell you?" she yelled.

100

On the drive back from dropping the Preachers off at the airport, Seth worked on his plan, rolled it over and over in his head until he was confident with it. If he followed it to the letter, everything should be all right.

He had lunch in his room watching the news about the theft of Jean Michel Basquiat's painting from The Butler. Reporters all stated the same thing, "The investigation is ongoing, and authorities are running down leads," which was cop speak for they didn't have a clue. Clicking off the television, Seth placed a call to Stony.

"Holy shit, old man! You actually did it. I can't believe it," Stony said with a giddy laugh.

Seth had never heard the young man in such high spirits. "Believe it. When I hand this over to you, my boy's debt is paid in full, right?"

"In full, indeed. Your boy's off my books after this. When do I get it?"

"I'll call you back in a few with time and place."

"What do you mean 'time and place'?" Stony asked impatiently. "Just have your boy bring it here, and let's be done with it, Harlem."

"First off who said Charlie was delivering it?"

"I just figured he would. It's his debt, granddad, not yours, right?"

"Yeah, it is, but him bringing it to you isn't going to happen at the moment."

"Why not?" Stony asked annoyed.

"Well mainly because there's still some things he and I have to do, but mostly, I don't trust you," Seth told him nibbling at the last of his fries.

"That hurts, old man."

"It was meant to."

"All right, New York, just make sure our boy is there."

"I'll call you later," Seth said and disconnected. There was no way Seth was going to have Charlie hand off the panting, and he was sure Stony knew that. "Nah youngin, Harlem ain't that stupid," Seth said to himself. He then dialed his grandson and set up their dinner date.

101

Charlie chuckled at his grandfather's good-natured grumbling. "I know you hated it that first night, but you have to admit that Stymie's isn't that bad, Pops. The burgers are good. You even said so yourself a few minutes ago."

"Yeah, yeah…that burger was good, and I suppose while the place lacks any type of panache, if I keep my eyes on my food it's somewhat tolerable," Seth said with a smirk and an eye roll.

"Then why did you pick this place for dinner?" Charlie asked with a chuckle. It felt great to laugh. For the first time in months, he felt as if there was hope.

"Because I know how much you love this place, so I figured I could grin and bear it for one evening. Doesn't mean I'm ever coming back here though."

Charlie laughed again and chomped down on another fry as he took in some of his old classmates and the antics at their tables. He didn't miss the silliness or their over-the-top antics. It all seemed childish to him now. This summer's drama had matured him in countless ways.

Charlie thought back to that first night at Stymie's with his grandfather. He had been high and panicked about his life and future. Now nearly all his tension and angst was gone, and his mind was clear. His grandfather had swooped in and saved not only him but his father too. Charlie felt sorry for all those who didn't have someone like his grandfather in their lives. In such a short time, Seth had taught him so much about what it meant to be a strong Black man. For that Charlie was grateful.

"Whatchu thinking about?" Seth asked.

"Everything you've done for me, Pop," Charlie said. "I can never thank you enough."

"No need to thank me, son. That's what family does."

"Family," Charlie said with a smirk. "You know, after mom died, it didn't feel like I had a family any more…not until you showed up. And with you and Dad making up, it's starting to feel like I have a family again, Pops."

His grandfather's features soften almost imperceptibly, but it was there in his eyes. "Well, there's still a lot of work to be done, but we're speaking again, and that's what matters."

"So I guess you're heading home soon, huh?" Charlie asked unable to hide his disappointment at the thought of goodbye.

"Yeah, tonight in fact," Seth said. "I'm all packed, and the tank is full."

"What? But we haven't even–" Charlie stopped, looked around, and thought through his words. Lowering his voice, Charlie began again. "We haven't dropped off the gift to our friends on the South Side."

His grandfather's eyes narrowed. "There's no 'we' in that task, son. I'll be taking care of that after we say our goodbyes."

"I thought I was going with you," Charlie whispered. "Like last night."

"No, son. This is different. You've done enough," Seth said, squeezing his grandson's shoulder. "Hey, what's that nice little lake called again?" Seth asked changing the subject.

"Berlin Lake?"

"That's it. That's it."

"Pop, don't change the subject. I'm onto that trick," Charlie said leaning forward. "I wanna go. I should go. I'm…I'm tryin to be the man you've been trying to teach me to be. Let me be that man, Pops."

Seth stared at his grandson amused that Charlie was finally starting to catch onto things. "Look, I need to step outside and make a phone call. I'll be right back, and you can keep trying to convince me to bring you along, and I'll keep telling you no," Seth said taking one of Charlie's fries as he left the booth.

Charlie watched his grandfather through the diner's big windows. The expression on Seth's face flashed from indifference to irritation to anger and lastly to determination as he disconnected the call. After a few minutes, Seth wordlessly slid back into the booth and finished his soft drink, but the determined look hadn't left his face. "Everything okay, Pops?"

Seth eyed his grandson and knew what he had to do. "You trust me, Charlie?"

"What?"

"Do you trust me?"

"Of course."

"Good, then finish up because I need you to do something for me, okay?"

Charlie's smile showed more teeth thinking that his grandfather had changed his mind. "You got it, Pops."

102

At first Charlie hadn't understood and simply stared at Seth, unsure of what his grandfather wanted him to do.

"Boy, we don't have a lot of time. I'll say it again. Go in there, get what you feel you need, and get back out here as fast as you can. Don't say shit to anyone. You got ten minutes."

His grandfather's words repeated over and over in his head as Charlie raced up to his room and looked around in a panic. He flew to his closet, grabbed a gym bag off the shelf, and started throwing in random clothes and sneakers without thinking. He quickly ransacked his bathroom of toiletries before he rushed back downstairs. He heard the TV in the cave and was tempted to go see his father, but Charlie wasn't even sure what to say, and his grandfather had told him to hurry and keep his mouth shut. With a one last glance around the kitchen, Charlie ran back outside and climbed into his grandfather's car clearly confused.

"Pops, what's going on?" Charlie asked pushing his gym bag into the backseat.

"Buckle up. I'll explain it all to you in a few," Seth said before smoothly pulling away from the curb.

The ride back to the hotel was a silent blur, and when his grandfather wheeled into the spot next to his Jetta, Charlie was almost breathless.

"You still want to drive my car?" Seth asked turning to him.

Charlie stared at him wide-eyed and even more confused but nodded.

"Good," Seth said, "I want you to get behind this wheel and drive this car to New York for me. If this thing goes sideways tonight I want you protected, and getting you out of town and to Paulie is the best way to do that. Drive it there tonight and go straight to where the GPS guides you. Don't deviate at all, got it? Go straight there and

413

ask for Paulie. If The Pearl's not open by the time you get there, wait in the car."

"Wait. What?" Charlie asked growing more anxious. "I don't understand what's going on, Pop. What exactly do you mean 'go bad'?"

Seth sighed and looked at him. As the last strands of sunlight streaked across his grandfather's face Charlie could see the haunting worry in his Pop's eyes.

"You know that call I made at the diner?"

Charlie nodded.

"I called Stony to make final arrangements to do this thing, but Frank answered instead. My Plan A had been a hand-off with Stony, but Stony won't be there. Frank will. Handing over the painting won't be the end of this," Seth said with a sigh. "Frank will likely try to kill you, me, your dad, and maybe even Bailey just because." Seth let that reality settle for a moment before continuing. "So we're onto plan B, which is you getting out of town."

"What? Why? How do you know?"

"You and I are loose ends, and Stony wants your dad dead for what Browning did to his uncle. You ever wonder how you got wrapped up with these guys in the first place?" Seth asked.

Flashes shot through his mind of Stony's nephew daring him to take his small time bets with Gavin and Chad to the big boys, but he couldn't understand what his grandfather was implying.

"Charlie, this wasn't entirely your fault. They knew exactly who you were and who your father was. Their plan all along was to destroy this family because Browning targeted and prosecuted his Uncle years ago. You were a pawn, Charles, a means to an end for an angry young man with a vendetta."

That familiar fear was back. Once again it gripped Charlie with a viciousness that left him unable to speak or think.

"Frank demanded that you deliver the painting tonight instead of me. I told them okay, but if you go alone he'll kill you on sight and throw your body in the lake. I'm not about to let that shit happen. I stand a better chance of making it out of this alive, so hand me your keys. Frank will see your car, and hopefully that'll buy me the time I need." Seth said. "Now you get behind this wheel, and you get to New York. Don't speed, don't draw any unwanted attention, and don't look back, boy. You understand me? As soon as things die down, we'll get you to Michigan."

"What about dad and Bailey?"

"I'll call him on my way to give him the heads up. That's all we can do. I'll take care of the rest," Seth said.

Recognizing that once again his Dad's position made everything about this situation impossible, Charlie nodded and took a deep breath. "Okay, Pops. I trust you," Charlie said and slowly climbed out of the car. His grandfather did the same, and Charlie could see the obvious relief in his face. Charlie walked around to his grandfather.

"I'll see you again, right, Pops?" Charlie said, fighting back tears.

Seth's jaw clenched, and he glared at Charlie. "What did we talk about, son?"

Charlie swallowed hard and pushed down the emotions that had bubbled to surface.

"That's better. Now I won't lie. I hope so. But if you don't, know that I love you very, very much. Know that I always have. Remember everything we've talked about and what I taught you."

Charlie gritted his teeth and lunged at his grandfather for one last hug and whispered. "I love you so much, Pops."

His grandfather's bone-crushing embrace helped calm Charlie some. "I know," Seth replied before he let go and nudged Charlie into the Caddy. "Now go. Take this," Seth said handing Charlie a few hundred dollars. "Don't stop until you're in Harlem at The Pearl's doorstep."

Charlie nodded and started his grandfather's car as Seth shut the door. Once he adjusted the seat and mirrors, he pulled out of the parking lot and headed east, but after a few blocks Charlie turned into a strip mall.

The horrible possibilities of tonight flashed through his mind and chilled his soul. Charlie yanked at the steering wheel and screamed in frustration. Sitting there in the idling car, he took a minute to catch his breath and go over everything his grandfather had said, but he struggled with Seth's instructions. His head pounded. He was torn. Part of him wanted to rocket to New York, but part of him was terrified to leave. After a minute he inhaled deeply and through puffed cheeks exhaled. His grandfather had told him that it was time he took control of his life. With that thought guiding his actions, Charlie smoothly drove away from the strip mall. There was one last thing he had to do before he left town.

Seth wiped at the tears he couldn't stop after the taillights of his Caddy and his grandson faded from view. He loved that boy and believed he had a bright full future ahead of him if he could just get this noose off the boy's neck. Steeling himself for what was ahead, Seth climbed in Charlie's Jetta, shifted into drive, and hit the gas as the sun blinked goodbye.

103

Hannibal and Monique left their favorite wing joint by the mall in Boardman and were headed across the parking lot to catch the latest superhero movie when his cell rang. It was Crow.

"Frank's on the move."

The Wolf's hulking frame came to a sudden stop. Those looking for parking waited patiently for him to move too intimidated to hit their horns. "Where he at?"

"He's rollin south toward Boardman. Hard to stay with him though. He's a bullet, and I ain't got enough horses under my hood."

"He alone?" the Wolf asked squeezing Monique's hand.

"Yeah, first time in days he's rolling solo. Don't mean he's staying that way, know what I mean?"

Hannibal did a sudden about face with Monique in tow returning to the borrowed Suburban. "Yeah, I get you. You did your job, C. Stay on him if you can, and let me know when he gets to Boardman or if anything changes," Hannibal said and disconnected.

"No movie then?" Monique pouted and then smiled wide with a flash of excitement in her eyes.

"Not tonight but I'll make it up to you, deal?"

"Deal as long as there's some action in our evening," she said scrambling into the passenger seat.

"Don't you worry about that. I promise you there will be."

104

As Seth followed the light traffic into the inky darkness of farmland and country roads, he called Paulie. "It's about to go down out here, so I'm sending the grand to you. He should be there early morning or so. If I don't make it out of this, do me the honor of looking after him?"

"You can do that your damn self when you get back here," Paulie replied gruffly.

"Let's hope that happens."

"You scared?"

After thinking for a second Seth said, "I'm apprehensive."

"You on Plan B?"

"Yeah."

"Fuck."

"If you don't hear from me in two hours get Charlie settled in. The Black Hat already took care of the paperwork Charlie needs to sign for my brownstone, my accounts, and my half of The Pearl. If necessary, I need you to take care of the details."

Paulie growled. "You come home, old man!"

"I'm a do my damnedest, Paulie, but if I don't…sometime in the near future pay a visit to Romare's on the South Side for me and make Stony pay what he owe."

"With interest, my friend. That's a promise."

"I did it right, right, Paulie?"

"You always did."

"I was a friend to my friends and an enemy to my enemies."

"Best friend I ever had and the worst enemy I've ever known. Now handle your business and get your Black ass back to Harlem where you belong."

Seth laughed. "Working on it. I love you, Paulie."

"I love you too, old man."

Seth disconnected and hoped he'd be able to see his friend and share another cup of coffee with him again.

His last call was to Browning. When his son's voicemail message came on, Seth was relieved. He didn't have time for Browning's questions. Plus a message gave his son an out if anyone asked what he knew.

"Charlie's on his way to New York and Paulie. He'll call home when he gets there to let you guys know he's okay. Please trust me on this, Brownie. This is the only way I knew to keep him safe. Remember that question you asked me last night as to why I came out here? Charlie got mixed up with some very bad people, son, people who wanted to destroy him to hurt you. I did what I could to fix things, but there's one more thing left to do. Hopefully it all works out. Protect yourself and that beautiful wife of yours. I love you, Brownie. I always have. I love you and that son of yours with all my heart," Seth said and ended the call. According to his GPS, Berlin Lake was just ahead.

Seth pulled Charlie's Jetta into the parking area at the far end of the lot. He glanced around the darkened lake. The full moon hung low which cast an eerie glow over the still water. Seth checked his Glock, chambered a round, and hoped he was still fast enough.

105

Hannibal tapped the "answer" button on his phone before the first ring had finished.

"Frank just hit Boardman. It looks like he's gonna head west on 224," Crow said.

Hannibal tore out of the mall parking lot. "Pull back, Crow. I'll get him. I'm already on 224. Thanks. We'll settle up later," Hannibal said before turning to Monique. "Frank should be coming up on us pretty soon the way Crow was talking. Keep your eyes open, baby."

"Does he know this truck?" she asked.

"Not this Suburban, so we good. The tint should help too," he said. His adrenaline was pumping hard, and he struggled to keep the truck at the speed limit.

Minutes later outside of Canfield, Monique's hand squeezed Hannibal's thigh "I think this is him," she said as headlights closed in behind them in a hurry. The car's blinker flashed and car maneuvered next to them.

Hannibal glanced over slyly. "Oh yeah, that's Frank's BMW." The car accelerated, passed them, and smoothly shifted back into the lane right into the Suburban's headlights before pulling away at a steady clip. The Wolf surveyed the darkness. "You know what's out here? I ain't never been over this way."

"There's nothing but country roads and a lake my family and I used to visit when I was a kid," she said.

"A lake, huh?" The Wolf hit the gas, and the truck lurched forward almost angrily. "I'm coming for you, Frankie boy," he whispered. "I'm comin for you."

106

Frank slowly pulled into the parking lot at the park next to Berlin Lake. The area was vacant except for the kid's compact car at the end shrouded in darkness with the moon glinting off its hood. He flashed his high beams and a set of headlights flashed back in response and stayed on. Frank sucked his teeth. "What's with the high beams, Chuck?" he whispered. Frank headed toward the lights and finally came to a stop twenty yards from the Jetta. They were closer to the brush than they were the lake.

Frank checked his Colt .45 and tucked the gun in his waistband. As if this was all routine, he casually got out of his BMW. He was ready to be done with this kid and Stony's revenge, so he could stay on his grind of making money. He took a few steps towards the other car. "Come on, Chuck. I ain't got time to be fuckin witchu out here in the middle of nowhere all night," Frank said loudly. "Pop the trunk. Let's get this done."

The driver's side door opened. When Frank realized who climbed out, he came to a stop and threw up his arms in mock frustration. "Damn, old man, I was just beginning to like you too. Fuck you doing here?"

Seth eyed Frank in a mixture of regret and resignation. He could have gunned down the baby-faced killer in cold blood as he'd walked toward the car, but despite what his son had believed for so long, Seth had never taken any life easily.

He stepped in front of the Jetta and stood between the high beams. "I never liked you, youngin. I'm here because I know why it's you and not Stony that's here. I ain't about to let you put a bullet in my pup's head."

Frank laughed and took a few slow steps to his left trying to minimize the effects of the headlights. "I'm just here for the damn painting. Ain't nobody puttin a bullet in anyone."

"You think this is my first rodeo, boy?"

"Whatever. You got the painting, so I can get the hell outta here? Place gives me the creeps."

"It's in the trunk," Seth said. "You got the ledger?"

"What ledger?"

"The one I told Stony I wanted. The one that has my grandson's name in it with a dollar amount scrawled beside it."

"I don't know shit about some ledger, Harlem. Now go get the painting before I get upset."

"You know I don't give a damn about your feelings, youngin."

"Look, nigga," Frank said as he raised his gun in a flash and shot in one swift motion.

Seth did the same as fast as he could.

Frank was faster.

The shot tore through Seth's gut, sending him flying backwards against Charlie's car and his Glock scattering off into the darkness as his shot ripped off a a nice chunk of Frank's ear. The young gangster quickly reached for his ear as blood started to flow.

Charlie saw his Jetta's high beams and could make out his grandfather and Frank, so he cut his headlights and slowly crept towards them. When he was about ten feet from Frank's BMW, he eased the Cadillac into park.

Suddenly shots rang out into the night. His grandfather slammed back onto the hood of the Jetta while Frank grabbed the side of his head. Frantically, Charlie reached into the side panel until he found his grandfather's gun. Clutching the weapon, he hit the horn, flipped on the Caddy's high beams, and jumped out of the car.

When Frank saw him, Charlie quickly raised the gun. He had no idea what he was doing, but he wanted to protect his grandfather.

Slowly he began to move towards Seth who was seated on the ground in front of Jetta trying to apply pressure to his wound.

"What up, Chuck? Put that thing down before you hurt yourself. Whatchu gonna do?" Frank asked trying to keep blood out of his ear.

"K-kill you," Charlie stuttered edging away from the safety of the Cadillac toward his grandfather. He could taste the bile in the back of his throat. He had never been this scared.

"C'mon, Chuck. We both know you ain't never killed no one. Hell, the night Turk got his head blown off you threw up everything you had in you," Frank said with a laugh slowly moving closer. "Now I'm supposed to believe you gonna pull that trigger? Shit prolly ain't even loaded."

On shaky legs Charlie made his way to his grandfather. "You wanna find out?" he shouted as his hand began to tremble.

Suddenly footsteps approached from behind Frank, and Charlie saw a monstrous frame step into the Caddy's headlights. Frank turned with his gun raised to see who was coming when a loud boom thundered along with another shot, both of which violently spun Frank to the pebbled asphalt. Charlie looked down at his grandfather holding a smoking .45 pistol with a weak but satisfied smile.

Hannibal slowly walked towards Frank to stand over him. "I knew you was a punk ass nigga. You ain't got no respect for your elders, you know that?" he said as Frank tried to crawl for his gun despite his wound to his shoulder from The Wolf's shotgun and the bleeding hole in his back. Hannibal kicked it under his car. "There won't be any of that shit, short stuff."

"Fuck you, nigga," Frank wheezed before coughing up blood. He slowly rolled onto his back and looked up at his nemesis. "Get it over with, fat boy."

The Wolf enjoyed Frank's pain and suffering. "Know this…App was ten times the man you are. You can take that to your grave, bitch." With no hesitation, Hannibal aimed the barrel of his AA12 shotgun to Frank's sweat-drenched forehead. "For App, nigga." he said and pulled the trigger, exploding Frank's head.

Charlie continued to press his shirt into his grandfather's wound. "He's dead, Pops," he whispered. "It's over. I'm gonna get you to the hospital." Charlie knelt down and tried to lift Seth who yowled in pain.

"Stop, Charlie! Stop."

A shadow fell over them. "Wow, that was like some Wild West shit," the hulking man said. "I saw the whole thing. You kinda quick, old timer, like Billy the Kid and shit." The man knelt down and looked at Seth's wound. "You know what time it is, don't you, senior?"

His grandfather nodded. "Yeah…I do."

"You two need any help? Want me to call someone for you?" he asked getting back to his feet.

Seth nodded his head. "Any chance you can make the Jetta disappear?" he wheezed.

"Anything in it that I might need to worry bout?"

Seth smiled. "Not a thing."

Charlie was about to say something but stopped himself.

"No problem, old timer. It's the least I can do. Thanks for the distraction, lil man. I appreciate it," the man said as he walked to the black truck that had quietly pulled up to the scene.

"Charlie, what the fuck are you doin here," Seth asked. "Don't you listen to anything I say? You could have gotten your ass killed, you know that?"

"Yeah…I do, but men don't run. Boys do."

Seth reached up to grab Charlie's neck and spoke with labored breath. "I…love you…so much, and I'm very proud of you. You're right, son. Men don't run. Glad you were listening."

Charlie's heart swelled hearing those words, but he couldn't focus on his accomplishment. "Can you move? We gotta get you to the car…to the hospital."

"No, Charles. It's too late for that. Now do what I said. Get in the car and go," Seth said with a grimace while Hannibal climbed in and started the Jetta.

"What? I can't leave you here," Charlie cried.

"That's exactly what you're gonna do. Just lay me down."

As gently as he could, he lowered Seth's head to the ground. Then the Jetta slowly backed away and followed the black Suburban.

"Thank you, son," Seth said breathlessly. "Wow, look at all those stars and that fat full moon. You don't see stars like that in New York. Now get going, and don't let your father know anything until you get to New York, not before."

Charlie, his face soaked with tears, hugged his grandfather one last time. "I love you, Pops."

"I love you more, boy. Get to Paulie."

Picking up the gun, Charlie slowly walked away and climbed in his grandfather's pride and joy and did the last thing his grandfather told him to do.

107

As the sun broke over the city, Charlie pulled up in front of the warm brick exterior of The Pearl. Charlie looked around the just stirring Harlem neighborhood. He cut off his tears for the hundredth time in the last six hours. He'd made the turns the GPS had told him to make, and he'd simply focused on getting from one mile marker to the next, putting one foot in front of the other. With a sniffle, he walked to the door and knocked. After only seconds, he heard someone disengage the locks before the door swung open to a tall, handsome older Black man who looked both relieved and grim.

"Charlie?"

"Yes, sir. Are you, Paulie?" Charlie croaked.

"Yeah, that's me, kid. God, you look so much like him. Get on in here. It's been a long night for me, so I know it's been an even longer one for you," Paulie said as he led Charlie inside to the bar. "I haven't heard from Seth, son," Paulie said gravely.

Charlie paused and glanced at his still bloodstained hands. "I know."

Paulie stopped and looked over Charlie with an eagle eye, taking note of his hands and the stains on his wrinkled light blue polo shirt. "Talk to me, kid. I've been hoping for the best but bracing for the worst. What do you know that I don't?"

Charlie looked up in resignation and exhaustion as a few more tears slipped down his cheeks. "I was there. I t-tried to s-save him, but I couldn't."

"Shit," Paulie said grabbing a handful of napkins.

Charlie sniffled. "I'm sorry."

"No need for you to be sorry, Charlie," Paulie whispered wiping his eyes. After a few minutes, Paulie got his bearings. "You hungry? You wanna take a nap or something? You can crash in the office. I've closed the place up for the day. We can talk about everything that happened when you wake up."

Paulie waved Charlie off when he started to speak. "Whatever it is, it can wait. Okay, kid?"

Charlie nodded and followed Paulie deeper into his grandfather's pride and joy.

108

Two weeks later after the daylong services for Seth Ezekiel Jackson had ended at The Pearl, Charlie sat at a table by the large plate glass window and watched the bustling Harlem street traffic while contemplating his next move. He was supposed to be in Ann Arbor in two weeks, but he couldn't summon even a spoonful of enthusiasm for college life right then. When his dad had arrived to attend the services he had been surprisingly compassionate and hadn't pressured him to come home. Though Charlie suspected Paulie's "private" conversation with him had something to do with that.

A hand on his shoulder tugged Charlie out of his thoughts. "Charles," Paulie said, "can you come with me for a few minutes. I know it's been a long day, but there's some people you need to meet. There are a few things we need to handle, and then you can go back to the brownstone."

"Sure," Charlie said following him up to the office.

There were two men waiting for them. One was short, slender, and impeccably dressed in a custom-tailored suit. He looked young and wore the smile of a Cheshire cat while the other man looked chiseled from stone. Charlie remembered seeing the onyx colored man at the services and had thought he should be playing middle linebacker in the NFL.

Paulie closed the door behind them and made the introductions. "Charlie this is Jonathan Washington ESQ aka The Black Hat," he said of the diminutive lawyer. "He represents the firm Broome & Crowe. He's my lawyer, he was Seth's lawyer, and now he's your lawyer."

Jonathan stepped forward and shook Charlie's hand. "It's a pleasure to meet you, Charles Jackson. I'm sorry for your loss. You were very important to Seth, and my law firm would like to take you on as a client. We normally don't represent someone as young as you.

428

In fact, you'd be the youngest client ever at the firm, but Seth meant a lot to us all, and because of that we've chosen to, for lack of a better word, 'grandfather' you in so to speak."

"Am I in trouble? Paulie, why do I need a lawyer?" Charlie asked, his voice raising an octave.

Muffled laughter filled the room, and Paulie answered as he dropped his large frame into his squeaky leather chair. "No, no, Charlie. You're not in trouble. As for why you need a lawyer, well it's better to have and not need than to need and not have. Jonathan, please continue."

"This is our associate, Bennett Church," Jonathan said. Church nodded politely to Charlie from his spot across the room before Jonathan continued. "After speaking last week with Paulie, I believe you're in possession of an item that you need to be relieved of. Broome & Crowe has secured an appropriate buyer and would be happy to broker the deal as well as handle the transfer, transportation, and financial transaction for you—with the appropriate fees, of course."

Paulie chuckled. "By fees he means robbery, kid. The legal kind though with pens and paper and shit, but thankfully they do good work," he said with a smirk. When Charlie looked at Paulie blankly, he replied softly, "The painting, kid. They got a buyer for the Basquiat."

Charlie's eyes widened. He'd forgotten all about the Basquiat. "Oh…okay, yeah. That's fine."

"Don't you want to know how much before you say yes?" Paulie prompted.

Charlie was about to shrug when he recalled Seth's words. The other men nodded watching Paulie school him on the art of the hustle. "Uh, sure."

"Two," said Jonathan.

"Two thousand dollars is cool."

Jonathan cleared his throat. "That's actually two million dollars, Mr. Jackson, after our fees of course."

For a second, Charlie forgot how to breathe. With a cough he recovered as smoothly as he could. "Uh…then that's even better. Okay."

All three men smiled, and Church approached Charlie. "If you'll hand over the package, Charles, I'll be going. I need to get on the road."

Charlie walked behind his grandfather's desk and picked up the large black duffle bag that had sat there since his arrival. The cumbersome package took him two hands, but Church deftly handled the expensive cargo with minimal effort.

Jonathan quietly made a quick call on his cell phone. "We're a go on the transaction. Please confirm the transfer." After a moment, he disconnected and nodded to both Church and Charlie. "It's done."

Church reached out and patted Charlie on the shoulder. "It's been a pleasure, Charles. From what I've heard you're a good kid. That's rare these days. If I can ever be of assistance to you don't hesitate to call your lawyer," the baritone voiced man said. "By the way, it'll get easier," he said with a smile as he slid on his sunglasses.

Before Charlie could reply, Church was gone.

"The money's been transferred into the primary account," Jonathan announced opening his leather briefcase. He handed Charlie a thick manila envelope. "As your grandfather's sole beneficiary, here is the summary of your grandfather's—now yours—accounts and holdings which does not include the two million just deposited. Take your time and review everything. I will call you tomorrow to arrange a meeting in the next few days to review everything and answer any questions you might have," he said. "Unless you have any for me now?"

Charlie stared at the envelope once again in shock.

Paulie motioned to the door, and Jonathan got the hint. He snapped shut his alligator skin case, squeezed Charlie's shoulder, and shook Paulie's hand before he left the office. Charlie sat down behind his grandfather's desk and removed the contents of the envelope. Inside were credit cards, a bankcard with pin number, and a twenty-five-page summary of Seth's accounts and investments. Leafing through the papers, Charlie swallowed. "Paulie…is all this mine?"

"Yes, it is. With this place, the brownstone, the Cadillac, and his combined accounts, the number on that paper is everything your grandfather accumulated over the years," Paulie said as he leaned back in his groaning chair.

"How?"

"The Known Men, son, we weren't choir boys by any stretch of the imagination. We did things that we weren't proud of, but we did good too or at least tried to, and most of those things brought us a lot of money. Yeah, we did our dirt, but we did our best to give back, Charles. We opened The Pearl and gave jobs to kids who would have either ended up in jail or in the morgue," he said pulling a bottle of Johnny Walker Black and a glass from his bottom drawer.

"Now tell me…what do you want to do, Charles? You don't owe anyone anything, and your grandfather would be the first to tell you to do you. So do you want to stay here…in New York? You can keep it all, or Jonathan and I can help you liquidate, and you can go back home, to Michigan, or wherever the hell you wanna go."

Charlie sat back and rubbed his face with both hands as he considered his earlier thoughts. "I…I think I'd like to stay. It feels right here in a way I can't explain."

Paulie smiled wide. "Yeah, New York can have that affect on people."

"No, not New York. I'm talking about Harlem, Paulie."

Paulie laughed. "She got her hooks in you already, huh, kid? That's just fine by me. Read through those papers…or not and sign everywhere there's a damn 'X'. The Black Hat loves his X's," Paulie said as he poured two fingers of whiskey into his glass. He leaned back and raised it to the picture on the wall before draining it.

"Be smart with that money, talk to Jonathan, and let him make that money work for you, so you don't have to work for it. Then maybe someday you can pass down what you have to someone like Seth did with you."

"What do you think he'd want me to do, Paulie?" Charlie asked solemnly.

Paulie put his glass down and smiled at the question. "Charlie, he'd want you to be a friend to your friends and an enemy to your enemies. He'd want you to do it right, whatever it is. Do it right and have no regrets."

"I will. I'll make Pop proud."

"I know you will, kid. I know you will. Hey, you got a buck?"

"Huh?" Charlie said bewildered.

"Do you have a dollar?" he asked again.

This time Charlie took out his wallet, pulled out a dollar, and handed it to Paulie.

"Congratulations," Paulie said, "you bought me out. The Pearl is yours outright. I'll talk to Jonathan to get the paperwork started, but as of today The Pearl is yours."

"WHAT? But I don't know how to run this place," Charlie said suddenly panicked.

"Don't worry. I said the place is yours, but I ain't going nowhere yet. I'll groom my replacement before I retire to live the good life. I got some money too, ya know, and it's high time I spent it," he said standing up to stretch his bulking frame. "Oh yeah, you gonna need to hire a new bartender soon too. The one down there is coming with me," he said with a big grin.

"No problem," Charlie said with a laugh.

"And another thing. If you want, you've been accepted into Columbia University as an English major. For the life of me I don't know why English but whatever," he said with a dismissive wave. "You can start the Fall Semester. You just need to call this number and register or some shit." The confused look on Charlie's face made Paul smile. "He'd make that same damn face too when he didn't understand something. Anyway, don't ask how. Just say thank you."

Charlie shook his head at the character that was Paulie and smiled. "Thanks, Uncle Paulie."

"C'mon, kid, let's lock up and go home. I'm beat. That was some turnout today for Seth, huh?"

"Yeah, it was pretty amazing to see so many people who cared about my grandfather. They all kept telling me stories about something he'd done to them or for them. He was definitely loved."

"More importantly, he was respected," Paulie said.

Charlie nodded and followed Paulie out of the office. Before he shut the door, he stared at the picture on the wall of Seth and Paulie in their heyday. Both wore big smiles under bigger fedoras in front of The Lenox Lounge. "Thanks, Pops, for everything. I won't let you down."

EPILOGUE

Charlie stared up at the brick building and wondered once again if it was the right time. His second year had started at Columbia, and he was back to working ten-hour days at The Pearl and juggling a full load of classes. Despite his brutal schedule, life was good.

Between his first year of classes, Charlie had learned the ins and outs of the restaurant business from Paulie, Marta, Roscoe, and Tamara. He'd proved to be a fast learner when it came to ordering, maintenance, customer service, and overall management, and the restaurant had quickly become his home away from home and its staff his second family.

Marta pinched his cheeks when he wasn't out of arms reach. Their talented chef was just as his grandfather had described, a passionate woman with a huge heart and skills that rivaled any of New York's five-star celebrity chefs. She'd disappeared after the funeral to mourn in her own way and at her own time. Not even Paulie had known for sure if she would be back. She was gone so long that Paulie had considered bringing in a new chef. When she'd finally walked through the kitchen doors, demanding to know who was overcooking a burger, it was like she'd never left. Though she was her typical ebullient self, Charlie noticed from time to time a sadness darken her face when she thought no one was looking.

On the advice of Paulie, as soon as Charlie had taken the reigns of the restaurant four months ago, he'd given Roscoe a massive raise and named him general manager. "The money won't mean shit to him. His attitude won't change, and it won't inspire loyalty either. He's already that. The kid's earned it, and the title will show him that you trust him," Paulie had said. He'd been right about it all, and Roscoe was fast becoming a close friend and a trusted confidant.

They'd also hired Ray-Ray as the new bartender after he had gotten himself clean and appeared on the doorstep, hat in hand, looking for the job Seth promised. The ex-heroin addict had surprised everyone with his people skills and dedication to his work.

Before Paulie had retired and left for good with Tamara, he'd introduced Charlie to Florida over a drink and explained both the fees of remaining a member of The Network and the benefits of the information only Florida had access to. "It may take him a day or two to get you what you need, but he'll get it to you," Paulie had said.

A few days after that introduction Florida had come into the bar, sat at the far end, ordered a whiskey neat, and asked for Charlie. Florida informed Charlie that Romare's had been burned to the ground and that the owner was nowhere to be found and feared dead. Apparently the only wall left standing in the smoldering remains had had the words "debt paid" scrawled on it in spray paint. Florida had peered at Charlie, finished his drink, and walked out, back into the Harlem streets. The news had struck him as odd at first, but minutes later he smiled. *You got the last word huh, Paulie?*

Charlie hadn't been back to Ohio except for a short trip at Christmas to visit. While they missed him, his dad and Bailey had been supportive of his decision to stay in New York and found a myriad of excuses for quick jaunts to the Big Apple. It was through them Charlie discovered Chad had foregone school and spent months in rehab with his parents actively involved in his recovery. When Charlie had spoken to him last month, he was relieved to hear that Chad was taking classes at Youngstown State and that his friend seemed to be getting his life together.

Charlie's friendship with Gavin had cooled considerably since Seth's services. He wasn't sure why, but according to his social media posts, Gavin was loving life and doing well in his classes at M.I.T. He didn't know if he would ever see G again, and that saddened him a bit.

Over the last year, Charlie had learned so much, not only about the business of running a New York City restaurant or about the demands of writing a good story but about himself. Tonight he was counting on that knowledge and everything his grandfather had taught him for a chance at a new beginning.

Clutching the flowers and swallowing his apprehension, Charlie walked inside and made his way to the fourth floor to knock on the door to room 4F. In seconds, Lily snatched the door open. "I told you no already five times Bernard. I'm not interested in–" she said before stopping short when she saw it wasn't Bernard at her door. "Charlie?"

"Yeah, soooo not Bernard," he said with a little grin. "Who's Bernard? He sounds adorable," he said with a chuckle.

"What are you doing here?" Lily asked placing a hand on her curved hip and raising a suspicious eyebrow at him.

"I came to see you. I was hoping we could take a walk, talk, hopefully catch up some. Oh and these are for you," he said handing her a bouquet of wild flowers.

While still skeptical, Lily couldn't resist and inhaled deeply. College had definitely agreed with her. Her beautiful complexion, long dark hair, and lovely eyes still melted him. She was wearing shorts, flip-flops, and a sweatshirt, and he still thought she was the most amazing thing on two legs.

She gazed at Charlie for a good second. Her eyes narrowed. "You look different, Charles."

Charlie leaned against the doorframe and let her take in the new him. Gone were the baggy clothes, flashy sneakers, and matching caps. Instead slacks, loafers, and a nice fitting button down shirt were his daily attire. This evening he'd chosen a fire engine red shirt, black pants, and black shoes.

"Even your eyes…they seem brighter," she said.

When he smiled in response, he saw her catch her breath and hoped that was a good sign.

"Wait a minute. How did you find me?"

Thinking of Jonathan, Church, and Florida, Charlie smiled and said, "I know people." He slipped his hands in his pockets. "Do you want to take a walk? If you're hungry we could grab some dinner."

"Sure, I could eat. Give me two minutes," she said with a shy smile. After a quick change, Lily grabbed her purse.

Though he wanted to jump for joy that she accepted and not sent him off with his tail between his legs, Charlie took a deep breath and tried to calm his racing heart as they walked side-by-side down the bustling dorm hallway.

"So where are we going, buster?"

Charlie's heart squeezed. That simple endearment made all the butterflies he had felt up to that moment vanish. He punched the elevator button and said, "Well...There's this great little place up in Harlem you might like."

About the Author

In 2014 Mark Eric burst into today's fictional landscape with a refreshing blend of realistic heroes within larger than life plots. He pours his creative energy onto the page in a way that both thrills and entertains as he infuses his stories with characters that become fond friends and dreaded enemies.

Eric's writing career has spanned 20 years across multiple genres and media. His fans will be delighted with his range and unique tales. His dynamic multicultural casts reflect the rising demand in American entertainment for a richer, more diverse mix of age, race, gender, and socioeconomic status.

Eric's first release, *Benders*, is contemporary science fiction of a gifted young Black man being pursued by one of the country's most politically influential men. He also released a collection of poetry July 2014. With two other novels in the works, Eric will be filling our traditional and digital bookshelves for years to come.

www.ingramcontent.com/pod-product-compliance
Lightning Source LLC
Chambersburg PA
CBHW020829030726
47496CB00001B/155